With te  n, the
buildup pense,
The Last Immortal is a thoroughly enjoyable ride.

"*The Last Immortal* was an impressive read. I enjoyed how it made me think about the possibilities of future science and through that gave me inspiration to think for myself where else science could go. I have read a lot of science fiction books yet few of them go into such detail of the mechanics of how things work in its theoretical space."
— Andrew C.

"If you are a fan of Terminator, Matrix, or Avatar you will undoubtedly enjoy this book. I appreciate sci-fi with concrete science behind it and provocative enough to make you consider the possibilities of the fiction. *The Last Immortal* induces you to ponder the very real possibility of life beyond Earth. Intertwined throughout the novel are very real questions of how the advancement of technology and the decisions that we make today may present future unintended consequences. All of this is done while weaving together multiple sub-plots and cool action scenes. Highly recommended!" — Monty C.

To my dear friend July!

THE LAST IMMORTAL

A NOVEL

KEITH W. MICHON

First Printing, January 2018

ISBN-13: 978-0692996379
ISBN-10: 0692996370

www.keithmichonauthor.com
www.thelastimmortal.net

Dedicated to my mother,
whose sudden passing many years ago caused me to listen
to her favorite classical music, which led to the inspiration
for this novel;

and to my father,
who kept asking how things were coming along.

A sincere thank you to my manuscript editor Helen Shik;
to my publishing coordinator and final review editor Jan
Combs; to Monty Combs, who read my book in its various
forms and provided me with awesome feedback; and to my
wife Kathy, because without her in my life, none of this
would have been possible.

Challenge yourself

CONTENTS

THE LAST IMMORTAL

CHAPTER ONE – THE MITELS ATTACK

Commander Janus Stone sat in the control room of planet Thrae's Global Defense Center, his mind racing as he tried to decide what to do next to save his planet from destruction. He watched anxiously, as rows of hologram technicians furiously tracked the movement of the approaching Mitel Fleet. A second, even larger contingent of technicians began scrambling Thrae's ground and air defense forces.

Janus stood an impressive six feet eight inches tall, with broad shoulders and hazel eyes, his short salt and pepper hair a stark contrast to his thick black eyebrows and eyelashes. He was courageous, intelligent and logically minded and he was an Immortal. After Thrae's decision to eradicate the immortality blueprint, Janus painstakingly changed his identity several times over the past one thousand years. One thing that hadn't changed: his lifelong devotion to the planet he loved.

The hologram Third Officer approached the elevated command platform where Janus was seated to report how the Mitel Fleet had planned its invasion to coincide with the recent solar magnetic storm.

"The disturbance created by the sun's pole reversal was unprecedented," he began. "The Mitels realized that the storm would reduce the geomagnetic field just enough to disrupt our deep space surveillance systems."

"So that's how they evaded detection until now," replied Janus, shaking his head in disgust. "They are extremely opportunistic. How long were they able to conceal their energy signatures?"

"Almost three weeks. The storm itself was the largest and most disruptive ever recorded. Our scientists have estimated that such an event takes place once every 473 thousand years."

Janus sat silently for a moment as he processed this latest information.

"The Mitel Leadership obviously took a huge risk," he said. "The storm could have shifted several degrees in their direction and caused extensive damage to their propulsion and communications systems. The Mitels are known for assessing and taking huge risks and as a result, their Fleet is right on top of us."

"Yes Sir."

"Thank you and keep me posted," responded Janus as he studied the light blue translucent features of the hologram Officer's face.

"I will Sir," replied the Third Officer before quickly heading back to the computer area.

Janus shifted his attention toward the three-dimensional images and data fields throughout the command center. He desperately wanted to come up with one last idea that somehow, some way, might save his planet from attack by the Mitel Empire. Janus had replayed the possibility of this moment several times in his mind over the last fifteen years since the first Mitel invasion. Back then, Thraens barely repelled the invading Empire. The loss of life and destruction of infrastructure during that assault was staggering. The realization that a second, *larger* invasion was now unfolding filled Janus with emotion.

His mind wandered as he thought about the remarkable history of scientific breakthroughs on Thrae referred to as the era of *Scientific Revelations*. He also reflected on the World Council's decision to reach out to other inhabited planets within Thrae's celestial neighborhood. The *Thraen Interplanetary Project* was meant to improve the quality of life of other advancing civilizations by sharing its technological knowledge. However, Thrae purposely did not reveal three of its greatest and most profound discoveries: *the secret of immortality (or 'IM'), living holograms and human hybrid technology.* The Mitel Leadership — a group of cunning but aging men — used the outreach program to steal weapons and propulsion technology from Thrae. By the time the World Council realized the true nature of the Mitel Leadership, it was too late. The Leadership had discovered that immortality existed on Thrae and they wanted it — badly — and began an aggressive intimidation campaign to force Thrae to release its secrets. They ordered Mitel commando cells to seize Thraen civilian transport vessels along Thrae's interplanetary travel routes. In return for their safe release, the Leadership demanded the immediate release of the IM blueprint.

The World Council refused to give in to the Mitel demands and attempted to retake control of its vessels. But like a reoccurring nightmare, the outcome was always the same: complete destruction of the transport vessel and total loss of life. Desperate to get the IM blueprint, the Mitel Leadership intensified their efforts. Embedded commando cells were instructed to carry out attacks on the planet to disrupt and kill as many Thraens as possible.

After a series of unusually horrific attacks, the World Council finally informed the Mitel Leadership that IM no longer existed on Thrae as it corrupted the planet. The Mitel Leadership flatly rejected the explanation and stepped up the frequency and intensity of their terror attacks. In response, the World Council commenced a worldwide military campaign to eradicate the Mitel terrorism network. While the mission was successful, the World Council stopped short of attacking Mitel directly. Instead, they chose to isolate it from the rest of Thrae's interplanetary network. But it was too late. Thrae watched from a distance as the Mitel military became second to none. The groundwork had been laid for the first invasion of Thrae.

In time, Janus realized that the decision not to confront the Mitel Leadership and its military had been a grave error. Despite Thrae's inaction, a small yet tenacious Mitel resistance movement slowly developed. Unfortunately, Thraen intelligence concluded that the Mitel resistance could not bring down the brutally repressive Mitel Leadership on its own.

To clear his head, Janus stood up from his black swivel console. He stepped forward and placed both hands on the top bar of the clear composite railing that ran along the edge of his command platform. He stared down at the rows of computers that functioned as the brain of Thrae's coordinated defense system.

We simply don't have enough time to establish our global defensive positioning in outer space. Not that it really matters. Without Battle Spheres to assume the bulk of our counter-attack, our planet faces the strong likelihood of being quickly overrun by the Mitel attack force.

"Excuse me Commander," interrupted the Third Officer. "Our outer defenses report that the Mitel Fleet is almost within attack range. The communications specialists indicate that they are not responding to any of our warning transmissions."

"That's not a surprise, but thank you," answered Janus. "Until further notice, we will operate under full battle mode protocol with no exceptions."

"Yes Sir!"

Just then, Janus heard the all too familiar whirling noise to his left.

"It doesn't look good my friend," said Markus Kilmar, Second in Command, in his unmistakable rough voice. "From what I can see, this Fleet is much larger than the last one. I really don't like the looks of this."

Markus approached Janus slowly, his bronze wedge-shaped containment shell hovering a few inches above the ground. The shell encased him from the waist down, providing artificial kidneys, liver, stomach and intestines. Without it, Markus would be dead. At 1,250 years old, he was now the oldest living Thraen, and despite everything he had been through, his looks were still striking. He had smooth tanned skin, pale blue eyes and thick, long, flowing gray hair reaching below his shoulders; and a neatly cropped matching beard and mustache that covered his large square chin. Like Janus, Markus was an immortal. He had also been born with the ability to transform into a rare and formidable hybrid Battle Sphere.

During the first Mitel invasion, Markus fought side by side with another Battle Sphere known as Zebulon Park. The two played a considerable role in defeating the attacking Fleet. Like Zebulon, Markus continued to engage the Mitel forces long after his plasma-energy reserves had become dangerously depleted. Near the end of the conflict, Markus suffered a series of punishing laser bursts which tore through the lower portion of his weakened outer defense shields. A quick rescue in outer space saved his life, but his extensive injuries left him crippled. Soon thereafter, Zebulon's Battle Sphere collided with a Mitel strike fighter. The impact knocked him unconscious — causing him to spin out of control.

Zebulon began to slowly morph back into human form. Luckily, his remaining outer defense shield lasted just long enough to protect him as he crash landed in a remote mountainous area. Several locals heard the impact and rushed to the crash site. When they arrived, Zebulon had not yet completed his transformation back to flesh and blood. Arcs of plasma-based current raced up and down the silver metallic shard mesh outer skin covering his entire body, indicating the initial phase of a Battle Sphere's hybrid transformation.

Zebulon was carefully transported to a local village where he remained in a coma for five days. When he awoke, his transformation back to human form had completed. Unfortunately — and as hard as he tried — he was never able to morph into a Battle Sphere again. Unable to transform, Zebulon lost any chance of being repaired. The hybrid part of his life was now over. He vanished without a trace soon thereafter, only to become a folklore legend. Markus, on the other hand, struggled through several surgeries and a long recovery. He remained in the public spotlight and continued to help his people as best he could.

Janus and Markus watched the images and data fields for several minutes. As reports poured in, it was clear that Thrae was in grave danger. The Mitel space cruisers made quick work of the Thraen outer defense system, a matrix of spherical defense globes located beyond the planet's atmosphere. They alone were simply no match for such a large scale surprise attack.

Janus reached over to his console and activated the worldwide military communication system.

"This is GDC Commander Stone. We are under attack from the Mitel Fleet. I know I can count on each and every one of you to defend our planet with determination and courage. Thank you and good luck —"

"Excuse me, Sir," the Third Officer interrupted anxiously. "The Mitels have penetrated our outer defenses and their multipurpose fighters are beginning to engage our ground defense systems. Orders, Commander?"

Suddenly, a series of large explosions from outside the Command structure shook the building. Dust drifted down from the ceiling, slowly filling the air. Janus and Markus had no idea that the unfolding events would take control of the invasion's outcome out of their hands.

Approximately one thousand miles away, at Thrae's largest global defense base, a space defense cruiser commenced its vertical takeoff, fully loaded with high-energy plasma defense weapons. As it lifted slowly from the launch area under the power of its electromagnetically charged superconductor disc antigravity propulsion system, a stray yet powerful Mitel cluster pod warhead struck the vessel. The Command Center and all its personnel were immediately vaporized. The catastrophic explosion, and associated system failure caused all shipboard weapons to activate.

Personnel on the ground watched in horror as the massive craft rolled out of control toward one of the base's weapons storage areas. The crash and resulting explosions instantly destroyed everything within a one-hundred-mile radius. The subsequent detonation of the base's underground weapons stockpile began a second and larger explosion that destroyed everything within five hundred miles.

Thrae's defense bases and fusion based energy generation stations, located in an alternating grid pattern every three hundred miles, were strategically placed away from several known super volcanoes across Thrae's interconnected land mass. The initial explosions set off a chain reaction along the grid which quickly formed an immeasurable, rolling energy wave that had the potential to destroy all life on the planet.

In attempting to repel the Mitel Fleet attack, the crippled space defense cruiser sparked the beginning of the destruction of Thrae.

CHAPTER TWO — THE END OF THRAE

Reports of the rolling energy wave raced around the planet. Markus and Janus quickly recognized what was happening and realized there was nothing they or anyone else could do to stop it. Janus estimated that the destructive wave would arrive in forty-five minutes to an hour. Fearing the end of the planet, his thoughts quickly turned to Chad, his one year old son. As a recent widower, Janus was solely responsible for his infant's health and safety. Given the unfolding events, it was clear he had to go get his son.

"I know what you're thinking," said Markus. "You have got to go get that boy of yours. Well go do it!"

"But —"

"But nothing. Take a base hover craft and go get him. I'll watch over things from here."

"OK. If we somehow make it through this alive, I'll find a way to make it up to you," promised Janus.

"I know, my friend, I know," nodded Markus.

Janus turned over command of the GDC to Markus before leaving the Defense Center's main control room. He hurried down a series of corridors, through the twin security entry doors to a nearby base hover craft. Janus powered up the craft, secured his safety harness, and quickly set out toward the local infant care facility.

Rising quickly, he scanned the sky above him. The air traffic grid was congested. The grid consisted of a series of invisible antigravity skyways located five hundred to one thousand feet above the ground. Small and medium sized transport craft entered and exited the grid at predetermined transition points and flew in queue to their preprogrammed destinations. It was statistically the safest way to travel on Thrae, although not the fastest.

Some ten miles off in the distance, Janus's eye caught the gleaming reflection from the region's most famous landmark — the Assal sky structure. At two thousand feet high and located in the exact center of the large population cluster of Tryden, it was the tallest vertical sky structure on the planet.

Thraen population clusters contained 40 to 80 gleaming glass covered sky structures. Circular at their base, the structures curved up into the sky to form a group of tightly bundled cylinders of different heights. The structures were positioned in a descending pattern from the cluster's center, with air traffic grids weaving their way between them. From a distance, the grids appeared as glistening rivers suspended high in the air.

In the four minutes it took Janus to reach the infant care facility, he watched people make their way toward the intricate network of underground defense shelters for protection. He shook his head in disgust. There was nothing that anyone could do to prevent this tragedy. Janus tried to block out as much of what was happening as possible. To do otherwise would likely make him unable to function.

Janus landed in an open area adjacent to the infant care structure. He jumped out of the hover craft, entered the facility, and ran up the two flights of stairs. As he burst in, only Chad and one young frightened infant care specialist remained. He had seen the young woman there many times before but suddenly realized that he didn't even know her name.

She gently handed Chad to Janus who hugged him tightly. Looking into the woman's teary eyes, Janus sensed that she knew a horrific event was unfolding.

"Do you have a place to go?" he asked.

She nodded yes, wiping away her tears.

"Then go now, and hurry," said Janus, squeezing her hand before she ran off. He picked up his son's belongings and carried Chad back down the stairs, trying to figure out what to do next. When he arrived outside, the hover craft was gone. It had been stolen.

How could I have been so careless? Janus thought.

There was no one in sight and it had become oddly quiet. Janus glanced up to see that the grid was still congested. He knew that time was running out. Suddenly, he heard a familiar whirling sound getting closer. A base transport hover craft appeared over the trees to his right. Janus grabbed his identification device from his jacket pocket and pointed it toward the craft. Having registered his signal, it quickly banked toward Janus coming to a stop in the open area next to him.

"Are you ok?" asked the lone pilot.

Before Janus could reply, the pilot noticed the Commander markings on Janus's uniform.

"Sorry Sir, I —"

"Don't worry. I'm lucky you came along. Are you heading back to the Command Center?"

"I am *now*, Sir," replied the pilot quickly.

"Great. Thank you," responded Janus as he struggled to climb into the hover craft, his son in one arm and his belongings in the other.

"Let me help you, Sir," offered the pilot, holding out his arms.

Janus handed Chad up to the pilot, climbed in and off they went. Janus scanned the scenery below as groups of people made their way toward the defense shelter entrances that dotted the landscape. Up above, the grid was at a complete standstill.

"They're hopelessly trapped," he muttered quietly. "They will be the first to see the explosion wave as it approaches, and there will be nothing they can do."

Janus turned away in frustration toward Chad who was sitting patiently in his lap. Looking into his son's eyes, Janus's mind began to race.

What can I do to save you my little one? he wondered. Then it occurred to him.

I'll put Chad in a USEP (Universal Speed Escape Pod) *and send him to another inhabited planet! It's his only chance.*

In his current position as GDC Commander, Janus's team had developed accelerated space travel technology under the guise of a safety and survival program. Janus painstakingly presented the outward appearance that the USEP program was simply developing a small high-speed escape craft following the World Council's decision to pursue a general policy of isolation for the foreseeable future.

The small experimental pod could travel extremely long distances through deep space, within a few days. The craft was surrounded by a series of interconnected plasma shields to protect it. The small pod was propelled faster than the speed of light by a large cylindrical graphene ring which spun furiously around the outside of the pod like a high-speed jump rope. As the ring spun at full speed, the USEP could bend both space and time by contracting space in front of the craft and expanding space behind it. Just before the pod accelerated at normal speed, four large ring components extended from underneath the pod via powerful positioning bars. The four curving cylindrical sections turned, rotated and locked together to form the ring itself. At the same time, the ring drive shaft extended from each side of the pod's midpoint before being clamped down on by two of the assembling ring sections. Once activated, the spinning ring would immediately cause the pod to accelerate faster than the speed of light.

The pod's plasma shields were designed to insulate the craft, occupants, and its contents by absorbing, attenuating, and filtering the tremendous g-forces generated by the high-speed travel. The plasma shields also temporarily stored kinetic energy which was used to power the craft's slip ring drive, plasma shields and lower-than-light speed engines. Janus had worked tirelessly on all aspects of the pod's design, development, fabrication, programming and testing. By now, he knew the craft better than he knew himself.

In time, the pod achieved speeds more than ten times the speed of light. But that was not the best part. During prototype testing, Janus and his small team stumbled upon the most crucial discovery of all: once the USEP reached approximately twelve times the speed of light, its gravitational field caused the craft to resonate at the exact same frequency as deep space. This allowed the pod to slip through space for light years at a time *in mere seconds,* analogous to electric current running through a wire. The slip would then trigger the spinning cylindrical ring to slow down and the craft to decelerate to less than the speed of light. Once the ring came back up to speed, the process would repeat. Extensive testing had confirmed that the instantaneous travel or *slip speed* (as it was referred to by the development team) would end when enough energy resistance caused the pod's resonating frequency to change as compared to its natural surroundings.

Despite the successful tests, lack of funding prevented the team from building and testing a craft large enough to carry a flight crew. As a result, the experimental pods were only large enough to carry the monitoring and test equipment and not much else.

The second challenge for the USEP development program was to create an artificial gravity system. Janus's design team eventually integrated a complex series of magnetic charges imbedded in several locations within the inner layers of the pod's plasma shields, that produced a self-adjusting magnetic field almost identically matched to the gravity on Thrae of 31.931 feet per second squared. The magnetic field provided an added benefit: it shielded the craft from the damaging effects of cosmic radiation as it hurtled through deep space.

Chad would fit! Janus thought. It was a desperate plan, but Janus could not come up with a better idea. The question remained: *where to send him*? There wasn't much time for him to work out the details.

The transport craft slowed down. Directly below was the GDC Command Center. Janus signaled the hover craft airman to drop him off in front of the main building. He jumped out before the pilot handed Chad and his belongings down to him.

"Good luck, Sir!" yelled the pilot.

"Thank you. You too," replied Janus as he turned and hurried toward the main entrance.

Stopping in front of the building, Janus entered the applicable voice recognition security codes before stepping ahead for an eye recognition scan. When it beeped, he quickly made his way through two sets of doors which slid closed behind him.

The Command Center was chaotic and loud as base personnel scrambled in every direction. Janus could not make out the instructions over the base intercom system. He hurried down a hallway that led to three HorVert (Horizontal Vertical) elevators. Upon entering the middle one, he quickly instructed it to head directly to the USEP facility. The elevator hummed downwards and then diagonally across the command facility. When he arrived, Janus hurriedly stepped out clutching Chad and his belongings. Looking around, he noticed that the area was deserted. *Not a big surprise,* Janus thought.

The USEP area had seen little activity in recent months due to the lack of funding. The area itself was housed in the last old Thraen defense fortress, the most heavily fortified building on the planet. With the advent of the outer space defense system, the old defense fortresses had been dismantled over time and recycled.

Janus rushed down a hallway to a large open room containing four rows of computer stations. Five USEP pod storage bays were located beyond the computers along a long, curved wall. He placed Chad on the floor beside him as he sat down to use a computer in the third row. As Janus began typing, he heard muffled explosions. He entered a code on a keypad next to the computer to call Markus in the command center.

"Markus, what's happening?"

"The Mitels decimated our outer space defense and their fighters are now attacking our surface forces."

Powered by sophisticated plasma engines, thrust vectoring and gyroscopic directional systems, the agile and durable Mitel Fighters could operate effectively in both outer space and atmospheric conditions. They represented the apex of Mitel's own engineering achievements.

"That's not good," replied Janus.

"No, it's not. We're trying to mount a counter-attack."

Another, much larger explosion shook the entire building. Small particles of dust and debris sifted down from the ceiling.

"Where might you be?" asked Markus.

"In the USEP facility."

"The USEP?" asked Markus, somewhat confused.

"I'm here with Chad."

There was a brief silence.

"OK, my friend. I understand now. Do what you need to do and give the boy a kiss for me."

A soft beep signaled that Markus had ceased communications.

Glancing around the USEP facility, Janus paused to gather his thoughts. He then began to type furiously, accessing the system computers. They confirmed that the pod in bay number three was partially energized and otherwise ready to go. Janus instructed the computer to begin the pod's launch sequence. It would take the computer a few minutes to cycle through the safety checks before the sequence was fully activated. In the meantime,

16

he picked up Chad and made his way further down the hall toward the nutrition area.

When Janus arrived, he grabbed a large empty storage bin on wheels from the corner. He lowered Chad into the container who shrieked with joy to have found a new play area. Janus wheeled Chad over to the long row of food storage compartments. He fumbled through his coat pocket for his silver metallic security medallion before holding the coin shaped object in front of the identification eye. One by one, Janus ordered various non-perishable foods and beverages, placing the packages in the bin next to Chad. As he did, his son touched and inspected each one. When he was done, Janus handed Chad his security medallion to keep him occupied.

Guessing that the initiation sequence was now complete, Janus pushed the container back down the hall to the large open area. The doors to bay number three had opened to reveal the sleek silver and white wedge-shaped pod with its raised GDC USEP emblem displayed in several locations across each side of the craft. The pod's curved nose expanded on either side toward the rear of the craft before transitioning into trapezoidal shaped wings. In the back, the pod contained a triangular vertical stabilizer on each corner and a propulsion slot that extended rearward — its opening located just beyond the rear surface of the wing tips. Stored tightly underneath the pod and wings beginning at its midpoint, sat four large quarter circle ring sections, curving rearwards, two on each side. The ring sections were arranged in an alternating pattern since they extended beyond the centerline of the pod, due to their size. Each ring section contained large GDC USEP emblems. Janus stared briefly at the pod with a sense of both pride and accomplishment.

Janus pushed the container through the bay opening and typed the six-digit code into the pod's keypad located next to the outer airlock door. With a whoosh, the door opened. He then inserted the same code into the second keypad positioned just inside the small airlock chamber. As the interior door swooshed open, the pod's inner lights powered up. Janus surveyed the interior of the pod, noting that it was relatively empty.

After unloading most of the contents of the cart into the pod storage bins located on either side of the craft, Janus left Chad in the container to return to the computer to program the pod for launch mode. After entering a series of instructions, he paused to take a deep breath.

Which far off planet should I send him to? Janus contemplated. *It doesn't make sense to send the small pod closer to the center of the universe given the more extreme conditions there, and I can't risk sending Chad outside of our galaxy spiral. The distances are much too great even for the USEP.*

Then it suddenly dawned on him. *There's a planet a little over six hundred light years further out along our galaxy spiral which is almost identical to Thrae. It's still a long way, but certainly within reach of the small pod, and well beyond the reach of the Mitels.*

Janus began to pull together the final details in his mind, when he began to panic.

The plan won't work! Janus thought. *I can't send an infant into outer space all by himself! The USEP is not advanced enough to carry out such a mission on its own. How could I have been so stupid?*

As Janus stared glumly at the pod, another large explosion shook the building. He jumped from his seat to check on Chad. Janus then heard the familiar beep of the facility communications system.

"Stone," Janus said in an agitated tone.

"It's Markus. Things do not look good. Our ground defense forces are overrun. And the explosion wave is approaching fast. I have ordered all nonessential personnel to the defense shelters."

"How long until the wave arrives?" asked Janus grimly.

"Twenty minutes."

Janus glanced back toward the storage container.

"How are things going over there?" asked Markus.

"Not well."

"And why not?" Markus asked sensing Janus's frustration.

"Because I don't think I can do it."

"You can't start the USEP's launch sequence?"

"No. I did that."

"You can't activate the large launch pod?"

"No, Markus, *that's not it*!" said Janus tersely "I can't do it. I can't just send my son away, across the universe, in a small pod by himself."

"I'm on my way."

With that, the communication system beeped again and Markus was gone.

Time was growing short and with no better plan in mind, Janus hurried back toward bay number three. He lifted Chad from the cart and placed him carefully in the pod before transferring the remaining food and beverages into the pod's side bins.

"What am I going to do?" Janus asked himself as he looked toward the pod's console computer.

While scanning the console readouts, he heard the familiar whirl coming down the hallway.

"What seems to be the problem here my friend?" bellowed Markus with his trademark smile.

Janus stared at Markus, but didn't know what to say.

"Listen," said Markus quickly, "your boy can't stay here, that's for sure."

"But I can't just send him up there," Janus began. "He can't feed himself, or operate the pod, find a suitable planet or even land the pod for that matter! It was a stupid and foolish idea."

"You are right on all counts — all except the last one."

"What do you mean?"

"I was thinking . . ." replied Markus slowly.

"About what?"

"How you could accompany Chad on his voyage."

"*What*?"

"You could keep him company, feed him and find a suitable planet along the way," Markus explained calmly.

"Well, even if I said yes, Markus, I won't fit."

"A hologram would fit comfortably."

Janus thought for a moment before answering.

"But how?"

"In bay number five," Markus said, pointing toward the wall. "There are about a dozen monitoring orbs in there. I can shoot your hologram image into one of them and then you will fit easily."

"Markus, I . . ." said Janus as tears began to fill his eyes.

"What, my friend?" frowned Markus.

"I have to stay here. I have to do what I can to help our people through this disaster," explained Janus weakly.

"Help them through this!" bellowed Markus. "You know as well as I do that no one is going to make it through this disaster alive!"

"We don't know that for sure Markus," protested Janus. "I need to stay here and help. I owe it to them. This invasion — this disaster — it's my fault. I need to stay here and help."

"You know that what you are saying is not true. You have dedicated your *entire life* to the people of this planet and have *always* put yourself second to the needs of everyone else. You have guided our people through good times and bad. You have also accepted, and never complained about, the unjust and wrong accounting of your accomplishments by the historical bureaucrats. And you have endured more than your share of tragedies while being reduced to quietly and humbly living a secret life among your people. Despite all of this, you have never lost your faith in this planet and its people."

Markus paused for a few seconds, letting his words sink in.

"Sejus, you need to go with your son."

Markus was the only remaining Thraen who knew Janus by that name and it sounded foreign to him. During the later stages of Scientific Revelations, when immortality began to unravel, Janus was known as Chancellor Sejus Theron, head of the World Council. That tumultuous and painful period in Thrae's history so long ago still haunts him. Janus stared at the pod. "Markus, I can't go."

"You have *never* changed my friend. You are as stubborn as the day I first met you."

Janus smiled weakly at Markus.

"Then *I* will go with the boy, Sejus," said Markus softly.

"Well, I —"

"Listen," interrupted Markus, tapping his knuckles against his shiny metallic wedge. "It's no secret that I despise this tin can that's keeping me alive. I also know my days in this device are numbered. I might as well have some fun floating around for a little while until I get the boy settled somewhere safe."

"Thank you, Markus. I couldn't think of a better person and friend to do this."

With that, Janus quickly made his way back to the third row of computers. With a series of key strokes, the doors to bay five glided open. Inside were a dozen gleaming silver monitoring orbs about a foot and a half each in diameter with three black or blue stripes — one along the top and on each side which met in the back to form an oversized arrow. Directly in the front was a shiny oblong screen.

The small orbs used a time-tested Thraen technology to achieve their antigravity propulsion: a spinning superconductor ceramic disc in its center, surrounded by a hermetically sealed film of frictionless helium-4 superfluid sonically stimulated with electromagnetic energy to produce *gravitational propulsion.* The angular momentum of the spinning disc controlled the direction and speed of the orb. Over time, Thraen scientists applied gravitational propulsion technology to a wide range of Thraen flight applications. Later, scientists developed electromagnetically charged plasma fluid chambers surrounding a solid superconductor sphere to achieve the same result.

"Go check on your boy," instructed Markus as the two of them stared at the orbs.

As Janus headed back toward the USEP pod, Markus whirled over to another computer in the middle of the second row and quickly began to type.

"I think I would look good in blue," Markus said to himself.

In a matter of seconds, a silver and blue monitoring orb activated and slowly rose above the floor. Markus directed the computer to transport the orb to a specific open area in the room. As it reached the designated spot, the orb stopped and hovered silently. Markus then programmed the orb to accept the Thraen hologram technology.

"OK, I think we are ready to go," he clapped.

Markus glided over to another computer at the end of the row. He entered a few commands causing an overhead panel to slide open. A large black L-shaped tubular machine with a complex array of cables and control boxes descended from the ceiling. On either end was a large convex shaped perforated cap. The device had always reminded Markus of a very large microscope. The machine had only one purpose: to transform whatever it scanned into an identical and similarly functioning three-dimensional hologram.

"Time to put me in," said Markus loudly.

With that announcement, Markus whirled over and positioned himself directly under the shorter vertical cylinder. As he did, Janus hurried back over to the second-row computer and positioned the monitoring orb directly in front of the longer horizontal cylinder.

"Are you ready?" asked Janus cautiously.

"Ready as I'll ever be," Markus smiled broadly.

"Once I do this, there is no turning back. You will be a hologram —"

"For the rest of my existence, I know."

Janus paused and stared silently at Markus.

"It's OK, Sejus. This is what I want to do."

Janus glanced back down at the panel and hit the button. There was a loud humming. Markus smiled and gave a brief wave, then disappeared. The machine quickly powered down and went quiet. Only a hint of gray smoke remained where Markus had once stood.

Janus shifted his attention to the orb. For a moment, it hovered quietly.

"Well, that wasn't so bad!" boomed Markus's voice from the sphere. "An incredibly sharp pain for a few seconds — like an electric shock — and here I am!"

With that, his orb raced around the room. Janus watched with amusement as the monitoring orb circled and bobbed up and down before it returned, hovering in front of Janus.

"It seems quite operational enough," announced Markus. "OK, one last thing."

A bright beam of light projected down to the floor from a small lens located just below the horizontal blue stripe on Markus's orb. From the ground rose a life size three-dimensional hologram of Markus. The opaque hologram glowed brightly, surrounded by a light blue hue. Janus stared at the hologram, amazed at how detailed and accurate the image was. The only difference was that Markus appeared fully human.

"Hey look!" Markus exclaimed. "What do you know, I have legs again! The machine recreated the lower portion of my hologram based on my DNA profile!"

Markus walked around in a tight circle before stopping for a moment to stare at his reflection in front of a bright reflective support column. "I think I'm even a bit taller!"

He walked over to the first row of computers and sat down. As he did, the back of his legs and lower portions of his torso began to sparkle brightly. "Let us see how well this works."

As he typed, wherever his fingers touched emitted the same sparkling light.

"See how the focused energy allows me to perform everyday tasks?" marveled Markus. "It feels a bit different though, a little tingly. I always thought the development of hologram technology was the best thing we ever created —"

Markus was interrupted by a series of large explosions that shook the building again. The power flickered momentarily but stayed on. A very fine dust filtered down from the ceiling and slowly filled the room.

"OK, Markus, I think it's now or never," said Janus anxiously.

The two of them walked back over to the USEP pod. As Janus looked inside he saw that Chad was scared and confused. Janus reached down, picked up his son and gave him a long hug.

"I love you my boy," said Janus as tears filled his eyes once again. Chad smiled back at his father.

Janus placed Chad back into the pod while Markus's orb floated through the door, followed closely by his hologram form. Markus sat down next to Chad and looked at him with a broad smile. He reached over and picked up the boy, emitting the same bright sparkling light.

"You are not scared of old uncle Markus now are you my little one?" he asked quietly.

Chad let out a big giggle as he touched Markus's nose making it sparkle. Chad laughed even louder.

"Looks like he has forgotten me already," said Janus.

"Maybe it's a good time to launch us then," replied Markus.

"I think you're right. Please strap him carefully into one of the cargo restraints."

"OK, my friend, I'll do it now."

Janus made his way back to the computer and pushed the button that closed the interlocking interior and exterior pod doors. The computer monitor indicated that the pod was ready to launch.

Janus switched on the communication channel.

"Can you hear me Markus?"

"I hear you loud and clear."

"Is Chad secure and ready?"

"Yes."

"And how about you Markus — are you all set?"

"Affirmative," replied Markus calmly.

"OK. After I launch you into orbit, I'll activate your departure sequence from here. The USEP will automatically propel you a safe distance from the planet before commencing faster than light speed. Once you reach slip speed, you should monitor and adjust your course if —"

"Janus," interrupted Markus.

"What?"

"I know."

Janus paused for a moment to stare at the pod. Another series of loud explosions caused the lights to flicker before the power went off. After a few seconds, the backup power engaged and everything came back on line with a loud whirl. Janus could see that the dust cloud was growing heavier.

They are getting very close, he thought.

Janus entered the pre-launch instructions into the computer. The number three bay doors slid closed while the pod was transported down a tunnel to a waiting multipurpose, reusable launch pod to piggyback the small spacecraft into outer space. It was oblong and contained triangular wings in the front and rear with matching trapezoidal shaped winglets. After it arrived, the USEP was robotically attached at the midpoint of the launch pod.

Waiting for confirmation that the pre-launch sequence was complete, Janus feverishly programmed the USEP's high speed exit trajectory toward the galaxy's outer spiral arm. He then instructed the computer to search for the precise coordinates of planet 5.1.18.20.9. Janus stared impatiently at the monitor for confirmation that the exit trajectory and general flight information had been uploaded into the USEP's computer. When confirmation arrived, he activated the small pod's low speed invisibility system — consisting of a series of plasma energy panels that formed a highly sensitive second skin around the entire pod. The panels absorbed all forms of scanning and radar energy which it expelled on the opposite side of the pod. This gave the illusion of an uninterrupted scan making the pod impossible to detect.

While the computer retrieved the destination planet's coordinates, Janus found himself staring at the launch initiation switch. *Good-bye Chad,* he thought, as so many memories flooded his mind. He closed his eyes briefly before activating the switch, commencing the launch.

Seconds later, the USEP streaked toward the sky on the back of the launch pod. Janus moved over to the tracking computer to monitor its progress. Racing through the upper atmosphere, the pod slowed down dramatically before automatically releasing the small spacecraft. Janus then activated its internal propulsion system, pushing the pod further into outer space. Once confirmation arrived that the pod had reached a safe orbit, Janus prepared to commence what was referred to in the USEP facility as the *sling shot.*

"Markus, can you hear me?" asked Janus over the encrypted communications system.

"Yes, I can," replied Markus.

"Good! I am going to start energizing the pod's slip ring for your departure. The last thing I need to do is upload the planets exact coordinates into the pod's navigation system—"

"Oh no!" interrupted Markus.

"What?"

"My monitoring orb has detected Mitel vessels all around us. There are so *many*!"

Janus did not panic. He glanced at the status of the data retrieval before shifting his focus to the pod's slip ring energizing process which reached *50, 55* then *60* percent.

"Still energizing," said Janus.

Hearing his father's voice, Chad began to cry. It was a long, sad cry that told Janus his son realized that his father was missing.

"Is everything still OK Markus?"

"Yes, we are fine," said Markus.

I hope you can forgive me some day my son, thought Janus as he struggled to concentrate on the launch.

"What's taking the computer so long to retrieve those coordinates?" Janus muttered in frustration.

As Chad's crying continued in the background, Janus refocused on the energizing status which had reached *85, 90* then *95* percent. *Come on, come on!* he thought.

At that exact moment, a red light flashed above Janus. It was followed by a series of long beeps. Over the intercom came the warning: "DANGER! EXPLOSIVE WAVE APPROACHING IN FIVE MINUTES! REPEAT, EXPLOSIVE WAVE APPROACHING IN FIVE MINUTES!

SEEK SHELTER IMMEDIATELY!" The long beeps continued and the message was repeated.

It's almost here, thought Janus.

"Markus," Janus stated firmly.

"Yes, my friend."

"The pod is fully energized. It's time to initiate departure. Are you ready up there?"

"We're ready."

Struggling to remain calm, Janus thought, *I need the planet's exact coordinates now!*

Chad's cries suddenly turned from sad to angry as he struggled to free himself from his protective harness.

"Calm down little one," said Markus.

But Chad simply became more agitated as he struggled to free himself. Markus watched with amazement as Chad's eyes turned bright white before a metallic silver shard mesh spread from his eyes that covered his head, then the rest of his body. Stunned at what he was seeing, Markus realized that Chad was beginning a hybrid transformation. Given its distinctive characteristics, Markus realized that the boy was not only a hybrid, but a rare Battle Sphere!

Chad studied Markus briefly before shifting his gaze to the many lights and three-dimensional displays located on the USEPs programming console. Suddenly, Chad emitted white beams of energy from his eyes that struck the center of the console. Sparks flew in all directions before portions of the console went dark. Markus quickly reached for Chad and unbuckled him from his harness, convinced he would destroy the pod at any moment! But, as he raised him up from his harness, Chad's attention was diverted back to the white sparkles where Markus was holding him.

"Calm down little one. It's going to be OK. I promise," said Markus softly.

Chad stared at the many sparkles being emitted by Markus's hologram. As he touched and played with Markus's sparkling white ears, Chad transformed back to normal.

In the USEP facility, Janus tried to focus over the noise of the alarm. Out of the corner of his eye, he noticed an indicator flashing *malfunction* in the lower left corner. Puzzled as to the problem, Janus frantically searched through the screen diagnostics, quickly determining that the invisibility shields had failed and the departure triggering mechanism had malfunctioned.

"Markus!" shouted Janus.

"I'm here," confirmed Markus. "We have a problem. I'm not sure why, but Chad worked himself into such a state that he began a *hybrid transformation*. Not only that, but it appears that your son is a *Battle Sphere*."

"Markus, that's impossible," scoffed Janus.

"It's true," began Markus. "Scans by my monitoring orb confirmed my suspicion. Unfortunately, before I could calm him down, he sent out a short plasma laser energy burst from his eyes which damaged the programming console."

"Markus, he's just a baby!"

"I'm shocked too, my friend. If I had not seen it for myself, I wouldn't have believed it either."

Positioned just above Thrae's outer atmosphere, a Mitel battle cruiser patrolled the area for any remaining pockets of resistance from the Thraen space defense forces. In the cruiser's Integrated Command Center referred to as the ICC, the scanning specialist noticed the

USEP's modest signature profile. His computer quickly identified the object as being a small Thraen pod. The huge battle cruiser was the newest weapon in the Mitel Fleet, commanded by a young but savvy officer named Zan Liss.

Zan, muscular and almost seven feet tall, was an awe-inspiring individual even as Mitel soldiers go. He was completely bald but had thick black eyebrows and a full mustache and goatee. Despite his imposing appearance, the young Commander's best attributes were his intelligence, leadership and practical understanding of a wide range of Mitel military technologies and tactics.

When Zan was six, Mitel soldiers stormed his family's home. He watched in horror as his parents were killed by lethal blasts from hand-held electro lasers. He is haunted to this day by the blank stare in his father's eyes as he lay dead on the floor. Zan was immediately taken into custody by the soldiers and brought to their base. Senior Officers sat him down and explained that his parents were cold blooded murderers who had ruthlessly butchered countless soldiers and security personnel over the years to evade capture. Zan sobbed uncontrollably. He did not want to believe what the Officers were telling him, but he was scared, confused and alone.

Zan was raised on the base by a series of military foster parents and in time, the vivid memories of his parents' violent death faded. He spent his free time working on Mitel Fighters at the base. His insatiable curiosity led him to become an expert mechanic, computer troubleshooter, and eventually a pilot. He also displayed a keen interest in military strategy, technology, programs and innovation. Base personnel would often shake their heads and laugh, saying that Zan could run the entire base all by himself.

In his spare time, Zan enjoyed a popular form of one to one combat called Closed Cage Club Fighting (CCCF) which was fought in a metal mesh enclosure called the *cage*. The only instrument allowed inside the steel enclosure was a five-foot long one inch diameter solid metal pole called the *club* — padded on either end to help avoid severe injury. CCCF allowed Zan to use his strength, speed and agility to its fullest potential. The competitions also provided an outlet for his subconscious rage surrounding the violent death of his parents. He was always matched against older and more experienced competitors, which often included cadets from the elite Mitel Military Academy. Zan never lost and took great pride in beating up the arrogant cadets. One day, he was told that a graduating cadet by the name of Lon Rexx wanted to fight him. Lon was also undefeated and in the process, had killed five opponents in the cage and badly maimed several others.

Zan had heard about Lon, and how his family had also been brutally murdered by the Mitel embedded Special Forces when he was just a child. Back then, at the last minute, Lon went to visit a friend which spared his life. In time, Lon was adopted by a member of the Mitel Leadership but his anger and rage proved to be too much to handle. Lon was eventually sent away to a military academy for young boys to figure things out, a plan that did not go well.

As the match approached, Zan trained relentlessly during the day and stayed up at night trying to figure out how one human could inflict such damage against another using only the club. On the morning of the match, he was nervous. As he climbed into the ring and saw Lon for the first time, he was taken aback by Lon's size and stoic demeanor.

Once the buzzer sounded signaling the start of the fight, Zan used his speed and agility to deflect and avoid several blows. After the first scheduled break, before the match was set to resume, Lon leaped forward and staggered Zan with a direct hit to the side of his head, rupturing an eardrum. As blood poured down the side of his face, Zan's pent up rage was unleashed like never before. Using his incredible strength, Zan attacked Lon relentlessly until he beat him unconscious. As trainers and staff rushed into the cage, Zan reached down and grabbed Lon's club, smashing it against a large pipe located along the side of the cage. Iron pellets flew in all directions from each end. Everyone in the cage immediately knew how and why Lon had killed his opponents: by cheating. Even though Lon was permanently barred from participating in further CCCF competitions, he went on to graduate with honors from the Mitel Military Academy.

As his reputation grew, Zan's natural leadership was quickly recognized by Senior Officers. At the age of 17, he became one of the youngest commissioned Officers in the Mitel military. Only four years later, he was a Mitel cruiser commander.

"Commander, my computer scanners have detected the sudden appearance of a very a small Thraen pod up ahead," announced the scanning specialist.

"What do you make of it?" asked Zan.

"I'm not sure. It seemed to have come out of no-where."

"Perform a detailed scan," instructed Zan, his voice deep and confident. "I want to know exactly *what* it is."

"Yes Commander."

In the USEP facility, a red indicator light blinked on and off next to Janus confirming that the pod was being scanned.

"Markus — sensors are showing that you've been detected."

Janus tried to reset and reactivate the pod's invisibility system and departure triggering mechanism without success. Just then, planet 5.1.18.20.9's coordinate data appeared on Janus's computer screen.

"Markus, I can't activate the departure sequence or re-establish the invisibility screens."

At that instant, the series of warning beeps were replaced with a long signal burst. Janus knew what this meant. The energy wave was about to hit the base.

"Markus," asked Janus, "Are you able to assess the extent of the damage?"

"I'm sorry Sejus, I don't know the USEP like you do," confessed Markus. "We appear to be adrift at the moment."

"What am I going to do?" muttered Janus.

He knew he was out of time and his plan had failed. His son would either be killed or captured by the Mitel Fleet.

I've got to get up there! Frustrated and worried, he found himself staring at the doors to bay number five.

"Markus, I have an idea." Instinctively, Janus switched computers and furiously went to work. He reactivated the hologram scanner and energized a second monitoring orb in bay number five. A silver and black sphere floated out from the bay. Janus positioned it next to the horizontal arm of the scanner, then jumped to the next row of computers and set the takeoff sequence for a second multipurpose launch pod. Knowing he would only have one chance, he set the destination coordinates to match the current trajectory of the USEP pod and programmed the launch pod timer for sixty seconds. As the doors to bay number three slid back open, Janus switched on the hologram scanner. With a deep breath, he sprinted under the vertical chamber. Within a few seconds, there was only a puff of smoke where Janus once stood.

Janus felt momentarily dizzy. Regaining his bearings, he could see the open bay directly in front of him. He knew he had to reach the launch pod before it took off. His black and silver monitoring orb streaked down the tunnel to the waiting launch pod. As he entered the launch area, he darted up toward the door at the top of the launch pod. The bright white electromagnetic glow at the base of the pod signaled that launch was imminent.

As his orb approached the launch pod door, a beam of light appeared from the left side of his sphere. An instant later, Janus's hologram materialized. He felt a strange, tingling sensation throughout his entire self. Janus refocused, reached over, and entered the program code into the pod's exterior keypad causing the outer airlock door to slide open. He moved inside and repeated the process, triggering the pod's inner door to open. Entering the pod, his monitoring orb notified him of a disturbance approaching only seconds away. Janus entered the emergency override code on the inside keypad, which quickly closed both pod doors.

Janus glanced around the pod while his orb floated silently next to him. Suddenly, the pod raced skyward. Janus looked out the windows directly opposite the pod door and saw the ground below falling away from him. He watched in awe as the energy wave consumed the base and everything else in its path.

In the distance, Janus saw the Assal sky structure and the rest of the large population cluster of Tryden. The air traffic grid was still heavily congested. He watched helplessly as the explosion wave raced toward the cluster before quickly engulfing it. As the wave continued, only the upper sections of the Assal sky structure remained visible, before slowly disappearing into the rising haze.

The launch pod streaked skyward as it passed through the upper levels of the rolling cloud of dust and debris that trailed the destruction. As the pod cleared the last remnants of the airborne debris, Janus looked out toward the horizon. He was shocked at the magnitude of the devastation. Countless fires raged out of control off in the distance.

This truly is the end of Thrae, he thought. Repulsed by the enormity of the catastrophe, Janus turned away.

From his computer console, the scanning specialist studied the results of his detailed scan.

"Commander Liss," announced the specialist, "the scan confirms that there is a single Thraen life form on board the pod."

"What is its trajectory?" asked Zan calmly.
The scanning specialist frowned as he turned toward his Commander. "It's just sitting there."

"Navigator, set a course for that vessel immediately. I want to find out how this Thraen suddenly appeared out of nowhere during our invasion, and I want to know what that craft is hiding."

"Doing it now, Commander," replied Ard Lindar, a 20-year old Navigator and third Officer in Command.

Even though Ard's early childhood was similar to Zan's — his father was also killed when he was very young — Ard's path to becoming a Mitel Officer was quite different. His mother remarried a Mitel Leadership member and Ard was sent away to attend the prestigious Mitel Military Academy, where he graduated near the top of his class. He had a love for history and was a deep thinker. Like Zan, he was tall, but much leaner, with short brown hair and charcoal black eyes that helped him hide his emotions.

Watching his stepfather closely, Ard developed a deep distrust of the Mitel Leadership, but he kept those feelings well hidden. Ard did however, look up to and respect Zan, given their common experiences early in life. He also marveled at how Zan so rapidly ascended the intensely competitive Mitel military ranks.

For his part, Zan considered Ard nothing more than a self-centered spoiled brat who, in his opinion, had been handed his career on a silver platter. As far as Zan Liss was concerned, Ard was of little use to him.

As Janus's launch pod reached the upper atmosphere, he was filled with emotion ranging from anger to sorrow. Then it suddenly dawned on him: even in his new state, he retained his ability to feel and express emotion. This revelation took him by surprise, but he also knew that he had to focus all his attention on the task at hand. Janus glanced back out the pod windows to see the launch pod entering outer space.

As the craft's propulsion system slowed down, Janus looked for the USEP. He heard sounds of the launch pod's thrusters firing intermittently. As the launch craft rotated, Janus continued to search for any sign of the small spacecraft. Once the launch pod completed its rotation, the shiny pod appeared directly in front of him.

The scanning specialist instructed his computer to update its initial scan. To his surprise, it confirmed the presence of a second pod.

"Commander," exclaimed the specialist, "A second, larger unmanned craft has appeared right next to the Thraen vessel."

"This is getting interesting," replied Zan, slowly stroking his lower jaw. "What else does your detailed scan show?"

"The smaller craft appears to contain an assortment of test equipment and other supplies. I am also receiving unusual energy signatures consistent with that of small monitoring probes."

"What can you tell me about the Thraen on board the craft?"

"The detailed scan indicates that it's a young male, probably a child, or an infant."

"A child or an infant?" responded Zan incredulously. "*All alone in space*? What nonsense is this? Does your scan reveal anything else, specialist?"

"The chemical composition of the Thraen . . ."

"What about it?" Zan asked impatiently.

"The scan warns that he possesses abnormally high levels of titanium, aluminum, beryllium, cobalt, manganese and cadmium," explained the confused specialist.

"Very interesting," boomed Zan.

"Commander?" Ard frowned.

"We have stumbled upon a *living Thraen hybrid!*" replied Zan. "We must intercept that craft immediately. I *must* get my hands on him!"

"Increasing intercept speed now," confirmed Ard quickly.

"Good, we cannot lose that vessel," Zan insisted.

Using his monitoring orb's communication system, Janus tried to contact Markus.

"Markus, can you hear me?"

There was no response. Janus tried re-transmitting over other frequencies.

"Markus," urged Janus.

"Hello, my friend, I can hear you," replied Markus.

Janus was relieved to hear Markus's voice. "We need to get the pod operational so that we can complete the departure. If not, we will be captured by the Mitel Fleet. We can't let them have my son, nor can we hand over a Thraen immortal *and* a Battle Sphere — especially one that doesn't even know how to defend itself."

"You're right, but how are we going to avoid such a result?"

Janus did not answer.

In the battle cruiser's ICC, the communications specialist intercepted the unencrypted transmission.

"Commander Liss!" announced the specialist excitedly. "I have intercepted and translated a transmission between the two crafts!"

"And?" replied Zan jumping up from his command console.

"The transmission confirms that the young Thraen is not only a hybrid, but a Battle Sphere *and an immortal!*" exclaimed the specialist.

"An infant Battle Sphere *and* an immortal?" exclaimed Zan, surprised and excited. "This is too good to be true! We *must* capture that craft at all costs!"

Zan paused briefly before continuing.

"Our *Leadership's* primary desire and objective has always been to secure the secrets of immortality at any cost. But just think — if we can seize the Battle Sphere *before* it can learn to transform and oppose us — the possibilities are endless! We could test and observe the Thraen as he grows. We might even unlock the secrets of the transformation process for ourselves!"

From inside his launch pod, Janus entered the keypad code causing the inner door to slide open. He entered the chamber, followed closely by his orb. After the chamber was depressurized, he quickly repeated the procedure for the outer launch pod door. As it glided open, Janus could see countless stars.

His hologram returned to his monitoring orb as it darted into outer space, brightly reflecting the light of the sun. As his orb approached the USEP, Janus glanced down at Thrae. The chain reaction blast had rolled across the entire visible surface of the planet. Pockets of yellow and orange haze dotted the globe. Janus looked away as he struggled to contain his emotions.

Reaching the pod's outer door, Janus once again projected his hologram. He entered the keypad's security code and the door glided open. Following his orb inside the small entrance chamber, Janus repeated the code on the inner keypad and the outer door slid closed behind him.

"Markus, I'm in your entrance chamber," announced Janus. "Push the black button to the left of the pod door and then enter the keypad security code. It will pressurize the chamber and open the inner door."

"Doing it now."

When the pod door opened, the sight of Janus's pod and hologram left Markus speechless.

"Is that all you have to say for yourself Markus?" Janus asked with a grin.

"My friend, I —"

"I know. Now we're more than friends. We're twins."

Markus laughed loudly as Janus looked over at his son, who reached for his father with a big smile. Janus grabbed Chad and hugged him tightly. Turning his attention back toward Markus, he began, "I 'm here to try to repair the console. The Mitel Fleet will be upon us very soon so we need to get to work fast. You can help me by keeping Chad occupied."

"That I can do," replied Markus quickly.

Janus looked around the USEP for the pod's tool case, which was secured about half way up the rear wall. As he reached over and removed it from its storage clips, it felt heavy. *That is a good sign*, he thought, opening the case. Upon quick visual inspection, it appeared to contain everything Janus anticipated he might need to perform temporary repairs.

"Excellent!" he said aloud, turning his attention to the programming console. After a brief visual inspection, it was clear that the center of the console was too badly damaged to be repaired quickly. 'We need to go to plan B."

"What plan is *that*?"

"Rewire and reconfigure the departure mechanism from underneath the console."

"Oh, that plan!" exclaimed Markus.

In the cramped quarters of the small spacecraft, Janus crawled underneath the console. As a hologram, he could now move in or through any space. He quickly removed the composite mesh access panels and began to identify and sort out the various cables and connections.

Systematically identifying and disconnecting a series of optical fiber bundles that led from the console to the departure activation mechanism, he grabbed a small cutting tool from the tool case and cut the damaged portion away from the console connections. Then using a fusion splicing tool, he reconnected and reconfigured the departure system connections. Janus identified four remaining optical fibers that triggered both the regular and high-speed flight system. Using extra mechanical splicing connectors from the tool case, he re-routed each of them to a series of unused modules located to the left of the programming console.

Pausing to take a visual inventory of the fiber bundles connecting several modules further under the console, he saw no other damage. Although there were countless lines and conduits going in all directions, Janus was confident that he had taken into account all critically necessary connections.

"Hopefully that'll do it," said Janus, sitting up from underneath the panels. "It doesn't look as though any of the cables and hardware further beneath the console were damaged. But there's only one way to know for sure."

Janus pushed a square blue button on the console activating one of the newly rerouted control modules. A loud humming sound could immediately be heard as the pod deployed the slip ring cylinder components and driveshaft from either side. Janus knew that the plasma shields would form around the entire craft immediately after the ring locked together.

"That sound is music to my ears," smiled Janus.

As the Mitel battle cruiser closed in on the pod, Zan gave the order to make visual contact. The USEP and the launch pod quickly appeared on the ICC's main viewing screen. Zan studied the screen image of the two crafts sitting side by side. A cylindrical ring could be seen around the small spacecraft.

"What *is* that?" Zan demanded.

"Commander," said the scanning specialist, "scanners are detecting a huge energy buildup in the smaller pod. It may be preparing to launch."

"Initiate the gravity control beam," instructed Zan. "We *must* seize that craft!"

Turning to the communications specialist, he ordered, "I want you to instruct any fighters in the immediate vicinity to assist in the capture!"

"Yes, Commander," replied the specialist.

Markus's orb suddenly detected the Mitel battle cruiser closing in on them.

"My friend, it appears that we have a large visitor," announced Markus in a serious tone of voice.

Janus paused for a moment and concentrated. His monitoring orb also picked up the signal. "A Mitel battle cruiser is right on top of us."

Janus glanced at the energizer gauge for the status of the departure initialization. The gauge indicated *65, 70* then *75* percent complete.

"Markus, we aren't ready for speed departure, but we need to get out of here *now*."

Janus reached over and pushed the second of the four buttons he had reconfigured. On command, the USEP shuddered then lurched forward under the power of its twin high output plasma thrust engines. At the same moment, the Mitel battle cruiser released two powerful, plasma-based corkscrew gravity control beams toward the small pod.

"Janus, my orb is picking up —"

"Gravity control beams," interrupted Janus "I detected them too."

As the small pod picked up speed, the gravity control beams narrowly missed their target.

"Commander, the gravity control beams failed to engage the Thraen pod," announced the battle cruiser's weapons specialist.

"*What*?" Zan snapped. "How is that possible?"

"The small pod is now moving away from the planet and picking up speed, Sir," confirmed the scanning specialist.

"Send more gravity control beams!" Zan demanded pounding his console chair with his fist. "We *must not lose* that craft!"

"Yes, Commander!"

"Lindar!" bellowed Commander Liss.

"Sir!" replied Ard.

"Accelerate this vessel to full closing speed!"

"Already done, Sir."

The battle cruiser's weapons specialist initiated a series of corkscrew gravity control beams aimed at the pod's projected trajectory. As Janus's orb registered their approach, he pushed the third button initiating maximum normal speed. The USEP lurched and accelerated faster as Janus and Markus braced for the impact of the gravity control beams. But nothing happened. One by one, the beams missed the small spacecraft. The weapons and scanning specialists nervously confirmed that the gravity control beams were still not engaging.

"*ARGGHH!* Useless technology!" yelled Zan in frustration. "It has *never* been accurate enough or powerful enough!"

"Commander," said the communications specialist. "I have confirmed that three high speed interceptors are responding to our request for assistance."

"*EXCELLENT!* Instruct them to intercept the small craft! Disable but *do not* destroy. We need to capture the Thraen alive!"

Upon receiving their orders, the three Mitel Fighters changed direction and began to close in quickly on the pod.

As the USEP accelerated, Janus felt the pod begin to vibrate. He knew that meant they were approaching maximum normal speed. There was a faint hissing noise coming from the back of the pod as the vibrations increased. He checked the energizer gauge which now read 90 percent. Just then, both monitoring orbs identified the approaching Mitel Fighters. Markus and Janus nervously glanced at one another.

"Markus, double check to make sure Chad is strapped in!" instructed Janus.

"Doing it now!" responded Markus, quickly inspecting Chad's harness.

"*Come on,*" Janus encouraged the small pod. "You can do it."

As he glanced at the console, it suddenly occurred to him that he forgot to program the planet's exact coordinates into the pod's navigation system.

"*Oh no!*" Janus moaned in frustration.

"What's wrong now?" asked Markus with obvious concern.

"I never transferred the planet's coordinates into the pod's computer!"

"Can you do it now?"

"No!"

As the three Mitel Fighters closed in on the USEP, the squadron leader announced, "We have visual."

"*Disable it!*" yelled Zan. "*Now!*"

The three Mitel Fighters fired a series of low energy laser bursts at the small pod, barely missing their mark. The fighter computers recalculated their target coordinates and prepared to fire a second round.

Janus saw the energizer gauge flashing the message that it had reached 100 percent. He lunged for the forth button and activated the departure sequence. The cylindrical ring rapidly sped up until it was spinning at lightning speed.

The pilot in the lead fighter registered the sudden increase in energy and instinctively fired a lethal burst of high energy laser directly toward the center of the pod.

From his console computer, the scanning specialist immediately detected both energy sources.

"Commander Liss, the Thraen craft is taking evasive action and our fighters are now shooting to destroy it!"

"NO!" shouted Zan.

"The small craft is emitting a tremendous surge of energy!"

Before Zan could respond, the pod's departure sequence commenced just as the lethal laser burst was nearing a direct impact. The small spacecraft instantly accelerated faster than the speed of light and was gone from view.

The outer space directly behind the USEP distorted like an invisible tsunami. The lethal laser burst exploded harmlessly against its approaching wake. In the cockpit of the Mitel Fighters, all three pilots simultaneously received indication of an approaching disturbance. They began evasive maneuvers, but it was too late. All three craft were hit simultaneously by the approaching distortion and instantly obliterated. By then, the pod had accelerated to a point where it was already leaving the Thraen universe.

Zan bellowed in anger, realizing that the small pod had escaped into deep space.

As the USEP accelerated beyond the speed of light, Janus's unsecured orb slammed against the rear wall. His hologram involuntarily terminated and returned to the orb, which rolled to a stop next to the side wall. All was quiet for a few minutes other than a faint hissing sound which was soon replaced by a tranquil humming.

Gathering his thoughts, Janus instructed his orb to hover from its position on the USEP floor. He peered out through his monitor to see Markus's secured hologram sitting right next to Chad. Markus looked over at Janus and let out a big laugh.

"What's so funny, Markus?"

"It's your screen." laughed Markus even harder.

"What about it?"

"It's got a big crack in it!"

Janus quickly hovered toward a section of reflective inner wall to inspect his damage. "Maybe this trip will knock some sense into me," he mused as he re-projected his hologram image.

Janus stared intently at his hologram reflection for the first time. His hologram deformed for a second or two before returning back to normal. It almost looked as if his body was being sliced along a diagonal.

"Now what?" he groaned.

"Well, hello there," laughed Markus from across the pod. "No need to go to pieces on me."

Janus rolled his eyes. "I hope the disruption in my appearance does not scare Chad."

"Oh, my guess is that he'll find it quite entertaining! I know I do," Markus chuckled.

As Markus spoke, Chad squealed with joy as he stared at his father.

"See? What did I tell you?" smiled Markus.

In the battle cruiser's ICC, the scanning specialist struggled to maintain contact with the fleeing craft.

"Sir," the specialist spoke weakly, "the pod is accelerating at an incredible rate. I have never seen anything like it."

Zan strained to keep his composure as he turned and walked slowly back to his command console before slumping into his chair. As he sat, dejected, the small

USEP craft accelerated into deep space, leaving behind a burning planet.

CHAPTER THREE – THE JOURNEY

Janus peered out a series of small trapezoidal shaped windows above the instrument panel. To his surprise, he could not see any stars, but rather a white translucent haze. Turning his attention back to the instrument panel, he watched the speed indicator climb steadily. It read *10.40X* then *10.80X,* confirming that the small pod was now traveling 10.8 times the speed of light. Janus glanced over toward Markus who was holding a sleeping Chad comfortably in his lap.

"I think we are getting close to slip mode," said Janus quietly. "Make sure that both you and Chad are properly secured."

"I've got the little one. Don't worry my friend," whispered Markus.

The indicator methodically climbed to *11.35X* then *11.95X.* A yellow indicator began to flash on the left side of the panel signaling that the pod was beginning to slip. The pod shuddered ever so slightly and then a few seconds later, began to rapidly decelerate.

That was uneventful, thought Janus.

The speed indicator rapidly decreased to *8.44X,* then *4.31X* then *2.02X.* The pod continued to decelerate until it reached *0.8X,* once again traveling slower than the speed of light. Outside the windows, thousands of stars could be seen shining brightly in all directions.

Janus quickly scanned the directional readouts and distance log. The USEP was now already two light years away from Thrae along the galaxy's spiral arm. The Mitel Fleet was no longer a threat. There was no turning back. Janus gazed over toward his sleeping son. *My little boy, I can't let you down. I must get you to your new home before you die out here in space.*

"OK Markus, since I forgot to load the planet's coordinates into the pod's computer, we're going to have to locate it ourselves."

"Understood. Any thoughts on how?"

"Any way we can," replied Janus somberly.

Satisfied with the USEP's early performance, Janus decided to search the craft. He made his way along the pod's floor deck and began to systematically open the storage bins in search of anything useful. The first bin was completely empty. *Not a good start,* he thought. The second storage bin contained one large and three smaller umbrella shaped deep space monitoring antennae used during test flights. The smaller antennae were used to pick up various radar, microwave and radio signals. *This is very promising. Hopefully, the interface modules are also on board.*

In the next bin, Janus found the interface hardware along with several signal-boosting components, items which he knew might come in handy. In the fourth and final bin were various fiber optic connectors, switches and adaptors.

At the same time, Markus began to rummage through Chad's bag. He found a few levitating cubes which changed colors as they taught the Thraen alphabet, and several of Chad's favorite holographic picture books.

Awakened by all the noise, Chad giggled with excitement as he watched Markus pull the various items from his bag.

Good, thought Markus. *These will help keep him occupied.*

Over the next few hours, Janus and Markus worked together to install and position the equipment while Chad played. When they had finished, Janus motioned for Markus to activate them. Markus entered the code sequence into the console computer. Several seconds later, the larger antennae emitted a flashing blue light at its base indicating that it was operational. After a brief hum, the three small antennae came on line a few minutes later. A series of repeating red signals along one side confirmed that they were scanning the universe ahead of them.

"Well, that's a relief," sighed Janus as his hologram leaned back against the USEP side wall. He continued to study the monitoring antennae for a time before his mind began to wander.

Janus reflected on Thrae's relentless obsession with advancing the productivity and durability of the human life form. At first, scientists simply hooked humans up to machines which severely limited mobility. Next they imbedded microchips into the human brain, spinal cord and limbs. Unfortunately, health problems eventually arose from the prolonged exposure to non-ionizing radiation and magnetic fields. Scientists also found themselves limited by the number of neurons necessary for implanting more complicated microchips.

Scientists ultimately went in another bold direction which tested the limits and blurred the lines between the human condition and machine. The first great leap forward — which ushered in the era of Scientific Revelations on Thrae 1,500 years ago — represented the apex of several generations worth of testing and manipulation of highly concentrated metallic and synthetic blood stream additives. Combined with DNA manipulation, scientists created several crossbreed blueprints — although they were never able to control someone being born with hybrid abilities, not to mention a particular blueprint. The transformation itself could only be triggered through concerted mental focus or an intense emotional stimulus.

To help achieve the hybrid configurations, scientists studied, tested and eventually harnessed each blueprint's latent but powerful psychokinetic abilities. This allowed transforming hybrids to attract enormous amounts of heavy metal trace elements and helium-4 from the surrounding atmosphere and ground areas. During the reverse transformation process, the metal trace elements and helium-4 were excreted back into the planet's atmosphere through the hybrid's porous outer surface.

The rarest, and by far, the most complex of these hybrids were known as Battle Spheres. They were so rare that only eleven had ever been identified. This was not to say that more had ever existed. Most hybrids went through life either not knowing about their latent abilities or unable to transform.

After the first failed Mitel invasion, news of the defeat spread quickly across the galaxy. The failed assault represented the first major setback for the expanding Mitel Empire. As a result, the Battle Sphere was unanimously recognized as the single most formidable fighting machine in the known universe.

After coming to grips with their failure, the Mitel Leadership painstakingly analyzed the ill-fated mission. In doing so, they focused their attention on the two Battle Spheres that were instrumental in the outcome. The

Leadership concluded that Markus Kilmar had been permanently damaged beyond repair while Zebulon Park had been destroyed. They also concluded that it was the *human aspect* of the Battle Sphere's decision making that had caused both hybrids to be neutralized. This information was relayed throughout the Mitel military and eventually became the foundation for a mandatory course in strategy and maneuvers at the Mitel Military Academy.

Despite the Mitel Leadership's obsession with securing the secrets of IM, they faced one insurmountable challenge: how to defeat the formidable Battle Sphere? In time, they realized that they would be unable to develop a comparable weapon and reluctantly made the decision to wait and closely monitor Thrae until they could determine whether more Battle Spheres existed. After monitoring the planet closely for almost a decade, the Mitel Leadership eventually decided that there were none.

The Leadership then spent most of the next five years preparing for a second, much larger invasion to defeat Thrae. Failing a second time was not an option. However, the question of how to implement a successful surprise attack remained. The appearance of the rare and overpowering solar magnetic storm gave the Mitel Leadership the answer.

Chad awoke crying and tugging at his pants. Janus instructed his monitoring orb to perform a scan of both Chad and the interior of the pod.

"Uh-oh," said Janus.

"Uh-oh, what?" asked Markus, his eyebrows furrowed.

"I think Chad has reached the limits of his waste dispenser!"

"Not good," replied Markus, shaking his head.

Janus reached into Chad's bag and pulled out a fresh dispenser.

"These things last about two weeks before they need to be replaced. We will probably need to rethink our list of the greatest Thraen discoveries!" laughed Janus.

"I think you're right," Markus chuckled.

Janus carefully removed Chad's pants and unfastened the white composite dispenser. A small light near the waist area was blinking red. Janus deftly installed the new dispenser around Chad, and the small light glowed solid green. Chad immediately stopped crying as he watched Janus's sparkling white lights.

"Yes, I bet that feels *much* better!" cooed Janus as Chad smiled back.

Janus then looked around the pod.

"What are you looking for?" asked Markus, somewhat confused.

"Where do we put the depleted dispenser?"

"Hmmm, that is a good question. How about putting it in one of the empty storage bins?"

"They're not sealed," explained Janus. "The odor won't bother us since we are no longer affected by such things. But I'm afraid the poor air quality will bother Chad."

Scanning the pod, Janus and Markus found themselves staring directly at the inner door to the pod entrance chamber.

"Markus, are you thinking what I'm thinking?"

"Yes, I think I might be."

"Jettison the dispenser —"

"Yes, indeed. That sounds like a fine idea."

Janus grabbed the used dispenser, and entered the access code to the pod entrance chamber. As the door slid open, he placed the dispenser on the entrance floor and quickly closed the door by re-entering the code.

"OK, time for dispenser launch!" smiled Janus.

As Janus entered the keypad code for the outer door, Markus saluted.

"Good-bye waste dispenser and thank you for your loyal service," Markus grinned.

The two of them listened to the sound of the composite dispenser being sucked out into space from the resulting vacuum. Janus inserted the code again and the door quickly closed.

"Well, that takes care of that problem!" Markus chuckled as he glanced over at Chad, who smiled and then giggled along with him.

Over the next seven days, the small spacecraft journeyed across the galaxy's spiral arm. In their cramped quarters, Janus and Markus passed the time watching hologram story books over and over with Chad. They also developed a few games, consisting mostly of tossing the levitating cubes back and forth. As Markus and Janus touched the cubes, their focused energy made them shine so bright that they blanketed the interior of the pod in blues and reds and greens. Chad giggled and laughed every time. He also enjoyed playing with the silver security medallion that Janus had given him back in the USEP facility.

After Chad fell asleep, Janus and Markus silently stared at the three-dimensional displays and read outs on the programming console, as they monitored the pod's progress. After a time, Janus turned and watched as Chad slept, still clutching a favorite hologram picture book. His thoughts drifted to the Hologram Protective Force, an integral part of their world's defense forces for well over one thousand years.

1,400 years ago, Thraen scientists worked closely with experts from several advanced technology fields to develop living hologram technology. The program was part of the Thraen Hologram Initiative (THI). Its goal was to develop a living being that was an exact holographic replica of a human. At first, researchers successfully scanned and created a three-dimensional hologram map of the entire human body down to the individual cell level. Scientists then modeled the body's electrical system by reproducing the positive and negative charges of potassium and sodium ions at the cell levels within the hologram itself. This elaborate signal grid enabled the hologram to send messages throughout its three-dimensional self, including its brain.

Next, through computer simulation and electrical current phasing, scientists created a fully functioning inner sub-hologram of the Thraen brain. Finally, and after decades of testing on animals, THI teams successfully transferred animals into the first hologram reproductions. This was achieved by infusing the entire body with an enormous gamma ray energy burst which instantaneously transformed the body into an almost infinite number of discrete electrical signals, activating the hologram.

The living hologram was infused with the electrical DNA of the living body form, including the brain's discrete memory, feelings, preferences and physiological traits. Once Thraen volunteers were effectively transformed into holograms, scientists began to explore the limits of THI. In time, holograms were applied to ever increasingly complex applications, culminating with the monitoring and assistance of hybrid blueprints. Not unexpectedly, the most sophisticated control center ever achieved was designed to support the Battle Sphere. After 100 years of development, the hologram transformation procedure became routine.

Instead of blood and tissue, holograms used modest amounts of electricity and plasma energy to maintain their physical structure and appearance. As a result of the streamlined design, the hologram's initial transformation charge lasted thousands of years because of the minor resistance/impedance of the hologram representation itself. For holograms to operate in the physical world, scientists created *focused energy*. Through subconscious thought, living holograms directed discrete electrical particles to become concentrated in specific areas such as the hands, arms, feet and legs. This created surface forces allowing them to perform physical activities.

Unfortunately, a living hologram's use of focused energy exposed them to the inherent dangers of the physical world. In a way, until living holograms activated their focused energy, they were like ghosts — able to move freely through the physical world without limitation. The resounding success of THI led the World Council to formally establish the Hologram Protective Force (HPF).

Thraen volunteers were carefully screened before being selected. Once transformed, they would achieve a form of immortality as their hologram likenesses would be preserved and projected for thousands of years in the exact form that existed at the time of their transformation. Once in hologram form, a Thraen dedicated his or her entire future existence to the support and protection of Thrae. After transforming, they were designated for assignment, sometimes being imbedded into the military hybrid blueprints.

In time, it became clear that a living hologram could be destroyed in a second way: the destruction of the technology the hologram personnel was now a part of.

There was, however, one possible exception.

While formal records no longer exist, scientists believe that long ago, a crippled Battle Sphere elected to extinguish its existence. They theorized that the Battle Sphere allowed its plasma propulsion core to be sped up to nearly the speed of light, resulting in the immediate buildup of large amounts of antimatter. They also speculated that the subsequent and instantaneous annihilation explosion — on a cosmic scale — triggered the hologram transformation process *in reverse.*

As GDC Commander, Janus became aware that the reverse transformation process represented a form of mythology among the HPF personnel who quietly referred to it as the *miracle of life* event.

It's still a mystery to this day, he thought as he stared at the center console. *But the decision to end one's existence — for any reason — is one that I will never agree with.*

As the small pod continued its long journey, Janus passed the time inspecting and repairing the damage to the console caused by Chad's temper tantrum. Janus hoped that he had repaired the pod's low speed invisibility system.

Only time will tell, he thought.

On the eighth day, the large and two of the small antennae were working intermittently. On the ninth day, they ceased working altogether. As hard as he tried, Janus could not bring them back on line with the limited tools and equipment on the USEP.

On the eleventh day, Janus studied the programming console longer than usual.

"We have now traveled six hundred and eight light years," Janus informed Markus.

"We should be very close to the planet then," replied Markus, sounding optimistic.

"Yes, but . . ."

"But *what*?

"Without exact coordinates, we are relying on the remaining small antennae and its signal booster to pick up the planet's radio waves."

"So what's the problem?"

"The *problem* is that radio waves dissipate as they travel through space. We'll need to be within a few light years of the planet to have any chance of picking up a recognizable signal."

"I see. That is going to make it pretty hard to find."

"Yes . . ."

Janus and Markus sat in silence as they contemplated their predicament.

"Markus, how are we on food and air supplies?" Janus asked, changing the subject.

"I would say we have at most, a week's worth of food and air left for the boy."

Janus suddenly stopped talking and froze.

"Markus, did you hear that?"

"Hear what?"

"That! *Shhhh.* Listen!"

There was a brief silence. Then, over the console speakers a slightly garbled voice could be heard speaking in an unrecognizable language.

"And the pitch is outside for ball one," the voice continued.

"*That*! Did you hear it?" demanded Janus.

"I did!"

"Curve in for a strike," the voice resumed. "The count is now 1 and 1 on the Yankee centerfielder."

"OK!" Janus exclaimed excitedly "We must trace that signal immediately and lock onto its coordinates!"

Janus fumbled with the console computer before directing the antennae to determine the direction and source point of the signals. He waited impatiently for the results to appear.

"The signal is coming from our right side approximately 2.1 light years away," Janus reported happily.

Markus immediately programmed the coordinates into the flight navigation system. Seconds later, the pod softly banked to the right.

Over the next few hours, Janus and Markus processed information received over a wide range of frequencies through the USEP computers. Using their monitoring orbs, they quickly decoded and translated the information into their own Thraen language.

"The atmospheric composition, characteristics and gravity of this planet are almost identical to our own," Janus began. "The diameter of the planet is slightly larger than Thrae, and the star it revolves around, referred to as *The Sun* is about the same age and size as our own, maybe ten percent smaller."

"The planet is somewhat closer to their Sun than Thrae is to its star, and completes one entire revolution around the Sun in only 365 days, rather than our 412," Markus added.

"What I find fascinating," responded Janus, "is that the planet completes one full spin in almost the identical amount of time as Thrae. Using this planet's time terminology, it's only 4 minutes shorter per day."

"Truly uncanny," nodded Markus.

Janus paused briefly as he continued to process additional data.

"This planet contains a single satellite called *The Moon*, which appears to interact with the planet very similarly to our own."

"And just like Thrae," Janus continued, "the length of day and Moon cycles both appear to have profoundly affected the mathematical development of this civilization. Their Moon completes 12 lunar cycles per year. Combined with the almost identical amount of time per day, the people of this planet have developed a very similar numbering system."

"Agreed," Markus commented, as they continued to pour over all the data being received.

"Markus, I'm 99 percent confident that Chad could survive in this environment without artificial means. In certain geographic and cultural settings, he could probably fit right in without being noticed."

"What about his immune system?"

Janus paused to think before he looked over at his sleeping child. "That's a good question. We must process as much scientific data as possible to make sure we don't miss anything. Their medical development is still in its infancy. There are significant health and environmental risks across the planet."

"Janus, look," said Markus, pointing toward the console.

The yellow light flashed, indicating that the pod was entering slip mode. The pod shuddered slightly for a few seconds and the light went off.

"Let's reconfirm where we are relative to the planet," said Janus.

He furiously typed his request into the console's computer. After a moment, the results appeared on the data screen.

"We overshot the planet by 3.2 light years. Even at our fastest normal speed, we are too far away to reach the planet before our supplies run out."

"What should we do?" asked Markus.

Janus thought for a moment. "I know it's not very scientific, but we are going to have to keep slipping until we get close enough to reach the planet under normal power."

"How?"

"Triangulation," replied Janus. "Based on where we end up after each slip, we will plot the next course in a triangular pattern around the planet. The computer keeps track of the trajectories and resulting distance from the planet, and uses probability theory to determine the next path."

Janus quickly typed a series of instructions into the USEP's computer. "Now we wait for the next slip."

The two of them went back to reviewing the planet's transmission data in silence. Every once in a while Janus's hologram crackled and repositioned itself as a reminder of their narrow escape from the Mitel Fleet.

When the yellow light flashed again, the pod shuddered briefly and the yellow indicator eventually ceased flashing. Janus quickly checked the console readings.

"We are even *farther* away from the planet," he groaned as he studied the new computer-generated coordinates, before entered them into the navigation computer. Within seconds, the pod slowly turned and headed in the path of the new coordinates. Janus turned his attention back to the radio wave transmissions, but they had fallen silent.

"Why have the signals stopped?" Markus asked.

"During the last slip, we traveled outside their effective range. This far out, the waves have attenuated to such an extent that it's impossible to pick them up. That is the reality of the vastness of deep space."

As they waited for the next slip, Janus and Markus watched Chad as he slept.

"Chad, your son," said Markus after several minutes. "He's the last of our kind."

"I know. That's another reason why we must find a safe place for him."

Once again, the yellow indicator light flashed and, as before, the small spacecraft slightly shuddered. When the slip completed, Janus checked the results. Markus noticed a look of excitement on Janus's face.

"Good news?"

"Yes!" replied Janus excitedly. "We're about two days away from the planet at full normal speed. I think we shouldn't risk trying another slip that may push us much farther away again."

"Agreed!" grinned Markus.

"Then it's settled. I'm disabling the slip departure mode and we will proceed toward the planet on normal power."

With a series of key strokes, the pod banked once again toward its final destination, while the slip ring unlocked, retracted and rotated the four large curved sections toward their storage location beneath the pod. Janus and Markus turned their attention back to processing the multitude of radio waves being transmitted to their monitoring orbs.

"Markus, the people of this planet appear to speak several thousand languages," said Janus.

"Yes, but there are three predominant ones — *Mandarin, Spanish* and *English*."

"I think it makes the most sense to learn those three languages first, don't you agree?"

"Yes," replied Markus. "And from what I can ascertain, the planet is called *Earth*. Don't you find that to be a strange coincidence?"

Janus paused for a moment and then his eyes lit up. "You mean the almost backward spelling of our world's name?"

"Yes," replied Markus.

"I guess so. But let's hope the technology and ways of their world are not backwards as well."

"You mean compared to *our* planet?"

"Yes, *our* planet."

"You mean our own *advanced* planet that very recently helped bring about its own destruction?" asked Markus sarcastically.

Janus paused as a very serious look came over his face. "I guess I shouldn't pre-judge this planet Earth, should I, Markus?"

"Probably not the best course of action at this point, considering *we're* the ones in need of a home."

Janus smiled slightly as he looked at Markus. "Your point is well taken my friend, Markus."

Over the next two days, the mood on the USEP was high. Janus and Markus intercepted and processed an endless number of transmissions from Earth. As they exchanged and compared their findings, they took turns feeding and playing with Chad while, at the same time, practicing the three new languages.

"Earth is composed of many separate governing bodies," said Janus.

"Yes. They generally coexist for periods of time until a dispute arises. Unfortunately, the method of dispute resolution appears to be quite inconsistent and ultimately violent."

"There's certainly a great deal of distrust between the governing bodies as they struggle for power and influence," added Janus.

"This world has not yet progressed to the point where common ideals and goals can be centralized for the good of the entire race," explained Markus. "There is an incredible amount of duplication of effort, waste and needless suffering."

"Given their current state of development, it's unclear to me if we would be welcomed by this planet."

"Agreed," replied Markus. "Given their folklore and current perception of alien beings, we certainly run the risk of being detained or harmed. What do you suggest we do?"

"We should land the pod in an environmentally friendly but sparsely populated area to minimize detection. Once there, we could remove and reuse as much of the onboard equipment as possible."

As the pod continued toward Earth, it propelled its way past the orbits of Jupiter and Saturn. Janus then navigated the pod through the asteroid belt before passing Mars.

"We're rapidly approaching Earth," announced Janus. "I'm reducing speed to minimum normal."

The pod responded immediately and continued to slow down as it quietly passed the Moon. Janus and Markus peered out of the series of forward facing windows. Directly in front of them was a large blue marble surrounded by the blackness of space and countless stars. Swirling patches of white clouds dotted the planet. Beneath the white patches, sections of green were also visible.

"Earth is beautiful," whispered Markus.

"It's truly incredible," added Janus. "Other than my little sleeping boy, it may be the most beautiful thing I've ever seen."

Markus glanced back down at Chad briefly before gazing out the windows again.

CHAPTER FOUR – TECHNOLOGY'S FALSE PROMISES

One thousand seven hundred years ago, Thraens voted to eliminate regional boarders and governments in favor of a single ruling body, the World Council. The vote represented the culmination of a movement that began soon after the *fourth* and final world war. The long and agonizing road to recovery from the devastation of that conflict galvanized the planet's population, fundamentally changing how they viewed themselves and each other. Fears, prejudices and regional misperceptions melted away in the face of a worldwide desire for lasting peace.

Thrae's technological journey restarted after the vote, but this time, it was different. Technical innovation thrived as information was shared around the world at unprecedented levels. Major worldwide infrastructure projects such as the hyper-speed electromagnetic railway system and antigravity air travel grid made it easy and inexpensive to travel almost anywhere on the planet. In time, cultures and values slowly merged, creating a uniform and cohesive world society.

The decision to adopt a World Council was ultimately an easy one. The unification represented a simple and logical progression: Thrae would *finally* move forward for the greater good of *all* people.

The lasting peace and cooperation led to a series of remarkable scientific advancements. Unfortunately, the most profound and recent Thraen breakthrough — the discovery of IM nearly 1,300 years ago — almost destroyed civilization itself. At first the discovery was hailed as a miracle. The uncoiling and realignment of Thraen DNA, which eliminated the eventual onset of the aging process, was subsequently stored as a genetic code in all immortals (IMs). Preventing the new DNA code from *recoiling* and mutating into life-threatening variations required all IMs to consume a daily combination of expensive medicines called the Serum.

During the early stages of IM, immortality was incredibly liberating. The concept of time became, in many ways, irrelevant. Existence was almost surreal. However, many alarming problems soon developed. The first and most obvious obstacle, which quickly dampened the initial euphoria, was the financial cost. Because the Serum was so expensive, only the wealthiest Thraens could afford it. This immediately upset the balance achieved approximately four hundred years earlier, and set in motion a new class structure on Thrae.

IMs plotted behind the scenes to change Thraen law in favor of IMs' long-term goals and struggled to manage and control the growing resentment of the non-immortals (or Terminals). The daily Serum doses also produced a buildup of a toxic chemical residue in IMs that poisoned the body. Many IMs eventually became weary of their existence or simply grew tired of struggling with the adverse effects of the Serum. They either committed suicide, or ceased taking the Serum which was a death sentence, as their DNA quickly recoiled creating one or more devastating health problems.

Once IMs reproduced with Terminals and Hybrids, it became alarmingly clear that the potent Serum adversely affected the genetic code of their children causing a dramatic increase in the rate of birth defects, stillborns and significantly reduced life spans. It also became apparent that the Serum contaminated robotic limb and organ cultivation technology, and rendered Hybrid powers unreliable, and at times, uncontrollable. The Thraen population was poisoning itself.

On extremely rare occasions however, the offspring of two IMs would inexplicably be born without need for the Serum. Markus was one of these rare individuals, as were both Janus and his wife Liana. Their first two children were not.

More than three hundred million IMs, Hybrids and Terminals died tragic deaths including Janus's two children, Zeya and Mistil. For Janus, Liana, and countless others, the sadness and struggle became almost unbearable.

The crisis led to one of the greatest and longest running debates in Thraen history: *What to do with IM?* While the solution seemed obvious, a small minority of wealthy IMs fought vigorously against efforts to outlaw or eliminate it. But as the Serum became increasingly scarce and public opinion grew more vocal, it became harder for IMs to retain power and positions of authority. Terminals vigorously protested around the world demanding drastic change. Regional factions plotted a course for independence. The World Council found itself facing elimination. IM was tearing Thrae apart.

In the end, it was not the protests, the threats of independence, or the dwindling resources that ended IM. Rather, the wealthiest, most powerful and defiant immortals simply died from one or more of the many adverse side effects of the Serum. With their passing, the opposition abruptly ceased.

This void, combined with overwhelming support of the people, permitted the World Council to order the elimination and purging of not only IM, but hybrid technology as well. The IM and the hybrid scientific blueprints were systematically and irreversibly deleted. In time, both discoveries became nothing more than Thraen folklore.

Due to the lingering stigma associated with IM, all remaining immortals went to great lengths to hide their identity. Over the next five hundred years, the world slowly returned to life as it existed before the discoveries. However, the suffering and turmoil caused by IM profoundly changed how Thraens viewed advanced technology. Thraens became more conservative, no longer believing that such exotic forms of technological advancements were in their own best interests.

After the first failed Mitel invasion, the negative view of advanced technology became even stronger. After painstakingly rebuilding from the global devastation caused by the first Mitel attack, the remaining world's population was convinced that the Thraen Interplanetary Project had been a grave error. The World Council put a moratorium on future space exploration. In doing so, Thraen leaders chose to isolate their planet from the rest of the universe for the foreseeable future.

As an IM, Janus was born into substantial wealth 1,200 years ago. But he did not choose that early existence — it had chosen him. When he was only fifteen years old,

Janus and his father witnessed a transportation accident unfold in front of them. A small altitude transport vehicle lost control and crashed as it transitioned from the antigravity skyway to the surface. While the exact details of the accident had long since faded from memory, Janus never forgot the look on the face of the young girl who died in his father's arms.

Despite their efforts, Janus and his father were powerless to be of any real assistance. As Janus stared down at her, he felt her eyes look deep into his soul as she passed away. The incident was burned into Janus's consciousness. Going forward, he decided to dedicate his existence to helping and improving the lives of all Thraens. As he got older, and the problems of IM intensified, Janus changed his identity in order to continue to publicly help and serve the people without distractions or persecution. Under a new identity known as Sejus Theron, Janus became active in local politics even though he secretly despised the political system. His ultimate goal — which he kept mostly to himself — was to use his position and power to better the lives of all Thraens. To Sejus, the betterment of Thrae and its people was his primary mission. Nothing else was more important to him.

At first, he was elected to the Ruling Advisory Panel of his local area. Sejus later rose to local Chairman before being elected to the Regional Governing Board. Sejus's popularity grew. He subsequently became a member and then Director of his continents' Legislative Panel before being selected to serve on the revered World Council.

Janus eventually became the Central ruler of Thrae: Chancellor Sejus Theron, head of the World Council. As luck would have it, he presided over the Council during the worst phase of the tumultuous fallout from IM.

Despite not discovering or developing IM, Janus still felt responsible for its failure and was powerless to stop it from spiraling out of control.

"I should have anticipated the consequences and taken steps to prevent all of the suffering. I was in a position of power but let myself become powerless," Janus once said to Markus.

To cope with his feelings of failure and guilt, Janus turned to meditation which inadvertently unlocked his own Hybrid powers. In doing so, Janus began to understand and appreciate the struggles that Hybrids endured. Over time, revisionist historians blamed the World Council members for IM's spiraling out of control. Today, Chancellor Sejus Theron is considered a traitor by most historians for leading the world down the path of self-destruction.

Janus was never really bothered by this rewrite of Thraen history. He remained more tormented by his personal inability to recognize the adverse side effects of the discoveries, as well as his failure to prevent the tragic suffering of his people. He was also saddened that his world, in choosing the path of isolation, had turned its back on developing any significant new space technology.

Janus understood that IM represented a struggle that Thraens did not want to see repeated. It was a clear example of how technology can quickly outpace the ability of a world's people and leaders to control and use that technology for good. Despite Thrae's isolation tendencies, Janus believed that in time, Thrae would heal and recover; and that Thraens would eventually change their position and once again reach out to the universe. Janus decided to bide his time until that moment arrived. After all, as an IM, if there was one thing he still had, it was time.

Janus enjoyed his role as GDC Commander. His life was stable. His marriage had reached a level of happiness as the two of them finally put their own personal tragedies behind them. Unfortunately, however, it was becoming harder for him to conceal his true identity. There were stares and whispers from colleagues and friends about his youthful appearance.

Liana and Janus gathered the courage to try to have a child once again. The decision was a tragic one. Liana died delivering Chad. Janus cried as he held his son for the first time, only minutes after holding Liana's hand as she passed away. Liana had been the driving force keeping Janus moving in a positive direction through all the difficult dark times. He had always admired her inner strength and grace under adversity, especially after the death of their two daughters.

As Janus held Chad, the medical staff explained that Chad may not survive. In his weak emotional state, unable to face one more tragedy, Janus decided that if Chad also died, he would end his own life.

The lead physician had strong suspicions that IM was to blame for Liana's death. A week later, the physician appeared in the doorway of Chad's hospital room. As Janus sat next to Chad's life sustaining enclosure, he sensed that he was being watched. Janus looked up to see the physician staring at him. Their eyes met and the physician nodded letting Janus know that he too was an IM. Janus knew then that his own secret, as well as the secrets of his family, would be protected.

After falling into a coma, Chad came close to dying on multiple occasions. Janus left Chad's life support enclosure only once to travel to the development area of the GDC headquarters to make sure that an experimental high-speed pod was activated and ready for launch. In the event Chad passed away, Janus had finalized his plans to immediately head to the GDC headquarters where he would pilot the small high-speed craft into the sun. As GDC Commander, no one would stop him or question his intentions. Watching Chad fight for his life, Janus was consumed by thoughts of his suicide plan. *It will be quick and relatively painless,* he thought. *I'll be dead from the heat long before the craft disintegrates and there will be no evidence that any of my prior identities ever existed.*

But those plans were unnecessary. Chad woke up one morning and quickly improved.

CHAPTER FIVE – A NEW WORLD

As the USEP approached Earth's outer atmosphere, Janus monitored the three-dimensional displays closely. He typed instructions for the computer to re-charge and reposition the pod's protective plasma shield.

"I'm programming the computer to saturate the pod's outer shield with a negative charge," Janus explained as he typed. "Since the planet's gravity will be pulling us down, the negative charge should help significantly reduce that pull. The shields are also being repositioned up front to form a curved surface to deflect a substantial amount of the heat generated due to friction."

"Understood," nodded Markus.

"I also programmed the pod's computers to calculate and set the proper entry angle. We don't want our descent to be too steep which will generate too much heat, or too shallow — causing us to bounce off the outer atmosphere back toward deep space."

"Let's hope the computer gets that one right."

"Let's hope. And if everything goes according to plan, we will touch down in eastern New Mexico of the *United States*. That will provide us with an open and flat landing terrain that is sparsely populated."

"My monitoring orb indicates that the weather conditions there are very calm," confirmed Markus. "Do you still think we can avoid detection?"

"I activated the low speed invisibility system after our last slip," replied Janus. "But the outer atmosphere of Earth is denser than Thrae's. I'm not sure the system will hold up."

"If not, then hopefully we will be mistaken for a small meteor or space junk —"

Markus was interrupted by several alerts flashing on the instrumentation console.

"OK Markus, we are entering Earth's outer atmosphere. Make sure the two of you are firmly secured. Things might get a little bumpy."

"Doing it now," replied Markus as he quickly secured Chad into his harness before making sure his own monitoring orb was securely tied down.

As he watched Markus fasten Chad in place, Janus felt the nose of the pod shift downward as it positioned itself for entry. He knew from experience that there were only seconds left before the pod would reach the upper atmosphere.

Learning his lesson from his last bumpy ride, Janus hastily secured his monitoring orb before looking back out of the pod's front windows. Janus saw the faint blue translucent color of the plasma shield in front of him. Beyond it, planet Earth grew larger as the USEP approached. As Janus stared over the curved horizon, the Earth's sun shined brightly.

Suddenly, the pod shook, causing the small antennae to vibrate and move along the floor.

"Markus!" Janus called out, reaching toward the apparatus. "Watch out for any unsecured items and make sure Chad is not struck by anything!"

"Will do!" replied Markus as he kept a close eye on vibrating equipment.

The pod entered Earth's outer atmosphere. As Janus strained to look out of one of the small pod windows, he saw a bright yellow glow that had formed over the plasma shields.

"Don't fail us now shields!" he pleaded.

The USEP began to shake violently causing the antennae to fall over and bounce toward Markus. Janus saw that two separate indicators were flashing bright red, signaling that the invisibility system had shut down. *Probably due to the heat,* Janus surmised.

"We've lost the invisibility system, Markus."

The pod shuddered fiercely, causing his orb to vibrate and shake in its protective harness.

"MARKUS!" shouted Janus.

Before he could say anything else, his hologram involuntarily disengaged and returned to its orb. Janus found himself looking across the pod through his monitoring screen. He watched helplessly as Markus's hologram somehow maintained its form while struggling to bat several bouncing items away from Chad. White sparkles lit up the pod. Janus could see the fear in his son's eyes. He felt helpless.

And then, everything became calm.

"The pod made it through the outer atmosphere!" exclaimed Janus after successfully projecting his hologram form. "Is everyone OK?"

"The boy is fine, Janus. A little scared, but otherwise OK. I'm relieved he did not get upset enough to initiate another transformation. That would have been disastrous."

Janus nodded. "Markus, you did a great job keeping the equipment away from Chad."

"All in a day's work," said Markus, his eyes now twinkling.

"OK, then. I need you to stay with Chad while I try to figure out what's going on."

His hologram quickly made its way to the computer console to study the readings. From what he could make out, the plasma shields were still operational, but the intense heat and vibration appeared to have damaged the pod's navigation and antigravity systems. The readouts also indicated that the pod did not slow down as it descended.

"Markus — I'm afraid we have more problems," said Janus tersely.

"What's wrong *now*?"

"The navigation and antigravity systems have both shut down, likely due to the extreme heat and vibration."

At the U.S. Naval Space Surveillance System Command headquarters in Dahlgren, Virginia, Major Michael Talbot stood at the rear of the main monitoring room drinking his first cup of coffee. It was 3:00 a.m. Major Talbot had come to work early since he had been unable to sleep. It had been a very restless sleep — one that bothered him for some unknown reason. It was as if his subconscious was telling him to go to work.

Major Talbot enjoyed his early morning coffee. He liked it very hot with skim milk and no sugar. He was a career military and family man who took equal pride in protecting his country and raising his four children. He was 40 years of age, stood six feet three inches tall, with very short blond hair, hazel eyes and a muscularly lean and trim physique.

Sir," said Lieutenant Miller.

"What is it lieutenant?" asked Major Talbot politely.

Lieutenant Jason Miller, a 32-year-old former Navy Seal, had suffered a severe back injury during a rigorous training mission five years earlier. Now a communications specialist and part-time UFO Investigator, he intently stared at his computer screen.

"Radar is picking up a small object in the upper atmosphere over California at about eighty thousand feet. It's moving northeast at high speed, appearing out of nowhere."

"How fast is it moving?"

"Approximately Mach 15, Sir!"

"What do you make of it Lieutenant?"

"I'm not really sure, Sir. It's small enough to be a meteor, and the surveillance data indicates an angle of descent of approximately forty degrees."

"That sounds more like one of our old space shuttles, Lieutenant," said Major Talbot.

He looked over Lieutenant Miller's shoulder at the computer monitor.

"At that speed, it's moving a bit too slow to be a meteor. Let's keep a close eye on this one, shall we?"

"Yes, Sir," replied Lieutenant Miller.

Inside the USEP, Janus typed furiously.

"I'm trying to engage a system override, Markus. I think our best chance is to land the pod manually."

"Anything I can do to help?" asked Markus.

Chad began to cry, as if sensing that they were in danger.

"Try to calm Chad down so I can concentrate."

Markus touched Chad's feet and toes, causing his hologram fingers to sparkle. Chad gradually stopped crying as he reached out toward the shimmering light.

Janus paused, struggling to remember the override sequence. He tried one set of instructions, then another, then another without success.

At the Command Headquarters, Major Talbot continued to sip his coffee as he stood behind Lieutenant Miller.

"What's the status of the UFO now, Lieutenant?"

"It's moving at the same speed, Sir, and it's now over Arizona. Tracking data indicate that it's now at seventy thousand feet and descending rapidly."

"What is its current trajectory?"

"Modeling shows that it should touch-down in the Atlantic about two hundred and fifty miles off the coast of Maine, Sir."

"Do we have any vessels in that area?"

"I'll check, Sir" responded Lieutenant Miller, switching to a second computer to his left. He quickly checked the database. Major Talbot watched quietly as Lieutenant Miller scrolled down through several pages worth of screen data.

"No, Sir," he confirmed once he reached the end of the data list.

"Good. We don't need to issue an emergency warning since it will fall harmlessly into the sea. It's a meteor all right, but a very slow one at that," smiled Major Talbot as he patted Lieutenant Miller on the shoulder.

"Aye, aye, Sir," Lieutenant Miller grinned as Major Talbot walked back toward the rear of the room to pour himself another cup of coffee.

As the USEP raced toward the Earth's surface, Janus realized he had to set the code to match the project number for the old high speed development program! With a great sense of relief, he regained his focus. He quickly entered the code and confirmed that the pod was now operating on manual flight.

"Markus, *I did it!*" said Janus excitedly clapping his hands.

Markus let out a nervous laugh which caused Chad to giggle.

"But we aren't out of trouble yet," cautioned Janus, typing furiously once again. Using the override system, Janus tried to reactivate the navigation controls. They responded instantaneously.

"Navigation is back on line," shouted Janus as he feverishly typed instructions to initiate the high-speed landing sequence. The navigation computer immediately assessed the current flight data and repositioned the pod's plasma shields for landing. The pod shuddered slightly, as two triangular shaped wings deployed from its lower section.

"Markus, the pod has activated the forward wings."

"What?"

"The forward wings, they're what the humans on Earth refer to as *delta wings*. The plasma shield was designed to expand around them as they deployed. The wings slow us down for landing."

"Excellent news," Markus grinned. Chad, who was staring at Markus, giggled and reached up to touch Markus's face.

The pod decelerated and Janus reactivated the antigravity system. It also came back on line but not at full power. Despite the limitation, Janus's orb confirmed that the pod was noticeably slowing down.

"OK, we are going to need a little more help," said Janus. "I'm initiating a series of curves to slow us down prior to landing."

Janus instructed the small spacecraft to bank right on its first curve.

"*Sir*! Major Talbot, Sir!" shouted Lieutenant Miller from across the room.

Major Talbot, having poured himself his second cup of coffee, quickly walked back over to Lieutenant Miller, trying not to spill his hot drink.

"What is it Lieutenant?"

"Sir, the UFO is slowing down," he explained incredulously. "I can't be sure, but it appears to be banking back and forth."

Major Talbot was taken aback by this news.

"How is that possible, Lieutenant?"

"I don't know, Sir."

Major Talbot leaned over Lieutenant Miller's shoulder to get a better look at the computer screen. "What's it doing now?" he asked.

"It's over Pennsylvania at about thirty thousand feet, still traveling northeast but now at about Mach 3, Sir."

Major Talbot stood upright and paused for a moment. *What the hell is this thing?* he thought. *There must be a way to find out.*

"Lieutenant, prepare to scramble a couple of jets to intercept for a visual."

"Yes, Sir."

Major Talbot's mind raced as he tried to figure out what the UFO could be. *If it was a black ops mission, it would not be trying to touch down in Pennsylvania or upstate New*

York. Maybe it was one of ours in distress. No, that can't be, we would have received the heads up on that by now, he thought.

"UFO at twenty thousand feet still traveling northeast but it has slowed to Mach 2," confirmed Lieutenant Miller as he glanced up. "It's descending very rapidly, Sir."

In the USEP, Janus realized that if they did not land quickly, they risked overshooting the land surface altogether. Recalling that he hadn't tried to reactivate the invisibility system, Janus quickly instructed the console computer to re-arm the system. It came back on line instantly.

"UFO at ten thousand feet still traveling northeast, but now at about Mach 1 over western New York, Sir," Lieutenant Miller reported, but then hesitated and rechecked his screen.

"What's wrong, Lieutenant?" asked Major Talbot.

"It's the UFO Sir — it just disappeared into thin air!

"*It what*?" snapped Major Talbot.

"OK Markus. Prepare for landing," ordered Janus. He looked out the front windows. It was pitch black, but he could make out clusters of lights on the surface below.

Got to find a flat open area.

He glanced over at Chad and Markus to make sure they were both firmly secured. The console displays indicated that the pod had dropped below one thousand feet and had slowed to three hundred miles per hour.

Janus closed his eyes to concentrate. He instructed his orb to search its vast data files of Earth's geography and topography. He located and isolated the topography for the immediate vicinity. Even then, the data streamed past his consciousness faster than he could process it. He instructed his orb data bank to filter and identify unpopulated flat open areas of one half to one mile in length in ten mile increments in front of the USEP.

Janus opened his eyes to check back and forth between the windows and the instrumentation console. The pod was at an altitude of five hundred feet, then four hundred feet and had slowed to 200 miles per hour; then one hundred seventy-five. At three hundred feet he again closed his eyes and with the help of his orb, identified several possible landing sites.

Still too high, he thought.

Janus once again glanced down at the console. The pod was now at an altitude of one hundred fifty, then seventy-five feet. He closed his eyes one more time and suddenly received confirmation of a long open field immediately in front, but slightly to his left.

That's it!

"Hold on, Markus! Here we go!" shouted Janus.

Janus banked the USEP slightly to the left and then lifted the pod's nose. The pod began to vibrate as Janus struggled to keep it on course. With a loud bang, the pod skipped across the mud and dirt of the open field. It bounced a second time, and then a third and fourth time before skidding across the field.

Come on shields, hang in there!

The pod shook intensely. Chad screamed, as loud grinding noises could be heard from outside the craft. The shields were failing under the extreme friction from the uneven ground.

I hope the ring components under the craft will take the brunt of the landing.

In what seemed like an eternity, the pod slowed down and then finally came to a stop.

It worked! Janus shouted.

He looked over at Markus and Chad. Markus was still seated up against the pod wall holding Chad tightly.

"Is Chad —"

"He's fine! A little scared, but he's — Janus look: smoke!" shouted Markus, pointing toward the console.

"We need to get out of the pod and salvage whatever we can!"

Markus unstrapped Chad from his harness as Janus quickly released both monitoring orbs. Janus entered the keypad code and the doors slid open. Chad coughed as the pod filled with smoke.

"Markus don't forget Chad's bag!" barked Janus as he moved into the entry chamber. He quickly entered the keypad code to open the outer door.

Janus stepped out of the USEP followed by Markus and Chad. Seconds later, the two monitoring orbs sped out of the opening into the night sky.

Flames darted from underneath the pod's nose area.

"Quickly Markus, move away from the pod!" he warned.

As the flames spread, the open field was illuminated in a yellow glow. It was a large corn field. The soil was soft and lumpy, having been recently turned.

"Take Chad over there," said Janus pointing toward the edge of the corn field.

Markus nodded and floated across the open field until he reached the tall grass along its perimeter. Janus quickly climbed back into the pod to salvage whatever he could, before the fire engulfed the entire craft. As smoke poured out, Markus watched from a distance. Janus unloaded all the antennae and supporting equipment before removing as many of the quick disconnect modules on the computer console as he could. Racing against time as the fire grew more intense, he unhooked several keyboards in and about the main console and carefully but quickly placed them outside the USEP. Lastly, Janus tossed all the available tools and other loose test equipment he could find onto the ground.

By now, the front end of the pod was fully engulfed in flames.

"Janus, it's time to retreat!" urged Markus.

Exiting, Janus directed his orb to initiate its modest antigravity beam to pick up and transport all the equipment and tools away from the burning spacecraft. Janus motioned to Markus to follow him along the edge of the field.

By the time they reached each other, the entire pod was engulfed in flames. As they watched silently, Markus carefully handed Chad over to Janus who hugged his son tightly.

"I guess we're here to stay," said Markus softly.

"Well, at least we *are* here," replied Janus quietly.

Markus smiled and turned to Janus. "You know what I like about you, Sejus?"

"What?" Janus asked faintly.

"That even *you* can be positive from time to time," Markus chuckled softly.

Janus nodded and eventually cracked a smile before starting to look around. "It's probably not a good idea to remain here any longer," he said.

"Agreed," replied Markus as he also examined the woods surrounding the corn field.

"It appears that we won't be able to salvage anything else from the pod. Let's go."

Janus and Markus made their way across the large corn field in the dark. As they moved along, their orbs hovered silently behind them followed by the rescued equipment. As Janus cuddled Chad gently, the sparks emitting from his focused energy lit up the ground in front of them.

It was almost a full Moon and the sound of intermittent tree frogs and crickets could be heard off in the distance.

"It's bright enough that we don't need the orbs to provide any light," Janus remarked.

After the trio reached the tree line beyond the perimeter, Janus and Markus stopped for another look back at the pod. It was still burning, but not nearly as brightly as before.

"Maybe it won't burn away after all," said Janus somewhat surprised.

Janus instructed his monitoring orb to scan the area, which he compared to his orb's Earth database. The match came back almost instantaneously.

"Markus, we are near Coopers Falls, a town in upstate New York along the Hudson River. My scan shows that there are several humans and dwellings about two miles in that direction," Janus said, pointing toward the woods.

"It's fifty-eight degrees Fahrenheit in Earth temperature. That's a little too cool for Chad. Markus, please hand me a blanket from his bag."

Markus fumbled through Chad's bag and handed Janus a small blanket which he wrapped around his son. As he did, Chad squeezed against his father a bit tighter. Janus then instructed his orb to continue scanning the area as the three of them made their way into the woods.

"Sejus, what are you thinking?" asked Markus after a brief silence.

Janus stopped walking and looked at Markus.

"I'm trying to come up with a plan for Chad," he said. "He obviously, he needs to be taken care of."

"Yes, of course. And I think we are doing a fine job," replied Markus with a smile.

Janus looked up at the Moon and the stars before glancing back at Markus.

"Chad needs to be taken care of by real living people Markus, not a couple of holograms projected from metallic orbs."

Markus didn't answer.

"Listen, Markus, maybe we could find a way to fend for him in the short term. But what do we do as he begins to grow up?"

"We can still take care of him," protested Markus.

"Can we Markus? I'm not so sure about that."

Markus strained to glance back toward the burning spacecraft.

Janus placed his free hand on Markus's shoulder.

Markus turned to look at Janus with tears in his eyes.

"What do you want to do with the boy, Sejus?"

"There is what they call a hospital emergency room about twelve miles away. I think we should leave him there with a note."

"*Leave* him there?"

"Markus, listen. This is not easy for me, but I've been thinking about what to do ever since we located Earth. I am not suggesting that we abandon him."

"Well, what then?"

"We leave him at the hospital so that the medical staff can make sure he's OK."

"And then?" Markus asked tentatively.

"According to my database, this civilization has a system that allows for certain people to adopt children without identifiable parents. These people are screened and approved by the local authorities."

"Your plan is to give Chad *away*?"

"Well, sort of."

"What do you mean, *sort of*?"

"We would watch and protect him from a distance and at the right time —"

"We take him back!"

"Well, no."

"*No*? Then *what* Sejus?" protested Markus, clearly disturbed.

"At the right time, we reveal ourselves to him. It will be up to Chad to decide what he wants to do. If he rejects us, at least we will know that he is safe and happy."

Markus thought for a few moments, then asked, "Sejus, my friend, what about the Mitel Fleet?"

"What about it?"

"They are going to come looking for the boy, I am certain of that. Back on Thrae, my orb picked up a series of transmissions confirming that the Mitel cruiser had discovered that Chad was both a Battle Sphere *and* an immortal."

Janus glanced down at Chad and then back out toward the burning pod. "I received those transmissions too, Markus," he acknowledged. "Given the fierce determination of the Mitel Leadership, I'm certain they will scour the remnants of our planet for clues to locate us. And since the USEP facility was housed in the old fortress building, there is an excellent chance that the remaining pods will have survived the explosion wave relatively intact, not to mention our database disclosing the location of this planet."

"I agree," said Markus.

"That means the Mitels will reverse engineer the faster-than-light speed travel technology," Janus began. "And since the Mitels know that Chad is a Battle Sphere, they will not simply send out a small reconnaissance craft. Rather, they will develop the technology until they figure out how to propel a contingent of much larger spacecrafts."

"But that will take time."

"Yes," said Janus. "Our design team's preliminary modeling predicted that much larger vessels will *not* be able to travel as fast across the universe as our small pod."

"How long do you think it would take them?"

"Given the distance we traveled, I would expect that it would take them six Earth months to travel the same distance across the universe," said Janus.

"That's not a long time."

"No, it's not. In my opinion knowing full well that the Mitel Leadership will direct significant resources to achieve that goal, I estimate that it will take them ten, maybe fifteen Earth years to be in a position to send a large enough fleet capable of reaching this planet."

"What do we do then?" asked Markus.

"I don't have an answer for you right now," Janus replied with an unexpected smile. "But I have some time to come up with a plan."

Markus first smiled back at Janus, then began to laugh quietly.

"OK then, it's settled," said Janus. "Let's get started toward the hospital. It will be light soon and it's best that we travel under the cover of darkness."

"Agreed."

"My monitoring orb indicates there is a road about a half mile in that direction," said Janus pointing toward the woods.

Markus and Janus made their way into the pine tree forest. As they weaved their way along, Janus and Markus occasionally looked back toward the burning pod as it grew smaller and increasingly obscured by the tree trunks and branches until it was gone from view. They reached the end of the forest, coming upon a paved road.

"What next?" asked Markus.

"First, we need to find a place to temporarily store our equipment," replied Janus calmly.

"Yes, but where?"

"In these woods, the cover is very dense and the ground is dry."

"OK then, let's do it," nodded Markus.

They quickly retraced their steps back into the forest until the road was no longer visible. It was very still and quiet. Janus slowly lowered the equipment onto the soft pine needles of the forest floor with the aid of the antigravity beam. When they returned to the road, Janus stopped momentarily to reconfirm his recent orb scan.

"This way," pointed Janus.

They continued along the road in silence for about fifteen minutes. They passed two small houses, faint lights showing through the windows. When they came upon a third house, they saw a white van parked along the side of the road. The house was completely dark.

"What's that Sejus?"

"It's a crude surface transportation device, propelled by a petroleum-based liquid."

"Could it be of assistance to us?"

"Let's find out," smiled Janus as he carefully handed his sleeping son to Markus.

Janus cautiously approached the van on the driver's side. He tried to open the door but it was locked. Janus concentrated for a moment to make sure he did not activate his focused energy, and reached through the door. Activating his hand's focused energy he fumbled briefly before pulling a handle that unlocked the door.

"Nice trick," whispered Markus.

Janus flashed an amused grin as he opened the door. He briefly studied the dashboard while his orb performed a quick scan of the interior, then he instructed it to hover inside the van and provide a stream of light toward the driver's side of the dashboard.

"OK, here goes," Janus whispered as he reached under the steering wheel. He quickly located and grabbed the wiring harness. Using a sharp piece of hard plastic he found lying on the carpet, Janus cut the ignition, engine starter and battery wires. He then tied the battery and ignition wires together. When Janus touched their exposed ends with the starter wire, the van started up immediately.

"Well done, my friend," Markus chuckled.

"Quickly Markus, get in," instructed Janus pointing toward the passenger seat.

Markus hurried around to the other side of the van and carefully climbed in with Chad while his orb quickly darted into the rear area.

"One last thing," Janus twisted the steering wheel back and forth until he heard the steering lock pin break. He tentatively placed his foot on the gas pedal and the van lurched forward. When he pushed the pedal a bit harder, the van accelerated onto the road.

"Can you see where you're going?" asked Markus.

"Not really," said Janus as he fumbled with the knobs on the dashboard. "The sparkling from the focused energy is making it pretty hard to see."

"My monitoring orb indicates that there should be a headlight button to your left," said Markus.

"Got it!" confirmed Janus as the headlights came on. "That's much better. Now we can find the hospital."

Janus used his orb's positioning software to navigate toward the hospital.

"This machine has very dark windows. That should help us avoid detection," Markus observed.

"I think they're called *tinted* windows," replied Janus.

"I see. And by the way, my data indicates that you should be driving on the right side of the road."

"Oops," replied Janus, quickly steering the van to the right. A few minutes later, they stopped behind a car waiting at a red light. When the light turned green, the car sped off.

"I guess that means we should move ahead," Janus concluded.

"Evidently," replied Markus.

Suddenly, the light turned yellow.

"Now what do I do?" asked Janus.

"Hurry!"

Janus pushed down hard on the gas and the van roared across the intersection.

"I think landing the pod was a lot easier," grumbled Janus.

"If you say so," Markus grinned.

Suddenly, two bright lights approached from the opposite direction.

"What is that?" asked Markus.

"I believe it's another surface transportation device like ours," responded Janus.

"Not very safe," concluded Markus as the car whooshed passed them in the opposite lane.

As they got closer to the hospital, the buildings had become larger and taller.

"We're almost there Markus. By my calculations, we have about a half Earth hour of darkness remaining, so we need to act fast."

"Janus, there it is!" exclaimed Markus as the hospital came into view.

Janus turned into the hospital parking lot and drove slowly toward the Emergency entrance. He stopped the van in the entrance's circular loop. All was quiet.

"I think we should park this device over there," said Janus pointing to a series of bushes and small trees to the right of the entrance. "We can use the vegetation to hide us as we approach the entrance."

"Sounds good to me."

Janus drove the van around the entrance loop into the parking lot before parking along the curb at the far side of the shrubs. He turned off the engine and headlights. They sat in silence for a few moments as Janus's monitoring orb scanned the area.

"It's very quiet here," said Janus. "My orb's scanners don't detect any activity in the parking lot, but there appears to be one — maybe two — security personnel at the entrance. Given their positioning, they don't seem to be concentrating on the entrance doors right now."

Janus glanced over at Chad who was still sleeping. "OK Markus, if we are going to do this, then now would be a good time."

"Are we just going to leave him *sleeping on the ground* Sejus?" Markus asked, with concern.

Janus paused for a moment as he looked in the rear view mirror. "Of course not. Check to see what items are located in the back of this machine."

Markus carefully handed Chad back over to his father before floating through his passenger seat to the back of the van while his orb provided a stream of light.

"There are all kinds of things back here. There are some empty cartons, bottles, boxes and a large plastic tub. There are also several small blankets, paper and writing instruments."

"OK, great. We can use just about all of those," replied Janus quickly. "Line the large plastic tub with the blankets. But first hand me a writing instrument and some paper."

Markus handed a pen and paper to Janus who paused before writing while he held Chad against his shoulder. After a few minutes, Markus returned to the front of the van with the tub containing the blankets.

"How is this?" Markus asked.

Janus looked at the tub and blankets.

"That should be fine, don't you think?"

"Yes," replied Markus as he looked back down at the sleeping baby boy.

"Uh, Sejus . . ."

"What?"

"We must not forget to remove the boy's waste dispenser!"

"Good point. Finding a young child sleeping in a plastic tub wearing an extraterrestrial waste dispenser *might* raise suspicion," Janus said sarcastically.

"Agreed," smiled Markus.

Janus carefully removed the dispenser and placed it on the van floor. Janus placed Chad into the tub, kissed him on the forehead, and then carefully positioned additional blankets around him to make sure he was comfortable. Chad squirmed momentarily but did not awaken.

Janus instructed his monitoring orb to perform an updated scan. The orb confirmed that the area was all clear.

"OK Markus, let's go."

Markus floated through the passenger door before turning around to open it. Janus handed the tub gingerly to Markus before getting out the same side. They carefully made their way through the bushes until they reached the emergency room entrance. Janus instructed his monitoring orb to perform one last scan before placing the piece of paper in the tub next to Chad. When he confirmed that everything was clear, Janus cautiously stepped out into the lighted entry foyer and gently placed the plastic tub on the cement walkway in front of the main doors. He arranged the blankets one more time then quickly returned to the bushes.

"Now what do we do?" Markus asked.

"We wait by the transportation device until someone comes out to get him."

Just then, the main doors opened and a security guard in a blue suit and cap stepped outside. He spotted the tub, kneeling to inspect it.

Janus and Markus returned to their orbs and hovered silently in the shadows. As they did, the security guard turned his head and scanned the bushes for several seconds before turning his attention back to the tub.

"What the heck do we have here?" he said to himself slowly lifting the top blanket.

"A *baby* . . . holy cow!" he said in disbelief.

He then saw the note.

The guard read the note out loud "MY NAME IS CHAD STONE. PLEASE FIND ME A NICE HOME."

The guard placed the note back into the tub before standing up to survey the parking lot. He pulled a flashlight from his belt and shined it in the bushes. Janus and Markus hovered silently out of sight behind the shrubs. The guard then turned the flashlight back toward the entrance loop. Not seeing anyone, he put his flashlight away, picked up the tub, and walked back inside the hospital.

"Good-bye for now," whispered Janus. "I'll be watching you my son."

Janus's hologram then reappeared, followed by Markus.

"Markus, we need to go before anyone comes to search the area more thoroughly," said Janus.

"Agreed," said Markus, glancing back toward the van.

The two quickly made their way back to the white van trailed by their monitoring orbs. Janus opened the driver's side door and again reached under the steering wheel. Within seconds, the van restarted.

"Now what?" asked Markus quietly as he settled into the passenger seat.

"We need to return this transportation device."

"Why?"

Janus glanced over to Markus.

"To minimize to possibility of Chad being linked to our crash landing."

"I'm not sure I understand," Markus frowned.

As Janus drove the van out of the parking lot he explained.

"We took this device from an area very close to the landing site, correct?"

"Yes but —"

"If we return it there, we will hopefully eliminate any possible connection between Chad and the crash site."

"OK, I understand now," replied Markus, "but what about the damage we caused to this machine?"

"My hope is that it will be explained as vandalism."

"Ah, yes *vandalism*. Sounds reasonable," smiled Markus. "Do you know how to get back there?"

"My monitoring orb has already plotted a return route."

As Janus drove out of Coopers Falls, the two sat in silence. As they drove through a long stretch of wooded road, Janus noticed Chad's disposal dispenser. He quickly pulled the van over to the side of the road.

"Why are we stopping here?" asked Markus.

"Markus, hand me the dispenser," Janus instructed.

"What are you doing, my friend?" Markus asked as he handed him the dispenser.

"Getting rid of the evidence," said Janus as he disappeared into the woods returning moments later without the dispenser. "Hopefully that will not be found for a long time," he said as he restarted the engine. Down the road, the home of the van's owner was still dark. Janus slowly came to a stop and turned off the motor and headlights. The two quickly exited the van followed by their monitoring orbs. It was just beginning to get light.

Janus and Markus returned to their small metallic orbs before silently speeding off into the woods to retrieve their belongings, and make one last stop to see if there was anything else they could retrieve from the damaged pod.

CHAPTER SIX – A NEW FAMILY

The discovery of Chad by the hospital's security guard received little media coverage. The big story in the local news was the *mysterious crash* outside of town.

The United States military had cordoned off a two-square mile perimeter around the site. A *no-fly* zone was established. The gossip in Coopers Falls was that a UFO had crashed landed there.

A group of reporters gathered near the crash site. As the media waited anxiously, the lead investigator and his aides strolled up to greet them.

Major Talbot smiled as veteran reporter Joe Tetrault quickly stepped forward from the pack of reporters.

"I'm speaking here with . . ."

"Major Michael Talbot, US Navy Space Surveillance," answered Major Talbot calmly.

"Major Talbot, what can you tell us about the crash?" asked Joe quickly thrusting his microphone toward Major Talbot.

"Well, I," Major Talbot responded, pausing to glance at his interviewer's name tag. "Well, Joe, not much really."

"Why is that Major?" asked Joe quickly.

"Because there really isn't much of anything left. Between the re-entry, crash landing and ensuing fire, it's pretty much gone."

"I see," said Joe. "Major Talbot, the speculation out there is that a UFO crashed here. Can you comment on that?"

"If you call a piece of space junk falling back to Earth a UFO, then I guess your rumors are correct."

"Major, if it's only space junk," interrupted another reporter standing behind Joe, "then why has the area been cordoned off with such strict security?"

Major Talbot paused for a moment to scan the rest of the assembled media.

"Good question," he replied. "Some of the stuff that falls back from space contains all kinds of hazardous materials. Our job is to identify and isolate those materials as quickly as possible to ensure the public's safety."

"Have you determined what it was that came down then?" asked a third reporter. "A satellite, or part of an old space mission maybe?"

Major Talbot paused again before answering.

"As I said, there isn't really much of anything left after the initial impact and subsequent fire. We are still gathering debris and quite frankly we may not know for quite some time just what it was that came down. In the meantime, you can rest assured that the public is not in any danger. If you don't mind, I am going to refer additional questions to my very able assistant, Lieutenant Jason Miller."

Major Talbot smiled and waved to the cameras before walking back toward the crash site. As he did, he could hear the several reporters shouting out additional questions to Lieutenant Miller.

"I hope I sounded at least *somewhat* convincing," Major Talbot muttered to himself, as he walked away from the reporters.

That spacecraft didn't come from Earth thought Major Talbot. *And whoever, or whatever, piloted the craft survived the landing since a substantial amount of equipment and parts are missing.*

As he walked back toward the crash site, Major Talbot looked up at the sky and let out a deep sigh. *Given what we know so far, the details of this crash must remain a secret.*

Major Talbot shook his head as he considered what he should do. An important part of his job was to locate and investigate UFOs, piece together the evidence and come up with answers. Another part of his job was to keep that information away from the public to prevent widespread panic.

I need answers, and I need them quickly.

At the Coopers Falls Hospital, Chad Stone was an instant favorite. Because he only had eight fingers and eight toes, Doctors put Chad through an extensive battery of tests to determine the full extent of his physical defects. They quickly determined that Chad had an enlarged brain and lungs.

Doctors were also very surprised to discover that his heart had five chambers instead of four. When blood tests revealed that Chad had incredibly high levels of titanium, aluminum, beryllium, magnesium and other metals, the medical staff theorized that Chad's parents had lived under hazardous conditions.

Doctors assumed that his parents became aware of Chad's condition and decided to abandon him at the hospital. Efforts to track down anyone associated with Chad proved fruitless.

Chad's prognosis was bleak. The doctors who examined him concluded that Chad would likely die well before reaching the age of five due to blood contamination. But what surprised and confused everyone at the hospital was the incredible amount of energy Chad had. Given his diagnosis, Chad should have been listless and sickly.

In time, the medical staff became keenly aware of how smart Chad was. With his wild and wispy curly white hair, Chad was soon given the nickname *little Einstein*. Over the next several months Chad was kept under close observation while his condition remained stable. Doctors were at a loss to explain how Chad was still alive.

After a series of contentious meetings among the doctors, they decided to find adoptive parents for Chad. Over the next seven months, several couples inquired about Chad. Many of them came to the hospital to meet and hold him. Unfortunately, each couple decided not to move forward with an adoption once they were informed of Chad's medical issues. The hospital staff realized that little Einstein's bleak prognosis meant that he would never have a normal life. Instead, he would spend the rest of his short life in and out of hospitals. The staff tried to hide their emotions but the feelings of sadness and helplessness were universal.

About two weeks before doctors planned to abandon the adoption effort, Jim and Molly Johnson visited the hospital. Jim, a tall and lanky outdoorsman, was a physics professor at the local community college. Molly was a first-grade teacher at the Bickford Street Elementary School in Coopers Falls.

Jim and Molly had tried to have children on their own for a long time; until it was finally determined that Molly was physically unable to do so. Molly, an avid runner and health enthusiast, took the news very hard. She never was one to easily accept limitations being placed on her from anyone or anything. Despite the devastating news, she and Jim were determined to have a family.

At the hospital, Jim and Molly met with Kathy Duvall, about the adoption process. Kathy smiled and stood to greet them.

"Hi, I'm Kathy," she said reaching out her hand.

"Hi Kathy, I'm Molly, and this is my husband Jim." She quickly shook Kathy's hand before sitting down.

"Hello Jim. Thanks for coming," said Kathy "I presume you have been made aware of —"

"Chad's physical problems?" interrupted Molly.

"Well, yes," replied Kathy somewhat apprehensively.

"Yes, we have," said Jim softly. "Obviously we are concerned about his health."

"But we have heard so many wonderful things about Chad," said Molly. "So much so, that we felt compelled to come in today."

"Well *good*," said Kathy enthusiastically. "Quite honestly, Chad is doing great. It appears he is completely healthy and happy. It's as though Chad's abnormalities are normal to him, *does that sound weird?* Quite frankly, the doctors are at a loss to understand why. He is also incredibly smart," said Kathy "We call him —"

"Little Einstein," interrupted Jim, "yeah, we heard about that."

"No, you don't understand," laughed Kathy. "Chad is beyond incredibly bright. I mean, the medical staff says he's like, *out of this world* smart."

Jim's eyes immediately lit up. He glanced over at Molly who was already looking at him with a smile. She reached over and took Jim's hand and squeezed it tightly. The decision had been made. They were going to adopt Chad.

On the day Jim and Molly arrived to pick up Chad, Kathy came down to see them just in case they had any last minute questions. As Jim and Molly were getting ready to leave, Kathy asked them to wait. She disappeared for a few minutes and returned with something in her hand.

"I almost forgot," said Kathy.

She reached out her hand toward Jim.

"What?" asked Jim.

Kathy placed the round silver medallion in the palm of his hand.

"I want you to have this," she said. "We found it in the container with Chad the night he was left here."

Jim studied the medallion closely. There was a series of strange markings on either side, which reminded him of a form of hieroglyphics, but only different. Each marking contained a series of intersecting geometric lines and curving shapes.

"Do you know what this is?" asked Jim while he continued to study the object.

"No," shrugged Kathy, "we just assumed it was his."

"OK, thanks," smiled Jim.

He waved goodbye to Kathy before walking briskly to catch up with Molly as she walked toward the main entrance holding Chad.

"I can't believe we actually did this!" said Molly excitedly as they left the building.

"Me too," replied Jim. "It's going to be great, no matter what happens."

They strapped Chad into the car seat. Molly sat in the back seat while Jim slowly drove the newest member of the family home.

The years passed quickly. When Chad turned five, Jim and Molly were convinced that the hospital's initial diagnosis was incorrect. The medical staff called his thriving health nothing short of a miracle.

As Chad grew, it appeared that he was going to be tall. In time, his wispy curly white hair eventually turned black, filled in and became straight and quite thick, as had his eyebrows and long eyelashes. Jim and Molly let Chad grow his hair as long as he wanted since it seemed to go hand and hand with his inquisitive free spirit. Chad was a gentle soul who went out of his way to help others. Molly often said that it was as if Chad felt responsible for the safety and well-being of just about everybody.

When Chad turned eight, Jim and Molly took Chad on a two-week early-summer camping trip on the islands of the thirty mile long Lake Edward. They had recently purchased a used twenty-one foot inboard-outdrive motor boat. Jim obtained camping permits for two separate islands over the two-week period and was really looking forward to getting away for awhile. It had been an unusually busy semester and he needed to unwind.

At dusk the day before the trip, Jim and Molly carefully packed the tent, non-perishables and cooking gear into the back of their station wagon while Chad played in the back yard. Molly peaked out back from time to time to check on him. She smiled watching Chad run around the back yard chasing a remote control airplane he had received as a birthday present. Molly and Jim were amazed at Chad's insatiable interest in all things that could fly. From birds to planes to helicopters and jets, Chad seemed instinctively drawn to flying. Jim often joked that Chad would probably fly around himself if he could.

As Chad watched the plane circle in the air, something in the woods caught his eye. He stopped and looked toward the trees along the rear of the property as his remote-controlled plane fell harmlessly on to the grass. Chad stared intently at the lower branches for a few moments. Sensing something was there, he walked slowly toward the trees.

Suddenly, a silver and black metallic ball darted out from behind the closest tree and hovered in place momentarily. When Chad instinctively stepped forward, it quickly maneuvered through the maze of trees, disappearing into the forest. Chad stared in amazement for a few seconds before running as fast as he could toward the front yard.

"Dad, Mom!" yelled Chad with excitement.

Jim stopped packing the gear into the back of the station wagon and glanced toward Molly.

"Dad, Mom!" yelled Chad again as he raced toward them.

"Chad, what's wrong?" asked Jim.

"I saw a shiny flying ball!" exclaimed Chad.

"A what?" laughed Molly.

"I saw a shiny black and silver ball flying around the woods!"

"Really?" replied Jim somewhat amused and confused.

"Yeah!" said Chad. "It was floating in the air behind a tree. And when I moved toward it, it flew away into the woods real fast!"

Jim looked at Molly.

"Molly —"

"I saw it!" interrupted Chad "Come see!"

Chad turned and raced toward the back yard.

Jim followed Chad out back. When he caught up to him, they walked slowly toward the edge of the forest. It was getting dark and the crickets and tree frogs were chirping loudly.

"It was right there!" said Chad as he pointed at the trees.

Jim stared into the forest. Even though he tried to ignore it, he had the distinct feeling that he was being watched from a distance. It gave him goose bumps.

"Listen buddy," said Jim softly. "It must have been a balloon —"

"No!" protested Chad loudly. "It had a shiny *TV screen* on the front of it!"

"*A what?*"

"A shiny screen."

Jim looked at Chad for a moment before smiling nervously. It was not like Chad to make things up or tell stories.

"What do you think it was little man?" asked Jim quietly.

"I don't know," replied Chad weakly.

His face then lit up.

"Maybe it was from Mars!"

Jim laughed softly.

"Maybe so little man. And maybe it is here to keep an eye on *you* and protect Mom and me!"

"*Really?*"

Jim rubbed his hand through the thick black hair on top of Chad's head.

"Listen buddy, you need to start getting ready for bed because we are going to get an early start tomorrow, OK?"

"OK, Dad," smiled Chad.

Jim watched Chad race back across the yard, up the rear steps and into the house. After picking up the remote-controlled plane, he stared into the woods for a few more minutes. As Jim walked back toward the house, he could not help but feel that someone or *something* was still watching him from the woods. Molly noticed the serious look on Jim's face as he returned to the car.

"What's wrong honey?"

"Um, nothing really, why do you ask?"

"You have this look on your face like you are troubled about something."

Jim did not want to worry Molly unnecessarily, especially since he had not seen anything himself.

"Oh, I was just deep in thought making sure we are not forgetting anything," explained Jim before reaching into the back of the wagon to organize their supplies.

"If we do, we do," said Molly. "Let's just go and have some fun, OK?"

"Sounds good to me," smiled Jim.

After they finished packing, Jim and Molly *finally* got Chad to take a bath and get settled into bed. After kissing Chad goodnight, the two of them crawled into bed.

"Boy," sighed Molly. "Chad would *not* stop talking about the shiny flying ball he saw out in the woods."

Jim did not respond at first.

"What do you think he was talking about honey?" asked Molly.

"You know kids at that age," replied Jim quietly. "Their imaginations are constantly running at full speed."

"What did you tell him when you guys went out back?"

"Oh . . . I said that it must have been a balloon."

"That's what he said you told him. He *also* said that you told him that *maybe* it came to *watch* over him and protect us."

"I was just humoring him."

"Well, I don't think it's such a great idea to say he's being watched. It's going to give him nightmares!"

"Sorry Molly, I guess I wasn't really thinking."

The two of them lay in bed silently for a few minutes listening to the crickets and tree frogs through the open bedroom window.

"Molly?"

"What?"

"I was thinking earlier. I can't remember Chad lying to us before."

"Well, he's just a kid. They do that sometimes. I mean, it was either that or his imagination running wild, right?"

"Yeah, I guess you're right," yawned Jim.

He rolled over on his side to try to get comfortable. A few minutes later, they were both fast asleep.

CHAPTER SEVEN – FAMILY VACATION

The next morning, everyone was excited to hit the road. It was a beautiful summer morning, without a cloud in the sky. Chad came bounding down the stairs.

"Ready to go little man?" asked Jim.

"Yeah!" yelled Chad with excitement.

After a quick breakfast, they all climbed into the packed station wagon. Jim hit the gas slowly and heard the familiar clunking sound of the hitch ball against the trailer coupler.

"And we're on our way!" said Jim triumphantly.

They drove leisurely along the winding country roads from Coopers Falls to Lake Edward. When they arrived at the boat yard, Jim unloaded their gear into the boat before backing the trailer down the ramp and into the water. He unlocked the winch and slowly lowered the boat into the water. Jim scampered onto the bow, around the windshield and into the deck area. With a quick turn of the ignition key, the engine started. Chad watched his father through the station wagon's rear window. After Molly finished parking, the two of them walked down to the dock where Jim was waiting. The motor gurgled as the boat idled next to the dock. Jim helped Chad, and then

Molly, get in the boat. Once he pushed the throttle forward, the engine growled.

They made their way out of the bay and into the open lake. It was a magnificent view — the lake was a deep blue speckled with an occasional whitecap. Fir covered brown mountains curved gracefully toward the sky on both sides of the lake. A few of the islands that dotted the lake were visible in the distance. Jim pointed toward a larger island fittingly named *Dome Island* for its curved appearance caused by the densely packed pine trees that covered its entire surface.

"That's our first stop!" announced Jim.

Circling around the island, Jim immediately recognized their dock from the picture in the brochure. With a big smile, he turned toward Molly and Chad and pointed excitedly.

"That one over there!"

He cut the engine back to idle as the boat approached the dock, causing the bow to lower into the water. The waves quickly washed under the boat, nudging it further forward. Jim steered the boat until it was parallel to the dock.

As the boat edged closer, Jim cut the engine and made his way toward the bow. He quickly grabbed one of the boat's white dock fenders by its nylon rope and placed it over the side before reaching out to grab one of the many dock posts. Jim nudged the boat up against the dock until the fender was pinned in between the two. He then grabbed the extra nylon rope and tied it securely to the dock post. Jim quickly repeated the process with a second fender near the rear of the boat before stepping gingerly onto the dock.

"OK, everybody out!" instructed Jim.

The three of them explored their campsite for a few minutes before unloading the boat and setting up the tent. Other campsites were visible in different directions. At one site, there was a bright blue tent; at another, a large yellow tent. The gray cinderblock restroom building located toward the center of the island was also partially visible. However, there was no sign of any campers.

"I guess everybody is out and about," Jim said to no one in particular.

Once the tent was set up and the food and other supplies unpacked and stored at the campsite, the three of them went for a walk around the island. They followed a well-worn dirt path that snaked its way between the pine trees.

"Be careful," cautioned Jim. "Keep a look out for exposed tree roots — I don't want anybody tripping and getting hurt."

The dirt path eventually weaved its way down toward the rocky lake shore. A gentle lake breeze blew across the island. It was delightfully quiet except for the soft rustling sound of the breeze in the tree branches.

Up ahead, another couple and their young daughter — who appeared to be about Chad's age — came walking toward them. As the families converged, Jim stopped and introduced himself.

"Hi, guys, how are you doing? My name's Jim and this is my wife, Molly."

Jim then looked around for Chad who was now standing behind him looking somewhat apprehensively.

"And this is our son Chad," he added with a grin.

"Nice to meet you Jim," responded the man. "I'm David — and this is my wife Joanne — and our daughter Melissica."

"Hi Melissica," smiled Molly.

"How long are you guys here for?" asked Jim.

"The rest of the week," replied Joanne.

"That's great," said Molly. "We're here for four days ourselves. Maybe we can get together and have a cook-out."

"That sounds like a great idea," said Joanne. "*Maybe* Melissica will make a new friend."

"We're in the big yellow tent up the path," motioned David. "Why don't you guys stop by later?"

"That sounds great," smiled Jim.

With that, the families waved goodbye as they each continued their leisurely trek around the island.

"They seem really nice, honey," whispered Molly.

"Yes, they do," nodded Jim. "Melissica is a real cutie."

Molly then looked down at Chad.

"What do you think Chad? Maybe you can make an island friend during our vacation?"

Chad looked up at his mother, his eyebrows now furrowed.

"What's the matter Chad?" asked Molly.

"She's a girl!" blurted Chad.

"What's wrong with that little man?" laughed Jim.

"Nothing, I guess," replied Chad quietly.

"Well good," smiled Molly. "Let's just wait to see what she is like, OK?"

Chad nodded and smiled weakly.

"I'm getting hungry!" announced Jim. "How about we go back to our campsite and make us some lunch?"

"Yay!" yelled Chad running back toward the tent.

"Watch out for the tree roots!" Jim warned.

After lunch, Jim took Molly and Chad for a boat ride north to Sandy Bay, a favorite spot for boaters to drop anchor, soak up the sun and play in the waist deep water.

The water was crystal clear and the sand was soft and smooth.

After returning to camp, they quickly changed and headed over to the Erickson's big yellow tent with hamburgers, hotdogs and a small cooler of beer.

Despite Chad's earlier hesitation, he and Melissica became fast friends. They ran together around the tent, through the trees and then along the trail to the dock — all within the watchful eyes of their parents. They sat together for a time on the edge of the dock with their feet in the water while motor boats crisscrossed out in the distance, the sun sparkled against the waves.

"Your name is *Melissica*?" asked Chad quietly.

"Yeah," replied Melissica slowly. "Everybody makes fun of it."

"Really? Why?"

"They say I have two names *squished* together."

Chad's eyes suddenly brightened. He lifted his arms slightly as he showed Melissica his two four-fingered hands.

"People make fun of these too," smiled Chad.

"*Wow*! Do they hurt?"

"No. I mean, they *do* if I bang them against something."

Melissica laughed.

Chad then wiggled his feet up in the air.

"I only have eight toes too," said Chad pointing toward his feet.

"Oh my god!" gasped Melissica as her face grew serious. "What *happened* to you Chad?"

"I was born this way. I guess it's kind of like how you were born with your name."

Melissica looked at Chad for a moment.

"Well, *I* think they look just fine."

"Thanks," Chad blushed.

They stared at the lake in silence for a few minutes before Chad turned to look at Melissica. She had beautiful hazel eyes and thick brown shoulder length hair. Her complexion was very light with freckles on her cheeks.

"I like your name," Chad said softly.

"Thank you, Chad," smiled Melissica before the two of them laughed.

After a late dinner in front of a campfire, the families said good night. Jim, Molly and Chad headed back to their campsite. Exhausted from their first day, they all crawled into their tent. As dusk turned into nighttime, Chad and Jim peered out through the tent window up toward the stars.

"Dad?" whispered Chad.

"What son?" Jim asked in a hushed voice.

"How many stars are there?"

"Probably more than anyone can count. It's a big universe out there and —"

"How big *is* it?"

"Pretty darn big."

"You mean *really* big?"

"Not just *really* big, but *really, really* big," explained Jim. "The universe is measured by how fast light can travel in a year. Astronomers have used the relationship between distance and the speed of light to view portions of deep space that are almost 14 *billion* light years away.

"Wow," whispered Chad.

"Yup, they call that the *observable universe*," explained Jim. "Scientists also think that the universe is like a giant expanding ball which means — "

"That the universe is at least 28 *billion* light years in diameter."

"Yes," smiled Jim "And it continues to expand all the time."

"That's pretty cool!"

"It sure is little man," smiled Jim.

"But where are all the *aliens*?"

"The *aliens*?"

"Yeah, you know, *other life forms* — where are they?" asked Chad eagerly.

"That's a great question," replied Jim thoughtfully. "The universe is *so* big that it's pretty likely that we are not the only ones in it. But nobody really knows for sure where they might be —"

"Why not?"

"Well, first of all we would need to locate a planet that supports life."

"And then what?"

"We would need to figure out a way to communicate with them," Jim began. "Scientists think there might be a habitable planet circling a star called Alpha Centauri B. But it is still more than four light years away. On top of that, there may be as many as 1,000 to 1,600 other stars within fifty light years of Earth."

"Like our sun?"

"Some, yes."

The two of them continued to look up silently at the stars for a time.

"Our own Milky Way is a spiral galaxy that is about 120,000 light years wide that contains over 400 *billion* stars. Scientists believe that there are larger spiral galaxies out there which contain over a *trillion* stars."

"How many galaxies *are* there?" whispered Chad.

"Astronomers think there may be as many as *170 billion* galaxies in the observable universe."

"Then other worlds like Earth must be out there," concluded Chad.

"That's right."

"Do you think they are looking back at us right now?"

"I wouldn't be surprised."

They got in their sleeping bags.

"Dad?" whispered Chad.

"Yes Chad?"

"If the planet is like ours, do you think they *look* like us?"

"You mean the aliens that are looking back at us right now?" Jim chuckled.

"*Yes*," smiled Chad.

"Maybe, but it's hard to say."

"Why?"

"We don't know enough about the universe yet to be able to say," explained Jim. "Everything is so far away. As we invent better ways to see into the universe, maybe someday we'll find out — and come face to face with extraterrestrials from another planet. "

"That's what I want to do when I grow up!" hissed Chad.

"What?"

"Go into outer space and meet extraterrestrials face to face!"

"Maybe you will Chad. But for now let's get some sleep, OK?"

"OK. G'night Dad."

"Good night Son. Love you."

"Love you too, Dad."

Within a few minutes, everyone was fast asleep.

For the next four days on Dome Island, Melissica and Chad were inseparable. As luck would have it, David's company had just transferred him from California, and they had purchased a house only a few blocks away from Chad's.

On the fifth day, it was time to pack up and move to the next island, a smaller island with only one camp site, in an area called The Narrows.

"OK," said Jim as they finished packing their gear into the boat "let's go find Squash Island."

"How do you plan on doing that?" laughed Molly

"Well, it has a red dock with a green bumper on one of the piers."

"Oh, the *red* dock. That should be easy," replied Molly sarcastically. "Aren't there over *twenty* islands up there?"

"Indeed," smiled Jim. "But it's on the east side of the lake. That should *narrow* things down."

"Let's hope," laughed Molly.

After the three of them climbed in the boat, Jim untied it from the piers. Melissica stood on the dock, waving to Chad as the boat slowly drifted away.

"Bye Chad," waved Melissica. "See you when you get home!"

Jim started the engine with a gurgling growl and slowly backed the boat up in a curving circle before flipping the throttle forward. Chad watched silently as both Melissica and Dome Island appeared smaller and smaller. Their boat entered The Narrows about a half hour later. Jim steered to the right toward the east side of the lake and closer to the small islands.

Suddenly, Jim pointed to a red dock with a green bumper.

"Yay!" yelled Chad.

As they approached Squash Island the trio studied its details. It was flat with a rocky shoreline. A clump of tall white pines stood on one end and a grove of oak trees on the other. The open middle section contained a wooden picnic table, tent platform and outhouse.

"It's our own private island," smiled Molly as she put her arm around Chad.

By now, Chad had become an expert at watching his father dock the boat. He lowered the fenders into the water before jumping onto the dock to tie the boat down. Within an hour, they had the tent set up and the boat unpacked. Jim and Chad spent the afternoon fishing off the north side of the island while Molly read a book.

Before dusk, Jim and Molly took an inventory of their remaining food.

"We need more drinking water, hotdogs and hamburgers for sure," said Molly. "We are also running low on toilet paper. I made a list for you to take with you in the morning."

"Sounds good."

"By the way, how are we doing on gas?" asked Molly.

"We are getting a bit low. I probably should gas up at the same time."

"OK, honey," nodded Molly as she unzipped the tent flap. Chad was already fast asleep.

"We wore him out today," whispered Molly.

"Yeah," nodded Jim. "It's been a great vacation so far."

The next morning after breakfast, Jim grabbed his list and jumped into the boat. He checked his map to confirm the name of the bay where the general store was located.

"Jim, here," said Molly as she walked onto the dock. "Don't forget your life vest."

"Thanks!" he smiled.

Jim tossed the vest into the back of the boat and set out toward the marina. He gassed up the boat before heading over to the general store. It took longer than expected, but Jim eventually located all the items on the list. He exited the store and noticed ominous dark clouds to the west.

A thunderstorm is rolling in he thought.
But I should be able to beat it back to the island in plenty of time.

As Jim stepped into the boat, a passerby stopped on the dock and stared. He was tall and thin and looked to be about seventy years old with short gray hair.

"What are you doing young fella?"

"Trying to beat the storm back to my campsite," replied Jim.

"You sure you want to go out now? It looks like quite a thunder storm is headed this way," said the old man.

"Yes, but I don't want to leave my wife and son alone on the island. If I leave now, I should beat the storm back to the campsite."

"Where are you staying?"

"Squash Island."

The old man thought for a moment.

"I don't know," he said eventually. "If I were you, I would wait until after the storm passes."

"Thanks for the advice," replied Jim. "Like I said, I don't want to leave my wife and son alone."

"Good luck, then!" waved the stranger as he went on his way.

Jim backed the boat away from the dock and headed back toward Squash Island at full speed. Once he exited the safety of the bay, the wind and waves increased dramatically.

This was probably not a good idea Jim thought as he looked at the menacing clouds now directly overhead. Out in the open water, the boat bounced hard over the rough waves, forcing Jim to slow the boat down considerably. The spray from the waves quickly soaked his shirt and shorts.

Jim glanced back toward the rear of the boat. The groceries were strewn about the floor of the boat and Jim realized that his life preserver was missing. He immediately slowed to an idle and scanned the water behind him.

"*Damn it!*" muttered Jim angrily. "I'll never find it in this weather."

A bright flash of lightning, followed by loud thunder echoed across the mountains being pelted by long sheets of rain. With strong gusty winds, Jim could barely maintain his balance.

Don't panic he thought.

Jim scanned the lake. No other boats were visible. He reached into his pocket for his cell phone only to realize that he had left it at the campsite. Just then, heavy rain reduced Jim's visibility.

I am probably closer to the marina than the island Jim thought. *I should turn around and head back.*"

As he turned the boat around, a huge wave crashed into the starboard side, capsizing it. Jim struggled against the waves, trying to hold onto the hull but it was too slippery. His heart pounded as he made his way along the hull to the rear of the boat.

Maybe I can find something there to hold onto, he thought.

Jim grabbed onto the vertical section of the engine outdrive and clung to it tightly as he tried to catch his breath. The rain was so heavy that he had lost his sense of direction.

Damn it! He thought. *How could I have been so stupid?*

Jim huddled against the outdrive housing as he desperately tried to figure out what to do next. Before long the boat began to sink.

Crap! Jim panicked. The boat disappeared into the water.

He struggled to tread water as waves repeatedly washed over his head.

I can't die like this he thought as his heart pounded.

"I've got to stay afloat!" he scolded himself.

After only a few minutes of treading water, Jim was exhausted. The rough waves continued to wash over him as he gasped for air. Growing weary, he started to sink beneath the surface. Jim tried to yell for help as he went under but nothing came out. He struggled with all his might to get back to the surface.

NO — PLEASE GOD NO!

He went under a second time. Water filled his nose and his ears, and time seemed to slow down and then stop. It was now eerily peaceful and quiet. Jim stopped struggling and looked up toward the surface just as a bright bolt of lightning flashed. A shiny silver metallic ball wobbling back and forth just above the churning waves. Jim reached his hand up toward the sphere before passing out.

Just above the waves, Janus's orb hovered in place. He had raced out to where Jim's boat had capsized, having followed the family to Lake Edward to keep a watchful eye over everyone. Janus's monitoring orb detected that Jim's boat was in distress, and he sped out over the lake to its last known position. Janus appeared from the orb and reached into the water to grab Jim.

"Got you!" said Janus as he pulled Jim out of the water. A quick scan revealed that Jim was unconscious and in physical distress, having ingested a substantial amount of water.

Janus placed Jim over his left shoulder which sparkled brightly on contact. As he did, Jim expelled most of the water from his throat and lungs.

Just then, another huge bolt of lightning flashed across the sky followed immediately by a clap of thunder.

That was close thought Janus. *Now if I can only get him to shore before we are struck by lightning.*

Staying just above the waves, Janus quickly headed to shore followed closely by his monitoring orb as sheets of rain fell. His orb scanned the shoreline off in the distance, locating a grove of pine trees near a road and several lakeside cabins.

That looks like a good location thought Janus.

Approaching the shoreline, he saw the outline of the trees through the rain. Janus floated over several large rocks at the edge of the lake and headed toward the grove of pines about twenty feet inland. His hologram floated under the trees and gently placed Jim on a bed of soft pine needles. Janus placed Jim on his stomach and he immediately coughed up the remaining water. Jim's eyelids flickered, but did not open. The monitoring orb ran another scan that confirmed Jim was OK. Satisfied, Janus terminated his hologram and glided out of view. From a distance, Janus instructed his orb to continue monitoring Jim's vital signs.

After about an hour, the storm moved east taking along with it the ominous dark clouds. The late afternoon sun reappeared, followed by several birds.

As Jim lay silent, rain drops trickled down along the pine trees until eventually landing onto the soft needles under the trees. A series of drips landed gently against Jim's face causing him to stir. He coughed several more times as he cleared his throat. Jim sat up very slowly as he struggled to focus his vision. His arms and legs felt heavy and tired. He blinked several times until his vision slowly returned to normal. Jim stared at the pine needles all around him before glancing up at the trees. Hearing the water gently hitting the rocky shoreline, he turned to see the glimmering lake.

Where am I?

Jim took a deep breath and looked down at his wet clothes. Suddenly it all came back to him. He remembered the thunderstorm, and falling into the water, the boat sinking, and fighting for his life.

Am I alive? He wondered.

Jim touched his unshaven face. Realizing that he was still very much alive, he forced himself to his knees before slowly standing up. Jim walked gingerly out from under the pine trees into the bright sunlight. He looked around trying to get his bearings and heard a passing car off in the distance.

Jim walked slowly in the direction of the sound. He navigated his way up a slight incline and through some brush until he reached an old paved highway. There was a faded, single yellow line down the middle. Jim looked up and down the road in both directions noticing a cabin off in the distance.

Hopefully they have a phone Jim thought.

He walked sluggishly along the side of the road toward the cabin. Jim heard another car approaching. As it came around the bend, he turned and waved. An old gray Ford pickup slowed down and came to a stop next to him. The driver reached over and rolled down his passenger window.

"Mister, are you all right?" the driver asked.

"I'm not sure," responded Jim still somewhat dazed. "I had a boating accident during the thunderstorm."

"Was anybody else with you?"

"No, I was alone."

"Where's your boat?"

"It sank out in the lake."

"Hold on — I'm calling 911!" said the driver reaching for his cell phone. In a few minutes a Lake Edward police cruiser appeared from around the bend. Just as the police officer stepped out of his car, an emergency vehicle also appeared. The paramedics examined Jim. Then a second police cruiser arrived on the scene. A tall police sergeant slowly got out of the vehicle and spoke with the responding officer. After a few moments, he approached Jim.

"Sir, my name is Sergeant Thomas. What is your name and can you tell me what happened?"

"Jim Johnson. I was trying to make it back to Squash Island in my motorboat before the thunderstorm hit," explained Jim.

"Go on Sir," instructed Sergeant Thomas.

"Well, conditions got really bad. The boat capsized and I was thrown into the water."

"Where did that happen?"

"I had left the marina bay. You know — the one with the general store across the street?" explained Jim.

"I know the one, yes."

"I was heading north on the open lake toward the narrows just as the storm hit. A big wave capsized the boat. I tried holding onto it, but it sank."

"How did you get to shore Sir?" asked Sergeant Thomas.

Jim paused for a minute and looked the police sergeant in the eye.

"I — I don't know."

"What else do you remember?"

"I tried to tread water but it was so rough out there. The wind and the rain were really bad."

"What happened next?"

"I started to go under water. I was exhausted."

He suddenly remembered the silver metallic ball hovering above him. It was like a dream but it seemed so real. Jim realized that somehow, some way, the metallic sphere had saved his life.

"*Sir*?" asked Sergeant Thomas.

Jim paused.

"No, I don't remember anything else," responded Jim after several seconds.

Sergeant Thomas looked at Jim suspiciously for a moment, studying his face and demeanor.

"I need to get in touch with my family," said Jim.

"Where are they, Mr. Johnson?"

"On Squash Island."

"I will arrange for a Patrol boat to take you out there to pick them up," said Sergeant Thomas politely. "In the meantime, I will file my report."

Sergeant Thomas studied Jim for a few seconds more before walking back to his cruiser.

"Thank you, Sergeant," Jim said, rubbing his head.

After about an hour, Jim was escorted by a New York State Marine Patrol boat back to Squash Island. They passed the area where Jim's boat had capsized and sank. As he sat silently, Jim kept thinking about the silver metallic ball. As the boat approached Squash Island, Molly and Chad ran out on the dock. Jim climbed out and embraced them.

"Honey! We were *so* worried about you," Molly said, tears running down her face.

"I know Mol — I'm *so* sorry," whispered Jim.

"When it started lightning and thundering, we were so scared," said Molly hugging Jim tightly.

"Oh honey, I know," Jim's eyes filled with tears.

"And when you didn't come back," Molly said, crying. As she wept softly, Chad also cried. The three of them hugged while Jim quietly explained how the boat had been lost, but that everything was going to be OK.

With the help of the Patrol officers, Jim and Molly loaded their remaining belongings into the Patrol boat. They headed back to the marina where their station wagon was parked. After unloading, Jim thanked the officers.

"Our pleasure, Sir," one officer responded with a smile. "We're just glad everyone is safe."

Jim, Molly and Chad watched silently as the officers climbed back into their boat and sped away.

By the time they finished loading up the car, it was dark. Chad quickly nodded off and fell asleep in the back seat while Jim drove home slowly along the back roads. No one noticed Janus's monitoring orb sitting on the roof of station wagon. The black and silver orb blended in with the moonlit sky. When they arrived home, Jim pulled up the driveway and turned off the ignition. He looked over at Molly who had also fallen asleep.

"It's sure good to be home," sighed Jim quietly.

He watched Molly sleep for a minute or two.

I should probably keep everything to myself for now he thought.

Jim rubbed Molly's shoulder gently to wake her up.

"We're home. We can unload the car in the morning."

With a yawn, Molly shook her head in agreement.

Chad, Molly and Jim slowly made their way up the front steps and into the house. As he closed the front door behind him, Jim glanced at the empty boat trailer one more time.

CHAPTER EIGHT — ENLIGHTENMENT

At the Arman Matrix, Mitel's largest military base commonly referred to as *the hub*, Director Zan Liss sat alone in the officer's section of the hub's expansive cafeteria. It was mid-morning, and Zan's stomach was growling. The cafeteria was located only a few minutes from his temporary office and contained a wide range of foods and beverages twenty-four hours a day.

Approximately one month earlier, Zan was promoted to Mitel Director with full military honors. One of only twelve directors, Zan reported to the Mitel Emperor who in turn reported to the Mitel Leadership. Despite the promotion, Zan was miserable.

This is going to be the most boring assignment of my career, he thought, sipping his energy drink. *This position will be nothing more than mindless, bureaucratic data shuffling.*

"Congratulations!" said Commander Ard Lindar, as he approached Zan, abruptly interrupting Zan's train of thought. Ard had not seen Zan since he was the Navigator on Zan's cruiser during the second Thraen invasion. He was now an accomplished cruiser commander in his own right. Ard's trademark wit and offbeat humor had not changed, and neither had his well-hidden distrust of the

Mitel Leadership. While Ard had continued to follow Zan's career with keen interest, he was unsure whether Zan cared enough to follow his. But given their common and tragic childhood — Zan's parents and Ard's father having all been murdered under suspicious circumstances — Ard felt compelled to stay in touch with Zan.

"Thank you, Commander," replied Zan glumly.

"Do you mind if I join you?" asked Ard.

"Of course not, please sit down," replied Zan halfheartedly.

"You must be excited about the promotion," Ard continued, as he sat down across from Zan. "It's a great honor and well-deserved."

"If you say so," replied Zan as he took another sip of his drink.

"What do you mean?" asked Ard incredulously.

"The position is nothing more than a glorified data specialist," scoffed Zan. "You have the *real* job, Commander. *You* control a Mitel cruiser and crew. Now *that* is something to get excited about."

"True," laughed Ard, "But you are now so close to the powers that be."

"So?" grunted Zan.

"Well," said Ard quietly as he scanned the room. "You have access to information that is available to only a precious few."

"And?"

"Don't you want to know what's *really* going on at the top?"

"At the top?"

"Yes."

"You should know much better than I. Your *father* is a member of the Mitel Leadership."

"My stepfather," corrected Ard. "That's a *big* difference."

The two sat in silence for a few minutes while Zan continued to sip his energy drink.

"Well," said Ard eventually. "I should get going — "

"Wait. What are you *really* trying to tell me?"

Ard again looked around before speaking.

"I have great respect for you," he responded. "And I know you don't think I'm much of a leader — "

"I never *said* that," interrupted Zan defensively.

"You didn't have to. But I never took it personally. I mean, you got where you are because of *you and you alone.*"

"But — "

"But nothing," interrupted Ard quickly. "But that's not why I came over here. Listen, I admit that growing up with a stepfather who is a Mitel Leadership member had its advantages. It provided me unique insight into some of the things that are going on. But it didn't give me open access to what is *really* going on at the top."

"I would have thought otherwise."

"The Leadership is incredibly secretive. But if you stop to look around — I mean *really* look — you will notice things . . . patterns."

"Like what?"

"The systematic brutality committed by the Mitel Leadership *against our own people* for one."

Zan studied Ard closely before responding.

"I grew up on a military base. That was my entire existence. Until this promotion, I have not lived among the civilian population since I was a child. The ongoing conflict with the resistance is the only thing I know of —"

"I'm not talking about the Mitel resistance, although I have a hunch that movement may have impacted both of us more than we know."

"What do you mean?"

"For many years I have been trying to find out about the circumstances surrounding my father's death."

"*And . . . ?*"

"The more I dig into it, the more questions I uncover."

"I thought your father was killed in battle."

"I thought so too, initially. But as I dug further, I discovered that my father was connected *to your parents*."

"Are you saying that my parents killed your father?"

"*No*, that is not what I am saying *at all*," replied Ard nervously as he glanced around again.

"Then what?"

"My father was trying to *help* your parents before he died."

"*Help them*? Help them how?"

"I don't know. I don't have the necessary clearance to find out for sure, but I have my suspicions."

"Which are?"

"I think that they all may have had ties to the Mitel resistance," whispered Ard.

"The Mitel *resistance*?" exclaimed Zan.

Ard cringed as he glanced around the cafeteria one more time.

"I have to go now," announced Ard, not wanting to share anything further.

"But —"

"Again, congratulations on your promotion!" said Ard loudly as he stood up. Zan watched Ard as he walked away.

Zan replayed the conversation with Ard in his mind over the next few days.

Does he know more than he is telling me? Zan thought, staring at his office computer. He was working later than usual. He took a deep breath and reached for the keyboard.

There is only one way to find out he decided.

Zan entered his ID and password accessing the strictly confidential Mitel database. He quickly scrolled down until he saw the heading he was looking for, MITEL RESISTANCE. From there, Zan was asked to enter a second password. He quickly unlocked his desk drawer and searched impatiently for his password device.

Zan grabbed a small black device and held it tightly until it recognized his fingerprint pattern. It flashed repeatedly before the directory opened. Zan stared at the blinking cursor for a time trying to muster the courage to continue. Zan eventually typed in Ard's father's name. He was stunned by what he saw.

Magnus Lindar
Date of Death: 2.35.2958   Age of Death: 31
Surviving Family: Evie Lindar, Age 28; Ard Lindar,
Age 3.
Method of Death: Assassination by electro laser
Credit: Mitel Embedded Special Forces
Reason: Resistance Fighter, Level IV
Location of Death: Alek Provence

Zan scrolled down the file reading about Magnus. Near the bottom, a flurry of entries detailed his ever-increasing involvement with the Mitel resistance.

He was a decorated Mitel soldier, thought Zan disbelievingly. *How is this possible?*

Zan looked up toward the ceiling, closed his eyes for a moment and let out a deep sigh. He knew what he had to do. His heart pounded as he typed his father's name. His eyes filled with tears as he stared at the results.

Dag Liss
Date of Death: 3.4.2958   Age of Death: 29
Surviving Family: Zan Liss, Age 6.
Method of Death: Assassination by electro laser
Credit: Mitel Embedded Special Forces
Reason: Resistance Fighter, Level V
(Commander)
Location of Death: Alek Provence

He stared at his father's picture for a long time. It was like looking in the mirror. He then typed in the name of his mother. The results were essentially the same.

Arina Liss
Date of Death: 3.4.2958   Age of Death: 27
Surviving Family: Zan Liss, Age 6.
Method of Death: Assassination by electro laser
Credit: Mitel Embedded Special Forces
Reason: Resistance Fighter, Level V
(Commander)
Location of Death: Alek Provence

Zan reached out and touched his mother's picture on the screen.

Deep down, he had always wondered why his parents had been killed. But he did not have the courage to face the truth — not until now — and not until he had worked his way up the Mitel hierarchy. He pounded his fists on the desk in anger. The sheer force of the blow caused the front legs to splinter. He began to sob, his enormous shoulders heaving and shuddering violently.

Zan eventually pulled himself together and scrolled through the database to read more about his parents. They had met at age 14 and soon thereafter became Mitel resistance fighters. He scanned the pages upon pages of accompanying entries. It was obvious to Zan that his parents had dedicated their lives to the resistance. He then typed in 'Lon Rexx' to see what would pop up. The following information appeared:

Zan Rexx
Date of Death: 2.11.2957   Age of Death: 29
Surviving Family: Lon Rexx, Age 4; Jun Rexx, Age 4.
Method of Death: Assassination by electro laser
Credit: Mitel Embedded Special Forces
Reason: Resistance Fighter, Level V
Location of Death: Mitar Provence

"So, the rumors *are* true," Zan mused. "I guess everyone handles tragedy differently. In Lon's case, he became an angry maniac. Strange — Lon's father and I have the same first name — and he has a *twin brother*? Lon never mentioned either of those things."

Zan eventually signed off from his computer, but not before copying the contents of the four files onto an encrypted data capsule which he carefully attached to a metal necklace around his neck. He then moved to his office couch and went to sleep.

Over the next several days, Zan resisted the urge to reach out to Ard.

"Is this a test?" he asked himself. "Is the Mitel Leadership trying to gauge how I react? Could Ard be in on this? After all, his stepfather is one of them."

Zan eventually decided that Ard was not part of some elaborate plot, but rather just wanted to know what happened to his father. Ard also appeared to be trying to warn him to the escalating violence being carried out against Mitel civilians *by their own leaders*. In Zan's view, sharing opinions like that could easily have gotten Ard killed. He also realized that Ard appeared to be on to something. The dates of death — only a few weeks apart and in the same general location — were more than just a coincidence. While the files did not expressly confirm or deny it, Zan concluded that Ard's father must have been working closely with his parents before they were all killed.

No, murdered, he thought.

A week later, Zan was summoned to the Mitel Leadership Complex to appear before Emperor Oberon Leander. The Complex consisted of a cluster of heavily fortified buildings surrounded by a twenty foot high reinforced stone walls twelve feet thick. The Complex was guarded around the clock by the elite Mitel Special Forces. Zan had been warned not to make any sudden or unusual moves since snipers kept a close watch on visitors. After passing the initial checkpoint, Zan was escorted to a second security area for a full body scan.

After being cleared, he walked slowly across the complex grounds to the large administration building. Zan was a bit nervous as he approached the Emperor's chambers. After all, he had never met a sitting Emperor before. Upon entering he saw the back of Emperor Leander's head above his black chair located behind a large clear polymer table. The Emperor was staring out a window overlooking the stone and glass Leadership building. As Zan slowly approached the table, Emperor Leander cleared his throat.

"Director Liss, please — sit down."

Zan quickly did as he was told.

"The Mitel Leadership has heard a great deal about you. They believe that you are destined to do great things on their behalf. That is the primary reason why I summoned you here."

"Emperor Leander, I —"

"I am going to send you on a mission, one of great importance to the Mitel Leadership."

"Sir?" asked Zan cautiously.

"I want you to take a Mitel cruiser and accompany a transport vessel to planet Thrae. In my opinion, 300 Mitel strike fighters should be enough to do the job."

"What mission are you speaking of my Emperor?"

The Emperor spun his chair around to study Zan. Leander appeared tall and muscular. Like Zan, he was bald. His deep facial wrinkles seemed out of place for a man his young age. It appeared to Zan that the pressures of his position were taking a huge toll on his physical appearance. Emperor Leander locked eyes with Zan.

"I want you to destroy the Thraen resistance once and for all!"

"*The Thraen resistance?*" questioned Zan incredulously.

"Yes."

"But I thought we destroyed their planet years ago. I was there and —"

"On the contrary, the planet and its resistance forces are alive and well. So well in fact, that they are disrupting our military supply routes in the region. The Mitel Leadership wants them crushed *once and for all*."

"Yes, my Emperor," replied Zan.

"You will be given official orders and mission tactics. Prepare to embark by this time tomorrow."

"As you request, Emperor Leander."

"The Mitel Leadership wants you to use every weapon at your disposal, including the cruiser's formidable high energy cluster pods."

"Those pods can wipe out an entire population center," replied Zan quietly.

Emperor Leander smiled and nodded before responding.

"That is correct. Thank you and good luck."

With that, Emperor Leander spun his chair around to face the window.

Zan stood up and made his way toward the chamber entrance.

"Director Liss," said Emperor Leander causing Zan to spin around to see the top of Leander's head as he stared out the window.

"Sir?"

"The Mitel Leadership is counting on you."

"I will not disappoint —"

"Zan, it's important that the Mitel people not become aware of the Thraen resistance movement."

"Sir, I —"

"And the Leadership does not want the Mitel Resistance to find out that we are having difficulties thwarting the Thraen rebellion. They don't want to give the Mitel resistance — or our people — any more hope than they already have."

"Understood —"

"That is all."

"Yes Sir," replied Zan as he turned and quickly exited the Emperor's chambers.

Early the next morning Zan packed his gear into a large duffle bag and headed to the Arman Matrix in a small military hovercraft that was waiting patiently outside his quarters. On his way to the base, he contemplated his assignment.

This mission will face several hurdles and is prone to failure he thought. *The Thraen resistance will be tenacious and dangerous.*

Upon entering the Hub, Zan reported to the space transport facility. After a bumpy ride into space aboard a well-worn shuttle pod, the craft docked with the 1,550 foot long silver and white wedge shaped cruiser. The sleek and slightly bulbous craft had two sets of small triangular wings up front that transitioned into two very long narrow wings in the stern. Two vertical tails were located along the rear of the craft. After crossing through the airlock, Zan handed off his duffle bag to a young specialist and headed for the ICC. A smiling Ard Lindar greeted him.

"Good morning, Director," said Ard. "I did not expect to see you again so soon!"

"That makes two of us Commander," smiled Zan. "We have a lot to do before we depart."

"Agreed."

"So let's get started."

They split the pre-departure inspection checklist and over the next few hours scoured the vessel checking the operational readiness of major systems, propulsion and weaponry. They reunited one hour before departure to compare notes.

"Everything is operational and ready for launch from my perspective," confirmed Ard.

"Other than wear and tear due to the age of this cruiser, I agree," replied Zan.

"What do you expect," smiled Ard. "This is the Mitel military after all."

Zan smiled as he nodded in agreement.

The two-week voyage to Planet Thrae was completed without incident. During the trip, Zan and Ard reviewed and discussed the seemingly never-ending stream of intelligence reports about their battle plan. Zan resisted the urge to tell Ard what he had discovered about their parents. And while he continued to have strong reservations about the mission in general, Zan knew that he had little choice but to move forward. After all, the Mitel Leadership had little use for anyone who did not follow orders.

When he was alone, Zan researched highly classified data on the Thraen invasion eight years prior. His primary focus: the escape of the small Thraen pod into deep space. One computer database seized soon after the invasion had identified a planet known as 5.1.18.20.9 to be the small pod's destination. Unfortunately for the Mitel Leadership, it was located a staggering 600 light years away out along the galaxy's spiral arm.

They would need to travel across the universe at unprecedented speeds to reach that planet thought Zan. *I have a hunch the little pod did just that.*

He had replayed the series of events leading up to the pod's extraordinary acceleration in his mind many times. Zan was fascinated by the mysterious technology needed to achieve such speeds. His intuition told him that the little pod was part of a covert Thraen development program.

We would have heard about it otherwise, he thought.

After pouring over the confidential data files and images on the trip over, Zan was now convinced that the pod must have come from the old Thraen defense fortress attached to the Global Defense Center located outside of what used to be the Tryden population center.

At least that is where I would have hidden it, he thought.

While the Defense Center appeared badly damaged based on the surveillance images, the old fortress looked to still be intact.

My first order of business here is to search that facility, Zan concluded. *If I can locate that technology, I may be able to use it as leverage with the Mitel Leadership in the event this mission goes badly.*

Zan noticed his intercom light blinking.

"Director Liss speaking," he answered.

"This is Ard," the intercom replied. "We are approaching Thrae."

"On my way."

Zan exited the HorVert Elevator at the rear of the ICC, and was immediately taken aback by the sheer beauty of the planet on the primary screen monitor. From outer space, it appeared to have healed itself quite nicely from the effects of the worldwide disaster eight years earlier. However, Zan knew full well that the planet's surface itself would tell an entirely different story.

"Commander Lindar!" barked Zan.

"Sir?"

"Prepare a landing pod to be shadowed by four to six strike fighters. I want you and a security detail to accompany me to the surface to check out the old Thraen fortress."

"But Director Liss," replied Ard somewhat confused. "Our intelligence shows that facility is abandoned."

"Call it a hunch."

Zan stared out the window as the pod approached the planet's surface. The destruction was beyond description. While trees and foliage had returned, they did not conceal the pervasive devastation that stretched out as far as the eye could see.

The pod slowly landed adjacent to the old fort, while Mitel Fighters raced by overhead. Zan and Ard exited accompanied by eight heavily armed soldiers. The group surveyed the perimeter before cautiously approaching the entrance of the headquarters building. It was dark and desolate, and there was dust and debris everywhere. The high intensity lights on the soldiers' helmets activated automatically as they entered. They slowly made their way to the development and test facility in the old fortress. Zan pointed toward the enormous dusty microscope-like device hanging from the ceiling in the middle of the room.

Strange he thought.

Suddenly, a dull metallic flash caught his eye from across the room.

"Focus your light on the far wall," Zan instructed.

He quickly made his way across the room and carefully stepped into one of the five bays along the wall. Even though it was covered in dust, Zan knew immediately that he had found what he was looking for. He wiped the dust off the fuselage, exposing the raised GDC USEP emblem.

He quickly moved on to the next bay, smiling broadly seeing a second pod. Both appeared to be fully intact.

"These are nothing more than unmanned monitoring pods" said Ard, somewhat bored.

Zan did not answer as he continued to inspect the pods.

"With all due respect, this can't be why you wanted to come down to the surface," continued Ard. "Is it?"

Zan looked directly at Ard before responding.

"Order a transport pod and several technicians to come here immediately. I want to bring these two pods back to the ship."

"But —"

"Now!" barked Zan.

"Yes, Sir," replied Ard as he fumbled to turn on his helmet communicator.

It took several hours for the laser technicians to cut a large enough opening in the thick fortress ceiling. One by one, the pods were carefully hoisted through the opening by a hovering transport pod. From inside the facility, the group watched as each pod disappeared into the belly of the transport vessel before it turned and slowly headed skyward.

"OK let's make our way back to the landing pod —"

Suddenly, a flash of ball lightning laser fire appeared from multiple directions. Within seconds, the laser technicians and all eight soldiers were dead. Before Zan and Ard could react, they were hit with powerful stun blasts.

When Zan awoke, he was blinded by several helmet lights shining directly on him.

"Get up, Mitel garbage!" demanded a deep voice.

Zan struggled to his feet. He felt groggy and unstable from the stun blast. As Zan tried to focus his vision, he noticed Ard standing next to him. By the look of Ard's bloodied face, Zan knew that he had been beaten.

"Are you OK?" asked Zan quietly.

Ard slowly shook his head yes.

"Before I decide to vaporize you," barked the deep voice, "tell me why you're here!"

"Why didn't you vaporize us already?" asked Zan calmly.

"Because you are Commanding Officers," replied the voice. "But you will be joining your comrades very soon!"

"I already told you — *I* am the Commander!" said Ard. "He is just my *very large* assistant."

Zan shot a strange look at Ard.

"Shut up!" yelled the voice as he hit Ard forcefully in the shoulder with the butt of his laser gun causing him to fall to the ground in agonizing pain.

"Wait!" shouted Zan. "He is only trying to protect me! *I* am the Commanding Officer."

"We searched both of you while you were unconscious," replied the voice in a much calmer tone. "Your second in command awoke first and was a bit uncooperative. We put him in his place."

Zan struggled to control his emotions as he stared into the bright lights.

"We know you are much more than just a Commander," continued the voice. "Again — why are you here?"

Zan thought for a moment before responding. He looked down at Ard who was still struggling to shake off the pain.

"We were sent here to destroy your remaining resistance forces," replied Zan calmly.

"With a cruiser and 300 strike fighters?" scoffed the voice. "It is going to take a lot more than that, I assure you."

"I would not be surprised."

"Yet you still came?"

"If you knew my superiors, you would realize I had no choice in the matter."

"Knowing how the Mitel Leadership operates, that is *certainly* not surprising."

Zan thought for a moment before responding.

"My parents were resistance fighters on Mitel. So was his father," explained Zan, "which is something I learned quite recently."

Ard looked up at Zan in disbelief.

"Why are you telling us this?" demanded the voice.

"Because the same struggle you face here is going on back on Mitel."

"So then why are you not *with them*?"

"That's a good question," replied Zan quietly. "I was six when my parents were murdered in front of me by Mitel Special Forces. He was only four when his father was killed by the same unit."

Zan's eyes lit up as he remembered the data capsule on the chain around his neck. He reached for it, but it was gone.

"I had a data capsule around my neck," said Zan. "It contains highly classified information which will prove that I am telling you the truth."

"We have analyzed its contents," replied the voice. "That is probably the one reason why you are still alive."

"Then you know it's true."

"Yes, but *again*, here you are anyway — on behalf of the Mitel military — to kill us all."

Zan paused for a moment.

"Well, maybe I can do something about that."

"What do you mean?" asked the voice cautiously.

"Mitel intelligence has provided us with the exact coordinates of your major bases of operations," Zan began. "I have been ordered to use whatever means necessary, including our cruiser's high energy cluster pods, to eliminate those positions. If you let us live, I will give your resistance forces time to withdraw from those locations before we strike."

"Where does your intelligence say the targets are?" asked the voice.

Zan looked down at Ard before answering.

"There are six primary targets — Retba, Kotor, Amer, Salar, Taha and Bagan."

"Your intelligence is quite good," the voice replied. "But even if we were foolish enough to agree, how do we know we can trust you?"

"If you kill us, our forces will attack anyway. The Mitel Leadership will simply send more cruisers and strike fighters until they finish the job."

"You're not answering my question!" demanded the voice.

"If I return to Mitel unsuccessful in my mission, I will be killed. You might as well do it now if you don't trust me."

"But if we do as you propose, how does that help *our* cause?" asked the voice firmly.

"I report directly to the Mitel Emperor," Zan began. "Upon my return, I will inform him that my mission was successful. The Emperor will relay the information to the Mitel Leadership. They in return, will leave your planet alone for the foreseeable future. That should give your resistance forces time to regroup and become even stronger."

"Don't move," said the voice as he walked away.

"I would not take too long if I were you," cautioned Zan.

"And why is that?" asked a second voice.

"The soldiers you killed have an imbedded tracking device," explained Zan. "If our cruiser cannot contact them, they will come looking for us."

Upon hearing the news, the second resistance fighter quickly walked away in the direction of the first. A few minutes later, they returned.

"I have been authorized to tell you," the first voice began, "that Salar and Kotor will be completely abandoned 48 hours from now. After that time, you will be able to attack each facility."

"And the others?" asked Zan.

"They are to be left alone."

"I cannot do that," replied Zan shaking his head.

"You are in no position to negotiate!" replied the first voice tersely.

"Actually I am," replied Zan. "For the reasons I've already given."

"Then you will need to be *off target* with your weapons," explained the second voice.

Zan considered his options.

"I will probably have some explaining to do, but I'm willing to take that risk."

"Very well then," said the first voice. "Take off your jacket and shirt."

"What?" asked Zan.

"Do as I say!" snapped the first voice.

Zan quickly took off his jacket and shirt revealing his heavily muscled torso.

"Do you think it will even fit?" asked a third voice.

"It is going to be tight," replied a forth voice.

Two resistance fighters stepped forward from the darkness and placed a silver metallic device around Zan's torso. The device consisted of six metal mesh belts connected symmetrically around a circular silver canister about two inches thick and six inches in diameter. There was a large red dot at the center of the canister's face. The resistance fighters placed the canister against Zan's chest and quickly pulled the six belts two at a time around his shoulders, under his arms and mid torso. The belts were then connected snugly, one by one, to a metal hexagonal buckle against his back. Zan grimaced as the harness was clipped into place. The resistance fighters then stepped back into the darkness.

"You can put your cloths back on," instructed the first voice.

"What is that thing for?" asked Ard.

"It is a small, but incredibly powerful bomb," replied Zan as he put his shirt back on.

"You are correct," replied the first voice. "When you complete your mission as agreed, it will be deactivated and released. Consider it our *binding contract* if you will."

"How will I know when it's deactivated?" asked Zan.

"The red dot will blink," said the third voice.

"Regardless," interrupted the first voice impatiently. "The device will simply unbuckle on its own. If it detonates, you will never know — I guarantee you."

Zan nodded silently in agreement.

Suddenly, the bright lights of the resistance fighters faded as one by one, they withdrew from the large room.

"Oh, by the way," said the first voice from off in the distance. "The harness is made entirely of graphene. You will blow several holes in your own body before you are able to cut it off."

Seconds later they were gone. Zan and Ard stood in near complete darkness, with only a faint light shining down through the hole in the roof of the old fortress. Zan slowly bent down and helped Ard to his feet.

"Can you walk?"

"Yes," Ard grimaced.

The two slowly made their way out of the complex and toward the landing pod.

"Can you fly this thing?" asked Ard.

"I can fly just about anything," smiled Zan. "It comes with being a military base rat."

They climbed in and sat in silence as the craft took off.

"How will you explain how we lost the men?" asked Ard eventually.

"The *truth* — that we were ambushed by Thraen resistance fighters," replied Zan.

They sat in silence for a time until the pod approached the upper atmosphere.

"When were you going to tell me about my father?" asked Ard eventually.

"I don't know. Look Ard, when I found out, I wasn't entirely sure I could trust you. I mean after all, your father is a member of the Mitel Leadership."

"*I told you* — he is my *stepfather* — big difference."

Ard paused momentarily.

"And the Thraen resistance fighters . . . why did you tell them instead?"

"It got us freed, didn't it?" replied Zan matter-of-factly.

Zan steered the pod into outer space toward the cruiser.

"What are you going to do?" asked Ard quietly.

"About the mission?" Given the fact that I am wearing this exploding graphene girdle, I think my options are somewhat limited."

"No, not that . . ."

"You mean about the two small pods I found?"

"No, but what was that all about?

"Consider it a small insurance policy for when we get back."

"What do you mean?"

"It's a long story. Would you place one of them in a strike fighter storage container and hide it in the cruiser's shipping area for me?" asked Zan.

"Yes of course," replied Ard quickly, his eyebrows furrowed. "But —"

"And have it offloaded secretly when we get back."

"Yes again, but I still don't understand."

"As I said, it is a long story," smiled Zan. "Don't worry though — I'll explain everything to you at the right time."

"*Ok,* but what are you going to do?"

"About telling the Mitel Leadership?"

"No."

"OK then," Zan sighed. "What am I going to do *what* about *what*?

"About our parents, and the Mitel resistance, and what *we* should do going forward."

"Oh that," replied Zan quietly. "I haven't figured that out yet."

Ard sighed in frustration.

Zan and Ard delayed launching the attack for 48 hours. Using his Commander's access code, Ard overwrote the computer's predetermined target coordinates into the weapons database just far enough off the mark as to spare the four other resistance bases from destruction. Zan also met with the Mitel Fighter commanders and explained that updated intelligence showed that the two remaining targets contained the majority of the resistance resources.

When the agreed upon delay had passed, Zan gave the command to commence the attack. The Mitel strike fighters attacked the two resistance targets in waves leveling them to the ground. To the surprise of the grouping Commanders, no strike fighters were lost during the attack. They congratulated each other on a successful surprise attack.

At the same time, the cruiser launched a series of cluster pods each containing several powerful guided missiles. Once the pods successfully penetrated through the planet's outer atmosphere, the pods automatically released their missile cluster. The missiles quickly activated and separated before streaking toward the four pre-programmed targets. Ard personally took control of the weapons console to monitor the progress. After the last missile cluster detonated on impact, Ard confirmed that each target had been destroyed. Six hours later, the cruiser and transport vessels began their voyage back to Mitel.

As he stood shirtless in his sleeping quarters, the red light on the front of his harness started blinking. Zan waited helplessly for something to happen.

If this thing detonates, the entire cruiser will be destroyed! And there is nothing I can do to stop it!

Seconds later, the harness automatically unclipped and fell harmlessly to the floor. Zan slumped down into his chair. He stared blankly at the harness as he scratched the irritated skin on his chest and shoulders where the device had been.

Well, they kept their end of the bargain. The next thing I must do is get rid of the evidence.

Zan put on his shirt, quickly placed the harness into a small duffle bag and made his way down a series of hallways toward a small garbage receptacle located at the rear of the cruiser. He smiled and waved to the crewmen as he passed.

When Zan reached the garbage receptacle, he looked up and down the hallway before stuffing the entire duffle bag into the receptacle chute. When it closed, Zan immediately pushed the activation button ejecting the bag into outer space. He let out a big sigh of relief as he made his way back to his quarters.

Upon his return to Mitel, Zan was immediately called before the Emperor. He entered the chamber to find Emperor Leander once again sitting in his chair staring out the large picture window toward the Mitel Leadership Building.

"Welcome back Director Liss," said Emperor Leander without turning around.

"Thank you, my Emperor," replied Zan.

"The Mitel Leadership is eager to speak with you."

"They are?" asked Zan cautiously.

"Yes. They want to discuss several details concerning your handling of the Thraen mission."

"I would be happy —"

"They want to know why you did not follow the explicit orders."

Zan's heart began to pound as his mind raced to come up with a response.

"I certainly —"

"It is not me you need to answer to. They are waiting for you in the Forum Hall across the way. I would not keep them waiting if I were you."

"Of course, my Emperor," replied Zan somberly.

He walked briskly out the main doors, across the complex grounds toward the imposing stone and glass Leadership Building. Several security guards surrounded him as he entered.

"Director Liss?" asked one of the guards.

"Yes," replied Zan hesitantly.

"The Mitel Leadership is expecting you," replied a second guard.

A third guard pointed a hand held scanner at Zan, before motioning him to confirm his identity on the retinal scanner. A light on the left side of the device quickly flashed green.

"Follow me, please," said the first guard.

As Zan followed him up the wide marble staircase, two more guards followed closely behind him, their footsteps echoing loudly. Upon reaching the second floor, the first guard motioned Zan toward a set of enormous stone doors, which opened to reveal the Mitel Leadership Forum Hall. Across the large room, eleven men sat behind a large curved stone bench five feet above the forum floor. Standing in front of the bench were three enormous security guards.

I wonder which one is Ard's stepfather Zan thought as he entered.

Ard had described him as somewhat older, with a slight build and thinning gray hair. All eleven men fit that description. As Zan approached the bench, one of the guards motioned for him to stop. Two of the guards that had accompanied him up the stairs took positions on either side of him. As he stood motionless, Zan sensed the third guard standing behind him.

"Director Liss, we have been eagerly awaiting your arrival," said the Leadership member directly across from him.

"I am honored to be here," Liss replied.

"We have reviewed the intelligence reports from your recent mission *in detail*," said a second member. "We have also reviewed your written report."

"We have many questions," said a third member.

"I am happy to answer —"

"We are trying to determine whether you intentionally deviated from our mission orders," interrupted a fourth member. "If you did, then this meeting will not end well for you!"

Zan glanced nervously around the forum hall.

I cannot overpower these guards. And even if I did, I would not get very far. I must remain calm.

"Please explain!" demanded the first member.

"I will do my best," Zan began hesitantly. "Once we reached Thrae's outer orbit, I ordered a detailed series of surface scans to confirm the data contained in my mission plan. The results of those scans did not agree with the intelligence data."

"And why do you say that?" asked the second member.

"The scans showed concentrated heat signatures and energy levels which, in my opinion, confirmed that the resistance had centralized and consolidated its positions into four primary locations — Retba, Amer, Taha and Bagan."

"We read that in your report," asked the fifth member. "What happened to those scans?"

"I don't know."

There was a brief but deafening silence.

"Without those scans you understand, it is impossible for us to reach the same conclusion Director Liss."

"Yes."

"It also makes it impossible for us to give *any* credibility to what you tell us, Director," said the third member. "Do you understand?"

"Yes I do. But you put me in charge of the mission, and —"

"We gave you express written orders to carry out a mission of great importance to this Leadership!" barked a sixth member, his voice echoing.

"Understood," Zan replied quietly.

The Leadership members looked at each other quickly, some shaking their heads in dissatisfaction.

"Continue, Director Liss," instructed the first member.

Zan cleared his throat before speaking.

"I gave the order to target each of the four locations with a rotating series of cluster pods," explained Zan. "Subsequent scans of the blast perimeters for each target showed no sign of life."

"But again, there is no data to confirm the location of the blast coordinates," said the third member impatiently.

"Understood. I don't know why those coordinates were not logged. What I *can* tell you is that I personally confirmed the predetermined locations prior to the attack, with the aid of Commander Ard Lindar."

Out of the corner of his eye, Zan noticed a member on the far left quickly shift his position.

That must be the stepfather he thought.

"We sent you to Thrae with 300 Mitel strike fighters," said the sixth member. "Yet you used them sparingly. Why?"

"On the voyage, I came to learn that we had already lost over 500 fighters to the resistance," replied Zan. "In *my* opinion, those losses represented a significant drain on our precious resources —"

"We do not disagree," interrupted a seventh member.

"Given that fact and based on the surface scan results, I made the decision to send several fighters to destroy the two remaining resistance positions. Those positions were reduced to rubble without the loss of even *one* of our fighters."

"*And once again,* no data exists to support your assessment!" replied the fifth member tersely.

"That is not *true,*" replied Zan forcefully. "My report included several images taken after the fighters had completed their bombardment. The precise locations of those images were also included and matched the predetermined locations contained in my mission plan."

The members of the Mitel Leadership again looked around at each other. From where he stood, Zan sensed that he had not convinced some of the members.

"You are a very smart man," said the first member eventually. "You were promoted based on your unique background and impeccable record."

"Well I —"

"And now, with your top-level security clearance," interrupted the second member, "we presume you have searched the restricted database and confirmed that your deceased parents were Mitel Resistance Commanders."

"I have . . ."

"Your parents helped plan and carry out the assassination of countless military personnel," said the fifth member bitterly. "They were also responsible for the destruction of significant military resources."

Zan did not respond.

"Our question to you then," said the third member bluntly. "Given your parents — and *now* your mission abnormalities — how can we ever trust you going forward?"

Zan stood silently for several seconds.

"Because you can," he replied eventually.

"And why is that?" asked the fourth member impatiently.

"With all due respect, I was *six years old* when my parents were killed," replied Zan firmly. "I was raised, educated and trained on one of Mitel's largest and best military bases."

Zan then paused briefly.

"I serve the Mitel Leadership now," he added.

"Those are merely words," scoffed the fourth member. "And this Council is *not* impressed by words. We make our decisions based on *actions*."

The Mitel Leadership members suddenly began to bicker. While Zan could not follow the conversation, their tone and demeanor became increasingly hostile. He knew that he had to change the direction of the conversation, and do it quickly.

"I would like to bring something of great importance to the Leadership's attention," said Zan loudly.

The members immediately stopped arguing and stared at Zan. The first member then nodded.

"Go ahead Director Liss . . ." he motioned.

"Before the assault on Thrae, I personally went down to the planet's surface."

"For what reason?" asked the second member suspiciously.

"On the voyage to the Thraen planet, I spent a great deal of time reviewing data and images from the invasion eight years ago," explained Zan. "If you recall back then, it was my cruiser that identified and almost captured the escaping Thraen infant —"

"*The immortal hybrid!*" blurted the third member. "He escaped in a small pod at speeds far beyond any known technology!"

"To a planet we believe to be some 600 light years away, *far beyond our current reach!*" added the seventh member.

"That is all true," replied Zan. "But, based on my research, I was convinced that the small pod was an *experimental prototype*. Eventually, my instincts told me where I should look to find another one."

"*And?*" asked the first member curiously.

"I am happy to report that I in fact located a pod, completely intact, in the old stone fortress outside of Tryden. We lost a number of soldiers to the Thraen resistance securing its release, and I have brought it back for the Mitel Leadership."

The Leadership members erupted in excitement.

"We can reverse engineer it!" blurted the third member.

"And scale up the propulsion technology to retrofit our fleet," added the second member.

"We can send a task force across the universe to planet 5.1.18.20.9 and capture the immortal hybrid!" said the fourth member.

After the members settled down, the first member looked at Zan.

"This is very good news, Director Liss," he began. "Perhaps we were a bit hasty in our rush to judgment."

Zan nodded quietly.

"Unless I am overruled by my fellow council members," the first member continued, "I believe that it is only fitting that you be put in charge of the pod's reverse engineering program as quickly as possible."

"I would be honored to do so," replied Zan quickly.

"Excellent!" smiled the first member.

"And the Thraen resistance?"

"What about it?" scoffed the second member.

"Well, I for one —"

"I think it is fair to say," interrupted the first member, "that the propulsion development program will now be our planet's *primary focus*. What might remain of the Thraen resistance following your mission is of little consequence to us now, wouldn't you agree Director Liss?"

"Yes," replied Zan quickly.

"Then I think we are done for now," nodded the first member.

"Thank you," replied Zan.

He quickly turned, walked past the three guards and through the huge stone doors which closed behind him.

"What do you think?" asked the first member.

"He is friendly with my stepson, Ard Lindar," said the member far to the left. "Ard was the cruiser commander on his Thraen mission."

"And?" asked the third member.

"Ard's father was also a resistance fighter," replied Ard's stepfather.

"We have many military personnel who are orphans of resistance fighters," responded the second member dismissively.

"Agreed," nodded the first member, "but none have been high ranking officers. I think it is wise to keep a close watch on them going forward."

"Yes, agreed," nodded the members.

Over the next several months, Zan settled into his newest position — overseeing the enormous reverse engineering project associated with the captured USEP. With Ard's help, the second USEP was inconspicuously off loaded from the cruiser and transported to a small research and development facility tucked away in the black mountains in the north.

Zan carefully set in motion a small and secretive development program staffed by a handful of trusted, but now retired, mechanics who had acted as surrogate fathers to him when he was growing up at the Mitel base. Zan trusted each of them with his life. He knew they would do a much better job reverse engineering the small pod than any of the Mitel scientists and engineers assigned to his primary program. Given the enormous amount of attention directed at that program, he was confident that his own small program could be kept under wraps.

For the first time since he was a child, Zan found himself living among the general Mitel population. As the weeks and months passed, he noticed subtle acts of punishment being carried out by the Mitel Leadership against his own people. Men and women were forcibly removed from their living quarters and taken away. Other times, their lifeless bodies were carried out. On one such occasion, he came face to face with a little boy who reminded Zan of himself. The look of confusion and fear on the boy's face was heart wrenching.

While Zan grew increasingly upset, he remained torn between his own self-preservation and helping his people. Zan knew that he was being watched closely by the Mitel Leadership. If he did *anything* that could be interpreted as aiding the Mitel resistance or acting against the interests of the Mitel Leadership, he would end up killed, like his parents.

Zan knew he must ignore the killings and repression. He often sat alone at night in the darkness of his living quarters staring out the window at the stars. This night was no different.

"I have got to find a way to help my people," he muttered clenching his fists. "*I must!*"

CHAPTER NINE – ANOTHER CLUE

After the incident on Lake Edward, Jim was haunted by nagging questions about that day. How did he survive the storm on the lake? What was the silver metallic ball hovering above him just before he lost consciousness? Was it the same object that Chad observed in the woods behind their house?

These unexplained events reignited Jim's interest in the mysterious crash just outside of Coopers Falls. For months he read about every detail he could find about the crash. He found an interview between Major Talbot and the local media. He researched the U.S. Naval Space Surveillance System Command headquarters located in Dahlgren, Virginia.

Why were Major Talbot and the US Navy Space Surveillance there in the first place? And why was a "no fly zone" established? Jim wondered. *If the debris really was from Earth and contained hazardous materials like Major Talbot said, how could the material be dangerous to a curious pilot up in the sky? It doesn't make any sense.*

Everything about the crash appeared to be cloaked in secrecy. Try as he might, Jim couldn't track down any formal report on the incident. Other than the initial news reports, he couldn't find any additional documentation that the crash had even occurred.

Major Talbot did say that it might be impossible to identify the source of the wreckage, but I don't buy that argument concluded Jim.

Jim became obsessed with obtaining answers. He was convinced that there was much more to the story than the bits and pieces of information disclosed by the US Military through its spokesperson on the scene.

Jim decided to visit the crash site. He carefully inspected the open field and surrounding area several times for any signs of debris. Other than a few old bottles, cans and an old rusty wrench, he found nothing.

I'm wasting my time he thought.

By the end of the summer, Jim had the nagging urge to go to the old crash site one more time. He tried to ignore it, but eventually his unresolved curiosity got the better of him. When he arrived, he noticed that the field had been recently plowed to turn the soil. Jim made his way along the clumpy topsoil looking from side to side. When he reached the other end, he walked ten paces along the edge before heading back across the field. It took Jim fifteen passes to cover the entire field.

On his final crossing, something shiny caught his eye about ten feet beyond the plowed area. As he approached, he saw a metal object partially buried in the ground. Jim reached down and easily pulled it out of the soil.

Jim studied the metal object closely. It was triangular, about twenty inches long, twelve inches wide and a half inch thick. He brushed it clean, exposing various raised markings which appeared to be some form of hieroglyphics. They consisted of a series of complex combinations of horizontal, vertical and curved lines and shapes. The markings appeared to have a geometric influence, although no two were the same. The lines and shapes intersected and crisscrossed each other in random patterns.

Suddenly he realized the markings matched the ones on the silver medallion he received at hospital. As he studied the markings, Jim's heart raced.

What is this? Jim thought.

He placed the object in his backpack. As he headed back toward his car, Jim had the distinct feeling that he was being watched. It reminded him of the night Chad told him he saw the black and silver ball in the backyard.

Jim stopped and stood motionless as he looked off into the woods for a time.

Nothing there he thought.

Jim swung the backpack over his shoulder and walked briskly toward his car. As he did, he could not shake the feeling that he was being watched by someone or *something*. When he arrived home, Jim rushed upstairs and compared the metal object to the silver medallion.

Oh my god he thought, *the markings are almost identical.*

The next day, Jim drove down to Albany to meet with Frank Campbell, an old friend and former colleague who now owned and operated a material testing laboratory. Jim showed Frank the triangular object he found, hoping Frank could help figure out what it was. They reminisced about their college days while Frank examined the metal object. He was intrigued by the raised markings on the object's surface. Frank ran several tests on the object in the lab and told Jim he would call him as soon as the results came back. He offered to keep the object and run further testing but Jim declined. A few weeks later, Frank called Jim on his cell phone.

"Hey Jim, sorry for not getting back to you sooner, but it's been a little hectic around here lately," explained Frank.

"No problem, Frank. I really appreciate you taking the time to do this. What did you find out?"

"Well, I must say, I've been doing this for thirty years and have never come across anything like this."

"What do you mean Frank?"

"The metal piece you brought in — we really don't know what it is."

Jim was silent for a moment.

"I'm not sure what you are saying Frank," Jim said, his heart pounding.

"Well, the object *looks* like metal. But that is really an exterior coating of some kind. The inner material closely resembles *graphene*, which is one of the strongest materials known to man," explained Frank.

"OK then, it's probably graphene," shrugged Jim somewhat disappointed.

"It sure looks like it is Jim. But there is *one* problem. The technology for making something this size doesn't exist."

Jim did not answer.

"Where did you say you found this?" asked Frank.

"Uh, along the side of a country road," replied Jim as his mind raced to come up with an answer.

"OK, well I would be very interested in doing more testing on it for sure. I mean, the markings on the thing are unusual. It's almost like the thing is from another planet, you know?"

Jim laughed nervously.

"Yeah, that would be funny. *E.T. comes to Coopers Falls*," laughed Jim awkwardly.

"Yeah, right," Frank chuckled. "Well OK Jim, I'm sorry I don't have anything more concrete to tell you at this point. Let me know what else I can do."

"I certainly will Frank and *hey*, it was great seeing you."

"Same here Jim. Say hi to Molly for me."

"I will."

Jim put his cell phone on the table and rubbed his face as he considered what Frank had told him.

It all makes sense now he thought. *His hands, his heart, the blood stream abnormalities . . . he was left at the hospital the same night of the crash. My god, my son . . . where is he from?*

Jim sat back and took a long deep sigh.

Who should I tell? Who can I tell? Who would believe me? And what if I'm wrong? I must keep this to myself until I figure out what to do.

He retrieved the metal object and silver medallion from his bedroom closet, wrapped them in a cloth and carefully hid them in a basement storage container.

Over time, and as his teaching load increased, Jim had less and less time to figure out what to do next, although he did manage to spend several evenings online researching different forms of hieroglyphics. Despite his efforts, Jim could not find anything that remotely matched or explained the unusual raised markings displayed on the triangular metal object and silver medallion.

Because the silver metallic ball was not seen again, life slowly returned to normal. Jim and Molly received insurance money from the boat but decided not to buy another one right away. Instead, Jim used the money to construct a home telescope observatory on the back of the house so that he and Chad could look out into space.

It took some time to decide what to buy and the construction costs were greater than initially budgeted, but they purchased a fifteen-foot dome observatory which was placed on top of a dormer style addition to the rear roof. Jim also purchased a fourteen inch Newtonian telescope with a German Equatorial Mount. The observatory dome rotated a full three hundred and sixty degrees. After the installation was complete, Jim and Chad spent most Sunday and Wednesday evenings using the telescope.

Chad excelled at school. He was at the top of his class academically from grades 4 through 9. His teachers described him as a brilliant and compassionate student who possessed an insatiable appetite for information and a willingness to help everyone. At the age of sixteen, he was already six feet five inches tall with a muscular, lean build. It was easy to locate Chad in a crowd not only because of his height, but because of his light complexion and long black hair.

Unfortunately, Chad did have his detractors. As would be expected, his physical malformations were known throughout the school by teachers and students alike. With eight fingers and eight toes, Chad tried to ignore the occasional whispers of 'freak' as he walked by certain lockers in the school hallways and the gym's locker room.

Chad was an ongoing target of school bullies. He tried to always remember what his dad once told him: bullies focus on others so that they don't have to deal with their own problems or insecurities.

"It helps them feel better about themselves," Jim had said.

As time went on, Chad and Melissica grew to be best friends, the kind that could tell each other anything, knowing that they could trust each other to keep a secret. They walked to and from school together and ate lunch at the same table. They often did their homework together during and after school. Chad would help Melissica with her math and science homework and Melissica, who was fast developing into a talented writer and artist, helped Chad with his English assignments, papers and art projects. They also shared the common bond and understanding that comes from being teased regularly about something. The one thing Chad could never tell Melissica however, was how his stomach filled with butterflies whenever he was around her.

Every August, Melissica accompanied Jim, Chad and Molly on their annual summer camping trip. Chad faithfully watched Melissica's fall soccer games and spring lacrosse matches at Coopers Falls. Chad also dragged Melissica along to many of the volunteer programs he regularly signed up for. With Molly's help, Melissica planned a surprise birthday party for Chad's thirteenth birthday.

Two weeks later, Melissica came to Chad in tears. She had just been told that her father was being transferred again. This time, they were moving to Minnesota and they were leaving in one week. When the day quickly arrived, Chad sat glumly across the street on the curb as a misty summer drizzle hung over the town. The lousy weather only added to Chad's depressed mood.

He watched silently as the movers methodically loaded the Erickson's furniture and belongings into the moving van. Since Chad did not have any experience saying goodbye, he simply told Melissica that he would see her later. Melissica gave Chad a big hug and whispered, "I am going to miss you," before getting into the back seat of their car.

Chad's heart broke as he watched the moving van and Melissica's car drive off. She waved to Chad out the rear window as the car slowly followed the van down the street. The car then turned the corner and was gone. Chad fought back tears as he ran home. He did not stop running until he reached his bedroom, slamming the door shut behind him. The next day, he did not get out of bed until after lunch.

Two weeks later, Chad received a letter in the mail from Melissica. He excitedly tore open the envelope and read the letter. Melissica told Chad all about her new house and town. She also shared with Chad how much she missed him and how he always made her feel better when she doubted herself.

Since Melissica loved to write, the two of them began exchanging letters and pictures on an almost weekly basis. Melissica would end every letter with *remember how we used to . . .* followed by a vivid memory of their time together. Chad would smile broadly as he read her description even though his heart ached a little bit each time. They would also talk on their cell phones about whatever came to mind. Chad loved to hear Melissica's voice as she described the various people she met and new places she visited. Chad began to email and text Melissica almost daily and they would also frequently video chat. But since Melissica loved writing so much, letters remained an important way for the two of them to communicate.

In time, Melissica's dad was transferred to Dallas. Once again, Melissica was uprooted and moved to a new place. Melissica told Chad that he was the one constant in her life and she was so grateful for that.

Not long after arriving in Dallas, Melissica told Chad about how her parents argued a lot about money and her mom's resentment over the constant moving. After her dad took another job in Phoenix, she said that things were getting really bad between them. As money became tight, Melissica's parents imposed strict limitations on use of her cell phone.

Just after Chad's sixteenth birthday, Melissica's calls, texts and letters slowed down considerably, and eventually stopped. He knew she was having a hard time dealing with her parents and everything else that went along with their constant relocating. Despite not hearing from her, Chad kept on writing. He told her about his failed science experiments, one of which he thought was going to burn down the school.

Chad never told Melissica about all the awards he had received. It really did not occur to Chad to discuss them since he did not put much stock in awards as he was just doing things he loved to do. Chad also believed strongly that it was his responsibility to help others. While he could not put it into words, he felt responsible for the happiness and safety of everyone.

Busy with his many projects and volunteer work, Chad wrote to Melissica less often. He was also spending more time with his friends hiking, biking and going to Lake Edward to hang out in the tourist village and on the beach. As August rolled around, Chad realized that he had not written to Melissica almost the entire summer.

One evening while he sat at his bedroom desk, Chad wondered how Melissica was doing. He quickly reached under his bed and pulled out a large box containing all Melissica's letters she had sent him since she had moved away from Coopers Falls.

Chad sat on his bed rereading her letters and found a photo of Melissica that was taken when she was fourteen.

On the back it said "I miss you! Love, Melissica." Chad wondered if she was happy and if she had a boyfriend.

She is so beautiful he thought to himself. *I need to write her again before school starts and before she moves again!*

Chad carefully put the letters and pictures back into the box and placed it under his bed. He sat down at his desk and wrote her a quick letter just to say hi and that he was looking forward to the start of school in a few weeks. Chad mailed the letter the next day.

Just before the start of school, the letter came back marked "return-to-sender" with no forwarding address. That night, Chad tried to call Melissica but the number was no longer in service. Chad tossed his cell phone on his bed — distraught — feeling like a part of him had died.

How could she just disappear like that without telling me? Chad thought. *It is not like her to do that.*

Chad checked the mailbox every day hoping to find a letter from Melissica telling him where she was but a letter never arrived. Chad also noticed that Melissica stopped updating her face book page. He regularly checked his cell phone for a missed call, email, text or voicemail. Still nothing.

"I am really sorry you haven't heard from Melissica," Molly told him as she and Jim served leftovers for dinner. "I'm sure she's busy with school starting and all."

"Maybe she found herself a boyfriend," said Jim. "I mean, it's going to happen eventually Chad."

"*Really* Jim?" quipped Molly impatiently.

"I was only trying to —"

"*What?* Make Chad feel worse than he already does?"

Feeling embarrassed, Jim glanced over at Chad.

"Sorry, I did not mean to be so insensitive —"

"Can I please be excused from the table?" interrupted Chad quietly.

"But you haven't eaten much of your dinner, protested Molly softly.

"I'm not really hungry."

"It's OK Chad, you can go," said Jim glancing awkwardly toward Molly.

Chad went outside and sat on the back steps, staring at the clouds in the evening sky. Chad wondered if Melissica was doing the same thing.

CHAPTER TEN – THE CHALLENGE

Zan sat at his desk, letting out a long sigh. The Mitel Leadership had just summoned him to appear before them in two days. After five years of intense effort, the development team had successfully reverse engineered the small Thraen USEP. Under Zan's guidance, the slip ring technology was modified and scaled to fit every Mitel military space vessel — from the smallest pods to the formidable Mitel cruisers and enormous transport vessels.

Zan thought about the challenges he had overcome to bring the program to fruition. He smiled to himself as he considered how invaluable his own secret project had been to the success of the reverse engineering program. Because his team had consistently stayed one step ahead of the much larger project, Zan was able to advance the official Mitel program. Zan was recognized as a pioneer in the field of high speed space propulsion. He received many awards which he quietly and proudly passed on to his mechanics.

Zan also thought about the many setbacks he had overcome along the way. As the Mitel resistance grew, they relentlessly targeted and destroyed several prototype craft. Several key test pilots, scientists and technicians were targeted and killed. Zan himself narrowly escaped death during one attack, losing his left eye in the incident. Even though the mechanical replacement eye functioned better than the original, the mental scars lingered.

They are using our own terror campaign techniques against us Zan thought. *It is ironic on many levels.*

He had recently heard rumors of the sudden disappearance of Emperor Leander. Zan believed that Leander had fallen out of favor with the Mitel Leadership for his failure to crush the Mitel resistance.

I am not naive enough to believe that he is still alive Zan thought as he stared back down at the encrypted notice. *Could I be next?*

Zan decided to travel to his secret development facility in the mountains one more time before the meeting.

I might not get another chance he thought as he quickly packed a duffle bag before jumping into his hover vehicle. When Zan arrived, he was greeted on the elongated landing strip, carved into the mountain, with hugs and laughter by his hand-picked development team. They spent the evening discussing the status of their pride and joy — two prototypes of the second generation USEP. They were sleek, significantly larger and faster than the original USEP. As a final tribute, his team added the identical markings and emblems of the original Thraen pod. The only difference was that it was now labeled "USEP²".

"Nice touch," smiled Zan as he patted Dru Aldar, his lead mechanic, on the back. Dru, short and stocky, was bald with a gray goatee. He was the closest thing to a father Zan had ever known.

Soon thereafter, the two prototypes were carefully placed into unmarked storage containers for shipment. At dusk, a large transport vessel approached. The large humming craft circled the storage building before hovering in place as the first storage container was tethered. It was then carefully raised toward the belly of the craft. A few minutes later, the second container was also lifted into the transport vessel, accompanied by Dru and three assistants. Zan waived to the men as they disappeared from view. He watched silently as the transport vessel sped off toward a restricted storage facility on the Arman Matrix military base.

As Zan turned toward the facility to join the remainder of his team, an enormous explosion knocked him to the ground. Dazed, Zan sat up, feeling the intense heat against his skin.

"NOOOOO!" screamed Zan in pain as he tried to get up, but was unable due to the searing heat. Suddenly, Zan was grabbed from behind and pulled to a safe distance from the inferno.

Several heavily armed Mitel resistance fighters quickly encircled him. One of the fighters stepped forward.

"Get up!" demanded the lead fighter, a man much larger than Zan.

Zan struggled to his feet, wiping blood from his face. Zan felt the fury within him rising until he could no longer hold back his anger.

"The people you just killed were my friends! They had families, spouses and children! What did they ever do to you?"

"They were agents of the repressive Mitel regime," responded the lead fighter sternly.

"*No, they were not*!" shouted Zan defiantly. "They were helping me with a secret program!"

"They were still employed by the Mitel military. It was their choice to do so —"

"You — *all of you!*" shouted Zan. "You are nothing more than *terrorists!*"

The lead fighter cocked his head slightly as he studied Zan for several seconds.

"Your parents," replied the lead fighter eventually. "They would be heartbroken to see what you've become."

"What?" asked Zan "My *parents?*"

"Yes, your parents. You were their *only* child. If they were still alive and leading the resistance, they would find the inner strength to target you for elimination, for your role in assisting the repressive Mitel regime."

Zan silently shook his head.

"With all due respect," he replied. "*You* seem to be doing a pretty good job on their behalf."

"If we really *wanted* to kill you, you would be dead already."

"What are you waiting for then?" asked Zan sarcastically. "After all, I *am* a dedicated servant of the Mitel Leadership!"

The lead fighter studied Liss intently.

"Deep down, I know you don't believe that," he replied calmly. "Your true feelings — they are just the opposite."

Zan did not immediately answer.

"*Who are you?*" he asked finally.

"My Name is Zi — Zi Liss."

"*Liss?*" asked Zan incredulously.

"Yes. I am your father's younger brother."

"I didn't know he had a brother. He never mentioned you —"

"It was best to keep such information secret. The Mitel Leadership routinely wipes out entire families once they find out one of them is a member of the resistance."

"I see," replied Zan softly. "What do you want from me?"

"Become part of the resistance," urged Zi. "Help defeat the Mitel Leadership once and for all. You have the ability to lead us. Probably more than any other person on this planet."

"It's not that easy —"

"Deep down, you know you should do it. Not just for yourself, and your parents, but for every innocent Mitel man, woman and child."

"And if I *don't*?"

"The Mitel resistance will not stop until we are victorious. Going forward from here Zan Liss, you will either be with us or against us. The choice is yours."

As he spoke, the resistance fighters began to withdraw beyond the light of the burning storage building and into the darkness.

"Zi, how will I know how to find you?" shouted Zan.

"Don't worry," Zi replied from off in the darkness. "We will always know how to find you first."

Then they were gone.

Zan turned and stared at the burning building before walking to his hover vehicle.

The next morning, Zan — still stiff from the night before — entered the Mitel Leadership complex. After passing through the initial checkpoint and full body scan, he walked across the Leadership grounds to the stone and glass Leadership building. Zan was once again escorted up the wide marble staircase to the Mitel Forum Hall by several enormous security guards.

As the massive stone double doors swung open, the group entered the Mitel forum hall. All eleven Mitel Leadership members had eyes on Zan as he approached. A guard motioned him to stop in front of the large curving stone bench.

"Welcome, Director Liss," said the first member. "The Mitel Leadership has been anxiously awaiting your visit."

"I am honored to be here," nodded Zan.

"Good! We have been following the progress of your program very closely. From everything we have seen, the reverse engineering and associated application of those systems to our own fleet has been a resounding success. I would like to congratulate you on behalf of the entire Leadership panel."

"Thank you," replied Zan.

"We would also like to reward you for your outstanding achievement."

"Sir?"

"You are being promoted to Emperor."

"But with all due respect Sir, what about Emperor Leander? He obviously —"

"He is *not* your concern!" scolded a second member. "You will not be hearing from him ever again!"

"But, I —"

"Director Liss," interrupted the third member. "Please understand that we are not offering you the position based on the success of the propulsion program alone. Emperor Leander is ultimately being replaced for his failure to stop the rise of the Mitel resistance."

"If you are not interested in the position," said the fourth member. "I am sure we can find another suitable candidate who is."

"Understood," replied Zan.

"We have called you here today for three reasons," said the first member.

"And those are?" asked Zan.

"First, to confirm that you will accept our proposal to become the new Mitel Emperor," continued the first member. "If you do, you will enjoy all the benefits of being the leader of the Mitel people, answering to no one *other* than the membership of this chamber. If you accept, you will also assume the responsibilities of the position which, most importantly, are to follow the commands of this Leadership panel without question or concern for the consequences. Do you accept, Director Liss?"

"I do," replied Zan without hesitation.

The first member smiled before continuing.

"*Excellent*. We are confident that you have the potential to be one of the finest Emperors Mitel has ever seen."

"I will do my best to not disappoint you."

"We are counting on that," replied the second member.

"The second reason that we called you here today," began the third member. "We want to be *very* clear that as Emperor, you must eliminate the Mitel resistance once and for all."

"That will not be an easy task since it appears that they are growing in numbers and resources," replied Zan.

"You are correct," blurted the fifth member.

"And that brings us to the third and most important reason," said the first member. "We want you to personally guide a large attack force across the universe to planet 5.1.18.20.9 and retrieve the young immortal Thraen."

"The one that escaped our invasion force years ago?"

"Yes."

"And, you want me to take the newly retrofitted fleet to secure his return."

"That is correct," smiled the first member. "Our members desire to secure the secrets of IM. We also urgently need to defeat the growing threat of the Mitel resistance. By seizing the young Battle Sphere, we can achieve both goals."

"I'm not sure I understand."

"If we capture the young Battle Sphere, we can force him to do our bidding. He could single handedly eliminate the Mitel resistance," the first member explained. "At the same time, we could extract the IM code from his body for our own use. You see, Emperor Liss, as time goes on, the resistance is growing stronger, and the members seated in this room are only growing *older*."

"Understood," replied Zan. "But how can we ensure his compliance?"

"If necessary, you will seize the members of his inner circle," replied the third member, "and use the threat of harm *or worse* to ensure that the young Battle Sphere does exactly what it is told."

"Assuming the voyage across the universe is successful," said Zan cautiously. "The young Thraen will be challenging to find."

"True," acknowledged the first member. "But we will secure his quick release by employing the same technique that helped make the Mitel Empire what it is today."

"I don't understand."

"Terrorism tactics, Emperor Liss," explained the sixth member. "If the Thraen is not handed over *immediately*, you are to use our powerful cluster pods to destroy several of that planet's largest population centers. After that show of force, the world will locate the young Thraen and deliver him and his inner circle to us."

"But a preemptive strike of such magnitude, aren't you concerned that he could be killed in the process?"

"Even an inexperienced battle sphere will be able to avoid such an attack."

"And his inner circle?"

"He will protect them."

"But what if he has not learned to develop his powers? What if he is still just a boy?"

"Then he will be very easy to capture, don't you agree?" smiled the fourth member dryly.

Zan stood silently for a moment.

"What if the planet is more technologically advanced than we are?" he asked eventually.

"We don't believe that to be the case," replied the third member.

"And why not?"

"If they were," replied the second member. "We would have heard from them by now."

"Not necessarily —"

"Emperor Liss," interrupted the first member. "As I said earlier, we believe you have the *potential* to be one of Mitel's greatest Emperors. We are confident that you will be able to secure the return of the young immortal Thraen and deal with the planet accordingly."

"*Deal with the planet*?"

"Yes," smiled the second member. "Before you return, you must destroy it."

"But *why*?"

"To eliminate the threat of competition."

Zan nodded silently.

"You will depart one week from today," instructed the second member.

"*One week?*" replied Liss incredulously.

"Yes," replied the first member quickly.

"The resistance will try to sabotage *anything*, if given enough time and opportunity to do so!" interrupted the fifth member.

"As you command," replied Zan quietly.

"Thank you," smiled the first member broadly. "That is all."

Zan quickly exited the Forum Hall followed closely by the security guards, the huge stone doors silently closing behind them.

"What do you think?" asked the first member. "Can he be trusted?"

"Yes. We have already discussed that many of our best officers are orphans of the resistance," replied the second member.

"True. But I've heard that he has been in contact with the resistance."

"*Really?*" asked the third member. "Where did you get this information?"

"Commander Lon Rexx."

"Rexx? He is nothing but a liar and a cheat."

"He is also a ruthless murderer," added the fourth member.

"But he is loyal to our cause," replied the first member.

"Which allows us to overlook his character flaws?" asked the third member skeptically.

"To a point," smiled the first member.

"Lon's father was also in the resistance," pointed out the second member. "I really don't see any reason to be concerned."

"Maybe you're right," acknowledged the first member. He then turned to the junior member.

"Gen Zandt — I want you to accompany the fleet."

"Why me?" asked the junior member incredulously.

"To monitor our new Emperor and ensure strict compliance with our orders. I also want you to select six of our best imbedded Special Forces personnel to serve as your body guards. You are free to travel on whichever cruiser you desire, except the Emperor's."

"Why not his?"

"That should be obvious. You are to travel separately in case we need to *destroy it*," smiled the first member.

"As you command," nodded Gen stoically.

The next week was a blur for Zan. Pulling together and launching an attack force in such a short period of time was a monumental challenge.

Near the end of the week, Zan sat alone in the Senior Command café in the Arman Matrix. There had been no formal celebration surrounding his promotion, not that he wanted one. Relocating to the base for the week helped him feel a little less vulnerable to assassination.

Zan stared blankly at his protein drink for a long time while he considered all the loose ends that still needed to be addressed. He was already starting to feel pressured in his new role and worried that he was forgetting something critical that could jeopardize the mission.

"Do you mind if I join you, *Emperor*?" smiled Ard.

"Please do," replied Zan.

"Congratulations. You are a most worthy choice!"

"Thanks," smiled Zan. "Now, if I can just figure out how to pull off this mission, I may stand a chance of keeping my job for more than a year."

"The mission is quite a challenge that's for sure."

"Indeed it is," replied Zan, turning serious. "Our Leadership is obstinate, but they don't fully understand the complexity and danger of this undertaking."

"Agreed, but I —"

"I mean, the retrofitted battle cruisers, transport vessels, supply and weapons craft have not yet been fully tested."

"Understood, but —"

"I am very concerned that the larger vessels will not hold up structurally over such staggering distances. And their slip rings — they ended up a bit larger and slightly outside the design operating envelope of our computer simulations."

"Well I don't think that is a cause for —"

"*And* the tandem slip ring design for the transport vessels — you know — with the open center section design and pulsating plasma bridge . . . I worry about their reliability not to mention whether they can keep up with the rest of the convoy.

"But —"

"What if it takes us much longer to make the round trip? We won't have enough fuel, or water for drinking *and* to produce oxygen. There simply was not enough time to install enough additional solid fuel oxygen generators. As it is, each vessel is going to be crammed with twice the number of solid fuel canisters. I mean —"

"Zan — *slow down*. I have concerns about the mission too. But my cruiser is flight worthy and the crew is excited and ready to go."

"You say that now," scoffed Zan. "But what if your cruiser becomes disabled? Out in deep space, the rest of the convoy won't be able to stop and wait for you to complete repairs. You will be left behind to face certain death."

"That's always a possibility I guess. But with you in charge, I'm sure that this will be the most prepared mission of all time."

"I *doubt* that," grunted Zan. "There just isn't enough time to plan for everything."

"Agreed, but your whole development program, wasn't it implemented with this exact type of mission in mind?

"I suppose so."

"OK then," replied Ard. "Things will be fine. You just need to promise me one thing."

"What's that?"

"Promise me we look out for each other out there?"

"I promise," smiled Zan.

A few days later, the Mitel Fleet was ready to go: ten battle cruisers, twenty massive Mitel Fighter transport vessels and twenty-six supply crafts. Before their departure, Dru and his three assistants oversaw the loading of two unmarked storage containers into the recently refurbished launch bay at the rear of Zan's main battle cruiser. During the retrofit portion of the reverse engineering program, Zan personally oversaw the modifications to his cruiser and made sure that only he and his mechanic crew had unrestricted access to the rear bays.

Without any formal announcement and in an unusually low-key fashion, the Mitel Fleet launched its mission as the vessels completed their sling shot maneuver in rapid succession.

Here we go thought Zan as he accelerated Cruiser Number 1 beyond the speed of light. It felt good to be in command of a cruiser again after so many years behind a desk.

The mission began on a positive note as the Fleet moved forward in close proximity to one another. Communications systems were fully functional and at first, the larger vessels kept up with the rest of the fleet. However, on the second day, the large transport vessels began falling behind. On the third day, Zan received the stunning news that a supply vessel had exploded. Rumors quickly spread across the fleet that the vessel had been blown up by Mitel resistance fighters.

They believe so strongly in their cause that they are willing to give their lives thought Zan from his command console. *They probably smuggled explosive devices on board during our loading procedures. They have obviously infiltrated the military. By how much will determine whether this mission stands any chance of success.*

On the fourth day, four more explosions destroyed two enormous transport vessels and two supply craft. Each transport vessel, approximately four thousand feet long contained three stacked flight decks which housed 100 Mitel strike fighters per deck. The fighters entered and exited through a large slot at the rear of the vessel that incorporated a permeable plasma shield to buffer the decks from the effects of outer space. From a distance, the vessel appeared as an enormous and partially squashed cigar with a tapered profile that widened from front to back. The vessel contained two large wings and matching winglets on either side of the stern and three matching vertical winglet tails equally spaced across its stern.

"We just lost 600 Mitel Fighters!" blurted Zan from his console. "That represents ten percent of our attack force. I want every inch of every vessel searched for signs of the resistance! If we don't eliminate the threat, this mission is doomed!"

Over the next several hours, more than two dozen resistance fighters were discovered and killed. Several explosives were also found and jettisoned into deep space along with the bodies.

On the fifth day, three more supply vessels were lost.

"We have *got* to find a way to stop them!" muttered Zan in frustration.

Suddenly, a distress call was received from Cruiser Number 5.

That's Ard's cruiser thought Zan.

He rushed to a vacant seat at the communications console and sat down.

"Commander Lindar, can you hear me?" he asked over the interfleet communications system.

There was no answer.

"Ard . . . ? Can you hear me?"

Again, there was nothing. Zan's heart was pounding.

"Navigator!" barked Zan.

"Yes, my Emperor?"

"Plot a direct course for Cruiser Number 5."

"But Sir, we are about to enter into slip mode —"

"That will take us light years away from here! Abort slip mode. NOW!"

"Yes, immediately, my Emperor."

Suddenly Zan heard the garbled voice of his friend.

"This is Commander Lindar . . . resistance fighters posing as crew . . . multiple explosions . . . heavy casualties . . . propulsion system destroyed . . . losing auxiliary power . . . attempting to abandon ship."

The communication abruptly cut out.

"*Ard . . . ?* Ard — can you *hear* me?"

Nothing.

Zan felt his own cruiser shudder violently as it resisted entering slip mode. The ICC deck lurched at a thirty-degree angle while the cruiser struggled to execute a hard-right turn.

"Emperor Liss," said the Navigator urgently. "We must follow deceleration protocols or we risk breaking apart — "

"There is no time!" interrupted Zan. "Stay on course!"

"Yes Sir," replied the Navigator nervously.

As the cruiser continued to shudder, a loud hum could now be heard across the vessel.

Without auxiliary power, the escape pods won't be energized. They will run out of oxygen quickly. We don't have much time.

As the main battle cruiser completed its sharp turn, the violent shuddering and loud humming abruptly stopped.

"Maximum normal speed Navigator!" instructed Zan tersely. "We *must* get to that cruiser!"

"Yes Sir!"

"Ard, if you can hear me we are on our way!"

There was no response.

After ten agonizing minutes, the Navigator turned toward Zan.

"Emperor Liss, we are closing in on Cruiser Number 5."

"Give me a visual."

Zan studied the screen image of the crippled craft. Several large white spots could be seen glowing along its length. Seconds later, the craft violently disintegrated.

"Slow to minimum speed," ordered Zan. "Perform a detailed scan of the immediate area!"

"Doing it now," replied the Scanning specialist.

After several seconds, the results came back negative.

"Try again specialist," instructed Zan impatiently.

Could it be they didn't get out? he panicked.

"Still nothing my Emperor," replied the Scanning Specialist solemnly.

"ARRRGH," growled Zan angrily.

"Wait," said the specialist quickly.

"What?"

"Five small pods, located almost directly behind us."

"Turn the cruiser around and lock onto them with our gravity control beams!" shouted Zan. "Quickly!"

"Doing it now Sir," the Navigator confirmed.

"Energizing gravity control beams," added the Weapons Specialist.

Zan watched impatiently for the small pods to come into view.

"Initiating gravity control beams," announced the weapons specialist.

Zan stared anxiously at the specialist.

"The beams are engaged and retrieving the pods now," confirmed the specialist.

With that news, Zan raced to the HorVert Elevator at the rear of the ICC. The elevator whirled toward the rear of the cruiser before heading down to the lowest level. As the doors opened, Zan rushed to the primary launch bay. As he entered, he looked through the large reinforced clear acrylic panels. The last of the five small pods had just been pulled into the bay from outer space. As the silver bay doors slowly slid closed, countless stars shined brightly against the blackness of deep space.

Zan waited impatiently as he listened to the familiar hiss of the bay pressurization system. After what seemed like an eternity, the "all safe" light flashed yellow releasing the clear acrylic sliding doors. He quickly entered the bay along with the chief medical officer and several assistants, transport and safety personnel.

One by one, the doors to the small escape pods were opened. Zan watched as dazed and injured survivors were helped from the first, second, third and fourth pods by the medical staff.

Where is he? As the technicians struggled to open the last pod door, Zan made his way toward the front of the crowd. When the door was finally opened, he heard a faint hiss as air rushed into the small cabin.

He looked inside to find the occupants lying on the floor. Zan saw the face of his friend.

"Is he?" Zan asked apprehensively.

"Alive, yes, but unconscious," confirmed Rad Aarden, the cruiser's Medical Officer.

Rad studied his scanning device as he stepped past Zan into the cabin followed by several staff members. At eight feet four inches tall and almost four hundred pounds, Rad was a giant. The extensive black hair that covered most of his face and body made him look more animal than human. Zan watched while Ard and the others were carefully placed on wheeled life support tables and whisked away. He could not help notice that Ard's face was badly scratched and bruised.

"Take good care of him," Zan instructed.

"We will," nodded Rad.

Zan quickly headed back to the ICC. When the elevator doors opened, he looked around quickly.

"Navigator!" bellowed Zan. "Plot a course in the direction of the rest of the fleet! We must move at maximum speed. We have some catching up to do."

The next morning, Zan visited Ard in the crowded medical unit. When the doors to Ard's private but cramped sleeping area slid open, he smiled broadly.

"How are you feeling?" asked Zan. "The medical staff tells me you also have a fractured wrist."

"I'm doing OK." replied Ard.

"Look, I . . ."

"Thanks for coming back for us."

"Not a problem," replied Zan. "I was thinking as I was on my way here, and it is kind of funny actually —"

"What?"

"That you were right. You had just graduated from the *prestigious* Mitel Military Academy and assigned to my cruiser as a young officer. Once I found out your father was a member of the *Mitel Leadership,* I thought you were nothing more than a spoiled brat —"

"*Stepfather,*" interrupted Ard with a weak grin. "I keep telling you there's a *big* difference."

"Yes, you do."

"Well it's *true,* at least for *me,* anyway."

"Understood," smiled Zan.

"And now what do you think of me?" asked Ard cautiously.

"I realize now that I was wrong," replied Zan quietly. "You are brave, resourceful and loyal. Your father, Magnus — he would be very proud of you."

Ard quickly looked away.

"I am not so sure that would be the case."

The two were silent for a time.

"What is the latest with the resistance?" asked Ard eventually, trying to change the subject.

"Things have quieted down — at least for now," Zan replied. "Not sure what that means, if anything. In addition to your cruiser, we have already lost *two* transport vessels and six supply craft. Morale across the fleet is low. If the attacks continue, we will not remain a viable attack force much longer."

"Well, if it's any consolation, we left Mitel with more than enough firepower to decimate a planet like Thrae."

"Understood; but in their infinite wisdom, the Mitel Leadership also left our own planet vulnerable to attack in the process."

"I know," replied Ard softly. "Now what?"

"*I* must focus on catching up to the fleet," said Zan as he turned to leave. "*You* need to concentrate on getting better."

"Will do," replied Ard just before the doors to his medical quarters slid closed behind Zan.

CHAPTER ELEVEN — DISCOVERY

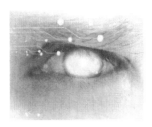

On the first day of tenth grade, Chad walked down the main second floor hallway searching for his assigned locker. When he found it, he dropped his backpack on the floor and opened the locker door which stuck a little bit.

Oh great, he thought to himself. Chad removed a few textbooks from his backpack before stuffing the bulky canvass bag into his locker. As he heard his name called by an oddly familiar voice, he turned to see a beautiful girl standing in front of him holding her books at her chest. She had a big smile on her face.

"Hi Chad," she said again.

"Um, do I *know* you?" asked Chad with a confused look on his face.

"I think so," she said nervously rolling her eyes toward the ceiling.

"I'm sorry but —"

"Chad! It's *me!*"

Chad looked at her face closely. The beautiful hazel eyes looked familiar.

"*Melissica?*"

"Yes!" she laughed.

Chad gave her a big hug before stepping back to look at her again. She was now about five feet nine with an athletic build, and the same shoulder length thick brown hair she had the last time he saw her.

"But I mean *how? Why?*" asked Chad eagerly.

"It's a long story," Melissica began. "You know that my dad kept getting transferred around the country, right? Well, my parents were fighting a lot and they eventually got divorced. Anyway, I live with my mom now and we came back here at the end of the summer when she found out she could have her old job back."

"That's great! I mean, I'm really sorry to hear that your parents got divorced and all."

"Thanks," laughed Melissica. "And I'm so sorry that I stopped writing and calling. I was pretty depressed there for a while."

"No problem," replied Chad. He almost had to pinch himself to make sure that this was really happening.

"Guess what?"

"What?" smiled Chad.

"My mom *finally* got me a new cell phone with unlimited minutes!"

"Very nice!" said Chad with an amused grin.

"I think so too!" I am now officially part of the twenty first century!" laughed Melissica.

"It's about time," teased Chad.

"Yeah, I know, right?"

"Well, um . . ." said Chad.

"Well?" asked Melissica a bit nervously.

Suddenly the first period bell rang.

"Hey!" said Chad.

"What?"

"What period do you have lunch?"

"Fifth"

"Me too. Do you want to have lunch together?" Chad asked enthusiastically.

"I would like that," smiled Melissica.

"Great, I —" Chad replied as he quickly turned and walked right into his open locker door.

Melissica put her hand over her mouth but could not stop from laughing.

"*Stupid design*," blurted Chad closing his locker door.

"Sorry Chad, I didn't mean to laugh."

"No problem, see you at lunch," Chad grinned before jogging down the hall to class.

At lunch, it was as though Melissica had never left. They laughed and joked and talked. Chad described the various friends and people he knew and who he thought were the best teachers. When the bell rang, they agreed to get together after school over the next few days.

After catching up with a few friends right after school, Chad headed home. He took his regular short cut through an apartment complex and behind the L-shaped Temple Bethel. There was a row of pine trees in front of a tall chain link fence behind the temple, creating a small secluded area. It was a warm and sunny afternoon and he was eager to tell his parents the good news about Melissica.

As Chad turned the corner behind Temple Bethel, he was confronted by four boys. He recognized Kevin Cane right away. Kevin was tall and heavyset, about an inch or so shorter than Chad. Kevin was in and out of trouble at school and in town. He was also known to be a bully.

"Hi *Chaddy*!" sneered Kevin. "Where are *you* going in such a hurry?"

Chad abruptly stopped and studied the three other boys who stood in a wide semicircle behind Kevin. He had seen them around school, but he could not remember their names. Chad sensed two more boys coming up quickly behind him.

They must have followed me from school he thought.

"Hi Kevin," Chad responded a bit defensively. "I was on my way home. Plenty of homework tonight, you know?"

"No, I wouldn't know about that," laughed Kevin sarcastically while the other boys snickered.

"Yeah, well, I have a lot to do tonight," replied Chad.

"Oh, *is that so*?" hissed Kevin.

"Yup," said Chad cautiously.

Kevin studied Chad intently for a moment, his left fist clenched.

"Well, I got to get going," said Chad.

"Not so fast," replied Kevin lunging forward. He grabbed Chad's shirt and shoved him toward the building while the other boys quickly circled closer behind, blocking his exit. Chad felt his heart pounding as he steadied himself.

"What is your *problem* Kevin?" asked Chad tersely.

"*You* are the problem!" Kevin snorted.

"I don't understand. What did I ever do to you?"

Kevin paused before glancing back at the other boys. Chad sensed that Kevin was a bit reluctant but was probably trying to prove to the other boys how tough he was. Chad tried as hard as he could to stay calm.

Maybe Kevin will back down Chad thought.

Then, one of the boys standing behind Kevin pointed at Chad. He was about medium height with curly black hair. "It's because you are a fucking freak, that's why!" he said angrily.

Kevin looked at the boy briefly who motioned for Kevin to proceed. Kevin quickly turned back toward Chad and stepped toward him, his fists still clenched.

"Kevin, why are you doing this?"

"Why? Why am I doing this?" replied Kevin angrily. "Because I don't like you. And like he said, you are a freak!"

Kevin lunged at Chad, swinging his arm awkwardly. Chad dropped his backpack and deflected the blow with his arm causing Kevin to lose his balance.

"*Ha, ha*" laughed a few of the boys. A third whistled and clapped. That only made Kevin angrier. He was not going to allow Chad to make him look like a fool in front of his friends.

"You *little* shit," cursed Kevin under his breath as he lunged forward a second time. He kicked Chad in the leg before punching him squarely in the mouth. The blow jerked Chad's head back and within seconds, he felt excruciating pain and the warm sensation of blood in his mouth.

"Beat the shit out of him Kevin!" yelled one of the boys.

"Kevin, look I —"

Kevin swung wildly hitting Chad in the ear as he tried to duck away. Kevin then punched him a third time in the chest as Chad darted quickly to his left.

"*Woo hoo!*" yelled a boy from behind.

Chad's ear hurt as he glanced around for a place to run, but there was nowhere to go.

"C'mon Kevin, kick his ass!" yelled another boy.

Kevin pulled out a long pocket knife and waved it toward Chad. Chad noticed a crazed look in Kevin's eyes.

"ENOUGH!" he yelled at the top of his lungs, anger swelling up inside of him.

Suddenly, Chad felt very strange. His stomach felt full as a tingling sensation raced through his body. His hybrid transformation was commencing. The metallic elements and bloodstream additives were interacting with every aspect of his physical being, triggering his conversion.

His stomach was filling up with electromagnetically charged plasma fluid. The stomach lining quickly morphed into an oblong chamber forming the basis of his antigravity propulsion system. Seconds later, his gall bladder became encircled by the expanding chamber as it hardened into a magnesium-based superconductor sphere.

Before Chad could say another word, his eyes widened and turned metallic silver. In a matter of seconds, the metallic silver quickly spread across his face and down his neck in a mesh pattern that resembled shards of glass.

Kevin stood frozen as he stared at Chad in stunned disbelief.

Chad looked curiously at the expression on Kevin's face as the bloating sensation intensified. He felt his skin hardening. The sensation was oddly familiar, like a leg or arm was falling asleep. At that instant, his eyes began to glow a very bright white.

The look on Kevin's face turned from disbelief to shock to fear. He dropped his knife. Chad then turned his attention to the rest of the group standing behind Kevin.

"*What the hell*?" said one of the boys as he instinctively stepped backwards. The other boys did the same as they looked on in fear and disbelief. They were staring at something crazy — something unbelievable — and that something was him! Chad glanced down at his shirt and pants. To his surprise, he did not notice anything unusual. He then raised his left arm. It was entirely covered with metallic silver shards. He saw two sets of intense white lights reflecting off his arm, like headlights. Chad then lifted his other arm which was also covered in the same metallic silver shards. He glanced back toward the group. He stepped forward.

"Holy shit!" yelled one of the boys who turned and fled followed by another then another until they were all gone.

Only Kevin remained, standing like a statue directly in front of him, frozen in terror.

"*Get out of here!*" yelled Chad angrily.

Kevin's eyes rolled back in his head as he fainted and fell to the ground with a loud thud. Chad stood over Kevin as he lay on the ground next to his knife. After a moment or two, he felt his anger receding and turned his attention back to his silver metallic arms.

This is unbelievable he thought, as he touched his face, which felt hard and bumpy.

Chad backed away from Kevin and turned to face the windows at the back of the temple. Seeing his reflection, he could not believe what he saw. His face and hair were covered in jagged silver and his eyes bright white lights. Chad stepped toward the windows staring at his reflection. He turned his head from side to side while he studied his silver features with nervous curiosity.

A moment later, the bright white beams disappeared, leaving his eyes metallic silver. He then watched in amazement as the metallic silver shard mesh receded up his arms then up his neck and down his head and around his face until only his eyes remained silver. His eyes eventually returned to normal. By that time, the tingling and fullness sensations were gone.

Chad heard a groan. He turned around to see Kevin awakening. Before he came to, Chad grabbed his backpack and hurried along the rear of the building. Approaching the corner of the temple, something caught Chad's eye from above. Looking up, Chad saw a silver metallic ball hovering silently near the top of the flat roofed building before suddenly darting around the corner. Turning the corner, Chad watched the ball race higher and higher into the sky until it was gone from view. By now, the other boys were nowhere in sight. Chad quickly peeked back around the corner at Kevin one last time to see him still lying on the ground.

When Chad got home, he walked briskly up the driveway and onto the back porch. Fumbling for his house key, he noticed that the back door was ajar. Chad stepped back, glanced toward the garage and saw his mother's car, which meant she was home early.

Chad quietly entered the kitchen and looked around. When he did not see her downstairs, he quickly sneaked through the dining room and raced up the front stairs to his room closing his door carefully behind him. Suddenly, Molly called from down the hall.

"Hi Chad. How was your first day of school?"

Chad did not answer. He went to his mirror and checked the bruises on his face and ear.

"Honey, is everything OK?" Molly asked as she approached his room.

What should I tell her? Chad thought. *I don't want to frighten her. I need to figure things out first.*

"I'm fine Mom," replied Chad through his closed door. "School was OK. I've got a lot of stuff to organize."

"Can I get you anything to snack on?" asked Molly from directly outside Chad's bedroom door.

Chad felt hungry, but he did not want his mother to see his face — at least not yet.

"No, I'm good," replied Chad.

"Are you *sure*?"

"Yup."

"OK. Hey, don't forget. Tonight is observatory night with Dad," reminded Molly as she turned and headed downstairs.

Chad groaned to himself as he touched his ear and face. *How am I going to hide this from Dad?* He then turned and flopped on his bed. A few hours later, Jim arrived home from work. As he came into the house, he called up to Chad.

"Hey Chad — you ready to look at the heavens?"

"Sure!" Chad yelled back, still lying in his bed.

"Hi Honey," Jim said to Molly as she greeted him in the kitchen.

"How was your day?" Molly kissed Jim affectionately.

"The usual, I guess," grumbled Jim. "I'm just trying to get everyone interested in the curriculum at the start of the new semester."

Jim paused as he noticed Molly's eyebrows were a little furrowed.

"What's wrong?" he asked.

"I'm a little worried about Chad," replied Molly.

"Why — what's going on?" asked Jim in a concerned voice.

"I'm not sure. He went up to his room as soon as he got home and hasn't come out since. Not even when I offered him a snack."

"*Whoa*, something must be wrong," laughed Jim, "that kid never misses a meal."

"I know, but —"

"Well, it's almost dark out. It's just about time for us to check out the stars. I'll try to find out what's going on, OK?"

"Let me know," sighed Molly.

With that, Jim went upstairs. As he passed Chad's room he knocked on the door once. "See you up there, *OK?*"

"Ok," answered Chad hesitantly.

Sitting at his desk, he listened as Jim made his way down the hallway and up the stairs to the observatory. About fifteen minutes later, Chad came up the observatory stairs to find his father tinkering with the telescope's settings. He quietly walked across the room and sat down next to Jim.

"What's new?" asked Jim without looking up at Chad.

Chad did not answer.

Jim continued to focus on the telescope. "Hey, I was hoping we could peek at Saturn's rings tonight. Maybe that will put you in a better mood — "

"Uhh . . . hey Dad?"

Jim stopped what he was doing and looked up. His eyes grew large as he noticed the welt on Chad's ear and the bruises and cuts near his mouth.

"Jesus Chad! What the heck happened to you?"

"I kind of got into a fight on the way home from school," replied Chad weakly.

"*Kind of* got into a fight? It looks like you got hit by a bus!"

"Well, Kevin Cane probably qualifies as a bus, or maybe a truck."

"What are you doing messing with that Cane kid? You know he is nothing but trouble," lectured Jim.

"I *know* that Dad. He and a bunch of other guys were waiting for me behind Temple Bethel after school."

"Who else was there?"

"I don't know them by name. I've just seen them around school."

"Well, what happened?" Jim asked impatiently.

"Kevin called me a 'freak' and then started hitting me."

"*I can see that.* What did *you* do?"

"I got mad, really mad."

"You got mad? Did you hit him back?"

"No," said Chad defensively.

"*No*? Why not? I mean — *no that's good* — I guess."

"I did get Kevin to stop and I got the other guys to run away," explained Chad cautiously.

"*OK,* good, but what did you do to make them leave you alone?"

"Well, it's really not what I did actually. Something just sort of happened . . ."

Jim stared at Chad who was now wringing his hands together. Jim could sense that something 'big' had happened.

"Chad? Did you do something illegal?"

"No."

"Did you call the police?"

"*No!*"

"Then what did you do Chad?"

"I don't know how to tell you this," Chad began. "After Kevin hit me, I started to change somehow. My eyes glowed like bright beams of light and my skin turned into pieces of metallic silver and it felt different — it was like it was hardening or something. And my insides felt like they were going to explode at any moment."

Jim was speechless, as he stared at Chad.

"The guys behind Kevin freaked out and took off," Chad continued. "I yelled at Kevin to leave and he fainted!"

Chad took a deep sigh, and waited for his father's response.

Jim looked down at the floor and then back at Chad, running his hands through his hair. Chad knew that when his father did that, he was confused or nervous or both.

"Listen Dad," said Chad softly. "I know it all sounds crazy — but after the guys took off — I walked over to a window at the back of the temple and looked at my reflection and saw it for myself."

"Chad, I'm not sure what to say."

"Dad, it's all *true*. I know how it sounds, but it happened. You *have* to believe me!"

"Well I —"

"Dad, listen, when Kevin pulled a knife out, that's when I could feel myself getting *really* angry. And that's when it all happened. It was like my anger or the feeling of being threatened somehow triggered whatever happened to me."

Chad's face suddenly brightened.

"You should have seen the looks on their faces," he laughed nervously. "It was like they had seen an alien or something!"

Jim just stared at Chad.

"And Dad, after I changed back to normal, I saw *it* again!" exclaimed Chad.

"Saw what?" asked Jim cautiously.

"The silver metallic ball! It was hovering above the Temple. It was as if it had been watching the entire time."

"You saw it?" asked Jim, his eyes lighting up with excitement.

"Yes!" replied Chad eagerly. "Then it darted around the corner and disappeared into the sky!"

Jim reached into his back pocket for his wallet. He carefully removed a folded piece of paper and handed it to Chad.

"What does this have to do with me?" asked Chad while he read the newspaper article.

"Chad, the baby in the article. It's you," Jim said softly.

Chad looked at his father. He always knew that he had been adopted. But he was never told about the specific details as to how or why.

"I was left *in a box* at the hospital?"

"Yes," replied Jim.

"But why are you showing this to me *now*?"

"You were left at the hospital the same night *something* mysteriously crash landed outside of town," explained Jim. The U.S. military immediately showed up and closed the area off as if they knew that something very unusual had crashed there. I tried to research the incident on line, but got nowhere. It was almost like it never happened."

Chad looked at his father intently.

"But Dad — I mean — there are stories like that in the papers and on the internet *all* the time."

Jim stood up.

"Stay here, I have something to show you," he instructed anxiously before rushing down the stairs.

He reappeared holding something in a towel. Jim sat back down and unwrapped it. He then carefully handed the triangular metal object to Chad.

"What is this?" asked Chad curiously.

"I am not really sure. I found it at the crash site —"

"Universal Speed Escape Pod."

"What?"

"It says so on this piece of metal," Chad explained.

"You can read those markings Chad?"

"Yes."

"But how are you able to do that?"

"I don't know," he replied.

Jim's heart was now pounding furiously.

"Listen, Chad. I found that at the crash site years later and brought it to an old friend of mine who does materials testing. He said that it is made of a material called *graphene*. He also explained that our world does not have the technology to produce something like this, and probably won't for a long time."

Chad's eyes widened. He looked up at his father.

"Holy crap Dad, *seriously*?"

"I'm *very* serious," said Jim as he reached over and handed Chad the silver medallion from the hospital. "This was in the box with you the night you were left at the hospital. It has similar markings as the metal object —"

"Global Defense Center."

"What?"

"That is what it says on the coin: Global Defense Center," replied Chad.

"Are you two finishing up?" Molly called from downstairs. "It's getting late. It's a school night, remember?"

Jim turned toward the stairs and shouted, "We are almost done, Honey!"

"Listen Chad, about the silver metallic ball, I think I saw it too," Jim confessed.

"You did? When?"

"When we were on vacation at Lake Edward years ago," said Jim. "It showed up out of nowhere when I was struggling in the water during that storm out on the lake. I am pretty sure it saved my life."

"Why do you say that?" Chad frowned.

"There is no other way to explain how I survived. I was drowning and the last thing I remember before waking up on shore was seeing a silver orb hovering directly above me. It had this oval shaped monitoring screen on the front of it —"

"Yes Dad, this one did too!"

Jim let out a long sigh while he ran his fingers through his hair.

"I think that the silver metallic ball, and the crash, and the hospital, and what happened to you today, are all linked somehow. I mean, if you are from another planet that would certainly explain all of your physical differences, not to mention your blood —"

"My *blood*?" What are you talking about?"

"Well, when you were little, the doctors told us that you have incredibly high levels of titanium, aluminum, beryllium, magnesium and other metals in your blood. I guess we should have told you that sooner, but it had no effects on your health, so we never brought it up again."

They sat in silence for a few minutes.

"Are we going to tell anyone?" asked Chad eventually. "How about Mom . . . should we tell *her*?"

Jim looked toward the stairs briefly and then back at Chad.

"My guess is that she is going to freak out *big time* when she hears about what happened. Maybe we should wait on that until we figure out what to do next."

"OK."

"I just can't figure out who else we should tell. The police will think we are absolutely bat-shit crazy, and could you blame them?"

"Probably not," Chad frowned. "What should I do about school tomorrow?"

Jim let out a big sigh.

"Let's just pretend for now like nothing happened," he replied.

"Pretend like *nothing happened*?" asked Chad skeptically.

"Chad look — Kevin and the other boys are in and out of trouble all the time, right?"

"Yea, so?"

"They have little to no credibility with anyone who knows *anything* about them, including the police and the school administration, right?" explained Jim. "Why worry about what they might say. If you stay calm and act like nothing happened, other than maybe the fight itself, you will be fine."

"Ok, I'll give it a try," replied Chad weakly.

"The next thing we need to do is figure out what happened to you today," concluded Jim. He then stood up and motioned for Chad to do the same. Jim then stepped forward and gave him a big long hug before placing one hand on each of Chad's shoulders.

"Everything is going to be alright son," Jim promised. "Don't worry. I am here for you and we will figure this out together, OK?"

"So, you really don't think we should tell Mom yet?" Chad asked one last time.

Jim ran his hand through his hair again.

"We certainly don't want to lie to her," Jim began. "But we also don't want your mother to worry unnecessarily. How about until we figure out what is really going on, we tell her that you were rough housing with a few guys at school and things got a little bit out of control. I mean, it's not too far off if you think about it?"

"I guess that's OK for now," shrugged Chad.

"OK good, let's call it a night," replied Jim as he motioned Chad to head downstairs. As they reached the bottom, Jim turned off the lights.

The next morning Chad walked slowly to school. He was anxious, apprehensive and didn't know what to expect. When he arrived at school, he went directly to his locker. Everything so far seemed normal, other than the occasional stares at the bruises and cuts. Chad quickly transferred the books from his backpack into his locker before stuffing the canvas bag into the bottom. Chad double checked that he had everything he needed for the first few periods before heading up the hall toward class. As he turned the corner, he came face to face with Kevin, who seemed very much afraid of Chad. Kevin said nothing and quickly turned down the hall.

At lunch period, Chad sat alone, reading a book about the history of space shuttles when Melissica sat down next to him.

"What happened to you?" she said, noticing the cuts and bruises on his face.

"Hi Melissica," replied Chad, slowly putting down his book. "I kind of had a run in with a few school bullies last night behind Temple Bethel."

"*Jerks* — who were they?" she whispered angrily.

"I only recognized one of them by name, not that it really makes a difference I guess," shrugged Chad.

"Did you tell anyone?"

"I told my dad."

"What did he say?"

"He told me to sit tight for now."

"Sit tight? *Really*?" frowned Melissica. "Those guys should be reported to the police!"

"You don't understand —"

"What is there to understand? It's against the law for people to go around hitting other people."

"I know Melissica. But it's complicated —"

"*Complicated?*"

"Listen let's talk about this later, OK?" replied Chad awkwardly. "I don't think the cafeteria is the best place to discuss this."

"Fine," responded Melissica impatiently.

"Thanks," smiled Chad weakly. "I'll call you later. Everything is going to be OK — I promise."

Melissica stood up quickly.

"Promise me you'll be careful?" she asked.

"I promise."

What Chad did not know was that the father of one of the boys from behind the temple was a special agent for the Federal Bureau of Investigation. When his traumatized son came home and explained what had happened, he immediately got on the phone with his superiors in Washington. They in turn referred the incident to the United States Naval Space Surveillance System Command.

Major Talbot's phone rang as he walked into his Virginia office the next morning. He carefully placed his hot coffee on his desk, dropped his black briefcase on his side chair before reaching across his desk to answer it.

"Michael Talbot speaking."

"Major Talbot, David Jansen, FBI Washington Bureau."

"Good morning David, what can I do for you?"

"Well, it is more of the reverse, really."

"What do you mean?" asked Major Talbot, settling into his chair.

"We received credible eyewitness reports of some form of UFO or ET behavior yesterday."

"Where?" asked Major Talbot, carefully sipping his hot coffee.

"Coopers Falls in upstate New York."

Major Talbot was silent as he recalled tracking the UFO that had crashed in the cornfield there several years ago. The wreckage was being secretly reverse engineered by a team of talented engineers and physicists. Because of that incident, faster than speed of light travel was now more than a possibility — it was on the horizon.

"Major Talbot, Sir. Are you there?"

"Sorry David, I'm still here," replied Major Talbot, snapping back to the present.

"You should receive an email report detailing the incident before the end of the day. Maybe you can make some sense of it."

"OK, thanks. I will be on the lookout for it." He turned toward his filing cabinet and after a brief search, pulled out a file on the Coopers Falls incident and scanned it once more. Shortly after Major Talbot received and reviewed the email detailing multiple witness reports of the *transforming silver being with the glowing eyes*, he made plans to visit Coopers Falls to locate and speak with the subject teenager, Chad Stone.

Chad was sitting in the school library when his cell phone beeped. It was a text message from Melissica:

> Hearing rumors about a fight between a bunch of high school boys and an alien behind Temple Bethel. Is there something else you want to tell me about last night?

Chad stared at the message. Feeling a little self-conscious, he looked around the library but nobody noticed him.

Don't get paranoid he thought before glancing back down at his phone

Probably shouldn't put anything in writing he thought.

> Let's talk later. Meet you at the corner of Main St. and Grove Ave. after last period. OK?

OK

For the rest of the afternoon, Chad agonized over what to tell Melissica. When they were younger, he remembered how they could tell each other anything. Back then, he knew he could trust her to keep a secret.

But that was then. Chad did not really know Melissica, despite having stayed in touch. He needed more time to get to know her before he freaked her out with the truth about his transformation and stories of floating silver metallic spheres. After last period, Chad grabbed his backpack from his locker and headed out the main entrance.

As he set out along Main Street, he sighed nervously. Main Street itself, like much of the town, was lined on either side by tall oak and maple trees. But what made the street unique were the huge Victorian mansions from a bygone era. Most of them were now professional offices or apartment buildings, but their beauty had been carefully preserved.

Stopping at the corner of Grove Avenue, Chad noticed Melissica walking toward him on the other side of Main Street. She smiled and waved as she crossed the street.

"Let's walk for a bit," said Chad calmly when Melissica stopped next to him.

"Sounds good to me," she replied and the two of them walked in silence for about a block.

"*Sooo*?" asked Melissica curiously.

Chad smiled weakly as he shot a nervous glance toward her.

"Listen," said Chad. "The guys I scuffled with last night are bad news. The ringleader is a guy named Kevin Cane. They are into drugs and who knows what else."

"But why are they are going around making up stories about you being an alien?" frowned Melissica.

Chad paused before raising his left hand.

"Remember these?" replied Chad, nodding toward his four fingers.

"How could I forget?" Melissica chuckled.

"Well, don't forget that it makes me a target of crazy rumors and stories, especially from sore losers."

"I hear what you're saying."

She stopped and looked at Chad intently as her left eyebrow rose slightly. Chad felt as though she was looking into his soul.

"Are you *sure* there isn't something else about the fight that you want to tell me Chad Stone?"

Chad laughed nervously not sure how to respond.

"Well, there is something . . ."

"*Yes*?" asked Melissica anxiously.

"When we were younger — I never told you something, even though I wanted to very much."

"*What* Chad?"

"I would get nervous butterflies in my stomach every time I was with you," blurted Chad awkwardly.

Melissica blushed and quickly looked away.

"I'm sorry Melissica, I didn't mean to embarrass you."

"You didn't embarrass me," smiled Melissica.

She quickly leaned over and kissed Chad.

"Listen," said Melissica. "I promised that I would make dinner tonight *and* I have a lot of homework to do. Promise me again that you'll be careful."

"I promise," Chad grinned.

Melissica waved goodbye as she turned and started walking home. Chad sighed again as he watched her walk down Main Street.

By midweek, Chad felt things were returning to normal. Kevin and the other boys were avoiding him. The alien rumors died down and Melissica did not question him again. Chad decided that these were all very good signs. After last period, Chad stopped by his locker and shoved his books and binders into his backpack and headed home.

Chad no longer used the shortcut behind Temple Bethel. Instead, he took the longer route home along Main Street and up Grove Avenue. As he made his way, he heard a car coming up behind him. The car approached and slowed down. Chad sensed that he was being watched.

The vehicle pulled up alongside him. Chad quickly turned to look at it. It was a dark brown sedan with tinted windows. The driver was wearing aviator sunglasses and looking right at him. Another man wearing sunglasses sat in the passenger seat, watching him too. Something inside told him that this was *not* a random driver. Chad's heart started pounding.

"Stay calm," he muttered to himself as he looked away from the car and readjusted his backpack. Chad instinctively started walking faster and after several seconds, the car picked up speed and continued up the street. Chad watched as the car signaled and then made a right turn.

Chad let out a big sigh and slowed down a bit. Suddenly, the brown car reappeared up ahead. As it approached, it slowed down again. This time, Chad studied the car closely. He noticed that the white license plate read *U.S. Government* and *For Official Use Only* in small letters. As it passed, the two men in the car continued to stare at him. Only this time, the man in the passenger seat was talking on a cell phone. Chad started to walk faster again, his heart now pounding furiously. He quickly glanced back over his shoulder to see that the car had pulled over down the street. Chad continued to walk home as fast as he could. When he arrived Chad looked up and down the street. The sedan was nowhere in sight.

Chad jogged up the driveway and up the back stairs. He stepped into the kitchen, quickly locked the door behind him before heading up to his room to start his homework. Chad looked out his bedroom window for a few minutes. There was no sign of the brown car.

About an hour later, Molly came home. A few minutes later, he heard her coming up the stairs. Molly knocked on Chad's bedroom door.

"Come in."

Molly opened the door and stuck her head inside.

"Hi Honey, how was school today?"

Chad wanted to tell her all about what had happened, but decided he should wait until Dad got home.

"It was OK. You know, the usual."

"Well I'm making meatloaf for dinner, *OK?*"

"Sounds good Mom," replied Chad as he forced a smile.

Molly closed the door and continued down the hall to her bedroom to change clothes. When dinner was ready,

Molly called up to Chad who did not come down. After her third request, she brought a plate of meatloaf and steamed broccoli up to Chad.

"Sorry, Mom," Chad apologized as she walked in with his dinner in one hand and a glass of iced tea in the other.

"It's OK honey," smiled Molly. "I remembered that tonight is astronomy night. I figured you would be trying to get all your homework done early."

"Yeah," Chad grinned.

"OK, he should be home from work within the hour. How is it going?"

"I'm getting there."

"Good boy," Molly replied softly as she kissed him on the top of his head. When Jim got home from work, he grabbed a few bites of meatloaf before heading up to the observatory. He knocked on Chad's door and said in a loud voice "*Meet you up there, Chad!*"

Chad rushed to wrap up his math homework. As he entered the observatory, Chad noticed that Jim was studying the astronomy resource book.

"How did things go at school today?" asked Jim without looking up.

Chad did not respond as he sat down next to his father.

Jim sensed something was not right and quickly closed the book and studied Chad's expression.

"Is everything OK?" asked Jim cautiously.

"I'm not sure, really," replied Chad softly.

"What do you mean? Did any of those boys say or do something to you today?"

"No," replied Chad quickly. "The guys seem to be avoiding me — which is probably a good thing."

"Yes, I agree. So, what's wrong then?"

"I think I was followed home from school today," blurted Chad.

"What do you mean?" asked Jim in a surprised voice.

"A brown car with tinted windows drove slowly past me a few times," explained Chad. "It looked like a police car, but it did not have any markings on it. Then I noticed that the license plate said *US Government*. Two men in sunglasses kept staring at me. It freaked me out."

"What did they do?"

"The car eventually stopped up the street. I just tried to stay calm and walk home as fast as I could. I didn't see the car again after that. I even looked for it out my bedroom window a few times after I got home."

Jim listened silently.

"Who do you think it was Dad? Am I in trouble?" asked Chad nervously.

"No Son. You are not in trouble," Jim said trying to reassure Chad and hide his concern.

"Do you think Kevin or one of the guys told somebody about what happened?" asked Chad quietly.

"Probably. But I don't think there was anything we could have done to prevent that. We need to remain calm and continue to act like nothing unusual happened."

"But if they come back, what are we going to do?"

Jim moved his chair closer to Chad and put his hand on his son's shoulder.

"Don't worry Chad. As long as I am around, you will be safe," replied Jim in a soothing voice.

Chad glanced up at the observatory opening before looking closely at his father.

"I know. I just want to understand what happened to me, you know?"

"Yes, I know. So do I. Listen, I am working on a research project and had planned to work from home the rest of the week. If you see these people again, text or call me from your cell phone, OK?"

"Well I —"

"I am serious Chad. You just call and tell me exactly where you are and I will drive right over, OK?"

"OK Dad," replied Chad nervously. "Hey Dad, I'm really tired. Is it OK if I just go to bed now?"

"Sure Son."

Jim gave Chad a big hug.

"Don't worry Son. Everything is going to be alright."

Jim let out a heavy sigh. He wondered who the men in the brown car were. Jim then replayed the events of the last few days through his mind.

I have got to get some answers to what is going on Jim thought. *In the meantime, I must protect Chad. I just hope to God that I can* he thought as he turned off the lights to the observatory.

The next morning, Chad woke up in a good mood. He headed to the kitchen where Molly had prepared a breakfast of scrambled eggs and wheat toast. Chad was running late so he stuffed the last piece of toast in his mouth, grabbed his back pack and headed toward the back door. As he rushed by the kitchen table, Jim motioned to Chad making a phone sign next to his ear. Chad smiled and gave the thumbs up as he disappeared out the back door.

Chad went through the school day without incident. He did not run into Kevin or the other boys from the fight. As Chad left school, he glanced up and down Main Street for signs of the brown sedan but it was nowhere in sight. He walked briskly up Main Street shifting his backpack until it was comfortable. As he turned onto Grove Avenue, he peered up the street.

Still nothing he thought. Feeling relieved, Chad looked up at the trees lining both sides of the road. When he looked back down, there it was. The brown sedan was slowly approaching him.

Chad's heart was now beating rapidly. As the car drove slowly passed him, Chad stared straight ahead then quickly peeked out of the corner of his eye. The same two men were watching him from inside the car. Once it passed, Chad fumbled for his cell phone and quickly texted his father:

> Heading home on Grove Ave by Ackley St. Brown car is following me again

Seconds later, Jim responded:

> On my way

Chad looked back over his shoulder and saw the brown car stopped up the street. He started walking faster. When he looked over his shoulder again, the car was turning around. Chad walked as fast as he could. Within seconds the car pulled up next to him and stopped. The two men got out of the car and approached him. As they did, the driver took off his sun glasses.

"Chad Stone?" he asked.

Before Chad could answer, Jim came barreling up the street in his station wagon. He pulled up abruptly in front of the sedan and hopped out.

"Chad! Is everything alright?" Jim asked sharply.

"I'm OK Dad," replied Chad in a relieved tone.

"Are you Chad's father?" the man asked.

"Who wants to know?" responded Jim tersely.

Major Talbot reached into his coat pocket and produced his black and white identification badge and showed it to Jim.

"Sir, my name is Major Michael Talbot, United States Navy and this is Lieutenant Jason Miller," replied Major Talbot removing his sunglasses.

Jim suddenly remembered the name from the old newspaper articles about the mysterious crash outside of town. He tried to stay calm and not let on that he knew who Major Talbot was.

"I'm Jim Johnson, Chad's father. How can I help you Major Talbot?" asked Jim quickly.

"We want to ask your son a few questions."

"About what?"

"There was an incident recently that took place behind Temple Bethel involving your son —"

"You mean the *fight*?"

"Well, yes Sir, I guess you could describe that way."

"I am aware of it. What about it, Major Talbot?"

"Well Sir, there are multiple eyewitness accounts that described very unusual and unexplainable behavior on the part of your son —"

"*Unexplainable behavior* Major? Could you please be a little more specific?"

Major Talbot reached into his coat pocket and pulled out a small pad of paper. He turned a few pages and began reading out loud. "Suddenly and starting from his eyes, Chad's face and skin turned this textured metallic silver color. Then his eyes glowed bright white, like mini-headlights."

Major Talbot stopped reading and looked directly at Chad before turning his attention back to Jim.

"Major Talbot, do you know *anything* about these kids?" asked Jim.

"You mean the eyewitnesses?"

"Yes."

"No Sir, I don't really."

"Do you know anything about my son?"

"I have learned a few things, yes."

"Did you learn that my son was born with physical defects?" Jim began. "And that because of those defects, my son has been harassed and bullied over the years by small minded people such as Kevin Cane?"

"Well, Sir, through various sources, I have been made aware of some of your son's physical abnormalities — "

"And did your sources also tell you that those boys who were picking on my son have had several run-ins with law enforcement?"

"Well, no Sir," responded Major Talbot defensively as he was taken aback by this new information. He glanced over to Lieutenant Miller who shrugged his shoulders.

"If you check with the local police you will find that they have been caught multiple times abusing drugs. If you check with the school, you will also find that they have all been suspended at some point for the same thing. My guess is that those derelicts and bullies were all high on something the day they decided to pick on my son. As a matter of fact, my son told me one of them even passed out in front of him. Major, do you have any eyewitness reports from anyone else? Perhaps more credible witnesses?"

"No Sir. I was unaware of this additional information," admitted Major Talbot as he closed his pad and slowly placed it back into his coat pocket. He then shot a quick glance toward Lieutenant Miller.

"Does the US Navy *also* make a habit of investigating claims by school bullies?" asked Jim tersely.

Major Talbot froze for a moment. Jim could see the muscles in his face tighten.

"No Sir, we *don't*" bristled Major Talbot. "Our job is to find explanations for unusual and unexplained phenomenon."

"Well maybe you should have done a little more homework on your *credible witnesses*," Jim retorted.

Major Talbot nodded silently.

"Do you have any other questions Major Talbot?" asked Jim firmly.

"No Sir, not at this time," replied Major Talbot humbly.

"OK then," said Jim. "Chad, get in the car and let's go home."

Chad looked Major Talbot in the eye as he walked quickly passed him. Chad threw his backpack in the back before getting into the front passenger seat. He watched his father walk around the station wagon and get in. Jim started the car, backed up quickly, before driving off. In the rearview mirror, Jim saw Major Talbot and Lieutenant Miller watch them drive away.

"What do you think they wanted?" asked Chad.

"The same thing we do: answers to what's going on with you."

They drove home in silence. As Jim pulled into the driveway, Chad looked at Jim.

"Hey Dad?" he asked quietly.

"What Chad?"

"Do you think they will leave us alone now?"

Jim let out a big sigh as he turned off the car.

"Only time will tell," he replied, unclipping his seatbelt. "Let's go inside. I think we've had enough excitement for one day, don't you think?"

"Yeah," replied Chad forcing a weak smile.

Chad grabbed his backpack and headed toward the back porch. Jim followed, and glanced toward the street to see the brown sedan drive slowly past. In the passenger seat, Major Talbot stared at them through his dark sunglasses.

CHAPTER TWELVE — REVELATION

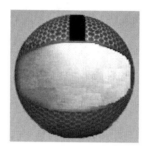

With no further sightings of the brown sedan, Jim researched human morphology in hopes of finding clues to help explain what happened to Chad behind Temple Bethel.

And Chad spent most of his free time with Melissica. On Friday night, Melissica came over to watch a movie. They ate popcorn and snuggled under a hand-made black and brown blanket that Chad's grandmother had knit.

On Saturday morning, Chad decided to go for a run to clear his head. It was a beautiful sunny morning and the air was clear and crisp. After stretching for a few minutes, Chad ran down Grove Avenue toward Randall Park about a mile away. The sprawling park had a large pond with a wooden foot bridge at its narrowest point, picnic areas, playgrounds and sports fields. On the far end, there was a dense wooded forest with dirt trails.

Chad headed up one of the dirt trails past an old Civil War Memorial toward the park's center. As he ran past the picnic tables, the pine trees became much denser. Chad had to pay close attention to the terrain to avoid the many sandy areas along the dirt road. As he approached one of the larger sandy sections, Chad glanced down to make sure he didn't lose his footing. When he looked back up, the silver metallic ball was hovering twenty feet in front of him.

Chad stood motionless as the object slowly approached. It had a single black stripe on the top and along each side, with an oblong silver screen across the front that had a large crack in it. Instead of being afraid, Chad was excited. He then remembered his father's instructions to contact him right away if he ever saw the silver metallic ball again. Without taking his eyes off the hovering sphere, Chad *slowly* reached into his pocket for his cell phone only to realize that he forgot to bring it with him.

Well that wasn't very smart, he thought.

The sphere suddenly turned around and darted along the dirt road deeper into the park. Chad ran after it. After about a quarter mile, the orb made a sharp left turn and was no longer in sight. Chad scanned the woods for any sign of the silver metallic ball. It was eerily quiet since people rarely visited this section of the park.

I've got to figure out what this thing is.

Chad took a deep breath as he made his way into the woods. He stepped gingerly through the maze of trees and dead branches. The forest floor was soft and squishy under his feet. It got darker as Chad ventured deeper into the woods. He glanced back toward the dirt road only to realize that it was no longer visible.

"Maybe I will go just a *little* bit further," he muttered before weaving his way through the forest about another hundred yards. It was somewhat brighter up ahead where there was an opening in the woods. Chad walked out into the circular opening some fifty yards in diameter and scanned the perimeter for any signs of the sphere.

The orb suddenly darted out of the woods and stopped about ten feet in front of Chad and hovered silently.

"Who are you?" asked Chad softly.

The orb continued to hover silently.

"I said — *who are you*?"

A beam of light projected from the orb as Janus's hologram appeared. Startled, Chad took a few steps back as he stared nervously at the three-dimensional figure surrounded entirely by a light blue hue.

"Hello Chad," smiled Janus.

Chad was frozen in place.

"How do you know my name?"

"My name is Janus," replied the hologram calmly just as a second silver metallic sphere sped out from the woods. It stopped and hovered next to the first one. Chad noticed that this one had blue stripes instead of black. A beam of light appeared from the same location on the second sphere. A Second later, Markus's hologram appeared next to Janus.

"This is Markus," motioned Janus.

"Hello Chad. How are you my boy?" asked Markus with a broad smile.

Chad stared at the two holograms standing side by side as he tried to muster the courage to speak again.

"What do you want from me?" he asked eventually, his heart pounding. Chad slowly reached down a second time into his pants pocket for his cell phone in the hopes that he may have somehow missed it before. It was not there.

"We are two of the three survivors from the planet Thrae," replied Janus calmly.

"Planet *Thrae*?" asked Chad.

"Yes. It was the name of our home, located approximately six hundred ten light years from Earth."

Chad, from his deep space astronomy research, thought about the configuration of the Milky Way's four spiral arms.

"There is a planet known as Kepler-22b located about that distance away along Earth's spiral arm. Is that it?"

"Not *that* specific planet, but in that general direction, yes," smiled Janus. "Your world refers to it as the constellation of Cygnus in the Orion Spur. There are a series of inhabited planets where we are from. And while it may seem a long distance away, in some ways it really isn't."

"That's *incredibly* far away. I don't see how —"

"We were advancing faster than speed of light travel which allowed us to get here in a very short time.

"Faster than the speed of light?" asked Chad skeptically.

"Yes. We also discovered that under certain ideal conditions above the speed of light, we could actually *jump* across space for light years at a time in mere seconds."

Janus's hologram suddenly sliced along a diagonal for a second or two.

"It's a long story," chuckled Markus as Chad smiled nervously.

"You said you are two of the *three* remaining survivors."

"Yes, I did," replied Janus.

"Who is the third?"

"*You* are, Chad."

"Me?" questioned Chad.

Janus raised his right hand to show his four fingers. At first, Chad was dumfounded. He stared transfixed at

Janus's hand before eventually walking toward him — as if being drawn by some invisible force. Chad raised his left hand and placed it against Janus's hand. The finger pattern matched exactly. He stared in amazement at the bright sparkling light that immediately appeared between their palms.

"Why is that happening?" asked Chad softly.

"We call it focused energy. It allows holograms to perform everyday tasks."

Chad suddenly had a flashback recalling seeing that light when he was young. Chad lowered his hand and stepped back from Janus. He realized the inescapable truth — *he was from another world.*

"It's true, isn't it?" asked Chad quietly. "I remember now. I remember the sparkles from when I was very little."

"Yes, Chad, it's true. Our small pod crash landed outside of Coopers Falls fifteen Earth years ago. You were just an infant."

"You mean the *Universal Speed Escape Pod*?"

"That's correct," smiled Janus. "I left a piece of the wreckage out in the field for your father to find."

"Why did you do that?"

"He needed proof of our existence to take adequate steps to protect you."

"Protect me? Protect me from *whom*?"

"From your government, for now."

"Major Talbot?"

"Yes. But he is only one of many," explained Janus. "The United States Military detected our small pod when we entered the Earth's atmosphere. They quickly located and confiscated the remains of our crash wreckage and correctly concluded that we survived the crash landing. They have been looking for us ever since. This means they

228

will also be looking for you once they connect *you* to the crash."

Chad let out a big sigh.

"Why do you appear as holograms?"

"It's part of the long story lad," replied Markus.

"Chad," Janus began. "When the Mitels launched a surprise attack against our planet, something went horribly wrong at one of our defense bases, triggering total destruction of our planet —"

"You mean the planet and everyone on it are *gone*?"

"Everyone from our planet is gone but *you* Chad. And in saving you that day, Markus and I chose to irreversibly become what you see now, hologram projections from a probe."

"But why have you come to me now?"

"That is a very good question. Before I answer that, you need to know more about yourself."

"You are an *immortal*."

"I'm a *what*?"

"You are an immortal being. It is what you think it means. You will live forever unless you choose to die or are killed," explained Janus.

"But why — I mean — how is that even possible? Immortality is something you read about in science fiction books."

"Chad, you were born with those characteristics, just as you were born with other very special abilities."

Chad tried to grasp what Janus was telling him.

"What *other* special abilities do I have?"

"You are also what our planet referred to as a *hybrid*."

"A *what*?"

"A hybrid. You can transform between man and machine. That's what happened behind Temple Beth El. You initiated the first phase of your hybrid transformation. In that instance, it was triggered by anger and your inner instincts for self-preservation."

Janus paused before continuing.

"You were born into an advanced civilization that, over a very long period of time, unlocked secrets of the body and mind that allowed for various ways to integrate themselves with machines. You possess unique abilities which you have yet to fully understand and control. But given recent events, Markus and I felt it was time for you to learn of your abilities for your own safety as well as the safety of others."

"So, you're telling me that *everyone* on Thrae was a hybrid and an immortal?" asked Chad suspiciously.

Janus glanced quickly at Markus before answering.

"No. We were never able to control who became a hybrid or the adverse consequences of immortality. In time, our technologies outpaced our ability to control them or use them wisely. Countless millions of our people died from unintended adverse effects of immortality before the process was eventually eradicated from our world."

Janus paused to look around the opening.

"Chad Stone, you are the last Thraen. You are also the last immortal *and* the last hybrid — and a very special hybrid I might add. And that is why they will come for you eventually."

"The Mitels?" asked Chad quietly.

"Yes."

"But *why*?"

"The Mitels are a rigid and militaristic society," Janus began. "And its leaders have an insatiable appetite for intergalactic domination. The Mitel Leadership's control over its people is absolute and they will stop at nothing to obtain the secret of immortality. In their blind and selfish determination to obtain that secret, they attacked Thrae twice."

Janus paused again before continuing.

"They refused to believe that we had long since eradicated the process and blueprint or *formula* if you will, centuries before their assaults. And as the three of us escaped in the small pod, our probe's sensors confirmed that the Mitels had not only discovered that you were on board our USEP pod, but they also established that you were both an immortal and a hybrid Battle Sphere. Once they locate and reverse engineer our faster than the speed of light technology — which they will — they will come for you."

Janus paused one more time before finishing his thought. "*My* fear is that this planet will then suffer the same fate."

The three stood silently, listening to the wind gently blow through the pine trees.

"Are you *sure* they will come looking for me?"

"Yes."

"You also said I am a hybrid —"

"Battle Sphere," Markus corrected him.

"*Battle Sphere*. And that's what I started to change into behind the temple?"

"That's correct," Janus replied.

"If the Mitels come here looking for me, what am I supposed to *do*?"

"You possess the ability to transform into the most formidable fighting machine in universe," replied Janus. "Back on Thrae, Markus was also a Battle Sphere. He helped defeat a massive Mitel attack force about sixty-five Earth years ago. If you practice and learn how to use your own Battle Sphere to its fullest potential, I have no doubt that you can singlehandedly destroy anything they send here."

Chad shook his head in disbelief as he sat down on the ground while Janus instructed his monitoring orb to run a scan of Chad's emotions. Chad looked back up at Janus with an expression of bewilderment and excitement.

Markus laughed. "Chad, Janus is telling the truth."

Chad studied Markus for a moment before responding.

"Well, is there anything else I should know?"

Markus glanced over to Janus who smiled briefly before turning serious once more.

"Yes Chad, there is one more thing. My full name is Janus Stone. I am your biological father."

Chad's eyes grew very wide as he looked up at Janus.

"*Seriously*?" Chad jumped to his feet.

"Yes."

"Just *look* at the two of you!" laughed Markus. "You have the same nose, mouth, chin, eyebrows, skin complexion and hair! It is pretty obvious from where I am standing anyway."

Chad was speechless.

"Chad, I've waited a long time to tell you this. I've rehearsed it in my mind hundreds of times," said Janus, "but as I expected, it's not any easier for me to tell you now."

"Is this why you have been watching me all this time?"

"Yes Chad."

"But I already have a mother *and* a father."

"I understand. And they have done a wonderful job raising you, and for that I am grateful — "

"And now you want me to go with you?" Chad said defensively.

"No, I'm not here to disrupt your life," explained Janus. "It's your choice to make. As I said, I'm here to inform you of your unique abilities and where you came from. I'm also here to warn you of potential future events."

"So, you *don't* want me to come with you?"

"No," replied Janus firmly.

"Why not?"

"I left you at the hospital because I wanted you to live a happy OK life. Or at least as normal a life as possible," Janus began. "I knew back then or rather I hoped that one day, we would see each other again. But I also knew that by leaving you, I forfeited my right to tell you what to do. That choice is yours."

Janus paused briefly before continuing.

"You are free to choose to embrace who and what you are. You are also free to continue to lead the life you have now. In fact, you probably could do both for a time."

Janus looked up at the sky briefly.

"Markus and I have been observing and looking out for you, Jim and Molly, ever since I left you at the hospital the night of the crash. At the time, I only wanted you to be safe and happy. I did not want you to be linked to our crash landing in any way. Your happiness is also why I saved your father when he was drowning on Lake Edward."

"That *was* you!"

"Yes it was me."

"My dad — he said he saw you when he was about to drown. He knew you had saved his life somehow."

"He is a good person as you say here on Earth. And in many ways, you have grown up to be just like him. Your mother would be so proud of you now."

"My *mom*? Did she die in the Mitel invasion?"

Janus tilted his head for a moment as he thought how to respond.

"No, she died in childbirth."

"Oh."

The three of them looked around in awkward silence for several seconds.

"Well, what now?" Chad asked eventually.

Markus glanced at Janus before answering. "If it were up to *me*, I would tell you that it is time to get ready!"

"For *what*?"

"Get ready to defend this planet against the Mitel Fleet. I am sure their leaders are more determined than ever to acquire the secret of mortality."

As Markus spoke, Janus's hologram sliced along a diagonal for a second or two.

"Why do you do that?" asked Chad.

"Do what?"

Janus's hologram deformed again.

"*That!*"

"Oh, that. During our escape, my orb was thrown around the USEP suffering minor damage to its projection mechanism," said Janus motioning toward himself. "We have tried to fix it a few times but we lack the necessary tools and parts. I have gotten used to it."

"I call him fuzzy!" laughed Markus.

"Listen, Chad," said Janus softly. "When Markus and I left you at the hospital, I knew that I may not get a second chance for you to be my son, but I never gave up hope wishing and waiting for the opportunity to talk to you and explain to you *who* and *what* you are. And with your help, we also have a second chance to do something that ultimately, I could not do back home."

"What's that?"

"Stop the Mitels!"

"Are you *sure* they will come here?" he asked softly.

"Yes, I'm afraid so Chad," Janus responded solemnly. "Based on my initial estimates, they may already be on their way."

"What if I'm not able to be a Battle Sphere? I mean — you say I can destroy a fleet of alien space craft! I don't see how that is remotely possible."

"Chad, you say that now," Janus began. "But you must believe that what I am telling you is true. You can transform into a fighting machine of *incredible* firepower, speed and maneuverability. You were born with these abilities. The medical professionals who analyzed you as a child diagnosed the materials that run through your body as contaminants. That could not be further from the truth. Those human engineering properties are what trigger and facilitate your transformation. You simply need to unlock and develop that power."

"But —"

"But nothing. I'm not saying it will be easy. You will need to train *very* hard. If you do that before the Mitel forces arrive, you will be surprised at what you can accomplish."

"The Mitels will be pretty surprised too!" Markus added.

"How would I train?"

"Markus and I can facilitate all of that. It will take time, and we must do it in secret so as not to put you or your parents in further danger."

"Are you saying my mom and dad are in danger?"

"Possibly," confirmed Janus.

"You mean from people like Major Talbot?"

"Yes."

"But why would they want my parents?"

"Chad, you are not from this world," explained Janus. "Even though you have adapted extremely well, you are something to be captured, examined, tested, and dissected. Your parents could eventually be detained and interrogated to locate and apprehend you. They may also be punished for concealing your identity."

Chad paused before asking another question.

"How was I able to read the inscription on the piece of wreckage that my dad found?"

"Like all Thraens, you learned our language in your first year of life," smiled Janus.

"Chad, listen," said Markus. "I know this is a lot to take in all at once. But I want you to know that Janus and I are here for you, just like your parents are."

"OK, but how will I know how to find you?"

"Don't worry about that," replied Markus. "We are always nearby. And we hear and see everything thanks to these monitoring orbs we call home."

"And Chad," Janus added, "when you are ready to see the abilities you possess, we will arrange a secret meeting place."

"Do you *really* mean that?"

"Of course!"

"Where would we meet?"

"Do you know the Davis farm on Dean Road outside of Coopers Falls?"

"Yes. I've been there many times. Mr. Davis is a nice man. I've helped him around his farm once and a while to earn some extra money."

"Well, about a half mile up from the main gate, there is a large grove of trees in the field on the left. Markus and I could meet you there when you are ready."

Chad's heart pounded with excitement. "Can we meet there tomorrow morning?"

"That sounds like a very good idea to me," grinned Janus.

"Great," said Chad "I'll see you there."

"*Oh*, and Chad —"

"Yes?"

"Be sure to bring a change of clothes."

"Why?"

"If we are successful and you transform, your clothes will not be of any use to you afterwards."

"Um, OK," replied Chad, intrigued.

With that, Markus's hologram returned to its orb and darted off into the woods. Janus paused until Markus's orb disappeared from view. He waved to Chad before he too returned to his monitoring orb and followed after Markus along the tree tops.

As he made his way back through the trees to the dirt road, Chad contemplated everything that Janus and Markus had said. When he reached the dirt road, Chad looked carefully in all directions to make sure nobody was around before he started running back toward the Randall Park entrance. As he did, Chad occasionally glanced back over his shoulder for any signs of the silver monitoring orbs.

CHAPTER THIRTEEN – TRANSFORMATION

The next morning, Chad had mixed feelings about what awaited him. He was excited to transform into hybrid form, yet anxious and nervous about the unknown.

Chad took a deep sigh, jumped out of bed and quickly pulled on a black tee shirt and gray sweats. On his way out the bedroom door, he remembered to grab a spare set of clothes. He stuffed a shirt and sweats into a small backpack he kept under his bed and headed downstairs. Molly was in the kitchen drinking a cup of coffee.

"Morning honey, are you ready for some breakfast?"

"I'm good Mom," Chad smiled weakly. "I promised Mr. Davis that I would help him today on the farm, remember? I really don't want to keep him waiting."

"I don't remember you telling me about that," replied Molly. "But OK. What time will you be back?"

"I'm not sure."

"Then please text me when you find out OK?"

"OK Mom, I will." Chad headed out the back door and down the rear porch stairs to his bike.

He quickly slipped his cell phone into his sweatpants pocket and attached his small backpack with a bungee cord to the rack above his rear tire. He then gave his bike a push, hopped on, and headed down the driveway. As Chad biked along, he alternated between peddling normally and raising himself above the seat to peddle faster. His adrenaline raced as he made his way out of town toward Davis farm. As he turned onto Dean Road, Chad kept a watchful eye for any signs of Major Talbot's brown sedan.

I do not want him following me today he thought.

When Chad reached the entrance to the Davis farm, he scanned Dean Road in both directions. It was still early and the country road was quiet. The metal gates at the entrance to the farm's dirt road driveway were secured with a long chain and key lock. Stone walls ran along the road on either side of the gates. Chad lifted his bike over the old stone wall and then scrambled over it himself. The stone wall rocks felt cool against his hands from the previous night's air.

Mr. Davis had a large farm. The dirt road driveway was long and straight with open fields on either side. Mr. Davis had stopped planting crops years ago, and over time, tall grass, wild flowers and weeds had taken over the fields. As Chad peddled along, he saw the large tree grove off in the distance. He continued up the dirt road until he was parallel to the tree grove before hopping off his bike to walk it through the tall field grass. As he made his way along, grasshoppers and crickets jumped in all directions to avoid him while moths and an occasional butterfly flew about. Chad noticed a light blue dragon fly following him that landed on his handle bars and sat motionless until his bike hit a bump, causing it to reset itself.

When Chad arrived at the edge of the grove of trees, he unstrapped his backpack and carefully laid his bike down in the tall grass, making sure it would not be seen from the dirt road. He scanned the fields for any signs of Janus or Markus. After a few minutes, Chad made his way into the dense tree grove to see if they were waiting for him there. He maneuvered around several tree trunks to a large opening. It reminded Chad a little bit of the secluded open area in Randall Park where he met Janus and Markus the day before. As he walked slowly to the opening's center, he looked skyward. The top branches of the trees formed a thin protective roof overhead with only a small blue hole in the center where the sky was visible.

"Janus? Markus?" Chad called aloud. There was no answer.

"Janus, Markus are you here?" he said louder.

Chad eventually made his way back to the edge of the field. Suddenly, there was a rustling sound to his left. The sound grew louder as it moved directly in front of him. He felt his heart pounding as he took a step or two back. Suddenly, Janus's silver and black monitoring orb rose out of the grass.

"*Holy crap* Janus!" blurted Chad. "You scared me!"

The orb darted toward Chad before stopping next to him. Janus's hologram materialized revealing a look of amusement on his face.

"Sorry about that. I scouted the area earlier and was waiting for you in the open field to allow the sun to charge my solar backup system."

Chad let out a big sigh of relief before suddenly remembering that he had forgotten to text his mom. He quickly pulled his cell phone from his pocket.

"I need to let my mom know when I'll be home," said Chad. He hit send before placing his cell phone back into his pocket.

"OK, what now?" asked Chad anxiously.

"Let's head to the center of the tree grove," instructed Janus.

As they entered the opening, Janus looked skyward toward the tree canopy above. "If everything goes according to plan, we will launch here," he explained. "I chose this location to provide cover for your Hologram Matrix. It will also materialize and operate from this location to minimize detection."

"My *what*?"

"Your *Hologram Matrix*," repeated Janus patiently. "It is also referred to as your Battle Hologram. It's the Thraen hologram team assigned to your Battle Sphere."

"Assigned to me?"

"Yes. You must be patient and let events unfold. If you transform here today, many of your questions and concerns will be answered."

Suddenly, Markus's orb appeared and hovered next to Janus. In an instant Markus's hologram materialized.

"Sorry I'm late. How's the boy doing today?"

"Hi Markus. I'm doing OK thanks!" smiled Chad nervously.

"That's my boy!"

Janus glanced briefly at Markus before looking back at Chad.

"Chad, I'm not sure what to expect from you today. *If* you successfully transform, I would like us to start your training immediately."

"*Us*?" asked Chad.

"Yes. I will accompany you into space during your initial training," replied Janus.

"That sounds good to me," smiled Chad. "But when you say you want to begin training, what do you have in mind?"

"We'll travel to your solar system's asteroid belt —"

"*Fly to the asteroid belt*?" blurted Chad incredulously.

"That's correct."

"But how will we get there? It's about sixty million miles away from Earth. I mean, I need to be home by dinner."

"Your Battle Sphere is capable of reaching the outer limits of your solar system in four to seven hours depending of course on the relative location of the sun and planets."

Chad quickly ran the numbers quickly in his head. "But that means we would have to travel near the speed of light!"

"That's correct," replied Janus. "At full speed, we should arrive at our first training area beyond the main asteroid belt in a little over half an hour."

"Holy crap!"

"For its size, a Battle Sphere is by far the most remarkable and powerful machine system in the universe. Your plasma-based energy core combined with your antigravity field will generate the sustained propulsion force necessary to achieve those speeds."

Janus paused briefly before continuing.

"It will be critical to reach maximum speed as quickly as possible to minimize the chance of being detected by Earth's monitoring systems. Your maximum speed, or what we call *all out* speed, increases exponentially before it trails off just below the speed of light in approximately five minutes. Think of it as an S-shaped acceleration profile. By my calculations, we should reach the inner band of the asteroid belt between Mars and Jupiter in about 12 minutes."

"Wow. And then what?"

"We'll practice high speed evasive maneuvering and test your weapons system."

"My *weapons system*?"

"Yes. Your Battle Sphere will be equipped with a complex laser weapons system. I want to test it out by firing at the asteroids in space — "

"We're going to the asteroid belt for *target practice*!" exclaimed Chad excitedly.

"Yes, but first things first. Let's see if you are able to concentrate enough to begin the transformation process."

"OK, fine."

Janus studied Chad's face as he instructed his orb to run a scan of Chad's current emotional state. After reviewing the results, Janus glanced over at Markus who shrugged.

"Chad," said Janus calmly.

"What?"

"I know you are nervous, and this is a lot to take in all at once. If you don't want to do this now, I fully understand."

Chad did not answer.

"The secret is to just relax and focus on your transformation. Channel your desire to transform into your hybrid self. It will take a few tries, and soon it will become second nature."

"What if I *can't*?" asked Chad apprehensively.

"Then we simply try another time."

Chad stared up at the trees, his palms getting sweaty.

"Listen Chad, you will be hesitant and anxious," said Janus in a soothing voice. "In many ways, that is a good thing my son. I would rather you be cautious and proceed slowly. But remember, I will be right there with you."

"How?"

"It's a little tricky, but I will attach my monitoring orb to the periphery of your outer spin surface. We will then fly up there together as a team. OK?"

"OK," replied Chad hesitantly.

"And once you transform, your Battle Matrix team will materialize and spring into action. In time, you will feel that they are part of you."

"I'm ready to give it a try."

Janus smiled. "That's what I was hoping you would say. There are millions of rock and metallic objects of all shapes and sizes in the asteroid belt. It's the ideal place to simulate offensive and defensive maneuvers of a Mitel attack. You must remain focused and follow the directions of your Battle Hologram team."

Markus gave the thumbs up sign.

"OK, let's get this mission started," announced Janus. "Your Battle Hologram team will most likely appear over there," he added, pointing at the opposite side of the tree grove opening. "Once I'm securely attached and confirm audio contact, I will transmit our travel coordinates to your Battle Hologram team. When I give the signal, you will launch, *OK?*"

"OK," replied Chad softly.

"Good. Now Chad, you must do exactly as I tell you."

Chad nodded again. Seconds later, a laser beam emitted from Janus's orb struck the ground several feet in front of Chad.

"First, stand next to where the laser beam is touching the surface," instructed Janus.

Chad did as he was told. He then glanced up toward the tree tops one more time while he nervously rubbed his hands against his sweatpants. Chad looked at Janus and flashed a nervous smile.

"Do as I do," said Janus who spread his legs about three feet apart.

Chad did the same.

"That's good. Now, raise your arms out to your sides so that they are a little bit above your shoulders like this."

Chad raised his arms.

"A little higher," instructed Janus calmly.

Chad obliged.

"Good. That's the pose you must assume once the transformation commences. Do you understand?"

"Yes."

"Now we are ready to start. Go back to standing normally and try to relax. Try to clear your mind."

Chad closed his eyes tightly and tried to relax.

"Don't force it, Chad. Relax. Take long deep breaths."

Chad reopened his eyes and started breathing deeply.

"That's it Chad. Keep breathing. Now I want you to focus on something that is very important to you. Focus your thoughts on something positive that you love very much. Can you think of something?"

"I think so."

Chad closed his eyes again and let his mind drift. At first, he thought about Melissica and her beautiful smile. His mind then wandered. He thought about how his mom used to read stories to him every night to help him fall asleep. He loved the sound of her voice as she read. It was so soothing and loving. Chad focused on the sound of her voice until he could hear her reading to him in his mind.

"Concentrate," said Janus soothingly. "Channel your thoughts and continue to breathe. Continue to relax. That's it."

Janus's hologram slowly approached Chad.

"Now I want you to try to focus everything on becoming one with your mechanical self and concentrate your mind on your own energy. Your energy potential is as great as your ability to focus on it."

Chad thought about his reflection in the window behind Temple Bethel.

"Chad, move your legs and arms into the position that I showed you," instructed Janus.

Chad did exactly as he was told.

"That's fine. Relax and focus your thoughts. Relax and breathe," coached Janus.

As Chad concentrated, Janus's voice began to fade. Chad felt weightless, calm and peaceful. It was suddenly very quiet.

Chad's eyes opened wide and changed to metallic silver. He felt his whole body begin to tingle as the silver metallic mesh pattern — resembling shards of glass — quickly spread from his eyes, covering the rest of his body before hardening. It felt the same as it did that day behind the temple.

Once again, the metallic elements and other bloodstream additives triggered his transformation into a Battle Sphere as they reversibly interacted with every aspect of his physical being. The transformation was now underway.

Chad felt bloated as his stomach filled with electromagnetically charged plasma fluid. His stomach morphed into the initial stage of the oblong chamber, encasing his gall bladder which hardened into a magnesium-based superconductor sphere, the combination of which formed the basis of Chad's own antigravity propulsion system.

He felt a slight itch just below his left ear where a small distress beacon switch had formed. Chad fought the urge to panic while so many strange sensations rushed through his body.

Stay *calm* he told himself. *Concentrate and try to relax.*

Chad's eyes turned bright white just before he levitated fifteen feet up into the air while his body generated a spherical electromagnetic field twenty feet in diameter. He suddenly felt very nauseous — like he was going to throw up. He opened his mouth and expelled a large stream of highly charged blue translucent plasma energy which was captured and distributed by the electromagnetic field, forming a bright blue translucent plasma bubble.

Feeling immediately better Chad looked down, surprised to see Janus standing several feet below.

"That's it Chad. Concentrate," coached Janus in a loud enough voice for Chad to hear.

As the transformation progressed, Chad's magnetic field grew stronger. He subconsciously activated his latent but powerful psychokinetic ability. The phenomena summoned heavy metal trace elements and helium-4 from all directions from the surrounding atmosphere and ground area. Swirls of shiny particles of titanium, aluminum, magnesium, cadmium, iron and beryllium entered the tree grove and whirled around Chad's blue plasma sphere.

As Janus watched, two new beams of white light streamed from Chad's eyes toward the ground directly across the opening. The same shiny particles appeared from all directions and swirled at that location like a large dust devil. Seconds later, a three-dimensional hologram appeared in the center of the whirlwind, and grew from the ground up to form a hologram cube matrix three squares high, three squares wide and ten squares deep. Each square was ten feet high and shined brightly with the same blue translucent plasma light that surrounded Chad. Human-like creatures quickly appeared inside the structure.

Staring at the Hologram Matrix, Chad noticed a small silver rectangular metallic strip float past him. He followed its path until it molded itself to the surface of the plasma bubble. Then a second strip floated by and then another and another as the process quickly accelerated. Glancing down at his body, Chad realized that the shard-like strips were *peeling off* his silver skin mesh. He watched dumbfounded as the peeling strips quickly shredded his clothes.

It doesn't hurt he thought as the strips peeled off his body in every direction. The floating strips quickly molded to the translucent bubble. As they peeled off, more layers of the hardened silver skin were exposed only to peel off again. The strips eventually formed the same intricate shard-like pattern against the outer plasma sphere. It was like watching a three-dimensional puzzle being assembled. Once the blue bubble was covered a few times over, the peeling stopped.

Seconds later, Chad once again felt incredibly bloated and feared he might burst from the inside out. *The final and most critical phase of his hybrid transformation was underway*. In a millisecond, like a controlled demolition, Chad's body expanded in all directions. His metallic bloodstream additives interacted with the swirling trace elements now being absorbed through his permeable silver skin. Chad's arm and leg bones, combining with the absorbed trace elements, transformed, expanded and extended before bowing outwards to form the vertical metallic support structure inside his silver mesh outer skin. Next, 11 of his 12 pairs of ribs expanded and bowed horizontally to form a secondary support structure that interlocked seamlessly with his vertical supports. This new metallic skeleton not only strengthened and supported the exterior surface of his Battle Sphere, it provided additional protection and support for Chad's mutating inner system architecture.

As the trace elements continued to be absorbed, the two longest pairs of Chad's ribs curved toward each other until they connected and morphed into an internal variable speed flywheel that spun just inside his support structure. The flywheel assisted Chad's antigravity propulsion system by coupling and uncoupling with what used to be Chad's sternum, causing the sphere to spin.

When engaged, the flywheel uses zero energy as it spins effortlessly in a thin bed of plasma fluid analogous to frictionless ball bearings. When disengaged, the flywheel is used to recharge Chad's plasma energy reserves.

As the transformation continued to unfold at lightning speed, Chad's lymphatic nodules, nodes vessels and ducts transformed into a complex monitoring system which controlled his internal operating systems.

His nervous system morphed into a sophisticated, plasma based outer defense shield. His muscles and clusters of nerve cells combined to become two hundred laser cannons that fired superheated high energy hydrogen plasma bursts fed from Chad's former intestines. The plasma pulses were contained by two layers of cross magnetic sheathing. The plasma pulses could be fired continuously at speeds more than six thousand miles per hour. Their destructive power was formidable. The plasma was excreted through mechanical pores in his outer skin surface. His new metallic nerve cells received and processed positioning, tracking and firing information from his Battle Hologram.

Chad's respiratory system converted into his Sphere's plasma energy generation and delivery system which also produced his laser cannon hydrogen based energy pulses. His cardiovascular system hardened to form a complex combination of wire like conductors.

During the transformation, Chad's head, including his brain, eyes and ears, remained largely intact to varying degrees, although they were now fueled by liquid plasma rather than blood. This realization kept Chad from panicking.

As he surveyed the tree grove opening, it appeared to him that he was still encircled by his initial translucent bubble — even though he had become an infinitely more complex and formidable Battle Sphere. He would learn later that his eyes had been mechanically copied, multiplied and positioned to six different locations on the outer edge of his spin surface to form a distributed aperture viewing system that acted like x-ray vision. This allowed him to see around the entire sphere at any time, during any conditions, day or night.

As he focused his gaze, a faint translucent square outlined in yellow formed. Beyond the square were several semitransparent "mini" screens displaying messages, data, and pictures that constantly changed and updated as he looked around.

A squat metallic cylinder extended a foot above the top and bottom of Chad's sphere. The sides of the cylinders were encased by glass arranged in a mosaic pattern that matched his silver outer spin surface. The cylinders changed colors based on Chad's emotional state — representing the remnants of his outward facial expression. The glass contained random patterns that eventually pulsated back and forth around the perimeter like a multicolored wave, before stopping and then repeating. The current blues and greens confirmed that Chad, while anxious, was otherwise calm. If he became agitated, upset or angry, the colors quickly changed to various shades of yellow, orange and red.

By now, the shiny particles swirling around Chad's sphere had all but disappeared. The silver metallic strip seams that made up his outer skin were clearly visible. The transformation was now complete. At over sixteen tons, Chad had successfully transformed into *the most advanced and intricate fighting machine in the universe*.

Without notice, his Battle Hologram initiated coupling of the variable speed flywheel to its sphere architecture, causing Chad's outer spin surface to rotate around the two interconnected cylinders. Chad studied the various screens and displays in his view, noticing a screen reading on his lower right that displayed an rpm reading of one thousand.

"Hey Janus, am I spinning?"

"Yes Chad, you are," confirmed Janus. "It is all part of your internal propulsion system."

"Then why can't I tell?"

"It's a natural part of your hybrid existence," Janus began. "Your cylindrical core remains stationary allowing you to view forward by default. You can change your view to any direction at any time by thought. If your Sphere receives an alarm warning of an impending collision, that view will instantaneously override your chosen view. Don't worry Chad, in time all of this will become second nature. By then, you will no longer need the Battle Hologram to initiate many of your command functions."

"OK . . ."

"And Chad, a simple but important concept to remember is the faster you spin, the faster your Battle Sphere can travel."

"Got it!" replied Chad enthusiastically.

"OK, on my command I want you to perform a series of movements. Do you understand?"

"Yes."

"Good. Now, try to turn around."

As he would normally do, Chad thought about turning his body around to reach for something. His orb quickly spun full circle in response, his digital readings and mini-screens flashing and changing instantaneously in the process.

"Well done. Now try to move up and then down," instructed Janus as he and Markus watched closely.

In response, Chad's battle sphere quickly moved vertically upwards about fifty feet, stopping short of the tree opening and returning to his original position.

"*Very good* Chad," smiled Janus. "Now try to move from side to side."

Chad thought about heading over to the side of the opening. As he did, his Battle Sphere darted sideways to the edge of the tree opening before coming to a stop once Chad realized he was out of room. Chad then reversed direction and zipped to the opposite edge of the tree grove before returning to his original position.

"Excellent Chad!" encouraged Janus. "One more thing. Circle the opening a few times."

On his mental command, Chad's Battle Sphere again proceeded to the edge of the opening and then whizzed around the perimeter several times going higher and higher. As he did, he clipped several branches with a series of loud cracks. Chad instinctively flinched as he hit the branches but to his surprise, he did not feel a thing. As he continued to race along the perimeter, the branches fell to the ground in bunches. Chad went higher and higher, then darted back down to his original position. Chad's nervousness was quickly replaced by relief and excitement as Janus smiled broadly.

"You are doing great my son. Under certain flight conditions, your Battle Hologram will direct and control your movements. However, you do have the ability to override the Hologram and go into what we call *free flight* by mere thought.

"Understood," replied Chad.

"Now I want you to wait —"

Before Janus could answer, Chad darted up through the tree opening and disappeared.

"The boy is a natural," Markus said.

Exiting the tree opening, Chad darted up into the sky as the sun reflected brightly off his new spin surface. To his left, he saw several tall buildings off in the distance in Coopers Falls. On his right, he noticed the mountain pass leading to Lake Edward. Far off in the distance, Chad could see the outlines of the green mountains of Vermont. Suddenly a small bird darted past him, dipping every so often. As Chad chased after it, his Sphere accelerated at a breathtaking pace. He passed the bird a few seconds later and watched with amusement as it dove down toward the ground with a startled squawk.

Chad accelerated as he reached the edge of the Davis Farm field before racing along just above the forest. He felt liberated from the constraints of gravity and free to fly wherever he wanted.

This is what it feels like to be a bird, smiled Chad.

The forest below gave way to another large field. Several black and white cows quietly grazed, tails wagging. As he raced by, Chad noticed a few bewildered cows looking up at him. Upon reaching the next forest grove, he curved back around to his left.

I better be careful not to let myself be seen by anybody, not yet anyway.

Chad slowed himself down as he dove toward the tops of the trees. He maneuvered effortlessly back and forth around the treetops, occasionally knocking down small branches along the way. As Chad approached the Davis Farm fields, he saw the familiar tree grove up ahead.

This is so awesome he thought.

Chad swooped down and raced just above the tall grass to minimize detection. Just before reaching the tree grove, he darted up toward the top of the opening, coming to a sudden stop at its center. He then slowly lowered his Battle Sphere down toward the ground and came to a stop, Chad saw Markus standing before him smiling broadly. Standing right next to Markus was Janus, his arms crossed, without even the slightest hint of a grin.

Uh-oh, thought Chad.

"Next time you decide to go for a ride, please let us know beforehand!" scolded Janus.

"Yes, Sir."

"Do you think anyone noticed you?"

"I don't think so. Well, maybe a few cows."

"Let's hope not," Janus said in a calmer voice. "As I started to say, wait patiently for a few minutes while I get us ready to go, OK?"

"OK, Janus," replied Chad as Janus walked over toward the Battle Hologram.

Janus noticed team Commander Mayla Tallis standing just inside the main entrance as he approached the structure. Mayla, who stood five feet eight inches tall, was athletic and exceedingly attractive. She had shoulder length dark brown hair, bronze complexion and charcoal colored eyes. She was surrounded by the same blue translucent haze as the hologram itself.

Stepping outside the Battle Hologram, Mayla glanced around in all directions as she tried to determine her location. She seemed confused.

"Hologram Team Commander Mayla Tallis," said Mayla as she studied Chad's Battle Sphere hovering over Janus's left shoulder some thirty feet away. She then noticed Markus's hologram and the two monitoring orbs.

"Hello Commander Tallis," replied Janus.

"May I ask who I am addressing?" asked Mayla cautiously.

"GDC Commander Janus Stone."

Mayla's eyes widened with surprise. "Janus Stone? *Global Commander Stone*?" she asked skeptically.

"Yes," nodded Janus.

"Excuse me Sir. But I do not understand why you are presenting yourself in hologram form. Nor do I understand why my system coordinates fail to register a location."

"I am in hologram form because my physical being no longer exists," explained Janus. "As to your second concern, your sensors do not register this place because you are over six hundred light years away from our planet."

"*Six hundred light years*? How is that possible?"

By now, Markus had made his way over to them.

"Mayla, this is Markus Kilmar. He is my second in command."

"Markus Kilmar? *The* Markus Kilmar?" asked Mayla. She knew Markus was one of the Battle Spheres that successfully defended Thrae from the Mitel Empire.

"Yes," replied Markus as he shot a glance toward Janus who stood expressionless.

"It is *truly* an honor to meet you," responded Mayla, nodding her head in respect.

Markus smiled weakly, again glancing awkwardly toward Janus, who continued to stare silently at Mayla.

"Why we are so far from Thrae?"

"Markus and I escaped our planet in an experimental pod which brought us to this planet. In order to escape, we had no choice but to transmit ourselves into the monitoring orbs you see behind us —"

"I'm confused. Why did you abandon our planet?"

"Unfortunately . . ." paused Janus as he searched for the right thing to say.

"Unfortunately, *what* Commander?" asked Mayla, now visibly confused.

"Our planet Thrae — it is no more."

Mayla's eyes opened wide before slowly welling up with tears.

"*That's impossible!*" she yelled. "You are lying! It cannot be true! I don't believe you!"

"I'm sorry Mayla. It's true. Thrae was destroyed in the second Mitel assault. One of our defense cruisers took a direct hit during takeoff and crashed into an unprotected base weapons storage facility. The magnitude of the ensuing explosion started a chain reaction fueled by the energy and weapons storage grid across the planet's surface. The rolling explosion wave destroyed all life on Thrae."

Mayla's face slowly turned from grief to anger.

"This is *your* fault! You and people like you!" she shouted. "You destroyed our planet!"

"*What?*" Janus replied defensively.

"I know *who* you really are!" She continued angrily. "My people, my ancestors, they told me about you! You are Chancellor Sejus Theron!"

Janus stepped back in surprise. He glanced at Markus who gave a slight nod signaling that Mayla be allowed to vent.

"It is *you* and *your kind* that destroyed Thrae!" Mayla shouted, tears running down her face. "You and all the other immortals — you thought you knew everything! You always felt that you knew what was best for our people and our planet! New discoveries, new break-throughs, each one a scientific *marvel* that was going to make life better for everyone — IM and Hybrid technology — touted by your kind as the greatest discoveries our race would ever see! They were going to *transform our world*!"

Mayla paused as she struggled to regain her composure. She turned and walked back toward the Battle Hologram before turning around to face Janus.

"But all these so-called breakthroughs ever really did was send our people down a path of destruction," lectured Mayla. "You and your kind never considered that potential outcome, until things got beyond your control. And now you're telling me it's all gone?"

Mayla wiped the tears from her eyes. Janus again glanced over at Markus, who quickly motioned for him to comfort her. Janus cautiously stepped forward and put his arms around Mayla's shoulders which sparkled brightly upon contact. To Janus's surprise, Mayla did not attempt to push him away.

"Team Commander Tallis, I understand that you are upset. You need time to grieve and fully process what I've told you. The loss of our planet was a horrible tragedy. We have all suffered an unimaginable loss," Janus said softly. "I know it will not be easy, but I need you and your crew to serve and protect this Battle Sphere. He is the last remaining immortal hybrid."

Mayla quickly stepped back from Janus, a flash of anger returning to her eyes.

"I don't care about the immortals or the hybrids. *Not* anymore," she replied firmly.

Janus paused to look over toward Chad's hovering Battle Sphere and then at Markus who remained expressionless.

"He is also the *last* living Thraen," said Janus before walking back toward Chad.

Mayla thought for a moment about what Janus just told her.

"What is your opinion on this Markus Kilmar?" she asked eventually.

"*My* opinion Commander Tallis? I think you are being too hard on him. Janus — I mean *Sejus Theron* — dedicated his life to improving the lives our planet's people. The loss of Thrae was *very* hard on him. He certainly did not choose to be born an immortal. The choices of our people were *their* choices. They certainly were not his alone."

"But *you* of all people," interrupted Mayla argumentatively. "How can *you* of all people, defend him?"

"What do you mean?" asked Markus defensively.

"You are *Markus Kilmar*."

"Yes, and?"

"You are one of the two immortal Battle Spheres that repelled the Mitels during the first invasion."

"I did help."

"Your bravery and skill are legendary. If it wasn't for you and the other Battle Sphere, the Mitels would have destroyed Thrae back then."

"Thank you Mayla, but I wasn't alone in saving Thrae."

"I don't understand how you can defend Chancellor Theron after all you have done for our world!"

Markus paused for a moment as he rubbed his chin.

"Commander Tallis," replied Markus quietly as his he looked intently at Mayla. "Where did you learn about these supposed things that Chancellor Theron did to our people?"

"As I said — from my ancestors. They passed down these accounts through generations of Thraen terminals. They wanted to make sure that we never forgot what really happened."

"I see. Are these the same ancestors who told you about me?"

"Well yes of course, but I don't —"

"And these ancestors, are they also the same ones who told you of the bravery of the other Battle Sphere who, I might add, did much more than I to save our planet from the Mitels during their first invasion?"

"You mean *Zebulon Park*?"

"Yes."

"My people certainly did not fail to give Zebulon Park the credit he deserves. Park was a selfless and brave Thraen who sacrificed his life to save our planet."

"Agreed Commander," smiled Markus, "except for the last part."

"I'm sorry but I don't understand."

"Commander, Sejus Theron was an immortal like me, correct?"

"Well yes, but I don't see how that changes anything."

"Would it make any difference to you if he was also known by another, more famous name?"

"Someone *more* famous than *Sejus Theron*?" asked Mayla skeptically.

"Yes."

"*Who then*?"

"Sejus Theron — *now* Janus Stone — is, or should I say *was* Zebulon Park."

Mayla was taken aback by this revelation.

"Yes Commander. Janus Stone, in one of several prior identities, was the *other* Thraen Battle Sphere that bravely defended our planet against the Mitels."

"But Zebulon Park *died*."

"No, he is in fact very much alive and standing right over there."

"Everyone said Zebulon Park was killed in battle."

"Bah! Bureaucratic revisionist history and nothing more," scoffed Markus. "He was badly injured, yes. But *killed* in battle? That did not happen."

"So, my ancestors were wrong?"

"Yes. About this and probably many other things."

"Why didn't he introduce himself or —"

"Or *defend* himself to you, Commander? That is not the essence of who he is. Janus loved our planet. He dedicated his entire life to Thrae. He didn't do it for praise or accolades. His satisfaction was derived from the happiness and success of our people. He bravely defended our planet and would have done so again if he was still able to transform."

Mayla listened to Markus as she watched Janus stand by Chad's hovering Battle Sphere. Chad sensed something was wrong.

"Is everything OK Janus?" he asked.

"I don't know," responded Janus with a sigh.

Mayla studied Markus's chiseled looks and long gray hair. She knew that he was very wise, sensitive and insightful.

"Why did he let it happen?" she asked quietly.

"Let *what* happen? You mean the destruction of Thrae?"

"Yes."

"I can assure you Commander Janus Stone did not *let it happen*. The destruction of our planet was set in motion a long time ago. We made a series of poor decisions culminating in the disaster the three of us barely escaped from. In my opinion the World Council underestimated the Mitels. After they terrorized our planet, we were too slow to respond. That only served to embolden their Leadership."

"What do you mean?"

"Well, after we neutralized the Mitel terror threat at home, we should have taken the fight to their planet and eliminated the threat once and for all. But we didn't and instead became an enabler."

"I see. But what about IM?"

"Yes that. While it was an incredible discovery, if we as a people had focused less energy on manipulating our physical being and instead, focused on enjoying the lives we were given, *maybe* things might have turned out differently."

"Are you convinced Janus Stone is not to blame?"

"Yes. As Janus Stone, Sejus Theron or Zebulon Park Commander, he suffered many personal tragedies including the death of his wife and two children. And yet, he continued to serve the people of Thrae in mostly unknown capacities. And what does he have left to show for his life of service? An unfair and undeserved legacy — and a dead planet, which he grieves for in silence every day. And *that* Commander Tallis is *my* opinion. Now if you will excuse me."

Markus walked slowly toward Janus.

"Markus," Mayla called out.

Markus stopped abruptly and turned to look back at her.

"Thank you," said Mayla softly. "I will give much thought to what you have told me."

"Good!" Markus said with satisfaction.

Janus stood silently as he was joined by Markus.

"What's wrong Janus?" asked Chad.

"Your Team Commander — she is understandably upset over the news that our home planet is gone."

"You told her just like *that*?"

"What else was I was supposed to do?" replied Janus defensively.

"OK, so you just introduced yourself and said *hi and oh by the way, our planet has been destroyed*," lectured Chad.

"Well, I —"

"Maybe you should have waited a little. You could have waited until the time was right to break the news."

"I guess maybe so."

"*Maybe*?"

"Alright Chad, I understand. You are right. I should have handled it differently. But I have always been honest and direct. That's my nature."

"I think I will go scout the perimeter," Markus told them, making his way toward the edge of the tree line. Chad and Janus paused and watched as Markus's orb weaved through the trees.

"Let me try talking to her," said Chad finally. "What's her name?"

"Team Commander Mayla Tallis." Janus walked toward Markus. Almost instinctively, Chad focused his thoughts on opening an encrypted communication link with the Battle Hologram.

"Hello?" said Chad.

"Battle Hologram communications, this is Teri" a male voice responded.

"Hi Teri. I'm the silver ball hovering in front of you."

"We figured that one out already," laughed Teri Anton, scanning and logistics specialist. Teri stood six feet five inches tall with wavy dirty blond hair and hazel eyes. He had a nose that was a bit large but still looked normal in proportion to his long face and wiry figure.

"*Very funny.* I need to speak with Team Commander Mayla Tallis."

"I can do that," replied Teri. "Let me locate her and patch her in."

Chad waited a moment or two in silence before receiving a response.

"Team Commander Tallis here."

"Hi Commander Tallis, this is Chad."

"I know."

"I want to apologize for my father. He can be very abrupt."

"There is no need to apologize on behalf of Commander Stone. Wait — *he is your father?*"

"Yes. He brought me here to Earth when I was a baby, as Thrae was destroyed. He's watched over me all these years."

"I see."

"He is convinced that the Mitel Fleet detected me during our escape from Thrae, and they will come here looking for me."

Mayla listened, but did not respond.

"Commander Tallis, I think Janus wants to save planet Earth from the Mitels if he can. I guess that is where we come in."

"What are our orders Commander?"

"Janus and I will begin target practice in the asteroid belt beyond Planet Mars of this solar system. Janus will give you the coordinates."

"We will commence your preflight weapons and system check," replied Mayla. "Please instruct Commander Stone to provide our team with travel coordinates and an anticipated flight plan. We should be ready to go soon after that."

"Thank you Commander Tallis."

"You are welcome," she answered before ending the communication transmission.

"Janus!" yelled Chad enthusiastically. "I think we are all set. Mayla asked for travel coordinates and flight information to the battle hologram. We need to get ready to go!"

"OK —"

"Oh, and by the way, when I was playing around with my audio feed, I overheard Markus say that you were also once a famous Battle Sphere named *Zebulon Park*? When were you planning on telling me about *that*?"

"I don't know. I didn't think it was all that important at this point —"

"Not important? Janus — it sounds like it was *hugely* important to the people of Thrae."

"I'm sorry Chad. Going forward, I'll try harder to explain *everything*."

"Thanks Dad," smiled Chad.

Janus terminated his hologram and quickly linked his orb's encrypted communication system to the Battle Hologram. He then proceeded to transmit both the predetermined course to the asteroid belt and the computer map of the entire solar system. His message was returned as confirmed. Janus then notified the Battle Hologram of his intent to accompany Chad's Battle Sphere. That message was also confirmed and returned with the exact position to locate his orb alongside the sphere just prior to takeoff.

Mayla reengaged communication between the three of them.

"Commanders, we have successfully completed all preflight diagnostics and we are ready to go. We are now entering active control status until further notice."

"Power levels are at full capacity," announced Teri. "We are ready to commence pre-flight sequence upon your command."

"OK, let's get started," replied Janus.

With a series of additional keystrokes, Teri sped up Chad's variable speed flywheel causing his Battle Sphere to spin faster and faster until the trees swayed. Chad tracked his rpm surge on the diagnostic mini-screen until it leveled off at one hundred twenty thousand.

Wow! he thought.

"Commander Stone, we are ready to begin the attachment procedure."

"Thank you Mayla . . . one moment please."

Janus glided his monitoring orb into position.

"OK, I'm ready," he confirmed as he inched his orb right next to Chad.

"Commencing synchronization," replied Teri.

Janus felt a slight jolt as the local magnetic field grabbed his orb and pulled it to within a hair of Chad's whirling outer spin surface.

"Synchronization complete," confirmed Teri.

"OK, great," said Mayla. "Since we plan to monitor you from this location, the last thing we'll need to do is attach a twelve pack to the Battle Sphere."

"*Twelve pack*?" asked Chad.

"It's a series of solar powered signal accelerators that allow for instantaneous communications and systems monitoring over very long distances," explained Janus. "Think of it as a series of mini cell towers . . . on steroids. We used them extensively for trade and travel routes back home."

"Cool."

Three technicians wheeled out the large module pack, before it was positioned by a modest antigravity beam and then synchronized to the back-side of Chad's Battle Sphere.

"Twelve pack in place and ready for automatic deployment," confirmed Teri.

"Activating outer shields in three, two, and one, *activation complete*," replied energy specialist Denton Millas.

Denton was energetic yet soft spoken and stood six feet four inches tall. He was muscular with gray eyes and light brown skin. His most distinctive features were his infectious smile, thick black eyebrows although the remainder of his head and face were void of any facial hair.

At that instant, Chad's Battle Sphere was engulfed by a blue opaque glow.

"Shields are fully operational," confirmed Denton, "and energy reserves at maximum."

"Commanders, we are ready for mission launch," added Mayla.

"Are you ready Chad?"

"I think so, Janus," he responded nervously.

"Now listen closely Chad. Your *all out* speed is *not* something you can jump in and out of easily. It is intended for longer range travel such as this. Your Battle Sphere moves fast enough under normal flight conditions."

"Got it."

"Launch sequence activated," confirmed Mayla.

"Takeoff in three, two, and one. *Launch*," said Teri.

Chad's Battle Sphere shot through the tree top opening, ripping away clumps of branches and leaves. Chad streaked through Earth's outer atmosphere in seconds. In the now silent tree grove, the Battle Hologram initiated monitoring its Battle Sphere's mission.

Standing alone Markus looked skyward as leaves and pine needles slowly drifted to the ground all around him.

"Way to go Chad," he said to himself.

CHAPTER FOURTEEN – TARGET PRACTICE

At the U.S. Naval Space Surveillance System Command headquarters, Corporal Keith Daniels noticed two intermittent radar blips on the screen. It appeared something small was traveling incredibly fast through Earth's atmosphere toward outer space. He tracked the object until it was fifteen thousand miles from Earth and beyond his tracking capabilities.

A quick computer analysis of the object's trajectory revealed that the signal originated in upstate New York at or near the base of the Adirondack Mountains. Corporal Daniels immediately texted his counterpart at NASA's Goldstone Observatory, located in California's Mojave Desert to see if she could pick up and track the object deeper into space. Corporal Daniels eventually received a response that the UFO had been located and tracked — disappearing from radar after about five minutes and almost five hundred thousand miles from Earth.

"Five hundred thousand miles in five minutes!" muttered a shaken Corporal Daniels. "What the hell was that?"

He immediately logged the information into the computer database for distribution to senior staff including Major Talbot

Under the watchful eye of his Hologram Matrix, Chad's Battle Sphere accelerated to its maximum cruising speed of 0.95X. Chad had slowly rotated his cylindrical core to gawk at the stars in every direction. At a 180-degree rotation, he watched as the Earth got smaller and smaller until it appeared as a bright star.

"How are you doing Chad?" asked Janus.

"Words really can't describe the beauty and sheer size of it all."

"Course adjustment in approximately one minute," Mayla reported from the Command Cube. Janus immediately compared the new directional coordinates against his monitoring orb's flight plan.

"Confirmed," he replied.

"Twelve pack boosters deploying on schedule and fully operational," noted Teri.

"Janus, what's next?" Chad asked.

"I will teach you how to override the Battle Hologram's flight programming with your thoughts Chad."

"You mean *free flight*."

"Yes. Your Battle Hologram will have limited ability to override your flight maneuvers if an imminent collision is detected. Think of it as walking briskly through a crowd of people who are moving in all different directions while being jostled by powerful wind gusts."

"OK, sounds a bit tricky."

"That's why we need to practice."

Chad would require a great deal of practice to learn how to operate in free flight under intense battle conditions. Chad also had to learn to trust his Battle Hologram team, which had complete control over the tracking, prioritization and destruction of one thousand targets at any given time.

Located just below the outer spin surface, the Battle Sphere's arsenal consisted of two hundred high energy laser cannons. Positioned in a grid pattern surrounding the sphere, each was capable of rotating through a series of five separate targets. The cannons fired through openings in Chad's shard mesh skin surface which represented the remnants of his porous skin cells. The sphere's permeable plasma outer defense shields, permeable from the inside out, allowed the passage of high energy bursts.

Each laser cannon emitted an incredibly destructive high energy plasma burst which on contact, immediately enveloped and destabilized the target's atomic structure, destroying it in seconds. In full battle mode, the sphere appeared as a tiny star emitting streams of bright white mini *stars* in all directions. The energy pulses curved as they exited the spinning orb before quickly straightening out and elongating as they raced toward their target.

A Battle Sphere could operate in full battle mode for approximately fifteen minutes before it became necessary to disengage, withdraw and reenergize. The recharging process could take anywhere from thirty to sixty minutes depending on how low the reserves had fallen. To recharge, the flywheel is disengaged causing the sphere to cease spinning until its internal energy reserves are adequately replenished. It is the Battle Hologram's sole responsibility to monitor a Battle Sphere's energy reserve levels. When the levels reach twenty percent, the Battle Hologram identifies and computes exit trajectories which must be executed before hitting ten percent reserve level, to ensure that the Battle Sphere can get to a safe location and reenergize.

In just over eight minutes, Chad's Battle Sphere streaked passed Mars and was closing in on the main asteroid belt.

"We're almost there. Mayla, should we initiate deceleration?"

"Implementing it now Commander."

"Chad. We will begin training in one of the asteroid pockets which your planet refers to as the *Trojans*. It is sparsely populated and should represent a good first exercise."

"Understood."

"Even at practice speed, they will be coming at us fast. As you become more proficient, I will teach you a trick or two of my own."

"Like what?"

"I developed a few maneuvers. My favorite I call the flip."

"What's that?"

"I used it when I was being closely pursued by a Mitel Fighter. I would do a 360-degree maneuver, instantly circling around behind the fighter."

"Cool!"

"Scanners detect the asteroid belt just ahead," said Teri.

"Alright Chad, we will pass through the main belt first," Janus explained. "Here we go — "

"Commander Tallis," interrupted Teri. "I've detected a broad and dense group of asteroids just ahead. Initiating target identification."

"Deactivate controlled deceleration," directed Mayla.

"There isn't time," said Cantor Tallon, propulsion specialist in his trademark deep voice.

Cantor, an extremely dedicated technician, stood a stocky five feet ten inches tall, with green eyes and pale complexion, long brown hair and matching beard.

Chad sensed urgency in Cantor's voice. Janus instructed his orb to perform a detailed scan of the immediate vicinity. To his dismay, it showed the grouping of asteroids bearing down on them.

"Chad, stay focused and let the Battle Hologram help us through this."

"Laser cannons energized and ready to go," announced Sami Larz, weapons coordinator. At a little over six feet tall, light brown complexion and short black hair, she always made sure all two hundred cannons operated flawlessly. Her father, a Mitel resistance officer had sought asylum on Thrae after the first invasion. Sami had signed up for the HPF on her sixteenth birthday, the first day of eligibility.

Chad scanned his mini-screens. Yellow dots with small identification labels appeared on several screens as his Battle Hologram identified and then tracked the approaching targets. Within seconds, the yellow dots on his screen multiplied, until they appeared as a swarm.

They seem to be everywhere Chad panicked and instinctively switched to free flight.

"He has taken over flight control!" blurted Teri.

"Combat stations everyone. Now!" ordered Mayla sharply.

"Chad, you must switch out of free flight *immediately*!" instructed Janus firmly.

"I don't know how!" replied Chad nervously as the asteroids raced by him.

Teri activated a thin band of high intensity search lights at the base of Chad's cylinders.

Chad immediately darted back and forth to avoid the approaching chunks of rock, metal and ice. Suddenly a huge asteroid appeared out of the darkness and he braced for impact. His Sphere shot a series of bright white energy bursts at the asteroid destroying it. The remaining debris deflected harmlessly off his translucent blue defense shields.

"*That was close!*" shouted Chad.

"Chad, focus!" ordered Janus.

"I'm *trying*," complained Chad as he continued to weave his way past the speeding objects. By now, the Battle Sphere's laser cannons were firing regularly. With each detonation, Chad's confidence in his Battle Hologram team increased. As he avoided one asteroid after another, his confidence in his own abilities also grew.

"You are performing extremely well, Chad."

"There are several thousand new targets approaching!" said Mayla abruptly.

"I register them too, Mayla," confirmed Janus.

"Command Cube, we are in combat mode until further notice!" directed Mayla.

As the second cluster bore down on his Battle Sphere, Chad's short-lived confidence evaporated. Sensing his panic, Janus ordered a quick scan of Chad's emotions.

"Chad, try to stay calm," said Janus. "Your Battle Hologram will quickly eliminate the targets."

As Chad's Battle Sphere converged with the enormous asteroid field, his 200 laser cannons fired rapidly in every direction. The light pulses curved away before streaking ahead to intercept the approaching metal, ice and rock. Seconds later, there were hundreds upon hundreds of bright white flashes as the approaching asteroids disintegrated. Chad weaved his way around the oncoming objects. But this time, he was being jerked in all directions as his Battle Hologram executed evasive maneuvers.

"You are doing an excellent job Chad. Keep it up!" encouraged Janus.

A quick glance at his mini-screens told Chad that the asteroid belt was thinning out considerably.

"Hey Janus, I think we made it. I can see — "

A huge dark chunk appeared out of the darkness. Janus's monitoring orb detected the large object just before impact.

"Chad! *Look out!*" yelled Janus.

But it was too late. The asteroid shattered on impact with his Battle Sphere, wrenching Janus's monitoring orb from the sphere.

"*Nooooo!*" shouted Chad.

He watched helplessly as his father's orb disappeared into the black abyss. Chad's weakened defense shield flickered before stabilizing a much lighter translucent blue color. Chad ignored his screen displays as he darted after Janus.

"Chad! What are you doing?" asked Teri while Battle Hologram technicians scrambled to detect and reprioritize the remaining targets.

Seconds later, a second, much smaller asteroid slammed into Chad's Battle Sphere, knocking him unconscious. The sphere stopped spinning and powered down. As a few remaining asteroids raced by, Chad's Battle Sphere disappeared into the darkness.

Standing in the forest opening, Markus noticed the increased activity in the Battle Hologram. He heard muffled shouts as Hologram technicians scrambled between cubes to various computers and monitoring equipment.

This is not good. Not good at all he concluded as he made his way toward the Battle Hologram's main entrance, followed silently by his orb. Mayla greeted him at the doorway.

"Is everything OK commander?"

"*No*. There has been an accident and we have lost contact with *both* Commander Stone and Chad."

"What?"

"We unexpectedly encountered two huge asteroid fields. Chad was struck twice. Janus's monitoring orb was separated from Chad during the first impact. We lost all contact with Chad after the second collision."

"Can you make contact with Janus?"

"No.

"What went wrong?" he asked calmly.

"Chad panicked and switched to free flight. That set in motion a chaotic training exercise which ended badly."

"I see."

"They almost made it through. Chad was exceptional. He dodged a significant number of targets. The Battle Hologram weapons specialists destroyed the rest — except the last two."

"What do you know about their condition or whereabouts?" asked Markus.

"We are tracking Chad's Battle Sphere. He is still functional, but is drifting and unresponsive. His defense shield is also down. We are trying to assess the damage."

"What about Janus?

Mayla paused before answering. "We don't know. We are scanning the area, but there are so many small objects in proximity to his monitoring orb."

Mayla's eyes began to well up with tears.

"It's *my* fault!" she blurted out as she struggled to control her emotions.

"Commander Tallis," replied Markus gently. "It was Chad's first time out. He was in over his head and panicked. That is not your fault."

"But it is my job to anticipate such things, and now Janus is likely lost forever."

"It sounds like you performed your duties admirably. Listen. Janus was aware of the risks. He chose to go out with Chad."

"Markus, I am sorry for my conduct earlier. It's just that everyone in the Battle Hologram pledged their *lives* to protect our planet and support all Thraen hybrids until the end of time. And now the planet is gone. Everything is gone."

"Everything is *not* gone Commander. You still have a Battle Sphere to support and an immensely talented team to supervise. As a matter of fact, I think you are going to find that you have a new planet to serve and protect."

"You mean *Earth*?"

"Indeed. For the fifteen plus years Janus and I have been here, I've realized that even the name itself is more than a coincidence."

"And what is the basis of your conclusion?"

Markus paused to look up at the trees through the translucent ceilings of the Battle Hologram.

"*I* think this planet in many ways represents what our planet was in its technological infancy. They are starting to discover the incredible possibilities that advancing technology can offer. Maybe somehow, someway we can help guide this planet and its inhabitants down the right path and *maybe*, help prevent the same mistakes we made on Thrae."

"I will give that some thought."

"I sincerely hope that you do Commander. In the meantime, I will let you get back to your duties."

"Yes, I should get back."

Markus followed Mayla into the Battle Hologram, up two flights of stairs to the uppermost level which housed the Diagnostics, Tracking, and Command Cubes. He stopped at the Command Cube entrance and immediately sensed the team's determination. Mayla continued around a large square translucent table toward Teri before stopping and looking back toward Markus.

"Markus."

"Yes Commander?"

"Thank you for your wise counsel."

"It's my pleasure. May I continue to watch? I promise to stay out of the way."

"Of course."

"Good then," Markus smiled as he stepped to the side to observe in silence.

Chad awoke in deep space to the sight of countless stars around him.

Where am I? He thought before his translucent diagnostic mini-screens caught his attention. As his Battle Sphere got back up to full spinning speed, it all came rushing back to him.

Janus! I need to find Janus!

Chad re-engaged communications with his Battle Hologram.

"Hello. This is Chad. Can anyone hear me?"

"Chad, Teri here. It's a relief to hear your voice. We are processing a series of diagnostic tests on your Battle Sphere,"

"Spin and propulsion systems appear to be fully operational," said Cantor. "We are running additional diagnostics just to be sure."

Mayla scanned the Command Cube monitors. Based on her experience, the data suggested that Chad's Battle Sphere was fully functional.

"We are confirmed," said Cantor, "all propulsion readings normal."

"Other than the shields still being non-operational, diagnostics teams report that everything is OK," announced Teri with a sigh of relief.

"Thank goodness," whispered Markus.

"Teri, has anyone heard from Janus?" Chad asked anxiously.

"Nothing yet, Chad."

"I *must* find him!"

Markus quietly moved closer to Teri's programming station until he was standing next to Mayla. From across the cube, Denton gave Mayla the thumbs down.

"Commander," said Mayla. "Your plasma defense shields are still not operational. You are in serious danger until we can bring them back on line."

"I need to find Janus. I am not coming back without him. And besides, I can't fly through Earth's outer atmosphere without the shields."

"Understood, but as Teri explained, we have not located Commander Stone's monitoring orb, and we cannot make contact with him."

"Then I will start looking for him."

Mayla glanced at Teri and then toward Markus who shrugged his shoulders and nodded that is was probably best that Chad continue his search.

"Affirmative," replied Mayla reluctantly. "In the meantime, we will make every effort to bring your shields back on line."

Chad maneuvered toward the last known coordinates of Janus's orb. As Chad moved slowly through the darkness, Teri reactivated the search lights on Chad's cylinders.

"This should help you a little."

"Thanks Teri."

"Be careful."

Chad inched forward looking for a sign of Janus's small monitoring orb. His mini-screens detected countless debris, remnants of the asteroids from the training exercise.

How will I find him?

Chad feverishly searched for Janus. One hour turned into two and then three. Chad feared the worst — *Janus was lost forever*. Suddenly, a blue glow appeared. In the Battle Hologram, Denton slapped his hands together.

"Plasma defense shields are back on line!"

Denton noticed that the Sphere's energy levels had fallen to twenty five percent. He removed his headset and looked across the command center at Mayla.

"Commander Tallis, Chad's energy levels have dropped to the return voyage threshold," he announced.

"Thank you, Denton," Mayla said as she glanced at Teri.

As their eyes met, they knew the time had come for Chad to abandon his search. After a long pause, Mayla got up the courage to relay the bad news to Chad.

"Commander."

"I heard him," Chad bristled, before seeing a tiny metallic reflection off in the distance.

"Wait a second. *I think I see something!*" he shouted.

Chad raced toward the source of the reflection. As he closed in, he saw the familiar black striped markings on Janus's silver monitoring orb.

"I found him!"

A cheer came from within the Battle Hologram.

"Janus. Janus! Can you hear me?" asked Chad.

There was no answer. Janus's orb was badly dented.

Oh no! What if? he thought, before pushing the negative ideas from his mind. *I've got to get him back home. Markus and Mayla will know what to do.*

"Chad, get close enough so we can reattach the monitoring orb," Teri instructed.

Chad inched has battle sphere closer to allow the Battle Hologram to once again synchronize Janus's monitoring orb with his sphere.

"Janus is not responding. His orb is damaged."

"Understood," Mayla responded. "We will get the two of you back here as soon as possible."

"We have programmed your return at full speed," added Teri. "And Chad?"

"What?"

"You need to stay calm."

Under full control of the Battle Hologram, Chad's Sphere raced past Mars and fifteen minutes later was approaching the Moon.

"Initiate controlled deceleration," instructed Mayla.

"Doing it now," replied Cantor.

"Commencing reentry," announced Teri.

Approaching the outer atmosphere, Chad's Battle Sphere decelerated further to Mach 22. After sliding through Earth's outer atmosphere, he raced through the fluffy cirrocumulus clouds toward Earth. Off to Chad's right, the curving view of the blue expanse of the Gulf of Mexico and the Atlantic Ocean was breathtaking.

At the United States Naval Space Surveillance System Command headquarters, Corporal Keith Daniels again noticed intermittent blips on his screen. Something small was again traveling very fast through the Earth's atmosphere. He tracked the signal as it descended across the continental United States heading west to east. Corporal Daniels lost the signal over Upstate New York.

"Damn it!"

Minutes later, he received an email from his counterpart at NASA's Goldstone Observatory confirming that she had again located and tracked a UFO from deep space which exhibited the same direction and velocity profile of the earlier event, *only in reverse*. Her email also indicated that the signal was lost at 70,000 feet and ended with the words: VERY STRANGE.

Corporal Daniels entered this latest information into the database for distribution to senior staff including Major Talbot.

In the Command Cube, the technicians prepared for Chad's landing.

"Initiating arrival sequence," instructed Cantor. The Battle Sphere was now rapidly descending.

Chad saw the Empire State Building and then the Hudson River. As the Battle Sphere decelerated moving north up the Hudson River, Chad recognized downtown Albany, then the racetrack at Saratoga Springs, and finally Coopers Falls.

The whirling Battle Sphere slowed to a stop above the opening in the field on Davis Farm and hovered briefly before descending through the trees. Markus, Teri, Mayla and Denton were waiting outside the Battle Hologram to greet him.

Chad's Battle Sphere stopped just above the forest floor. He watched his mini-screen track the deceleration of his spin surface down to 0 rpm before his translucent blue plasma energy shield dissipated.

Markus, Teri and Denton rushed to Chad's hovering Battle Sphere as Janus's damaged monitoring orb was desynchronized and released. Teri and Denton gently accepted the orb and brought it to Mayla to study.

"It is clearly damaged," Teri said as the Hologram team huddled around the orb for a closer look. In one location, the silver outer skin had been torn away revealing its inner circuitry. Teri glanced over at Mayla who was silent as she studied the orb.

"What do you think Commander Tallis?" Markus said eventually.

"It's suffered blunt force trauma. We need to run extensive testing on the inner components and circuitry to ascertain the full extent of the damage and to see whether," her voice trailing off.

"Whether what?"

"Whether it can be repaired. Denton, take it to the large Diagnostic Cube for evaluation."

"But, Commander, how will we get it into the Battle Hologram. I thought only Holograms can enter the Matrix."

"Janus is also a hologram. He is merely *encased* in the orb."

"It's certainly worth a try," nodded Teri in agreement.

The group followed Teri and Denton toward the entrance. Markus stayed behind with Chad. Janus's orb was permitted entrance into the Battle Hologram without any resistance from the translucent structure.

"How are you Chad?"

"Tired."

"Of course you are. I'm guessing you want to change back to human form as soon as possible."

"That would be great."

"OK then. Relax. Think of something soothing like crawling into bed after a long, hard day."

Chad closed his eyes and took a deep breath. He tried to relax as he focused on reversing his transformation process. He felt a warm sensation envelop his body. Within seconds, large amounts of trace elements exited his silver sphere from all directions. They swirled around his orb, passed through Markus's hologram before exiting the tree grove. Chad's support structure and system architecture instantaneously reverted to its prior human form while his magnetic field dissipated the last of the trace elements and helium-4 back into the surrounding atmosphere.

Chad's silver skin retracted to reveal a silver-colored human appearance inside the blue translucent bubble. He slowly glided to the ground and stared at Markus through his metallic silver eyes.

"Um, Markus . . ." said Chad, who was now all silver and completely naked.

"*Oops*, my boy, I know just what to do!" muttered Markus as his orb immediately streaked across the opening and into the trees. It quickly reappeared with Chad's spare clothes. By now, Chad was back to his normal self.

"Here you go lad. I put your tattered clothing in your backpack already."

"Thanks." Chad hastily got dressed.

They walked over to the Battle Hologram entrance.

"Sorry Chad, you will have to wait outside," Markus said as he entered.

"*What*?"

"Only holograms may enter the Battle Hologram."

"But Markus, I need to see him."

"I'm sorry Chad but —"

"What seems to be the problem?" interrupted Mayla as she approached the entrance.

"It's Chad, he wants to come in."

"So, what is the problem?"

"I've explained to Chad that only holograms may access the Battle Hologram."

"Chad is the *one* exception. The hybrid that the Battle Hologram serves and protects may of course enter," Mayla said with a hint of a grin.

"But of course," smiled Markus. "It has been so long, I have forgotten."

Chad smiled broadly and gave Markus the thumbs up.

"Follow me," instructed Mayla.

Chad glanced into each cube as he walked down the main hallway. Computers, monitors, scanners, testing and other equipment were everywhere. To his surprise, everything inside the Battle Hologram had the same bright translucent haze. Markus headed up the stairs to the Command Cube.

"Over here Commander," motioned Mayla from down the hall.

There were five hologram technicians hunched over Janus's monitoring orb. They had removed the front and side panels and attached diagnostic cables to the inner components.

"Commander, this is our large Diagnostics Cube," said Mayla softly.

"What are they doing?" whispered Chad.

"They are trying to determine the extent of the damage to Commander Stone's propulsion, processing and memory circuitry."

Chad and Mayla watched the technicians meticulously move the diagnostic cables from one component to the other in the orb. At each location, they paused to observe the output readings.

"Is Janus going to be OK?" he asked weakly.

"We don't know yet Commander. It will take some time to assess the damage."

Teri quietly joined them.

"Commander," said Mayla, "the analysis is going to take some time. Might I suggest that you wait with Teri? We will tell you as soon as we know something."

"OK Mayla." Chad glanced at his father's damaged orb once more before following Teri to his cube on the second level.

"This is my home," said Teri as they entered.

There were four separate scanning devices and three large computers. Several holographic picture images of friends and loved ones were displayed around the cube. As Chad looked closer, he noticed a holographic picture of a beautiful young girl about his age on the wall. As Chad approached, the hologram the girl smiled.

"Hi, I'm Chondra, who are you?" asked the hologram.

"Um, hi — I'm Chad."

"Hi Chad, it is a pleasure to meet you."

"That is — or was, my younger sister back on Thrae."

"Oh, I'm sorry."

"That's OK, Chad. I have been in the Hologram Protective Force for almost eight hundred years. My family died a long time ago."

"But you must still miss them and think about them even after all that time."

"Yes, sometimes I do. And with the holographic pictures I can still talk to my family — sort of anyway."

"Hey Teri," said Chondra "He's *really* cute."

"Behave yourself sis, he's my boss!"

"Sorry!" Chondra frowned. With that, her hologram returned to picture mode.

"The pictures contain computerized personality algorithms of my family," explained Teri. "When you join the Hologram Protective Force, each family member creates their own profile."

Chad turned back toward Teri who was now looking at one of his computer screens.

"You have been in the protective force *how long*?" he asked.

"A little over eight hundred Earth years."

"That's a *long* time."

"No not really. When you enter the Hologram Protective Force and serve hybrid immortals, time becomes relative."

"I guess it must."

They stood in silence for a moment as Chad continued to look around.

"Chad?"

"What?"

"I served your father's Battle Sphere. I mean up until the time he was badly damaged during the first war with the Mitels. I've been transferred around a few times since then, but my specialty is serving Battle Spheres. That's why I'm here with you now."

Chad stopped looking around and listened closely.

"Your father is a very good person. He cared for Thrae about as much as anyone could care for anything."

"I guess he did."

"But after the war ended, he was blamed for many things that were not his fault."

"Why was *he* blamed?"

"I don't know for sure. I guess it was easy to blame someone who did not promote himself or defend himself against his critics. Your father did not like to boast. Eventually he just went away. The rumor was he had died or taken his own life. But I was certain he was out there somewhere, still doing what he loves to do."

"And that is?"

"Improving our plant and pushing our people in new directions."

"That's what I've been hearing."

"Not everyone shares my sentiment. Take for instance, Commander Tallis. She is a fine commander, but I think she, like most of our people, believe your father helped push our race down a path of destruction."

"I don't understand. If that's the case, why is she serving in the Protective Force?"

"Because of her intense love for Thrae and our people."

"But I guess it's all gone now. I'm truly sorry, Teri."

"It is not your fault Chad. It is also not your father's fault. The Mitels are a wicked, hateful race. We found out too late about their true intentions, I guess."

"I guess so too. Hey wait, what time is it?" blurted Chad realizing that he was very late for dinner.

"Its 6:30 p.m.

"*Oh crap*! I have got to get home!"

"Then let's go."

Chad and Teri rushed to the Diagnostics Cube where Mayla met them at the entrance.

"Commander, I was about to come look for you."

"Is there any update on Janus's condition?" Chad asked, stopping abruptly.

"The tests are ongoing, but so far anyway, our scans have detected no significant damage to Commander Stone's orb."

"Great! And Mayla, I really appreciate everything you're doing."

Mayla nodded and smiled weakly.

"I really want to stay here with Janus, but I've got to get home before my mother comes looking for me. I should have been home from work an hour ago!"

"From *work*?" asked Teri with a raised eyebrow.

"Uh, well, it's a long story," smiled Chad. "Actually, I'm surprised she hasn't tried to call my cell phone."

"Your communications devices will not work in here," said Teri.

"Why not?"

"Because when you are in here, you aren't anywhere, actually."

"Oh, that's *not* good. My mom will be worried."

Markus walked down the stairs.

"Hey Markus. I've got to get home. I'm really late. Would you please keep an eye on Janus for me?"

"Will do."

Teri followed Chad to the battle hologram entrance.

"Hey listen, Teri. Thanks for everything."

"My pleasure Chad," grinned Teri as the two of them shook hands. "I meant what I said about Commander Stone."

Chad turned and ran across the clearing toward the trees and the open field beyond.

"Be *careful* riding home!" laughed Teri.

"*Ha ha!*" Chad joked as he disappeared into the trees.

In the Battle Hologram's large Diagnostic Cube, Mayla personally conducted the diagnostic scans and testing of the damaged orb. After several hours, she met with her team to draft a repair and re-assembly plan. The following day, as Mayla watched, the Hologram technicians restored Janus's orb. Seconds after being powered up, a beam of light projected from the orb to the floor causing Janus's three-dimensional hologram image to appear. Janus looked around the room, struggling to get his bearings.

"Welcome back Commander Stone," smiled Mayla.

"Hello Mayla. I am not sure I understand what's going on."

"Not surprising, Sir. You were in a serious accident during the training mission. Your orb was damaged and powered down."

"Where's Chad?"

"He is fine. He's at home. I will send Markus to notify him that you're fine. He has been very worried about you."

Mayla paused before letting out a big sigh.

"As a matter of fact, we've all been very worried about you. It took quite a bit of work. But other than a few remaining scratches and dents to your exterior surface, your monitoring orb is back to its former operating condition. Unfortunately, we couldn't eliminate your occasional distortion pattern. These technicians worked tirelessly to restore your orb."

"I cannot thank you enough, gentlemen. I hope that I can someday make it up to you."

"It was our pleasure Sir," the technicians responded in unison before exiting the cube.

"How are you feeling Commander?" asked Mayla.

"A little dazed. But otherwise OK."

"You may not recall, but Chad refused to leave the asteroid belt until he located you. His plasma defense shields were not functioning after the asteroid strike."

"That was a foolish decision on his part. It could have imperiled the entire mission!"

"I guess he is stubborn."

"Well maybe."

"Like his father perhaps?"

"Who suggested that?"

"I am sure you can guess."

"Markus . . ."

"You are correct Commander."

Mayla stepped toward Janus and looked at him intently.

"Commander, I —"

"You can call me Janus."

"Janus. I realize now that I was wrong about you. For that, I am ashamed. I would like to apologize to you."

"*Oh?*"

"Yes. I've come to realize that I should not have listened to what others were saying about your character and dedication to our planet. From what I have personally observed, you are nothing like how you've been portrayed."

"*Well*, you are not the first Thraen to have heard things about me that were — let's just say — a little off the mark. But it makes little difference now. Thrae is gone."

Mayla slowly reached her hand out to Janus. He paused for a moment before taking it. Mayla squeezed his hand and smiled.

"Janus?"

"Yes?"

"You and Markus are right."

"About what, Mayla?"

"We still have a mission. We must protect and defend the Battle Sphere."

She is so beautiful he thought as he looked at her.

"And, after a meeting with my crew last night, we all agree that we have a *new* planet to protect and defend: Earth.

Janus hugged Mayla. As they came together, the cube was drenched in a bright sparkling white light. Janus pulled away looking awkwardly at Mayla.

"Mayla, I —"

"There's no need to apologize, Janus. I enjoyed the hug."

Janus smiled and took her hand again.

"Thank you Mayla."

"But now, we have work to do. We must prepare for the upcoming training missions. We need to simulate as many of the Mitel attack formations as possible with Chad."

"Agreed."

"Good. I recommend we meet with the battle operations team as soon as you feel up to it."

"How about now?"

"That sounds good to me."

"Teri?" said Mayla into the intercom.

"Yes commander?"

"Please call a team meeting immediately to discuss the next phase of Chad's Battle Sphere training."

"Will do."

Janus followed Mayla out of the large Diagnostics Cube and walked with her slowly down the hall.

Markus watched them exit the Diagnostics Cube and walk together down the hall. He smiled in approval, before heading down the stairs and out the front entrance of the Battle Hologram. Once outside, Markus quickly terminated his hologram and returned to his monitoring orb before racing up through the tree grove opening and out into the fields in the direction of Chad's house. When he arrived, Markus hovered outside Chad's bedroom window, hidden from view of the street by the large oak tree. Markus saw Chad sitting at his desk, trying to concentrate on homework.

Chad's face lit up when he realized that Markus's silver and blue monitoring orb was floating outside his window. He jumped up from his desk and lunged toward his window. Chad fumbled with the lock before pulling up the bottom half of the wooden double hung window.

"Hi Markus," whispered Chad excitedly.

He glanced quickly up and down the street to make sure nobody else was around. Satisfied, he looked back at Markus' orb which by now contained his smiling face on the screen.

"Hello lad," said Markus. "I've come to let you know Janus is better."

"What a relief. I was worried sick about him."

"We were all worried my boy."

"Where is he now?"

"In the Battle Hologram Command Cube. He and Mayla were already meeting with the team to plan your next training missions."

"He never stops, does he?"

"He sure doesn't. Maybe someday, but I wouldn't bet on it."

"Thanks for letting me know Markus. Maybe now I can concentrate on my homework."

"My pleasure lad. Listen. What you did out there was very brave. You should be very proud of yourself."

"Thanks, Markus."

"Chad, I brought you up some snacks," Molly said from the other side of the door.

"That is my cue to get going. See you soon!"

Markus's orb darted away as Molly entered.

CHAPTER FIFTEEN – COMPLICATIONS

Zan stepped out of the HorVert elevator and made his way down the corridor to check on Ard. The fracture to his hand was worse than expected. Luckily, the regenerative bone brace was healing the damage ahead of schedule. Zan entered his ID number into the keypad. Ard sat at his desk, staring at his computer screen as the doors opened and Zan entered.

"Hello, Ard. What are you looking at if you don't mind my asking?"

"Oh, nothing really. I'm just doing a little research."

"A little research? Now I'm really curious," asked Zan as he flopped into the spare console chair across the room.

"I'm reading about the history of Thrae. It's a hobby of mine.

"I didn't know you had such an interest in the Thraen civilization."

"I have ever since I was a boy, actually. Not sure why but perhaps it's because my step father talked about Thrae so much. I can still picture the anger in his eyes every time he did."

"Why was he so angry?"

"Jealousy perhaps?"

"Could very well be. In the end, the Mitel Leadership got the better of that rivalry."

"Maybe."

"*Maybe*? You can't be serious."

"I'm not talking about the military conflicts," Ard frowned. "That part is obvious."

"Then what?"

"I'm talking about the paths each world took. Thrae was a free and open society that fostered an atmosphere of innovation. Their leaders were principled people. They possessed a genuine desire to reach out to other worlds — such as ours. And what did they find?"

"Please tell me," Zan smiled in amusement.

"They found the opposite: a repressive, unimaginative and tightly controlled society. In retrospect, I don't think the Thraens knew what they were getting into and by the time they did, it was too late."

"Maybe so. But you should be very careful who you express that opinion to."

"I know," Ard sighed. "But do you think it's too late?"

"Too late for what?"

"For our people. You know, to be free."

"I don't know."

The two sat in silence for a few minutes.

"What is the latest on the resistance?" asked Ard eventually.

"Things seem to have quieted down. At least for now.

"Hey! Did you hear who the commander is for Cruiser Number 2?"

"No, but I have a feeling you are about to tell me."

"Lon Rexx. Can you believe it? I mean that guy is absolutely insane, even for a Mitel warrior."

Zan did not respond.

"I remember him back at the Academy. His life revolved around CCCF. I mean he was obsessed. He killed a bunch of guys in the Cage. I think he retired undefeated."

"No, he didn't."

"And how would *you* know?"

"Because I beat him."

Ard was speechless.

"After our match, he was permanently barred from competition for cheating. He had killed his opponents by stuffing the end of his club with iron pellets."

Zan paused.

"That's all in the past. But, yes, I agree. He is crazy. Gen Zandt, the junior member of the Mitel Leadership is accompanying him as an observer along with six bodyguards. Hopefully he will keep Rexx in line."

"*Wow*! You *beat* Lon Rexx at CCCF. Now that's pretty impressive!"

Ard then turned serious.

"He has always been violent. I heard he *personally* executed all of the resistance fighters captured on his cruiser."

"That doesn't surprise me," grunted Zan. "The resistance appears to have infiltrated the entire fleet."

"I take it you don't think we've located all of them."

"Only time will tell. But no, I don't."

"Why does that answer not make me feel so good?"

"Maybe because we are out in the middle of nowhere trying to defend ourselves against an enemy we can't see."

"Yeah, that sounds about right. Hey, speaking of *enemies we can't see*, have you been studying the mission plan?"

"I have."

"And what do you think?"

"We have to capture the young Battle Sphere. I was thinking that we could — "

"That's not the part I am talking about."

"OK, then, what part *are* you talking about?"

"The part where we use cluster pods on the largest population centers to intimidate their civilization into handing over the young Thraen."

"Oh that. I discussed it with the Leadership before we departed."

"How did that go?"

"About as good as any conversation with the Mitel Leadership can be expected to go. They obviously want the Thraen at any cost."

"I get that. But unleashing the cluster pods on countless innocents? What does that make *us* Zan?"

"Mass murderers. But what alternative do we have? If we don't carry out our orders, we will be killed."

"Should we kill countless millions of innocent men, women and children to save ourselves?"

"Of course not," replied Zan his voice trailing off. "It's just that . . ."

"It's just *what*?"

Zan paused to look around the room.

"What am I supposed to do? Join the Mitel resistance? The Thraen resistance?"

"I'm not *asking* you to do anything Zan," Ard began. "I just think that at some point during our lives, we must confront who we really are and what we're doing. And if we're truly being honest, maybe we can somehow find the courage to do what's right."

"You make it sound easy."

"Zan, I never said it was easy. I'm saying that just because the choices are hard doesn't mean we shouldn't make them."

"You are probably right. Now if you will excuse me."

Zan was tired and out of sorts, so he headed to his own quarters to rest. He notified the ICC via the wall intercom that he was not to be disturbed for the next several hours unless it was an absolute emergency. As the doors slid open to his darkened quarters, Zan flopped onto his bed and let out a long sigh. A few minutes later, he heard a noise from across the room. Looking up, he saw Lia Saar, the ship's communications specialist, seated in his desk chair. Zan had noticed her the very first time she set foot on the ICC. Standing a little over six feet tall with long curly brown hair and pale green eyes, Lia was stunningly beautiful.

"How did you get in here?"

"My friends let me in," smiled Lia.

"Your *friends*?"

"I think you refer to them as the Mitel resistance," Lia grinned sarcastically. "Oh, and before I forget, your uncle Zi says hello."

Zan nodded in amusement.

"What do you want?"

"That depends on what Emperor *Zan Liss* decides to do going forward."

Zan did not answer.

"You should know that there are a few very powerful devices hidden on this cruiser. If you try to locate them or tell anyone else, we will activate them."

"Why haven't you done so already?" asked Zan indignantly. "For that matter, why haven't you wiped out our whole fleet already?"

"We could have," smiled Lia confidently. "But for now, we decided to cull it down to a slightly more manageable size. At least for the time being."

"I see."

"It took us a very long time," Lia began, her voice growing determined. "But we finally infiltrated the Mitel military enough to affect certain outcomes. During that long and difficult process, we were forced to look the other way while your Leadership brutally butchered our people. But now, here we are."

"Yes indeed. Here you are," Zan mused. "That phrase sounds oddly familiar."

"Why do you think your Leadership sent you on such a high stakes mission?" asked Lia directly.

"I have a feeling you're going to tell me."

"It's because they know that we are now a serious threat. The Mitel Leadership knows that it's only a matter of time before the Mitel resistance challenges them directly and when we do, we will free our people once and for all."

"OK," nodded Zan. "But that still doesn't explain why you're here."

"They sent you to capture the young Thraen Battle Sphere, correct?"

"Correct."

"And bring him back to Mitel to crush the resistance."

"Yes," nodded Zan.

"We obviously cannot allow that to happen," smiled Lia.

"Understood," replied Zan. "I will ask again: why haven't you wiped out the entire fleet by now?"

"As I said earlier, that depends."

"On?"

"On what Emperor *Zan Liss* decides to do."

"Why does *everything* depend on *me*? Look. If I don't carry out my mission, I face certain death at the hands of the Mitel Leadership. I don't have a lot of options."

Lia quickly approached Zan. She stopped right in front of him and rubbed his cheek gently.

"I like you Zan. Very much. I think you have the potential to do great things."

"That's what people keep telling me."

"Maybe you should listen to them."

Zan stared into her eyes. Lia abruptly headed for the door.

"Zi has told me many times that things have a way of working out," she said. "I have not always believed him, but we shall see if he is right in this case. In the meantime, I offer you a warning. If you value your own life and the life of your dear friend Ard Lindar, you will keep this conversation to yourself. Understood?"

"Completely," nodded Zan.

"Oh, and one last thing. It is not just your Mitel Leadership and the resistance that should concern you."

"Who else is there?"

"The Mitel military. If any of those devoted subordinates find out that you have been in communication with the resistance, they will kill you without hesitation."

"Understood."

Zan watched the doors slide closed behind Lia. With a huge sigh, he fell back on his bed and slept for several hours. When he awoke, he took a long shower, got dressed and headed for the ICC. Exiting the HorVert elevator, Zan immediately saw Ard standing next to the command console.

"Commander Lindar," smiled Zan. "It is good to see you up and about."

"Thank you, Emperor Liss," Ard grinned. "I heard you took a well-deserved rest."

"I did indeed. What news do you have for me?"

Zan flopped into the console chair.

"The fleet is making excellent progress. But we still have a long way to go."

"Understood."

Lia approached the command console from her communications station carrying an encrypted communications tablet.

"Excuse me, Emperor Liss," she said. "I have received a series of transmission logs from the rest of the fleet during your absence."

Zan looked intently at Lia.

"My Emperor?" she asked blankly. "Is something wrong?"

Zan studied her face as she handed him a tablet. There was no hint in her expression to indicate they had spoken several hours earlier.

"No. Thank you, Lia."

Lia returned to her communications station.

"What was that all about?" whispered Ard.

Zan paused to glance over at Lia before responding.

"Oh nothing. I just had a bad dream."

CHAPTER SIXTEEN – MORE PRACTICE

Chad and Janus traveled to the asteroid belt every Saturday and Sunday for a month, practicing evasive flight maneuvers, target drills, recharging and energy reserve management. Chad practiced the flip maneuver around several asteroids until he mastered it. Chad also studied late into the night during the week to avoid falling behind in school.

Molly was becoming suspicious after finding Chad's clothes nearly shredded to threads. So, Chad started disrobing down to his boxers before transforming into his Battle Sphere. After each transformation, Chad would simply toss the torn underwear into a trash can on his way home. When Molly asked what was happening to all of his underwear, Chad simply shrugged and said they must be going to the same place the missing socks disappear to.

Before each training mission, Chad met with his Battle Hologram team to discuss combat strategy and flight maneuvers. Afterwards, Chad, Janus, Mayla, Teri, Denton, Sami and several weapons specialists reviewed the day's activities. Chad's successes were reinforced and his mistakes were broken down and discussed further. The goal: to make Chad a *flawless* fighting machine.

Each week the Battle Hologram team painstakingly searched the asteroid belt for pockets resembling the three known Mitel Fighter attack patterns. The most common of the three is the *wave* pattern. Mitel Fighters launch their attack in a series of clusters designed to overrun and overwhelm their adversary. The second attack pattern, known as the modified wave, bypasses the target to search and destroy the target's supporting technology behind the attack zone. The remaining waves of Mitel Fighters would then alternate between direct engagement and bypass to minimize losses. A successful bypass would place Chad's Battle Hologram at risk of attack and if destroyed, his laser cannons would be useless.

The third Mitel attack pattern, called the swarm, is considered the most intimidating and typically used against a more heavily armed target. A large group of fighters would attack the opponent in a circular swirling pattern meant to surround and overwhelm the target. The Mitel Fleet often utilized this pattern to engage large space battle cruisers and coordinated air defense systems. To prepare for this possible formation, the Battle Hologram team drew up a flight plan that intentionally flew directly into dense clusters of asteroids. Chad's battle sphere would immediately respond with all-out weapons fire.

After a month of training, Janus felt Chad was ready for solo training runs. While the decision was not easy, Janus knew from experience that it was a necessary step in building Chad's confidence and proficiency.

Despite his steady progress, Chad occasionally lost focus under extreme battle conditions. Thanks to his incredible maneuverability, he avoided harm each time. During the subsequent debriefings, the Hologram team tried to pinpoint the root cause of any errors while reinforcing Chad's successes. Chad's skills steadily improved, eventually exceeding the lofty expectations of both Janus and Mayla.

As Chad got to know his Battle Sphere weapons specialists, he felt more responsible for their safety. And for good reason. Each weapons specialist is assigned to monitor and fire five separate cannons in their assigned weapons cluster. In the event the cluster is destroyed, the specialist would also be eliminated as their weapons station would power down and go black. The uniformity and brightness of a Battle Hologram during conflict was a grim indication of how the engagement was progressing. If the Hologram Matrix was littered with black cubes, then it was clear that their Battle Sphere was under extreme duress.

Knowing this, Chad worked tirelessly to refine his concentration and evasive maneuvering skills during battle simulations. He also learned to trust his weapons team.

Chad became especially friendly with weapons specialist Luna Adair. She was about the same height as Melissica with hauntingly beautiful gray eyes, metallic blue hair, with wiry shoulders and a voluptuous figure. Luna was energetic and regularly joked with him about his transformation, referring to him as the *silver sculpture*. In return, Chad would tell Luna that he could *see right through her jokes,* a reference to her translucent appearance. He also told her that she needed to work on her target practice.

However, Luna was by far the most professional and proficient weapons' specialist Janus had ever seen. At night, Chad would sometimes lie in bed and worry about a misjudgment during battle that would terminate Luna.

"I can't let that happen," Chad often told himself as he tossed and turned in bed. *I must never lose my focus.*

As his Battle Sphere returned from his latest solo training exercise, Chad noticed the Moon cycling its way toward a full harvest Moon. At that instant, he got the idea to place a protective plasma shield around it. Since his all-out speed deceleration was now complete, Chad switched over to free flight. He slowed to a stop, closed his eyes tightly, and concentrated intensely on the Moon. Chad sensed his energy reserves expanding rapidly. His psychokinetic ability caused large quantities of trace metals to swirl up from the Moon's surface into outer space to form the basis of the plasma shield. When he opened his eyes, Chad saw a slight blue hue around the lower half of the visible Moon.

Back in his Battle Hologram, Chad's monitoring systems lit up like a Christmas tree. At the same time, the Matrix spontaneously expanded as three rows and columns of cubes were added to monitor the new assignment. As Chad watched, the light blue plasma shield around the Moon slowly deteriorated. When it was completely gone, the Battle Hologram abruptly returned to its former configuration and Chad's readings returned to normal.

Inside the Battle Hologram, technicians scrambled to determine what had just happened.

"Commander, are you all right?" asked Mayla in an unusually urgent tone.

"I'm fine Mayla, why do you ask?"

"You switched to free flight. There was also an unusual energy surge emanating from your Battle Sphere causing our Battle Hologram to temporarily expand."

I should probably keep this whole experiment to myself thought Chad.

"That sounds interesting," he replied. "Maybe it was a meteor shower or something."

"No Commander. It was not."

"The aurora borealis?"

"Commander, please. This is serious."

"OK, OK. I was projecting a protective plasma shield around the Moon."

"You can do that?"

"Apparently I can."

"When did you realize this?"

"Just now."

"I see. And for what purpose are you doing this Commander?"

"Not really sure yet."

"And what was the result of this attempt?"

"A partial shield around the Moon for a few seconds," he said with pride.

"Commander, that activity significantly drained your reserves," replied Mayla while she continued to review Chad's recent energy history on the monitors.

"I understand. But didn't you just say the Matrix expanded momentarily as a result?"

"Yes. What's your point?"

"If I keep trying, maybe I can permanently increase the size of the Matrix for our benefit."

"I need to process this," replied Mayla cautiously. She glanced at Janus who had heard the exchange. Janus realized that everyone else in the room, including Markus, was staring at him.

"It's his Battle Sphere," shrugged Janus. "And quite frankly, he might be on to something."

"Are you starting to mellow in your old age my friend?" asked Markus.

"Maybe, but don't quote me on that."

Over Chad's next four practice runs, he attempted to project a plasma defense shield around the Moon. On each try, the plasma energy shield covered more and more of the Moon and lasted longer and longer before decaying.

His third attempt resulted in a three by three cube permanent expansion to the Battle Hologram. Each new team member indicated the last thing they remembered was preparing to be embedded into their next assignment.

Janus concluded that an unknown number of Thraen Hologram personnel must be embedded somewhere within Chad's Battle Hologram architecture. Despite an intensive search, the hologram team could not locate these additional Thraen holograms. It was eventually decided that only Chad had the ability to release the hologram personnel as his energy potential expanded.

On his fourth attempt, Chad successfully placed a protective shield completely around the Moon. This resulted in the addition of six more permanent cube rows. Mayla and her team were astonished. Chad had essentially doubled the size of the Battle Hologram through concentration and practice.

"I did it!"

"Great Job Chad!" laughed Teri.

Chad hovered in space proudly watching the plasma shield stay in place for twenty minutes before disintegrating.

I'm going to try to place a shield around Earth next.

At that exact moment, an amateur astronomer in the Northern California town of Eureka was gazing through her six-inch Newtonian telescope with an equatorial mount when she spotted Chad's hovering Battle Sphere.

She quickly snapped a series of photographs using her side mounted DSLR (Digital Single Lens Reflex) camera before Chad resumed course and disappeared.

She excitedly posted the images on Twitter with the hashtag label *#UFOSighting*. The pictures were quickly retweeted and posted by many on Facebook. Professional and amateur astronomers, who had been following the unusual Moon activity quickly followed, posting on twitter with the hashtag *#UFO shields Moon in blue?*

The next evening, the network evening news broadcasts also reported on the UFO sightings. Leading experts including Neil deGrasse Tyson, Kip Thorne, Stephen Hawking and world famous astrophotographer Ted Wolfe were all interviewed. Having reviewed the pictures in detail, Ted Wolfe concluded that they were authentic.

The headline on the New York Times Read:

UNEXPLAINED CELESTIAL ACTIVITY SPARKS GLOBAL CONVERSATION

The scientific community revealed that energy spikes had been detected near the Moon in recent weeks. Scientists and physicists alike were perplexed by the fact that the phenomenon only occurred on the weekends during the mid to late afternoon, Eastern Standard Time for North America. However, the scientific community did not consider the activity to be a threat to either the Earth or the Moon, despite being at a loss to explain how and why the events occurred. Some experts hypothesized that the energy disturbances were somehow linked to the mysterious sphere photographed the day and time of the strongest reading to date.

In response to the latest development, Chad and his Battle Hologram team agreed to stop projecting the plasma shield around the Moon. The following weekend, Chad resumed his normal practice routine. On Sunday afternoon, Chad finished up early and checked in on Teri. When he arrived at his cube, Teri looked up and smiled.

"Hey Chad, come on in," he motioned.

Chad sat down on a hologram chair.

"How is everything, Teri?"

"OK, I guess."

"I am sorry we haven't had much time to talk about anything other than the training missions."

"I know, but that is our top priority, right?

"Yeah."

Chad paused to look around Teri's cube again. He glanced up at Chondra's picture, but she did not make an appearance this time.

"Teri?"

"Yes Chad," he said as he entered flight simulation data into his computer.

"You said you served Janus during the first Mitel invasion?"

"Yes. Why do you ask?"

"I don't know. Just trying to get your perspective on Battle Spheres."

"How do you mean?"

"Are you aware of any weaknesses?"

"That is a definite no! To me, the Battle Sphere is the ultimate fighting machine."

Teri then paused to consider the question.

"The only vulnerability I can really think of is poor decision making by its hybrid Commander," he said eventually. "In your father's case, he made an error in judgment. And that resulted in him being badly damaged.

I firmly believe that he should have withdrawn one more time to recharge his energy reserves."

Teri paused and looked up at Chad.

"In the heat of battle, these types of decisions can have huge consequences. I think that is why Janus wants you to train so much."

Teri paused again before smiling.

"And hey, you are doing really great by the way."

"Thanks, Teri," grinned Chad.

The two sat in silence for a few moments.

"Teri?"

"What?"

"Can you think of anything *else*?"

"Well, I don't have firsthand knowledge of it myself, but there is a story that has been handed down through generations of Hologram Defense Force personnel. In the event a Battle Sphere chooses to end its existence due to significant damage or some other catastrophic situation, its Hologram support staff are returned to their prior form."

"You mean they are transformed back into people?"

"Yes."

"That doesn't sound possible," replied Chad dismissively. "If it were, Janus would have mentioned it to me already."

"Maybe you're right."

Teri thought how to choose his words before continuing.

"Listen Chad, it's great to serve in the Hologram Protective Force and I'm not afraid to cease to exist. But I sometimes wonder what it would be like to be a living Thraen again."

"I don't see how it would even be possible Teri."

"From what I have been told, it involves the Battle Sphere intentionally speeding up its plasma propulsion core."

"Speeding up its *propulsion core*?"

"Yes. When the plasma core is sped up, it begins an atomic particle scattering process that generates large amounts of antimatter. When the antimatter is released, it causes an instantaneous explosion, called *annihilation*. The amount of energy released could easily vaporize a planet. Anyway, the explanation I got was that the sudden release of energy somehow facilitates a reverse transformation. The Hologram Protective Force refers to it as the *miracle of life* process."

Chad and Teri suddenly sensed that they were being watched. Instinctively, they looked toward the door of Teri's hologram cube. Janus Stone was in the doorway.

"Explaining to Chad the hologram defense folklore Teri?" asked Janus in a slightly annoyed voice.

"Um, yes, I mean *no* Sir."

"Well, let me say this, your so-called *miracle of life,* is not an option for any hybrid, least of all a Battle Sphere. Do you know *why*, Teri?"

"No Sir."

"A hybrid fighting machine's *duty* is to protect and defend its people at *all* costs. There is no moral, logical or rational reason to do otherwise. It is an honor and a privilege to be in such a unique position. For a hybrid to *choose* to do anything less would be to neglect one's duty to protect and defend the innocent men, women and *children* who cannot otherwise protect and defend themselves."

Janus paused before continuing.

"The decision to end one's existence amounts to an act of cowardice. Do I make myself clear?"

"Yes Commander," replied Teri softly.

"Very good then," replied Janus and with that, he turned and walked away down the hall.

"What was that all about?" whispered Chad eventually.

"Janus is very committed to *the mission*. He always has been and always will be."

"What do you mean by *the mission*?"

"Protecting those who cannot protect themselves," explained Teri. "And he still blames himself for the destruction of our planet."

"But *why* does he blame himself?"

"I don't know the answer to that question. As I said before, he feels responsible for so many things that happened on Thrae. There is probably nothing anybody can say or do to change how he feels. But you know *what* Chad?" That's just who Janus is. He cared so deeply for our people. That is why I have such great respect for him."

"I do too," smiled Chad.

"Oh crap!" Chad noticed the time and jumped up from his seat.

"What's wrong Chad?"

"I'm late for dinner!"

"Oh no, not again!" Teri laughed.

"See ya later Teri."

CHAPTER SEVENTEEN – THE "FORT"

Janus and the Hologram team took the weekend off from practice. Chad woke up on Saturday morning with mixed emotions. He was sad, but also welcomed the opportunity to relax a little. Chad jumped out of bed, threw on his running clothes and headed to the kitchen where Molly and Jim were sitting and drinking coffee.

"Good morning honey. Are you ready for some breakfast?"

"No, not yet. I'm going for a run first."

"What about *work*?" asked Jim.

"Um. Mr. Davis said he doesn't need me this weekend."

"*Oh*, OK," replied Molly as she took a sip of coffee.

"Well, going for a run sounds like an ambitious plan this early in the morning," mused Jim. "Where to?"

"Probably through the park and back."

"That sounds good," encouraged Molly. "I'm going to make some pumpkin muffins. They should be ready by the time you get back."

"Save me two," he said closing the door behind him.

The morning air was crisp and cool, with the mild scent of an early morning fire somewhere in the neighborhood. Chad headed toward Main Street. The sky was a magnificent deep blue, the kind of blue that seemed to distort the height and depth of the trees as they sat drenched in its brilliance.

Turning onto Main Street, Chad passed several large Victorian-style houses that were a silent testament to more prosperous times in the town's history. The impressive structures were set back from the road and surrounded by lush green lawns and well-manicured shrubs. As Chad ran, he wondered who may have lived there and what their lives may have been like.

When he arrived at Randall Park, Chad headed up the dirt road past the old Civil War Memorial toward the center of the park and smiled as he thought about how Janus had appeared in front of him along the dirt road. Seconds later, Janus's black and silver orb hovered in front of him.

"Hi Janus!" said Chad with a wide grin.

Janus's orb hovered silently for a few seconds before darting into the woods.

"I guess that's my cue to follow you," Chad muttered to himself.

Chad followed Janus's orb through the dense pine trees to the circular opening where he had first met Janus and Markus. Janus's hologram was patiently waiting for him.

"*Hey*, I thought today was supposed to be a day off," laughed Chad.

"It is," smiled Janus. "I just thought maybe you wanted to see where Markus and I have been living all this time."

"That would be *awesome*! Where is it?"

"Farther into the woods in that direction, by a small pond," said Janus pointing toward the woods on the other side of the opening.

"I didn't know there was a pond out there."

"It's pretty well hidden. That's why we chose it. Follow me."

Janus terminated his hologram. His orb darted into the woods on the other side of the clearing.

"*Coming*," Chad smiled.

He weaved his way through the thickly wooded area. Every now and then Chad caught a glimpse of Janus's silver orb darting up ahead. Several minutes later, the woods opened to reveal an oval shaped pond. The water was as smooth as glass, reflecting the tree tops and sky above. The pond was edged by rocks of various sizes and shapes and transitioned into a wide sandy strip that ended at the edge of the forest. Chad noticed a simple stone marker off in the distance.

Janus's orb darted from across the pond stopping next to Chad. Seconds later, his hologram reappeared. As the two of them stood silently, Chad pointed toward the marker.

"Janus, what's that over there?"

"It's a stone grave marker. It is quite old, given the settlement history of this region."

"*Wow*. It's located in such a peaceful place."

"Indeed. Markus and I have been here with it for quite some time now. At this point, we feel as though it is a part of us. Behind me is our base camp."

Chad turned and looked but did not see anything.

"*Where?*"

"Look again," Janus smiled as the protective plasma shield dissipated to reveal several small dome shaped buildings in a hexagonal pattern. The structures were surrounded by numerous antennae and black triangular panels pointing skyward.

"How did you do that?"

"The plasma shield absorbs and redirects all natural light rendering our encampment invisible to the naked eye," explained Janus. "Our location is undetectable by anything on or orbiting this planet. For example, your planet's infrared technology, often used at night to locate heat signatures, is simply absorbed and recycled by the shield."

"That's cool." Chad walked toward the structures. There was the sensation of being above the ground as he entered the circular perimeter.

"Janus, am I — "

"Walking above the surface? Yes, that is all part of our enclosure. There's an antigravity floor that forms its base."

Markus's hologram emerged from the largest building.

"Hello Chad! How are you today?"

"I'm good, Markus, thank you." Chad continued looking around.

"What *is* all this stuff?"

"This is our base of operations. I guess you could call it our *Fort*," laughed Markus. "The various forms of equipment you see allow us to monitor deep space."

"How far can you detect something out there?"

"Suffice to say that it is much more accurate and sensitive than anything you will find here on Earth."

"But everything is so small."

"True enough, but our equipment is extremely accurate and very effective," explained Markus proudly.

"What are those things over here?" asked Chad pointing to several black triangular panels.

"They are solar panels that also help produce and recycle our plasma energy. They provide all of the energy needed to run everything you see here."

"Where did all this stuff *come from*?"

"Some of it your father and I salvaged from the USEP the night of the crash. The rest we constructed and modified over time as we searched the region for parts and materials."

Chad smiled and then turned his attention back toward the antennae.

"Any signs of the Mitel Fleet?"

"Luckily no," replied Janus. "But we've tracked quite a few asteroids, comets, satellites and other space debris."

Janus looked at Chad intently before continuing.

"But as I have said previously, it's only a matter of time before the Mitels make their way to this part of the universe. We need as much warning as possible, which is why we set up this observatory or *Fort* as Markus calls it."

"What are all the buildings for?"

"They provide shelter for the equipment during inclement weather. And in the farthest structure, we have accumulated a large assortment of nonperishable foods, bedding and other supplies. There is even a functioning lavatory and water reclamation system."

"Wow." Chad walked over to look inside the closest building.

"Is that a television?"

"Indeed it is!" responded Markus.

"You guys have a *television*?"

"I enjoy watching reality shows," Markus chuckled.

Janus rolled his eyes and shook his head as he turned away from Markus.

"Markus apparently has too much time on his hands," said Janus sarcastically.

"This place is great. But why are you showing me *now*?"

"In case you, or James or Molly need to seek refuge. The plasma shields and dwellings will provide shelter, protection and a way to avoid detection."

"You mean from the Mitels?"

"From anyone, or anything, that may be threatening you."

"Thanks, Janus."

After inspecting the Fort's vast array of hardware, Chad walked back toward the pond. He stopped at the edge and looked around some more before walking over to the grave marker. The lettering had long since eroded. As Janus approached, Chad heard the sound his hologram made as it deformed briefly.

"What are you thinking?" asked Janus.

"I just wanted to check out the grave stone. It's so peaceful and quiet here. It makes you wonder if it was planned that way, the location of the grave, you know?"

"I would venture a guess to say that it was."

They paused for a few moments, staring at the grave stone together.

"Janus?"

"Yes, Chad."

"Do you think the person who is buried here is still alive in some form?"

"That's a good question. I think the person buried here is in another dimension and form that we do not yet understand."

"Why do you think that?"

Janus studied Chad's face for a moment and gently smiled.

"We know that energy can change form. But we don't fully understand the limitations of those changes. We also don't know the limits of our own universe or the number of dimensions that exist within it. Perhaps someday we will discover those answers."

They stood in silence for a time.

"You should probably finish your run so that your parents don't worry about you," Janus suggested.

"You're probably right."

Chad waived to Markus and headed back toward the woods. Just before he entered the forest, he looked back over his shoulder. The plasma shields had already been reactivated. Like before, all Chad could see was the pond, the trees, and the lone grave marker.

After school the following Wednesday, Chad felt a nagging uneasy feeling. He kept trying to focus on other things but each time he did, the uncomfortable feeling returned. It was as if someone or *something* was trying to warn him. Feeling compelled to visit the Fort again, Chad walked down to Randall Park and made his way along the dirt road and through the two sets of trees. When he arrived at the pond, there was no sign of Janus or Markus or the equipment and buildings. Chad put his hand out as he made his way along the sandy shore. After a few minutes, he stood in the middle of where he thought the Fort should be.

Strange, I'm pretty sure that it was located right about here.

Chad turned and looked toward the pond to get his bearings.

Yes, it was right here! Where could they have gone?

A bit further around the pond, the Fort suddenly appeared. Markus emerged from one of the structures and waved to Chad as he approached.

"Hey Markus, I could have sworn you guys were over here."

"We probably were my boy."

"I don't understand."

"Our laboratory slowly rotates around the pond to avoid detection. It was one of Janus's many inventions."

"Got it," smiled Chad. He noticed a serious expression on Markus's face that he had not seen before.

"Is everything OK Markus?"

"No, not really."

"What's wrong?"

"Follow me." Chad followed Markus into the largest structure. Janus was looking at several monitoring screens.

"Hello Chad," Janus said, a serious look on this face as well, "the timing of your visit here today must be more than a coincidence."

"What do you mean?"

"We have discovered a large energy signal making its way in this direction —"

"*The Mitel Fleet!*"

"I am afraid so."

"*I knew it.* I had this strange feeling earlier today that something was happening, something very important."

"And you were right."

"When will they arrive?"

"By my calculations, they are a few Earth weeks away."

"Do you think anybody else has detected them?"

"No. Our antennae are powerful and accurate. We've also been able to concentrate their signals toward the exact region of deep space the Mitels would be most likely coming from."

"Understood," replied Chad softly.

"Earth's satellite technology will detect them very soon, given the size of their approaching fleet," explained Janus. "The Mitels appear to have successfully reverse engineered Thrae's high speed travel technology, which is probably why we weren't able to detect them earlier."

"Are we going to intercept them?" asked Chad quickly. "I mean, I could use my *all-out* speed and —"

"*Absolutely no!*" Janus said abruptly.

"Why *not*?"

"Several reasons. First of all, the Mitels will detect your approach and take evasive maneuvers to avoid your Battle Sphere while trying to surround you. Second, since they have the ability to travel faster than your Battle Sphere, it would be pointless to attack them unless we have the element of surprise —"

"But if we wait won't they simply encircle Earth?"

"Good question, but no. Earth is simply too big for them to effectively restrain your Battle Sphere. We can then employ the element of surprise from the planet's surface."

"How do you plan on surprising them?" asked Chad.

"We have set up several smaller plasma enclosures for you to seek refuge in," Janus began. "We have placed one on a small uninhabited island in the narrows on Lake Edward; another near an old abandoned military bunker located on Great Diamond Island off the coast of Portland, Maine; a third next to a pond in the White Mountain National Forest in New Hampshire; and a fourth at the base of a stone mountain face in the Adirondack State Park. They are all powered by the same solar devices you see here and along with a manual activation device on site if needed."

"When did you do all *that*?"

"Over the years, lad!" grinned Markus.

"From any of those locations," explained Janus, "your Battle Sphere can strike targeted craft formations and begin to weaken their defenses. After each attack, you can withdraw to a different hidden enclosure to recharge as we prepare for the next surprise attack."

"But Janus — if we let them come all the way to Earth's outer atmosphere — don't we risk them attacking and destroying this planet too?" asked Chad.

"That's a possibility."

"Then why —"

"The Mitels know that you are the last of your kind. Their hands will be tied to a great extent. At least until they capture you —"

"*Capture me*?" exclaimed Chad.

"*Or* withdraw and abandon their mission. We don't expect them to capture you. No Battle Sphere has ever been captured."

"Well that makes me feel a *little* better," sighed Chad.

"One more thing," instructed Janus. "Markus and I also placed three additional plasma enclosures on the Moon so that you could —"

"Hide there and attack their fleet as they approach Earth!" interrupted Chad enthusiastically.

"Correct," replied Markus.

"Where are they?" asked Chad.

"We placed an enclosure at each rim of the Moon's lighted surface and a third almost in the middle," replied Janus. "That way, we could be sure that at least two will be fully charged by your Sun and functional when needed."

"That's awesome!" smiled Chad.

"Let me tell you that placing those stations up there was no small task and we had a few challenges," explained Markus. "NASA has been photographing and mapping the Moon in great detail since 2009 using a device known as the Lunar Reconnaissance Orbiter."

"Did they *see* you?"

"We think so," Janus began. "To minimize detection, we placed the enclosures inside three separate basins referred to by astronomers as the Tycho, Thebit and Picard craters. Unfortunately, the structures themselves were exposed to surveillance and detection until we set up and energized the plasma shields."

"Which made them disappear," thought Chad out loud.

"Correct. We presumed the appearance and subsequent disappearance of the small enclosures raised suspicion within the United States Military community."

"It probably drove Major Talbot crazy!" smiled Chad.

Markus chuckled softly.

"I can hide there as they approach Earth and launch a surprise attack," said Chad. "It will be just like the asteroid belt!"

"That is what we were hoping you would say!" exclaimed Markus.

"And we won't have to contend with my all-out speed cycle."

"Exactly," smiled Janus. "And *that* is how we will severely weaken their fleet *before* they reach Earth."

"Hopefully they decide to give up at that point," replied Chad.

Janus and Markus looked at each other in silence.

"What?" asked Chad.

"The Mitels rarely *give up* lad," Markus said softly.

"Markus is right. They will regroup and eventually return —"

"*Unless* . . ." interrupted Markus.

"Unless what?" Chad frowned.

"Unless we completely decimate their attack force," replied Janus. "Only an absolute defeat will prevent the Mitels from returning."

The three of them looked at the monitors in silence for a time.

"Now what?" Chad asked.

"We must speak with your father," responded Janus.

"My *dad*?"

"Yes. The time has come to tell your parents what is going on. When you get home tonight, just go about things as usual. I will come by this evening when you're in the observatory with your father. We will see how it goes from there. *Agreed*?"

"I understand. I'm not sure how my dad will react, but he needs to know."

"Neither do I. But it's time to find out."

As they exited the structure, Janus put his hand on Chad's shoulder.

"Chad, listen to me. You have practiced very hard for this and have a fantastic Battle Hologram team. You're ready."

Chad looked up and smiled weakly at Janus.

"I think I am too. It's just —"

"You're scared."

"Yes, I guess I am."

Janus looked at Chad squarely in the eye. "If you *weren't* at least a little scared, I would be worried about you. Remember, I will be up there with you."

"*Really*?" said Chad as his face brightened.

"Yes. We will do this *together*."

"But it will be very dangerous for you."

"My choice to go up there with you is just that, and I do *not* want you to worry about me. Promise?

"Promise," said Chad softly.

"*Good.* Then I think it's time you got going," smiled Janus.

Chad waved goodbye as the Fort disappeared and he quickly rushed home. Sitting at his bedroom desk, Chad could not concentrate on his school work.

What's the point?

As he stared out the window, Chad reflected on his research project about evolution of the skyscraper in Manhattan over the past one hundred and thirty years. In doing so, Chad had painstakingly mapped out and memorized the streets and buildings throughout the City. By now, he knew them as well as anyone born and raised in Manhattan.

At school, Chad enjoyed telling friends and teachers little known facts about the architecture and development of the skyscrapers and other famous landmarks. Everyone joked that if he decided not to go to college, he could always be a tour guide. Chad would laugh and respond with a little known fact such as:

"Did you know that in 1927, Columbia University placed its solar observatory named the *Rutherford Observatory* above the 14th floor of Pupin Hall which contained a twelve-inch refractor telescope originally built in 1916 for the czarist government of Russia?" With everything going on, it now seemed like a pointless exercise along with the rest of his schoolwork.

At dinner, Chad was silent as he mostly played with his food. He did not touch his dessert.

"Is everything alright Chad?"

"I'm OK Mom, why?"

"You seem distracted and you really didn't eat anything. That's not like you."

"Um, everything's fine Mom, really. May I be excused from the table?"

Molly glanced quickly over at Jim who nodded his approval.

"OK honey, sure."

"Thank you."

He went up to his room. As Chad lay on his bed, he heard the faint clattering of dishes and clanging of pots and pans as his parents cleaned up the kitchen.

"See you up there," Jim said as he knocked once on Chad's door, making his way to the observatory.

"Be right up," replied Chad loud enough for his father to hear. He listened, as he has done for years, as his father climbed the attic stairs and walked across to the observatory.

Chad forced himself up from his bed, and headed up the attic stairs. As he entered, his father was sitting in his usual spot studying one of the several astronomy books he kept on a shelf next to the door. He immediately smelled the early night's fresh air. Looking up, he noticed that the shutter slot at the top of the observatory was already open.

"*Hey,*" said Jim as he looked up at Chad with a smile "how was your day?"

"A little unusual."

"What do you mean by *unusual*? Did something happen to you again?"

"No. I mean *yes*, but it's not what you think."

"Try me."

"It was nothing like what happened behind Temple Beth El, even though I guess it is all related."

"Did you see Major Talbot again?" asked Jim apprehensively.

"No."

"Did you see another car with US government plates?"

"No!"

"Then *what* Chad?"

"It's —"

Suddenly, Janus's black and silver orb was hovering just outside the open slot at the top of the observatory. It hovered a few seconds more before entering. Jim did a double take when he noticed the orb hovering near the ceiling.

"What the hell . . ."

Janus's orb slowly descended across the room. When it reached eye level, Janus's hologram appeared. Jim jumped up from his chair, knocking it over and dropping his book with a loud thud.

"Chad," asked Janus calmly. "Aren't you going to introduce me to your father?"

Jim stared at Janus, speechless.

"Dad, I want you to meet Janus. He comes from planet Thrae, which is a little over six hundred light years from here."

Jim, his mouth now slightly open, nodded hello.

"Hello James Johnson. It is a pleasure to meet you after all this time."

Jim did not respond.

"I'm sorry to appear so abruptly. But I thought it was time the two of us spoke."

"Who, err, I mean, what brings you *here*?" Jim asked nervously.

"Your son is the reason I'm here."

"Chad?"

"Yes. Unfortunately, Chad finds himself in the middle of a situation he did not create but one that will require him to take extraordinary measures."

"I don't understand."

"You see James, Chad is also not from this world."

"I figured that. I'm also guessing you didn't come here just to tell me that."

"Correct."

"Is Chad *your* son?"

"Yes, he is. But he is not any more mine than he is *yours*. Quite honestly, in many ways he is much more your son than he is mine."

Jim sat down and ran his hands through his hair before looking back up at Janus. As he did, Janus's hologram deformed and hummed for a few seconds before returning to normal.

"What was *that*?" Jim asked.

"It's a long story," replied Chad.

Jim looked over at Chad and then back up at Janus.

"Am I right to assume that you crash landed in the field outside of town about fifteen years ago?"

"Yes. That was our small pod," acknowledged Janus. I'm sorry that I did not make contact with you sooner. I didn't feel that Chad was ready to hear the truth about his past."

"Does the Military know you exist?"

"They're aware of our presence to some degree."

"Is that why you came here tonight? Is the Military coming back?" asked Jim.

"No not yet, but perhaps soon."

"Then *why* are you here?"

"I have come to warn you."

"Warn me about *what*?" asked Jim cautiously.

"The Mitel Fleet is approaching planet Earth. They will eventually be detected by your world community *including* the United States Military. That in turn will bring attention back to both you and Chad."

"*Who* is coming?" asked Jim with a confused expression.

"*The Mitel Fleet,*" repeated Janus patiently. "Our deep space surveillance technology detected their energy signature. While they are still a few light years away, they will likely reach Earth in about two weeks time."

"*Why?*"

"They are coming for Chad. And they will stop at nothing until they get him."

"*Chad?* Why Chad?"

"The Mitels have attacked our planet twice looking for two things. The second invasion resulted in our planet's destruction. Over two billion of our people perished."

"*Two billion* people were killed? *Why?*"

"The Mitels are a closely controlled militaristic civilization whose Leadership worships technology. They were desperate to acquire two secrets that our planet had long since discarded."

"What secrets could *possibly* be so important?" asked Jim incredulously.

"Immortality and the ability for a few of our people to transform into machine form. We call them hybrids."

"*Immortality and human machines?*" whispered Jim disbelievingly.

"To find the last of our people who is *both* an immortal and a hybrid," replied Janus.

Jim suddenly looked over at Chad, his mouth now wide open.

"Yes, James — Chad."

"*Oh my god!*" blurted Jim.

"Dad, I know it all sounds crazy. Remember when I explained to you how I turned all silver behind the temple?"

"How could I forget?"

"That's just the beginning. My body then morphs and expands into a mechanical ball called a Battle Sphere. I can fly close to the speed of light and fire two hundred laser cannons and until it all happened, I wouldn't have believed it myself. "

"*Whoa* . . . but how does it happen? *What triggers it?*" asked Jim quietly.

"Behind Temple Bethel, it was initiated by my anger. But if I focus intensely I can make myself transform."

"You activated your transformation much earlier than that," said Janus.

"*Really?* When?"

"As a baby in the USEP — you were agitated and angry after being launched into outer space to escape the Mitels. It was then that we realized that you were a Battle Sphere. Unfortunately, the Mitels detected your unique abilities before we escaped which set in motion the series of events that brings us here tonight."

"*Wow,*" replied Chad. "You knew back then what was going to happen."

"Yes," nodded Janus.

Chad looked back at Jim.

"We have been secretly training every weekend at the Davis Farm to develop my skills."

"We have been closely monitoring local communications," said Janus. "To this point anyway, there is no indication that we have been detected."

Jim's eyes lit up.

"All the stuff I am hearing about the *unidentified sphere* in outer space — and the energy disturbances near the Moon — was that you?"

"That was Chad. The world's military and scientific community will eventually find us and when they do, we need to be ready."

"And what about the Mitels?" asked Jim. "What are you going to do about them?"

"The Mitel Fleet is an impressive fighting force," replied Janus. "They are coming here for one reason: to seize Chad and they will destroy *anything* that gets in their way."

"But how can they be stopped?" asked Jim.

Janus looked over at Chad.

"Chad can stop them."

"How?"

"In his hybrid form, Chad is the most formidable fighting machine in the entire universe."

Jim sat silently for a full minute as he considered what Janus was telling him.

"But Janus, how can you be so sure he can do it?"

Janus hesitated for a few seconds while his orb ran a scan of Jim's emotions.

"Given the distance the Mitels are traveling, the force they can send here will be significantly smaller than what attacked our planet. And to prepare for them, Chad has been training intensely over the past several weeks. He has proven to me that he has the discipline, concentration and ability to surgically destroy a small to medium sized attack force all on his own. I can assure you that the Mitels did not plan on Chad being ready to oppose them."

"How can you be so *sure*?" asked Jim.

"I was once a hybrid Battle Sphere that fought the Mitels. I am intimately familiar with their military technology and combat tactics."

"Then why aren't you fighting them instead of Chad?"

Janus paused briefly before answering.

"My ability to transform ended during the first Mitel invasion," he replied. "It was a result of poor decision making on my part. The *only* credit I will give the Mitel Fleet — is that they allowed me to annihilate their forces until I made a foolish mistake."

"What happened?"

"Near the end of the conflict, I continued to attack them after my energy reserves were below safe levels. I ignored the repeated requests to withdraw and subsequently collided with a Mitel attack craft. I was lucky to survive, but the impact caused irreversible damage to my mechanical self. If I had simply listened, and withdrew to replenish my reserves, I would have finished them off without incident. In all likelihood the Mitels would have never attacked our planet a second time."

With that, Janus grew pensive as he stared up at the observatory's telescope.

"My mistakes were easily avoidable if I had not been so stubborn. I must live with the consequences of those decisions. But I will *not* allow the Mitels to destroy another civilization. Not *here*."

"I see," said Jim weakly. "And you are telling me that they are almost here?"

"Unfortunately, yes," nodded Janus. "It was opportune that Chad began his training when he did. Maybe it's more than a coincidence — perhaps *fate* or *divine providence*."

Jim let out another big sigh.

"Are there more of you?" he asked softly.

"Yes, there is one more like me. He is a three-dimensional hologram that projects from a monitoring orb such as mine. His name is Markus Kilmar."

"Don't forget the Battle Hologram team," said Chad.

"Chad is correct," smiled Janus. "His Battle Sphere is supported by a contingent of hologram technicians, all of whom are supremely dedicated to his success and well-being."

"This is all so unbelievable," replied Jim. "I keep expecting to wake up from my dream any second."

"I understand."

"What can I do to help?"

"We need to minimize Chad's distractions. You must also be ready to relocate to our modest but undetectable base of operations if government or Military officials come back looking for you."

"It's called the Fort. It's hidden deep inside Randall Park," explained Chad.

"Once events begin to unfold, conditions will become much more complex. We must be prepared to act quickly."

"How do you mean?" Jim frowned.

"When the Military detects the approaching Mitel Fleet, they will panic. They will come here searching for Chad. Eventually, the Military will make the connection between our crash and Chad's appearance at the Coopers Falls hospital the same night. They will ultimately link Chad to the approaching extraterrestrials."

"So you left Chad at the hospital to keep him from being linked to the crash?"

"That was a concern, yes. I also wanted him to be raised by parents that could provide for him in ways that I could not."

Janus paused.

"I also believe we have a moral obligation to help prevent your world from making the same mistakes we did."

"How so?" asked Jim.

"On Thrae I was deeply involved in our technology development. I firmly believed that the many profound discoveries we achieved were in the best interest of our civilization as a whole. I never thought — rather, I never *foresaw* — that our civilization would need to reject certain technologies to prevent self-destruction."

"Do you mean robotics?"

"No. Robotics technology on our planet was never intended to become the type of mechanical life form that you envision here on Earth. Our scientists focused on pushing the limits of our own human life form which resulted in a series of profound breakthroughs."

"You mean holograms and mechanical transformation."

"Yes. At first our scientists discovered ways to significantly enhance our people's productivity and life expectancy. It started with small imbedded chips on the brain and body, followed by robotic organs and limbs and blood stream additives. They then began experimenting with DNA manipulation and the interaction between human life form and the natural environment. This led to the ability to *trigger* the mechanical aspect of our human life form which formed the basis of our human hybrid technology."

"Which eventually got you to what Chad can do," replied Jim.

"Yes, but Chad represents by far the pinnacle of such technology. It took centuries to achieve."

"*Wow.*"

"In time, scientists discovered the complex *blueprint* necessary to achieve human immortality which we called IM. Along the way, they also engineered human holograms which arguably represented a *second* type of immortality. And, with the invention of focused energy, holograms were able to operate in the physical world. In my opinion, we created something superior to what you think of as robotics."

"That's incredible," whispered Jim.

"Indeed. But unfortunately, many complications surfaced."

"Such as?"

"As our technological advancements became more exotic, we lost the ability to anticipate or control the adverse side effects," replied Janus. "In a relatively short period, as our people began dying by the millions, we realized that we were poisoning ourselves."

"What did you do?"

"The only thing we could do. We expunged the underlying technology from our world. The eradication process itself was challenging and it took several generations for our world to heal itself."

Janus paused before continuing.

"And now . . . I see Earth embarking on a similar path. It is my hope that we can keep your world from making the same mistakes we made. But first, we must stop the Mitel Fleet."

Chad impulsively walked over and hugged Janus tightly. Jim watched in amazement as Janus sparkled and glistened on contact.

"We will do it Janus," smiled Chad.

Jim stood up and slowly approached Janus.

"I will do anything I can to help. Just tell me what to do."

Jim then slowly reached out his right hand and Janus did the same. As the two shook hands, Chad smiled broadly amid the twinkling sparkles.

"This went *much* better than I expected," sighed Chad. "We need to tell Mom."

"Yes we do," nodded Jim. "I should have told her a lot sooner, but I just didn't want to worry her needlessly if it turned out I was wrong."

Jim then turned back to Janus.

"What's next?" he asked.

"I think Chad should bring both you and Molly to our base camp within the next day or two."

"Agreed," nodded Jim.

"In the meantime," said Janus. "I should get back to Markus and continue to monitor the approaching Mitel Fleet."

With that, Janus's hologram terminated as his monitoring orb rose slowly toward the observatory's open slot and quickly darted off into the night sky.

After watching Janus leave, Jim turned to Chad.

"This is unbelievable. I mean *just unbelievable*," blurted Jim. He then stared at Chad intently.

"You OK?"

"I think so."

Chad's face suddenly lit up.

"*But Dad* — transforming into a Battle Sphere and flying to the asteroid belt in just minutes for target practice and being supported by a whole team of holograms just like Janus. It is exhilarating and incredible and a massive rush! You know that I have always loved everything about flying and *now* I am flying in ways that I couldn't have imagined!"

Chad paused before his expression turned serious.

"That part is like a wonderful dream," he said quietly. "It's just that, I'm afraid. I'm afraid of the nightmare that's coming at the end of this dream. Despite all the training and preparation, I have no idea whether I can do the things Janus and Markus say I can do — and need to do. I'm scared."

Chad then grew very quiet as he looked back up through the observation slot.

"What if I can't do it?" he said almost in a whisper, "then what?"

Jim's heart ached for Chad. He stepped forward and gently placed his hand on his son's shoulder.

"I'm scared too," has said softly. "But Janus — he seems convinced that your Battle Sphere can stop the Mitels. I just want you to know that your mom and I will do everything we can to help you — and I mean *everything*."

"Thanks Dad," Chad grinned. "I know I can count on you guys. I guess what keeps me from freaking out is how confident Janus and Markus are about the whole thing. They are unwavering in their assessment that I can do it. And they are also relentless in showing me how to avoid making the same mistakes they did. When I sit in bed at night, I tell myself that I need to treat the Mitel invasion like a three-dimensional video game. If I just do what I'm being trained to do, it will be over quickly and everything will be OK and things will hopefully go back to normal. But . . ."

"But what?" asked Jim quietly.

"No matter what happens, things will never really go back to normal."

"True, but I guess it depends what you mean by normal. If you mean going back to the way things were before Janus and Markus, then no, it won't. But maybe our world can move ahead after all of this with a new and wonderful normal. That is what we need to focus on."

Chad smiled and gave his father a big hug.

"I love you Dad."

"I love you with all of my heart Chad," Jim squeezed his son tightly.

After they hugged, the two of them looked out the observatory slot toward the stars that dotted the night sky.

"Chad?" Jim asked softly.

"Yeah Dad?"

"I'm not sure how I tell your mom about this."

"You can do it Dad," smiled Chad encouragingly "I know you can."

CHAPTER EIGHTEEN – THE CONFESSION

Jim crawled into bed with Molly. He then began the hardest conversation he had ever had. At first, Molly thought the whole thing was a practical joke. But her laughter was soon replaced by shock, fear, anger and utter disbelief. Molly also felt betrayed. It was as if Jim had taken a mistress, and had a secret life. She was angry that she was only finding out when things had become hopelessly complicated to the point where their lives were in danger. After talking the whole thing out, Molly hugged Jim tightly.

"We need to do whatever it takes to help our son."

Jim ran his fingers through Molly's hair.

"I agree," whispered Jim. "Janus wants us to visit his Fort. Chad will take us there. "

The night turned into morning and Molly and Jim went downstairs to get coffee. Chad was standing next to the kitchen table when Molly rushed forward and hugged him.

"I love you so much Chad," she whispered as her eyes filled with tears.

"I love you too Mom."

"Dad says you can show us where the Fort is. Can you take us today?" Molly said, wiping away her tears.

"I can be home a little before 3:00," Jim said.

"OK then, we'll go over to the Fort as soon as you get home from school," said Molly as she rubbed Chad's hair lovingly. "Are you hungry?"

"I'm all set, thanks. I need to head out early today to talk to Melissica, *OK?*"

"Are you sure she's ready to hear about all this?" asked Jim.

"Dad, you *know* how important Melissica is to me," pleaded Chad.

"Just make sure you do it in a place where nobody else can see or hear you, OK?"

"I promise. Mom, do you think I'm doing the right thing?"

"I think you should do whatever helps you deal with this."

"OK, then that's what I'm going to do," confirmed Chad, grabbing his back pack. He waved goodbye and made his way out the back door and down the driveway.

As Chad headed up Grove Avenue, a mist hugged the ground in response to the crisp autumn air.

As he stepped over the control joints along the cement sidewalks, his thoughts drifted randomly until he found himself thinking only about Melissica. The plan was to meet before school and explain to her what was happening. He had texted her after the meeting with Janus asking if she could talk before school. He suggested they meet at the main entrance to the Ridge Street Cemetery in front of the stone mausoleum. Sensing something was wrong, Melissica texted back quickly that she would meet him there.

Chad walked slowly as he approached the cemetery. The mausoleum itself was a beautiful yet simple stone structure made of rectangular granite blocks of various sizes mortared together in a random pattern, with a simple triangular steeple at the top. The left side roof had a saltbox design which added to its charm and beauty. There was something very calming about the cemetery that appealed to Chad. It was quiet and peaceful and tastefully dotted with fir and maple trees. He sometimes walked through the cemetery to clear his mind, studying the mausoleum building from different angles.

Chad arrived early, so he waited for her next to the stone mausoleum. Five minutes later, Chad saw Melissica walking up Ridge Street toward the cemetery.

"Is everything alright, Chad?"

"No, not really," he said, motioning her to follow him into the cemetery. Melissica tried to gauge his mood as they walked along the crushed stone drive.

"What's wrong?" she asked eventually.

"I'm not sure where to begin. I need to tell you something."

"OK."

"What's wrong Chad?" she asked softly.

"Remember when I had a run in with Kevin Cane and you asked me if there was something I wanted to tell you?"

"Yes —"

"What I really wanted to tell you was that I'm not from Earth. I'm from another planet — planet Thrae — which is about *six hundred* light years away from here."

"Come on Chad. This is really not funny." Melissica said impatiently.

"I wish it was a joke, Melissica. But all those rumors you heard about me. They're true."

"What do you *mean*?"

"The incident behind Temple Bethel — when Kevin Cane and the other guys said I changed into some kind of silver being with bright white glowing eyes."

"That was all made up. You even said so yourself —"

"I know I did. But I was *lying*. It *really* happened. I can transform into a machine!"

Melissica just stared at Chad.

"I'm able to transform into what is called a Battle Sphere. Which I've come to find out has really only one purpose. To obliterate whatever it considers a threat."

"Chad, I —"

"I *know* this all sounds crazy — and I know that I told you that I have been working weekends on Mr. Davis's farm outside of town, but that was also a lie. I have been biking over to his farm to transform and fly to outer space to train for a possible confrontation with Thrae's enemy, the Mitels. All the stuff you are hearing about in the news — the disturbances surrounding the Moon and the mysterious sightings of the sphere in outer space? Melissica, I did all that."

Melissica stepped back. Chad could see in her eyes that she was frightened and confused.

"Chad, listen — I'm not sure what's going on with you, but I think I need to leave — *now*!"

"Melissica, please listen. I am telling you the truth!"

"I *need* to go!"

"No, Melissica, please —"

Before Chad said another word, Melissica ran off. Chad started to run after her but quickly stopped once he realized that following Melissica would only make things worse. As he stood there, Chad suddenly felt foolish and helpless.

How could I have been so stupid?

Chad left the cemetery. He saw Melissica in the distance, heading toward the High School. Every once in a while, she would glance back over her shoulder as if to make sure that he was not following her.

It would serve me right if she calls the police or the FBI. Here I am Major Talbot — come and arrest me. I am the freak you have been looking for. OK, I can't start feeling sorry for myself. That won't solve anything.

Chad didn't think Melissica would tell anyone about their conversation, at least not right away. But to be safe, he decided to avoid her for now, and go home to wait for his parents.

I can show them the Fort and get my mind back on track, he thought. *By then, maybe Melissica will have calmed down a bit and want to talk about this.*

Chad took the long way home so that he would not run into anyone headed to school. Along the way, Chad found himself looking for the brown sedan. Chad felt vulnerable again and he didn't like it.

When Chad arrived home, he glanced up and down the street one last time for the brown sedan before going inside. Entering the kitchen, he dropped his back pack onto the kitchen table with a thud before slumping into one of the four wooden chairs around the table. Chad ran his hands through his long black hair trying to calm down. He stared at the wall clock next to the back door. Chad started to consider the whole concept of immortality.

Will I always keep track of time? And does time really have any meaning to me anymore?

Chad shook his head trying to push the questions out of his consciousness. But they were merely replaced by other concerns.

I need to keep training. I cannot think about failure or feel sorry for myself.

Chad's thoughts then turned to Thrae.

The way Janus described it, Thrae must have been pretty cool. Were all the people smart? What was it like for someone like me to live there? I wish I could have seen it.

Chad looked around the kitchen. He noticed how everything was carefully located along the countertop: the coffee maker, blender, microwave, toaster oven, storage containers, cooking oils were all neatly arranged, everything in its place.

What is my place? Where do I fit in?

Chad stood up, stretched, and headed upstairs to lie on his bed. It was starting to rain. He drifted off to sleep to the sound of rain drops hitting the window. Chad dreamt that his Battle Sphere was being pulled down by gravity as it attempted to reach the upper atmosphere. He eventually found himself sitting on a small silver beach ball as he struggled to get through a long dark tunnel. He tried to use his lights to find an escape route, but it was no use. Eventually, the tunnel opened to a small room. There was no way out.

Chad was awakened by the sound of his parents in the kitchen. He sat up in his bed and looked over at the clock on his bedside table. It read 2:45 p.m.

Holy crap! I have been sleeping for hours.

He jumped out of bed and hurried downstairs. Jim and Molly were surprised to see him home from school so early.

"Chad, are you alright?" he asked.

Chad glanced at Jim before looking toward Molly.

"What's the matter honey?" she asked.

"I tried to tell Melissica, but she freaked out and ran off."

"I'm so sorry honey," she said as she hugged Chad tightly.

"I never should have told her."

"Don't be too hard on her. I mean, I'm still trying to come to grips with the whole thing myself," said Jim. "Are you ready to take us to the Fort?"

"Of course," replied Chad.

Jim and Molly went upstairs to quickly change into casual clothes. Molly quietly expressed how worried she was about Chad. Jim reminded her that they had to do everything they could to support him.

"Like Janus said, we need to help him stay focused," explained Jim.

Within minutes, Chad, Jim and Molly climbed into the station wagon and drove to Randall Park. The rain had stopped and the sun was peeking through the clouds. Jim turned into the park entrance and drove up the dirt road past the stone Civil War Memorial. They drove past the many picnic tables located near the recreation building. There was no one in the park.

"Park over there," Chad instructed, pointing toward an open area just beyond the far edge of the picnic area. Just up the dirt road was the pine forest where Chad had first seen Janus's orb. As they got out of the car, Chad headed up the dirt road.

"This way."

Jim and Molly held hands as they followed Chad toward the pine forest. When he reached a familiar tree, Chad again motioned for the two of them to follow him into the woods.

"Through here."

The three of them navigated their way through the dense pine trees, rain drops from the trees above occasionally falling on them. When they reached the first clearing, Molly looked around.

"Where's the Fort?" she asked.

"We are not there yet Mom. Follow me," Chad said as he walked briskly across the clearing toward the trees on the other side of the opening.

"Come on guys."

Jim and Molly cautiously made their way through the dense forest. There was a bright light up ahead.

"We're almost there!"

They exited the woods. Molly admired the clear blue sky above and its reflection in the still pond in front of her.

"This is *beautiful*," muttered Jim. "I had no idea this even existed."

Chad looked around the pond for signs of the Fort. The grave stone off in the distance was still wet from the recent rainfall.

"Well?" Molly asked.

"Hold on," responded Chad as he scanned the perimeter of the pond.

Molly glanced over at Jim who shrugged his shoulders slightly. Suddenly, across the pond, the Fort appeared.

"There it is!" shouted Chad.

They made their way along the edge of the pond to the series of domelike structures. Markus stepped out from the largest one, waving as they approached.

"Hi Chad!" said Markus with a grin.

"Hello Markus," he said with a big smile. "These are my parents, Jim and Molly Johnson."

"I am pleased to finally meet you. Welcome to the Fort!"

"Hi Markus," Molly said as she stared at his translucent hologram.

"It takes a bit of getting used to," said Markus, noticing Molly's expression.

"I'm sorry. I didn't mean to stare."

"Not to worry. It has been quite some time since a woman stared at me."

"*Markus!*" said Chad, rolling his eyes.

Markus gave Jim and Molly a tour of the Fort, including the newest and largest structure at the far end of the other buildings.

"You can stay here if it becomes necessary to hide," Markus said.

"Thank you, Markus," replied Jim. "Let's hope it doesn't come to that."

Markus nodded in agreement before motioning them over to the next largest structure. As the group entered, Janus stood up to greet them.

"Hello James, Chad. This must be your mother."

"Janus, I would like you to meet my wife Molly."

Molly cautiously stepped forward. Janus reached out his hand to greet her, as she nervously reached out hers in return. Molly marveled at the bright sparkling lights emitting from where their hands touched.

"It is called focused energy Molly," explained Janus. "It allows Markus and me, in our hologram forms, to perform everyday tasks. Markus believes our world's development of hologram technology was the best thing we ever invented. There are days that I tend to agree with him."

Suddenly, Janus's hologram deformed slightly before returning to normal.

"What was that?" asked Molly.

"It's a long story," responded Markus from the back of the structure.

"Thank you both for coming here," said Janus. "I'm sorry that it's under such serious circumstances. However, I remain very confident of a successful outcome."

Janus paused.

"I also want to thank you for the wonderful job you have done raising Chad. I —"

"You don't need to thank me," smiled Molly. "But I must admit, the last 24 hours have been a blur. I want you and Markus to know that we are ready to do whatever we can to help."

"What is the latest with the Mitel Fleet?" Chad asked anxiously.

"They're getting closer," confirmed Janus before pausing to enter a series of instructions into the main computer.

"Over the past several years our monitoring orbs have been accumulating data regarding Earth's space monitoring capabilities. Based on that information, we expect your government to detect the approaching Fleet within the next two days. By my calculations, the Mitels will reach this planet in approximately nine to eleven days."

"Do you think they know for sure that Chad is here?" asked Molly.

"Yes. But I also believe that we still have the element of surprise."

"How?" asked Jim.

"They know Chad is a Battle Sphere, so they are unlikely to confront him directly. They will try to wear him down and capture him. However, we have placed protective shields in various locations."

"Allowing Chad to launch a surprise attack," concluded Molly.

"Exactly," smiled Janus.

"And to recharge his reserves," added Markus.

"The plan is for Chad to destroy large numbers of Mitel Fighters very quickly. Once they are neutralized, the larger space cruisers will be vulnerable to Chad's weaponry."

Janus paused.

"The one unknown is the size of their attack force."

"What do you mean?" asked Molly.

"If it is extremely large, the fight could get more complex. In that case, Chad will be required to recharge his core often to outlast them."

"Don't worry, I'll be ready," said Chad from the back of the structure.

"Janus, what can we do to help?" asked Molly.

"When Earth detects the approaching fleet the world communities will panic. And then your military will likely come looking for Chad. We need to make sure he stays focused. His Battle Hologram will need to remain undetected so that it can perform its support function."

"What then?" asked Jim.

"At the first sign of trouble, I suggest the three of you come here. You won't be detected from the outside world while you are in this place. You should transfer food and other supplies immediately to the largest structure, so that you can live there temporarily in relative comfort."

"We can do that," nodded Molly.

"OK, good. We must also devise a plan to get Chad over to the Davis Farm when the time comes to engage with the Mitel Fleet. Chad has been transforming there and is comfortable in that setting. The physical layout also provides a good location for the Battle Hologram to materialize. If that cannot be achieved, then we will operate from this location. Chad, are you *OK* with that?"

"I think so Janus. I mean, I love this place."

"Excellent. James and Molly, please feel free to start moving your supplies and belongings at any time. Early morning and early evening would be best to minimize detection. Markus and I, in our monitoring orbs, can transport the supplies from the dirt road via our modest antigravity beams."

Janus paused for a moment.

"Chad, it's important that you continue your training and remain sharp. We should plan on a practice session Saturday."

"Sounds good to me."

Janus stood up and led the group to the entrance.

"It's critical that you not reveal the Fort's location. Now if you will excuse us, we must get back to our duties."

Janus and Markus headed back into the structure, as Jim, Molly and Chad headed back around the pond. Jim glanced back toward the Fort as it disappeared.

"*Wow!*" he whispered to himself.

Chad, Molly and Jim navigated back through the woods in silence as each contemplated what Janus had told them. The only sounds were the occasional crackling of twigs and branches underfoot, as they weaved their way back through the dense forest.

When they arrived back at the dirt road, Chad slowly stepped out first and looked around. Up the road someone was walking their dog. He quickly motioned for Jim and Molly to wait. As the dog and its owner disappeared around the bend, Chad motioned for his parents to come to the dirt road. The trio walked briskly back to the car and drove home in silence as Chad and

Molly watched the sun set behind the trees. Chad's mind wandered to thoughts about the approaching Mitel Fleet.

In a cramped mid-level officer's quarters on Cruiser Number 2, Lon Rexx sat at a small rectangular desk with several monitors. Having surrendered his commander's quarters to Gen Zandt, he now found himself relegated to a seldom used area of the cruiser.

"If I was any further from my own quarters, I'd be in the engine room," growled Lon in disgust. "No matter, this allows me to communicate without fear of detection."

Suddenly, the faces of several Cruiser commanders appeared across the makeshift monitors.

"Fellow commanders, thank you for joining me," said Lon. "The time has come for us to finalize our preparations."

A few of the commanders nodded in agreement.

"As you all know, I have not hidden my feelings for our *current* Emperor. Unlike us, he never attended the Academy and in my opinion, he is mentally weak and unfit to lead our planet into this critically important mission. I, on the other hand, will do whatever is necessary to successfully complete our mission."

"Agreed," said one commander.

"I also don't have to remind you that very credible sources have indicated that Liss is a traitor with significant ties to the resistance. The very same people who are destroying our ships and killing our comrades," snarled Lon. "If we don't take matters into our own hands, he will help the resistance defeat us!"

"We hear you Rexx," barked a second Commander. "But get to the point. I can't stay on this encrypted channel very long."

"Very well then," replied Lon calmly. "As I said before we launched, I need everyone's backing in order to declare myself Emperor. Once in charge, we will work together to capture the Battle Sphere. I have been working on a plan that I am confident will achieve our desired result."

"And that plan is?" asked a third Commander.

"All will be revealed in due time. When the Battle Sphere is under our control, nothing will be able to oppose us. And once we seize control of Mitel, we will all have power and riches beyond our wildest dreams!"

The commanders again nodded in agreement. Suddenly, there was a beep from Lon's intercom.

"Rexx here," said Lon impatiently.

"Sorry to bother you Sir, but Leadership Member Zandt wants to see you in his quarters immediately," replied the ICC's communications specialist.

Lon rolled his eyes in disgust.

"Tell him I'm on my way," he replied.

The intercom then beeped a second time.

"We will continue these discussions in the very near future," said Lon.

With that, he pressed a button and the monitors went black.

CHAPTER NINETEEN – THE YOUNG SPY

Chad did not run into Melissica the rest of the week, nor did he go out of his way to look for her. At lunch, Chad sat alone in the school cafeteria and read a book about advanced propulsion theories. He glanced at his cell phone constantly, hoping for a message or call from Melissica. As the week wore on, Chad found himself thinking about her more and more.

On Saturday morning, Chad grabbed his set of spare clothes and came down to the kitchen. Chad was pleased when he heard that Molly and Jim were going to bring some supplies, camping cots and other equipment to the Fort. He hugged both of his parents before heading out on his bike to Davis Farm. It was an unusually warm fall morning and the air was humid. As Chad peddled along, he repeatedly wiped the sweat from his face and chin on the sleeve of his sweatshirt. When he arrived, Chad quickly lifted his bike over the stone fence at the farm's entrance.

I am getting pretty good at this, Chad thought as he scrambled over the stone wall. He reached down and grabbed his bike and headed up the dirt road. Chad did not realize that Melissica was quietly following him on her bicycle. Even though she peddled furiously, Melissica had barely been able to keep up with Chad. What kept her on course was the fact that she knew where Chad was headed based on his confession the previous Monday morning.

As Chad disappeared up the farm's dirt road, Melissica struggled to lift her bike over the stone wall. After a few tries, she shoved it over the top where it fell with a thud. She quickly scaled the wall, picked up her bike, and walked it over to the dirt road. When she saw Chad peddling off in the distance, Melissica headed after him. Before long, Chad stopped riding and was now making his way across the field toward the large tree grove. Melissica stopped and crouched down and waited a few minutes longer before cautiously peddling further up the road.

When she reached the spot where Chad had entered the open field, Melissica stopped and looked around for the best route to take across the field. It was very quiet, except for the sound of crickets. She eventually decided to approach the tree grove from the opposite side to avoid detection. She carefully placed her bike down in the tall grass and walked gingerly out into the field. Almost immediately, hundreds of small yellow moths were flying around in every direction.

Melissica tried to ignore the flying bugs as she made her way further into the open field. Eventually, the moths tapered off as she methodically circled around to the far side of the grove stopping every so often to scan the area. Melissica took a long deep breath before slowly approaching the trees. She crouched down as she moved closer and closer to the grove's edge, before stopping to listen. There wasn't a sound, so Melissica entered the tree grove, moving tentatively from one tree to the next until she saw a clearing. A translucent blue light caught her eye. Inching closer, she saw more lights through the trees which seemed to run along the edges of a structure. To her amazement, the building was completely translucent and appeared to be made up of a series of large cubes stacked on top of each other that ran across one full side of the clearing. Each cube had a translucent blue boarder and she saw people moving about inside the structure.

What is that? she wondered.

Suddenly, Chad exited the building followed by three other individuals who appeared to be carrying some type of portable equipment in their hands.

Why is he only wearing his boxers?

She didn't recognize any of the people with Chad. As she studied them, she realized that they were not really people at all, but some form of translucent beings. Her heart raced as she watched the group walk across the opening. The three translucent figures stopped and appeared to be monitoring Chad as he continued another twenty feet. Melissica crouched down next to the large tree, watching Chad until he stopped, turned around and stood motionless, his legs apart and arms stretched out above his shoulders in either direction.

What the hell is he doing?

Chad's entire body suddenly turned bright silver and his eyes glowed brilliant white. Melissica stared in utter disbelief as Chad slowly rose into the air just before a bright blue translucent sphere abruptly surrounded him. She heard a loud rushing sound as swarms of small particles entered the tree grove from every direction, encircling and swirling around the sphere.

Is he absorbing the particles? She wondered incredulously.

Within seconds, Chad's silver skin appeared to be flaking off in large chunks in all directions to the point where he was no longer visible.

Oh my god! He was telling the truth.

Melissica slowly stepped out from behind the large tree and moved forward until she found herself staring at the shiny metallic silver sphere from the edge of the opening. Two short cylinders lined with a mosaic pattern of glass fragments appeared at the top and bottom of the large orb just before the sphere began to slowly rotate before spinning faster and faster. The wind blew against her face and the tree branches swayed. When she looked back toward the sphere, a random pattern of blue and green lights flashed along the perimeter of the glass fragments.

Suddenly, out of the corner of her eye, Melissica saw two much smaller metallic balls dart out toward her. Instinctively, she turned and ran back into the woods as the two orbs zipped past her. Her heart pounded as she ran as fast as she could toward the open field. The two small silver spheres reappeared ten feet in front of her. Melissica abruptly stopped and stared at the two spheres which hovered silently. Within seconds, Janus and Markus materialized from their spheres and walked toward Melissica. She quickly turned and ran back toward the tree grove opening only to see the three other beings blocking her retreat. Melissica glanced back over her shoulder to see Janus and Markus walking briskly toward her.

"Leave me *alone!*" She yelled as she began to cry.

"Janus wait!" said Chad in a loud voice from the tree grove opening. "I think I know who that is —"

"Chad!" blurted Melissica as she looked back toward the whirling sphere.

Chad's Battle Sphere spun to a stop, the flashing lights disappeared and swirling particles were released back into the air. His silver skin peeled back to reveal the bright blue translucent ball with Chad's silver outline floating in the center with his arms and legs still outstretched. As the blue hue quickly faded away, Chad's silver body descended back to the ground.

"*Melissica*. What are you doing here?" asked Chad.

Teri turned and tossed a towel to Chad which he caught and wrapped around his waist as his silver skin quickly receded and his eyes returned to normal.

Chad hurried toward her, and noticed that she was trembling.

"Chad, why is this young woman here?" asked Janus.

"How did you find me?" Chad asked Melissica, ignoring Janus's question.

"You told me! Don't you *remember*?" snapped Melissica as she fought to control her tears.

"That's right, I did."

Melissica stopped crying but was still trembling.

"It's OK, nobody is going to hurt you," Chad said trying to sooth Melissica who stared at the five holograms standing around her.

"Melissica, let me introduce you," motioned Chad. "This is my *biological* father, Janus Stone. Standing next to him is Markus Kilmar. They brought me to Earth as a baby. Over here is Teri Anton, Denton Millas and Cantor Tallon. They are part of my Battle Hologram team."

Melissica smiled weakly as if to say hello.

"*Hello Melissica*," responded Teri, Cantor and Denton in unison.

"Chad, I'm so sorry I doubted you," mumbled Melissica, rubbing her tears on her sleeve.

"What? That I told you I was an alien from another planet?" Chad asked.

"You told her just like *that*?" interrupted Markus with an amused grin.

Chad looked over at Markus awkwardly.

"You just said *hi* and oh by the way — I'm from another planet?" continued Markus.

With that, Markus and the three technicians laughed loudly. Chad smiled sheepishly before stepping forward to give Melissica a big hug.

"This is so unbelievable," said Melissica softly. "I promise I will never doubt you again."

Mayla suddenly appeared from out of the Hologram Matrix and strode toward the group with a determined look on her face.

"Uh-oh," muttered Chad.

"Commander. What is the meaning of all this?" she asked sternly.

"Hi Mayla," responded Chad. "This is Melissica. She is —"

"I'm Chad's *girlfriend*."

"Mayla, I've known Melissica a long time," explained Chad now blushing profusely.

"Hello Melissica, I'm Mayla Tallis, Chad's Battle Hologram Commander. I'm curious. How did you get here?"

"Well," replied Melissica with a nervous smile. "Chad told me earlier this week that he came here to train, but I didn't believe him. I guess I had to see it for myself. I followed him here on my bike."

"Have you told *anyone else* about this place Chad?" asked Mayla directly.

"*No*," replied Chad quickly. "And I won't. *I promise!*"

"Thank you, Commander," nodded Mayla.

"It's imperative that this place remain a secret for now Melissica," instructed Janus. "Do you understand what I'm telling you?"

"Yes," nodded Melissica.

Janus instructed his monitoring orb to perform a detailed scan on Melissica's emotions.

"I believe we can trust her," Janus said after the scan was completed.

Janus glanced toward Markus who had been running a continuous scan since the moment she was detected.

"I'm way ahead of you my friend," smiled Markus. "My extended data scan leads me to conclude that she is being quite truthful."

"Well then," said Janus. "I believe it is settled."

"OK," said Mayla as she looked around at everyone. "Let's take a few minutes to regroup before we restart the aborted launch and training exercise."

"Sounds good to me," responded Denton, motioning Cantor to follow him back to the Battle Hologram.

"Chad — is there anything else I can do for you?" asked Teri.

"I think I'm good for now, thanks," replied Chad.

"OK great. Let me know when you are ready to start up again."

"Will do, Teri," replied Chad as he watched the technicians head back toward the Hologram Matrix.

"Is there anything I can do Commander?" asked Mayla.

"No, I'm good," Chad grinned. "Is it OK if I show her around?"

Mayla looked toward Janus who nodded his approval.

"That's not a problem," she replied.

"Great! Follow me Melissica," he said leading her toward the Battle Hologram.

As the two of them walked slowly toward the translucent structure, Mayla walked over and stood next to Janus.

"Do you *really* think we can trust her?" Mayla asked Janus quietly.

"Yes."

"What makes you so sure? Is this conclusion based solely on the results of your monitoring scans?"

"The scans have been almost flawless in their analysis of the human condition," explained Janus. "If Markus's extended data scan suggests that she can be trusted, then I am confident she can."

"Very well then," Mayla said, walking toward the Battle Hologram.

"What choice do we have really?" added Janus as Mayla walked away.

Mayla quickly stopped and turned around.

"What do you mean?"

"We can't keep the girl here against her will. That would trigger a massive search by the local authorities and our location would be revealed."

Mayla thought for a moment as she considered what Janus was telling her.

"You're probably right."

"There isn't much time remaining before the Mitels arrive. The girl clearly has an attachment to Chad."

"And it appears the feeling is *mutual*," Markus added.

"Well then," interjected Mayla with an amused grin "I will consult with my team about the potential need for a backup plan."

"Any backup plan must be consistent with our current goal," interrupted Janus.

"And *that is*?" asked Mayla with one eyebrow raised.

"To protect Chad from distraction at all costs," replied Janus. "At least until he successfully begins to engage the Mitel Fleet. Any significant disruption could jeopardize his ability to concentrate and transform. *That* would be disastrous. "

"Understood," replied Mayla. "In the meantime, would you care to walk around the forest grove with me?" she asked gently while reaching out her left hand to Janus.

Janus's stoic expression quickly melted away as he smiled affectionately at Mayla. He took her hand and they walked toward the trees surrounding the forest grove opening.

"I will scout the perimeter to see if we have any more visitors," smiled Markus.

"You do that," replied Janus while he and Mayla continued walking.

In a cramped mid-level officer's quarters on Cruiser Number 2, Lon Rexx was once again meeting with the Cruiser commanders.

"How are the preparations coming Rexx?" asked one commander.

"Everything is moving along according to plan," replied Lon in his deep monotone voice. "The only question we face at this juncture is whether to ask the Mitel Leadership Member to join us. I for one think it would make perfect sense to do so."

"Really, why is that?" asked another commander.

"He would be very valuable when the time comes to round up and eliminate the rest of the Mitel Leadership."

"But why would he agree to join us?" asked a third commander.

"Why wouldn't he?" replied Lon. "As the most junior Member, he has nothing to lose and everything to gain. Besides, what other option would he have? By joining us, he will ensure his own survival."

"But what if he doesn't want to join us?"

"Then he will be eliminated. In the unlikely event the mission doesn't go as planned, we will say that regrettably, he was targeted by the Mitel resistance. Two of his own bodyguards no less."

"How will you deal with the bodyguards?" asked the first commander.

"After such a long voyage, they have become complacent," replied Lon. "They guard the Member on a rotating basis, three at a time. One is stationed in his room at all times, while two others are positioned in the hallway outside. The three remaining guards are off duty until the shift change. If things don't go as planned, I will take care of all of them."

Several of the commanders nodded in agreement.

"Then it's settled," confirmed Lon. "The next time Leadership Member Zandt calls me to his quarters, I will *ask* him to join our cause."

Melissica's eyes widened like large saucers as they approached the Battle Hologram.

"This is so unbelievable. *What's it for*?"

"It's for me."

"For *you*? I don't understand."

"It supports my mechanical self."

"But how?"

"I'm not exactly sure. I think it's stored in my DNA somehow. When I transformed the first time, it essentially *awoke* and materialized. And it's with me in one form or another all the time."

Melissica tentatively walked closer to the hologram structure.

"*Wow*," she said as she stood right next to it. She cautiously reached out her hand to touch it, only to have her hand forced back.

"Why can't I touch it?"

"I'm not sure about that either. Only holograms can enter and exit it. Well, only holograms and *me*. I've also been told that if something bad happens to me, it will also happen to the Battle Hologram."

Melissica stiffened as she looked at Chad.

"But nothing is going to happen to you, *right*?"

Chad paused as if to answer, but didn't.

"Chad, nothing is going to happen *right*?" repeated Melissica firmly.

"I don't know."

"What do you mean *you don't know*?"

"Melissica, I tried to tell you at the cemetery —"

"Tell me what?"

"The Mitels are coming for me."

"Who?"

"The *Mitels*. They are enemies of Thrae. And they are traveling over *six hundred light years* to come here to find me."

"But I don't understand Chad. Why would the *Mitels* come all that way just for *you*?"

"Well, partly because of what you saw here today."

"They are coming all that way because you can change into a *spinning silver sphere*?"

"Yeah, I mean, that's only part of it," explained Chad defensively.

"Why are they are coming all that way for a *spinning sphere*?"

"It's called a *Battle Sphere*.

"Oh that's right. You mentioned that at the cemetery."

"And because I'm the last *immortal*."

"But *how*?" asked Melissica almost in a whisper.

"I was born that way. The Mitel Leadership wants the secret of immortality for themselves. Janus says they will stop at nothing to get it."

Melissica crossed her arms and frowned.

"*Look*," said Chad softly. "I know what I am telling you must sound really crazy."

Melissica looked back up at the Hologram as she considered what Chad was telling her.

"Why don't the Mitels just go to wherever you are from and get it?" she asked eventually.

"Thrae," smiled Chad weakly. "I'm from Thrae."

"*Thrae*," repeated Melissica. "Why don't they just go there to get the secret?"

"Because Thrae no longer exists."

"*What?* Why not?"

"It was destroyed during the second Mitel invasion when I was a baby."

"OK, but why not just give the secret of immortality to the Mitels so that they leave us alone?"

"It's not that easy. My home planet destroyed the *blueprint* and the chemical formula called the serum, for immortality a long time ago. It's gone."

"Then I don't understand. How are you *immortal*?"

"After the serum was discovered, Thraens were occasionally born as *natural* immortals, and didn't need to take the serum. I guess I was one of the *lucky* ones, not that the Mitels know or even care about that. Worst case, they will probably try to reverse engineer it out of *me* somehow."

"So now what?" she asked eventually.

"I must continue training for battle. Janus says that my Battle Sphere is our only hope of defeating the Mitels."

Tears were welling up in Melissica's eyes, as Chad stepped forward and gave her a big hug.

"I'm scared for you."

"I know. I'm scared too."

"Do your parents know about what's going on?"

"Yes. They met Janus and Markus but they have not been here, at least not yet."

"How do *they* feel about all of this?"

"Overwhelmed. And scared."

Melissica paused as she wiped her face again.

"I totally understand that. So why, why are *you* doing it?"

"Doing what?"

"You know, standing up to the Mitels all by your-self?"

"I'm not doing it all by myself," Chad replied eventually.

"You know what I mean."

"The Mitels are coming here for *me* Melissica, not for you, or Janus or Markus or anyone else here on Earth."

"But —"

"*But what?* Everyone else will be caught in the middle unless I do something. *Don't you see Melissica*? I have no choice."

Melissica stood silent for a moment.

"You do have choices," she responded eventually.

"And what might those be?"

"You could negotiate with them."

"Janus says they don't negotiate."

"Then tell them the secret no longer exists!"

"They *know* I'm an immortal. That's why they are coming."

"But you don't *need* to defend Earth," replied Melissica impatiently.

"But I have *no choice* —"

"Yes you do. And you don't owe this planet *anything*!"

"Melissica, you are not making sense —"

"Do you think the world is going to thank you?"

"No I —"

"Do you think countries are magically going to change somehow and be nicer to each other?"

"Melissica, I —"

"Chad, Earth can be a cruel and hard place to live. The world will go right back to doing what it always does — fight over land and money and power. Innocent people caught in the middle are killed or starve every minute of every day and there is nothing you or I can do about it."

"You don't know that!" shouted Chad in frustration.

"*You* are going to get killed for *nothing*!" lectured Melissica angrily.

"Melissica, hold on," said Chad in a softer tone. "*Please* listen to me for a moment. The Mitels caused the destruction of Thrae searching for the secret of immortality. Janus and Markus grabbed me and brought me here."

"But none of that is *your* fault," replied Melissica quietly.

"But that's *not* the point," Chad began. "Don't you see? I am standing up to the Mitels because I have the unique ability to do so *and* because Earth is my home now. Janus says that the Mitel Fleet will do really bad things to us if they are not stopped first. If I don't at least *try* to do it, Earth may end up just like . . ."

"Like Thrae," said Melissica softly.

"Yes. Teri and I talked about this recently in his hologram cube. Janus suddenly appeared in the doorway and explained to both of us that a Battle Sphere has a moral obligation to do everything in its power to protect those who cannot defend themselves."

"That's easy for him to say, isn't it?"

"No, *not at all*," frowned Chad. "Janus was a Battle Sphere himself as was Markus and they successfully defended Thrae against the Mitels during the first invasion."

"*Seriously?*" asked Melissica.

"Seriously," replied Chad glancing up towards the battle hologram. "Unfortunately, they were both badly injured during that attack and can no longer transform. But . . ."

"But what?"

"They would have given their lives in an *instant* if they knew it would have protected our people and planet during the second invasion. They would do the same now if it meant that the people of Earth would be protected."

Melissica listened but did not respond.

"Don't you see Melissica?" Chad asked earnestly. "This is really about the greater good of all mankind and not about someone's selfish viewpoint or agenda or fear or prejudice, or need for power. It is about helping others who can't help themselves. At the end of the day, that's how we should all strive to be remembered."

Chad paused to look Melissica directly in the eyes.

"Maybe the world will look up and take notice and maybe it won't," he continued. "Maybe things won't happen right away. But in time, hopefully the people of

Earth will come together and find their collective voice just like Janus says Thrae did. Do you understand what I'm trying to say?"

"I think so."

"Hey Chad," Teri said, popping his head out of the Hologram entrance, "ready to begin today's mission?"

"Sure. I'm ready when you are Teri."

"Good!" smiled Teri. "Denton and I will be right out with another tech to assist you."

"OK, great. Thanks Teri." Chad squeezed Melissica's hand tightly. "I didn't know how to tell you all of this back at the cemetery. It was probably good that you got to see things for yourself. Everyone here, they are fantastic, caring and dedicated. They are all doing everything possible to make sure things work out OK for *this* world."

Melissica smiled nervously.

"Are you going to be OK?" Chad asked.

"Yeah, I think so," replied Melissica. "At least for the time being anyway."

"Let's go Chad!" boomed Denton from the battle hologram entrance.

"I've got to go," Chad said as he headed back toward Denton.

Melissica watched Chad walk across the opening followed by Denton, Teri and Cantor. As Chad reached the other side, he turned around and stood with his legs and arms apart. Chad closed his eyes and stood motionless for a moment. Melissica could almost feel him concentrating. As before, Chad began his transformation. As Melissica watched, Janus and Mayla came to stand next to her. Markus soon joined them. By this time, Chad had already transformed into the silver metallic Battle Sphere.

While the particles slowly dissipated, the raised cylinders extended from the top and bottom followed by the random flashing light pattern. Chad's Battle Sphere then began to spin slowly, then faster and faster. Melissica again felt the wind blowing against her face and arms.

With a loud whoosh, Chad disappeared into the sky.

"*Oh my god!*" she exclaimed.

"Off he goes!" said Markus loudly as twigs and leaves fell to the ground.

"Young lady, will you be OK returning home by yourself?" Janus asked calmly.

"I think so," replied Melissica.

"Well just in case, Markus will follow you to make sure you arrive safely."

"No, that is not necessary, really. I'll be fine."

"No, I insist. Chad will want to know you got home safely."

Markus's hologram returned to his blue and silver monitoring orb hovering nearby.

"*Wow,*" whispered Melissica.

"Be careful Melissica Erickson," instructed Janus.

"I will," she smiled.

Janus watched Melissica walk across the forest opening. She stopped momentarily to look back at the Battle Hologram before waving at Janus and Mayla.

"Thank you."

"Remember Melissica," said Janus "If you ever need help, just call for us. We will be listening."

Melissica smiled and waved once more before disappearing into the forest followed closely by Markus's monitoring orb.

CHAPTER TWENTY – THE SHIELD TEST

Chad trained in the asteroid belt for several hours, losing track of how many targets he successfully dodged and destroyed. After obliterating a heavy band of potato shaped chunks of rock and ice, Mayla notified everyone that it was time to suspend operations for the day.

"Excellent work Commander Stone! The Hologram team will bring you back at all-out speed for debrief."

"Sounds good," an exhausted Chad replied. On the trip back, he cleared his mind and decided that the time had come to attempt placing a protective shield around the Earth.

If the Mitel Fighters launch a mass assault, he thought, *I could place the shield at the last minute. The fighters would be destroyed on impact!*

"Hello Teri."

"I'm here Chad. Is everything OK?"

"Yes, all good. Listen. I want to try placing a plasma shield around Earth, and—"

"Around the Earth?"

"Correct."

"But why?"

"So I can destroy as many Mitel Fighters as possible."

"I don't think that's a good idea, Chad. First of all it would take an *enormous* amount of energy to place even a temporary shield around the planet. Second, I don't see how that will deter the Mitels. And third, I don't know what the repercussions would be —"

"I do," interrupted Mayla. "In all likelihood, you will take most of Earth's satellite based communications systems off line while the shield is operational. That would most likely cause mass confusion and distress around the World. With all due respect Commander, it's ill advised."

"You may be right Mayla," acknowledged Chad. "But I want to place the shield around the planet *after* they begin their attack. If I time it right, their fighters will fly into it and be destroyed instantly."

"The shield could be used for other purposes," said Denton.

"Such as?" asked Mayla.

"It could also destroy incoming cruiser warheads."

"Good point," nodded Cantor.

Mayla contemplated Chad's idea.

"These practice attempts could send the people of Earth into a mass panic."

"By the time the Mitels attack, won't there already be mass panic?"

"Fair point."

"OK, great," said Chad. "Once you confirm I have exited all-out speed, I'll switch to free flight and give the shield a try."

"Understood, Commander," responded Mayla.

"How far out do you plan to initiate the shield?" asked Teri curiously.

"About a hundred miles."

"How did you come up with that Chad?" asked Teri.

"From what you guys have told me, Mitel Fighters are most effective within a five hundred mile radius of their transport vessels. They should still be going at a pretty good clip one hundred miles out."

"That makes sense."

"Let's see what I can do," said Chad.

"You are fifty thousand miles from Earth and closing rapidly," confirmed Teri.

"Disabling *all-out* speed mode," said Cantor.

"Thirty thousand miles and decelerating rapidly," confirmed Denton.

All-out speed mode is successfully completed," announced Teri.

"Five thousand miles and closing," stated Denton.

"Going into free flight," said Chad.

As Chad slowed his Battle Sphere to a stop approximately two hundred miles from Earth, he gazed over the blue, white and green horizon. Chad quickly focused his thoughts on projecting the plasma shield while his Battle Sphere spun in place. Mayla, Teri and the entire battle Hologram team watched the monitors as Chad's internal energy levels rapidly spiked. His psychokinetic ability triggered vast quantities of trace metals to swirl upwards from the Earth's surface through the troposphere and thermosphere before settling into outer space all around the planet to form the basis of the plasma shield.

"He's almost off the charts!" exclaimed Teri over the closed intercom system so as not to distract Chad.

"This is truly remarkable," Mayla muttered.

"Commander Tallis" said Denton.

"Yes?" answered Mayla looking away from the computer screen.

"It's the Battle Hologram. It is expanding again."

"Unbelievable!" whispered Mayla as she switched her attention to the Matrix monitoring systems computer.

At the U.S. Naval Space Surveillance System Command headquarters located in Dahlgren, Virginia, Major Michael Talbot was sitting in a swivel chair at the rear of the main monitoring room enjoying his late afternoon coffee. Ever since the youngest of his children went off to college, Major Talbot found himself spending more time at headquarters on weekends.

"Sir, I think you should see this," said Lieutenant Miller.

"What is it Lieutenant?"

"Our radar has detected a UFO approximately two hundred miles out in space," explained Lieutenant Miller.

"Give me some details," instructed Major Talbot.

"Well, Sir. Just like the other recent activity, this UFO seems to have appeared out of nowhere. When I first picked up its signal, the UFO was heading toward Earth much faster than an asteroid or comet, before suddenly slowing to a stop."

"It *stopped*? What's it doing now?"

"It's just hovering there, Sir."

"Can we get a picture of it Lieutenant?"

With that, Lieutenant Miller quickly typed instructions into his computer. In response, headquarters staff immediately initiated tracking and surveillance in conjunction with their counterparts at the National Reconnaissance Office. From approximately three hundred fifty miles out in space, one of the Military's Hubble style satellites closest to the UFO was repositioned to focus on its current coordinates. Once the UFO was located, the satellite was instructed to take images of the object.

The first images became visible on Lieutenant Miller's computer screen.

"It *looks* like a spherical satellite," said Major Talbot out loud. Then it suddenly occurred to him.

"Lieutenant, pull up an image of the UFO taken by the amateur astronomer in California last week. *Quickly!*"

"Doing it now Sir."

After a series of key strokes, the two images appeared side by side.

"*That's it*! It's the same object!" exclaimed Major Talbot excitedly.

"It sure looks like it Sir."

Two hundred miles out in space, Chad took one more deep breath before focusing with all his might on initiating the plasma shield. Several seconds later, Chad saw a light blue haze around the entire visible northern hemisphere. He did not realize that the shield had also spread across most of the southern hemisphere.

At the Naval Space Command headquarters, the computer screens suddenly went black, and most of the satellite communications systems went down. Everyone in the main surveillance room looked at each other in confusion as the alarm system sounded.

"What the hell just happened?" asked a confused Major Talbot.

"I'm really not sure Sir," replied Lieutenant Miller. "Nothing is responding. Our communications systems are being jammed somehow."

"Major Talbot Sir! My cell phone is not working!" said another analyst.

"Neither is mine!" said a third.

"We have lost contact with our satellite systems Sir!" confirmed another analyst.

This is crazy thought Major Talbot. *Who or what could be doing this?*

From space, Chad watched the partial plasma shield stay in place for about five minutes before rapidly deteriorating. At first, large spots appeared where the shield had dissipated; propagating their way across the planet until the blue hue was gone.

Not bad! He thought. *Not bad at all!*

"Chad?" asked Teri.

"I'm here Teri."

"OK good. We had lost all contact with you."

"It must have been the shield. It looked to me like it covered most of the planet! Did you register it?"

"*Did we register it?*" snorted Teri. "I think just about everyone here on Earth registered it Chad!"

"Woo-hoo!" yelled Chad with excitement.

"Chad, *listen* to me. You must get back down here *immediately*. The planet's entire surveillance system is coming back on line and will be scouring outer space to find the cause of the communication outage."

"On my way."

At the Naval Space Command headquarters, all systems instantaneously came back on line, as if nothing had happened.

"We are back up Sir!" confirmed an analyst sitting a few seats to the left of Lieutenant Miller.

"Lieutenant, get me another image of the UFO," instructed Major Talbot.

"Yes Sir!"

Lieutenant Miller typed furiously then shook his head in frustration.

"What's wrong Lieutenant?"

"It's the UFO, Sir. It's gone."

"Try the deep space antennae."

"Trying it now Sir," responded Lieutenant Miller as he sent search and locate instructions to his counterparts at the National Reconnaissance Office.

After several seconds, a response appeared on his computer screen.

"Negative Sir," replied Lieutenant Miller. "No. Wait!"

"What is it Lieutenant?" asked Major Talbot as he leaned over the Lieutenant's shoulder.

"I'm detecting a small blip just above the Earth's atmosphere heading toward Earth."

"Where?"

"Over northern New York State Sir."

"Are you sure?"

"I'll print the position data history in a moment, but yes, I'm positive on the location ID Sir."

"Very interesting."

"Sir?"

"Remember the UFO crash we investigated in Upstate New York about fifteen years ago?"

"Of course I do."

"And remember how we went back up there to investigate the eyewitness reports of a group of teenagers?"

"How could I forget *that*," smiled Lieutenant Miller.

"My hunch is that they are all related. Things might finally be starting to come together on this case."

Mayla, Denton, Teri and several other technicians rushed out to meet Chad as he landed. They waited impatiently as Chad completed his transformation.

"Commander, your plasma shield covered almost eighty-three percent of the planet on your first try!" explained Mayla excitedly.

"Unfortunately," added Teri, "you threw the world's communications systems into turmoil."

"Oops," Chad said with a grin.

"*It's actually a big deal, Chad,*" said Denton. "The world's scientific and technology community will be trying to get to the bottom of this. Our fear is that the trail will eventually lead to you."

"Well let's hope not. At least not before the Mitel Fleet shows up. Once *they* are detected, I assume all the focus will shift to them."

"Not necessarily," said Teri. "Earth's military may associate *you* with the Mitel Fleet, and that association is not ideal."

"As far as I'm concerned, Commander, whatever issues arise, it was well worth it," said Mayla. "As you said yourself, we might be able to use the shield to surprise the Mitels and destroy a significant number of their strike fighters."

"Agreed," said Teri.

"And look!" declared Mayla motioning toward the Battle Hologram "Our Battle Matrix is about to outgrow the protection of the tree grove!"

"Woo-hoo!" shouted Chad.

"I don't know how you are doing this Commander, but it is truly astonishing."

"Thanks, everyone," grinned Chad as he looked around the area. "Where's Janus?"

"He is back at the Fort with Markus monitoring the Mitel Fleet," explained Teri.

"Does he know about the shield test?"

"Yes," confirmed Mayla. "But he and Markus are still gathering advance Intel about the approaching Mitel Fleet. Their monitoring orbs are transferring the data to our Hologram computers so that we can incorporate the data into our battle planning."

"Commander," said Denton hastily. "I think it's probably time for you to get dressed and debrief. Before you do, call your parents and let them know everything is OK."

"Will do. Has anyone seen my phone?"

"It's in the Battle Hologram control room," replied Teri.

"Commander, don't forget to call Melissica too," said Mayla with a grin.

Lon paced impatiently in his cramped officer's quarters when the intercom beeped.

"Rexx here," he said lunging for the button.

"Sorry to bother you Sir, but Leadership Member Zandt would like to see you in his quarters immediately," replied the ICC's communications specialist.

This is it! he thought.

"Tell him I'm on my way." The intercom then beeped a second time.

Lon pressed the intercom button again.

"Luc here," answered the voice.

"It's me," said Rexx. "Meet me with the others at my main quarters. The time has come. Do you understand?"

"Completely. See you there."

After getting off the HorVert elevator, Lon waited impatiently for the three others to arrive. They then quickly made their way to Lon's old quarters.

"Are you ready?" whispered Lon.

"Yes," nodded Luc.

When they arrived, the two Special Forces guards raised their hands and waved.

"Hello Commander Rexx," smiled one guard. "Leadership Member Zandt is expecting you."

"Understood," smiled Lon. "Sorry to be late."

As the four men approached the door, the guards motioned them to stop.

"Only two are allowed in at a time," said the first guard.

"I know. But these men are here to help answer Leadership Member Zandt's questions."

"I am sorry Sir, but there are no exceptions."

"Understood," nodded Lon. "Luc, please accompany me into the meeting. Mir and Zen, wait here."

The doors slid open. Gen Zandt was seated across the room. The third Special Forces Guard stood in the corner, his electro laser stored safely in its holster.

"Thank you for coming," said Gen.

"Our pleasure. This is Luc Nord. Luc has been instrumental in helping integrate our mission plan."

"It is greatly appreciated," nodded Gen.

"Between the two of us, hopefully we can answer your questions."

"Good. My first question has to do with —"

"Before we begin, I would like to discuss something much more important."

"*More* important than the mission plan?"

"In my opinion, yes."

"Very well," motioned Gen.

"My fellow commanders and I have grave concerns about how the mission is progressing. We have sustained significant losses due to the ongoing terrorist activities of the Mitel resistance."

"I understand commander Rexx, but we have been dealing with it as best as can be expected."

"With all due respect Sir, I don't agree."

"Oh? Any why is that?"

"In my opinion, we are not addressing the root cause of the problem."

"Which is?"

"Emperor Liss."

"*Emperor Liss*? What about him?"

"My sources tell me Liss is a traitor with significant ties to the resistance. If we don't address things quickly, Liss and the resistance will defeat us!"

"That is a grave accusation, Commander Rexx. Who do you suggest replace him?"

"*Me.*"

"I see."

"And to that end, I have been putting together a plan which will enable us to capture the Battle Sphere unharmed."

"Excellent —"

"Which we can then use for our own purposes."

"*Our own purposes*?"

"Yes. And with your help, we will return to Mitel and use the Battle Sphere to seize power for ourselves."

"This is highly unusual —"

"Think of it!" interrupted Lon again, growing increasingly tense. "*Nothing* will be able to stop us!"

"Capturing the Battle Sphere intact is no guarantee of success, Commander," scoffed Gen.

"Nothing on Mitel will be able to defeat it."

"And just how will you get the Battle Sphere to do our bidding?"

"We will seize all of those in his inner circle and hold them all as hostages."

"If he in fact has a team," mused Gen. "And if they are not killed beforehand. There are too many variables here."

"How can you say that?" blurted Lon in exasperation.

"Who else have you discussed this with?" asked Gen distrustfully.

"Every cruiser commander other than the Emperor's cruiser," replied Lon quickly.

"So you are proposing a coup?"

"Yes."

Gen rubbed his chin as he considered Lon's request.

"I am afraid I cannot support such an action Commander."

"Your response surprises me," replied Lon.

Sensing trouble, the Special Forces guard reached for his electro laser but was not as quick as Luc, who pulled a specially modified "dwarf" electro laser from under his shirt, fatally shooting the guard. On cue, Lon activated a small beeper on his belt before opening the door. Zen and Mir quickly dragged the other two dead guards into the room.

As the doors close, Lon turns to Gen.

"I am giving you one last chance to join us," he growled.

"This is madness!" shouted Gen leaping to his feet.

"What is your decision?" yelled Lon menacingly.

"I demand to speak with Emperor Liss *immediately*!"

"Your decision is regrettable," hissed Lon as he lunged forward.

He grabbed the much smaller man with both hands and pulled him against his chest. In one quick motion, Lon retrieved a long dagger from his belt and thrust it deep into Gen's abdomen.

Lon gripped Gen tightly as he whispered into the dying man's ear.

"This is what happens to those who oppose me."

Lon pulled the dagger from Gen and wiped it clean on Gen's shirt before letting his lifeless body fall to the floor. Lon then turned to the three others.

"Wait here. You will ambush and eliminate the three other guards as they arrive for their shift change," he instructed calmly. "After that, I want you to jettison all of the bodies into outer space and have my quarters fully cleaned for my return."

CHAPTER TWENTY-ONE – CLOSING IN

Leading experts in the fields of astrophysics, astronomy, aeronautic engineering and telecommunications from around the world met in San Diego to determine the cause of the sudden communications outage. Rumors quickly spread that China, Russia or the United States was secretly testing a new high technology cyber attack. Rumors intensified to the point that the world's largest governments put their military on high alert. As it all unfolded, Chad and his parents tried to keep a low profile. Molly and Jim quietly moved additional supplies to the Fort.

Despite the heightened surveillance, Chad was still determined to practice placing a plasma shield around the Earth the following weekend. The Battle Hologram team debated the merits against the potential to plunge the world into war before the Mitel Fleet even arrived.

"The Mitel Fleet will be detected any moment now by Earth's long-range telescopes," Janus told the team on Friday. "Quite frankly, I'm surprised they haven't been located by now. But when they are, world attention will shift to the approaching Fleet."

Janus paused to look around the room filled with hologram technicians and team leaders.

"Because of this inevitability, I feel Chad must continue to practice placing his plasma shield around the planet. Since his abilities clearly surpassed anything we achieved on Thrae, the Mitel Fleet will be caught by surprise."

"But Janus," said Mayla, "don't you think Earth's governments, which already have a history of distrust for one another, might go to war thinking they are under attack from another country?"

"No. I don't, Mayla."

"Why not?"

"The Mitel Fleet of course."

"I don't understand." Teri said.

"Governments will shift their focus to the exterior threat," Janus began. "It is quite reasonable to assume they will conclude that the disturbances are being *created* by that threat. While it may not galvanize world governments to work together, they will, at the very least, focus their attention *independently* to quantify the threat."

The room was silent as Janus spoke.

"The diversion will allow Chad to continue to develop and strengthen his plasma shield in the short term. Once the Mitel Fleet gets close, he will have to stop to maintain the element of surprise."

The technicians and team leaders looked at each other and nodded their heads in approval.

"Then it is settled," said Mayla. "Chad will continue to practice and develop his plasma shield until we determine the Mitels are close enough to detect the presence of his Battle Sphere and plasma shield."

The next morning, the Battle Hologram team manipulated Chad's *all-out* speed algorithm sending his Battle Sphere streaking into outer space to avoid detection on radar. Within minutes, Chad reached Mars before circling back around towards Earth. Once his *all-out* deceleration was completed, he entered free flight mode before stopping approximately two hundred miles from Earth. Focusing his energy, Chad quickly projected a plasma shield around the Earth covering ninety five percent of the planet's surface for twelve minutes.

As the shield deteriorated, Chad's *all-out* speed was reactivated so he could fly back toward Mars to avoid detection. While he hovered beyond the far side of the red planet, Chad recharged his plasma energy reserves while Mayla, Teri and the rest of the team confirmed that the shield test had drained approximately seventy percent of Chad's Battle Sphere energy reserves.

"The energy draw is simply too great," said Mayla nervously.

She stood motionless in the Command Cube with her arms crossed.

"If he is forced to engage the Mitels immediately after initiating the shield, he will be at minimum energy reserves."

"But Commander," replied Denton from across the cube, "if the shield successfully destroys a significant number of warheads and Mitel Fighters, their battle operations will be disrupted. Chad won't need to immediately replenish his reserves."

"Yes, that is a possibility, but if the shield is not successful, he will be vulnerable."

After fully recharging, Chad swooped back to Earth under the direction of the Battle Hologram and repeated the maneuver. This time, the plasma shield covered ninety-nine percent of Earth's surface. On his third attempt, Chad successfully placed a plasma energy shield around the entire planet, lasting almost twenty minutes.

The entire Battle Hologram team cheered when Teri announced the latest shield data results. In all the excitement, Mayla walked over to Janus and gave him a long tight hug, lighting up the entire Command Cube.

Rumors quickly spread through the Mitel Fleet that Membership Leader Zandt had been assassinated by the resistance. Sitting in his command console on the ICC of Cruiser Number 1, Zan glanced up at Ard.

"What do you think about the assassination rumors Ard?"

"If it's true, why didn't Rexx tell us already? Given his history, I wouldn't be surprised if he strangled him with his own hands."

"Let's ask him then," said Zan as he turned on the interfleet communications system and typed in a four-digit code.

"By all means. After all, you're the boss."

Lon Rexx's face appeared on the monitor.

"Does this guy *ever* smile?" whispered Ard.

"Commander Rexx here."

"Commander Rexx, Emperor Liss speaking. I am here with Commander Lindar."

Lon nodded but did not respond.

"We have heard rumors that Leadership Member Zandt has been assassinated. Is it true?"

"Unfortunately, yes."

"What happened?"

"A formal investigation is underway, but it appears that two or more Special Forces guards were members of the resistance. In the ensuing shootout, Leadership Member Zandt and the guards were fatally wounded."

"I see. Where are the bodies now?"

"They were all jettisoned into space, naturally."

"Even Zandt?"

"Yes."

"By Mitel protocol, his body should have been sealed in a cryogenic tube and brought home."

"I am a cruiser commander, not a bureaucrat," Lon replied impatiently.

Zan did not immediately respond as he studied Lon's expression.

"Please forward me the investigation report as soon as it is available. Thank you Commander Rexx."

Lon nodded and the screen went black.

After a long silence, Zan asked, "well?"

"Well what?"

"What do you think?"

"About what Rexx just said?"

"*Yes*," replied Zan rolling his eyes.

"Off the record, I think Rexx would kill his own mother if he thought it would be of use to him — "

"That aside, do you believe him?"

"The fact that there is no evidence remaining seems a bit too convenient."

"Hopefully the report will shed some light on the actual confrontation."

"Maybe. But I can't recall a previous confrontation where Special Forces personnel acted on behalf of the resistance."

"Neither can I, but given the havoc they have caused on this mission, it wouldn't be a stretch to assume that they have finally infiltrated that elite unit."

"Anything is possible I guess. But my hunch is that Lon is up to something. Something big."

In Virginia, Major Talbot was monitoring the communications disruptions, convinced that Chad Stone was somehow involved. It was time to present his findings to the Pentagon and to request from the Joint Chiefs of Staff permission to detain Chad and Jim for questioning. *He must be piloting that craft* Major Talbot concluded. *Is he trying to create a diversion? Is he here in advance of others on their way and sending some form of location signal?*

Major Talbot's thoughts drifted back to his trip to Upstate New York to check out the eye witness reports of an alien.

Those boys really did see something behind the Temple. He concluded. *Jim Johnson knew about Chad's real identity when he confronted me. He was trying to throw us off the trail . . . but why?*

By Sunday morning, the internet was filled with theories, rumors and gossip about how or why the world's wireless communications systems were repeatedly being shut down. Every expert came to the same conclusion: a blue hue engulfed the globe as signals were disrupted, and then disappeared when service returned. At the Keck Observatory located fourteen thousand feet above sea level at the top of Hawaii's Mauna Kea peak, Francine Mulholland was collecting data from deep space. It was 11:30 p.m. on a quiet and starry night. Suddenly, Francine noticed a dense but un-focused group of lights that she had never noticed before.

That's strange she thought.

Francine tracked the objects and over the next several hours, continued to monitor and take pictures of the phenomenon.

The lights appear to be steadily moving she concluded.

Francine quickly sent an email to her collogues at the Great Canary Telescope some eleven hours ahead of her. The Great Canary, situated on the La Palma Mountain was the largest telescope in the world with a light collecting area of 34.3 feet. She gave the coordinates of the objects and typed:

DO YOU SEE WHAT I SEE?

As dawn arrived, she received a response:

YES, WE DO.

News of the mysterious light pattern spread. The Southern African Large Telescope or SALT, the largest telescope in the Southern Hemisphere also began tracking the light pattern. And then, both the Hubble space telescope and the Chandra X-Ray Observatory followed the movement of the unusual light grouping.

Finally, and in response to the growing scientific chatter, the National Reconnaissance Office satellites and the U.S. Naval Space Surveillance System Command began to monitor the strange pattern of lights. The light pattern was clearly moving and heading toward Earth.

Over the next few days, amateur astronomers around the world took photos and posted them online. Main stream media reported on the phenomenon as well. Speculation was rampant. Could it be a dense group of meteors or comets or some other kind of ancient space debris? On Thursday, as the lights moved closer to Earth, several satellite images were leaked to the press. The light pattern was not some form of naturally occurring event at all. They appeared to be a group of space craft.

On Friday morning, on the front page of the New York Post, the headline read:

E.T. IS COMING TO EARTH!

The headline on The Wall Street Journal read:

MYSTERIOUS SPACE LIGHTS CONCLUSIVELY
IDENTIFIED AS UFOS HEADING TOWARD
EARTH

USA Today also confirmed that the lights appeared to be some form of alien craft heading toward Earth. Their headline was:

WORLD EXPERTS AGREE: UFOS HEADING
TOWARD EARTH

As Janus predicted, the planet was now fixated on the approaching vessels. Chad's tiny and mysterious sphere was now all but forgotten by everyone except for Major Talbot. He was now convinced that the blue haze, the wireless communications interruptions and the approaching UFOs were all linked. And he was also sure that they were all connected in some way to Chad Stone and the UFO crash fifteen years ago.

On Friday afternoon, Major Talbot arrived at the Pentagon to brief the Joint Chiefs of Staff on the findings of his ongoing investigation. The meeting, while closed to the press, was packed with Military officials, Senators from the subcommittees on Cybersecurity and Emerging Threats and Capabilities, representatives from the Department of Homeland Security, CIA and the FBI. All eyes were on Major Talbot as he approached the Joint Chiefs who sat in a row at the far end of the chamber room on a raised platform behind a long mahogany desk. Behind them were a series of large windows that looked out over one of the internal court yards of the Pentagon complex.

As Major Talbot approached, he stopped and snapped a salute to the Joint Chiefs and cleared his throat. "Good morning Sirs. You should have the summary report of our investigation in front of you."

"As you know, we recovered the remains of a small UFO in Upstate New York fifteen years ago. Some of the materials were of a composition and strength that we have not yet been able to reproduce. We also recovered incredibly sophisticated electronics and an advanced propulsion system that a highly-classified NASA development team has been tirelessly working to reverse engineer for over a decade. Their progress to date is promising. It appears that travel faster than the speed of light is possible in the not too distant future."

Major Talbot paused for a moment.

"Based on the evidence obtained at that crash site, we believe that one or more of its occupants survived the impact. It was a rather small craft with a cramped cabin area, so it's unclear — "

"Why are you so convinced that the craft was manned, Major?" interrupted the Joint Chief Chairman U.S. Army General Frank Woods and JCS Chairman.

The Joint Chiefs of Staff consist of the Chairman, the Vice Chairman, the Chief of Staff of the Army, the Chief of Naval Operations, the Chief of Staff of the Air Force, the Commandant of the Marine Corps and the Chief of the National Guard Bureau.

"Well Sir, it appears the vessel had been stripped by the occupants. Various fiber optic circuitry and other parts were removed from the craft and we found tools and other objects in the field that appeared to have been dropped or lost in their haste to escape detection."

General Woods leaned back as he raised his eyebrows.

"I seem to recall that no footprints were ever found. Is that right, Major?" he asked.

"Correct."

General Woods smiled as he looked around the large room.

"That certainly does not support your theory Major, wouldn't you agree?"

Major Talbot cleared his throat again.

"I understand your skepticism Sir. And the matter remained essentially closed until recently but about six months ago, we were notified of an unusual incident only a few miles from the crash site in the town of Coopers Falls. A group of high school boys claimed that another sixteen year old by the name of Chad Stone changed from human form to a silver alien being — "

"A *silver alien being*?" Chief of Staff of the Air Force General William Grant interrupted with a snort.

"Um, yes Sir. The eyewitness accounts described the boy's outer skin changing to a silver metallic, and that his eyes glowed."

"Major, are you sure this isn't something the young men may have watched on an old episode of the X-Files?" asked a skeptical Chief of Naval Operations Admiral

Jonathan Black. He appeared to Major Talbot to be the youngest of the Joint Chiefs.

A slight laugh arose among the spectators.

"I am sure Sir."

"How is that Major?" asked Admiral Black pointedly.

"We looked into the boy's background —"

"Chad Stone?" asked Commander of the Marine Corp General Frederick Dempsey, as he flipped through the summary report.

"Yes Sir. It just so happens that as a baby, he was left outside the local hospital's emergency room in the middle of the night *only* a few hours after the crash."

"Leaving a baby abandoned at the hospital is an unusual and heartbreaking story Major, but certainly not proof that he is an alien," interjected General Grant.

"Agreed, Sir. However, our detailed review of Chad's medical records obtained from the hospital reveal many anomalies —"

"Such as?" interrupted Chief of the National Guard Bureau General Robert Doyle.

"Sir. Chad was born with four fingers on each hand and four toes on each foot. His heart has five chambers. The medical records reveal he has an abnormally large brain and lungs."

Major Talbot paused briefly to take a sip of water.

"The most important and startling finding is that blood tests showed Chad Stone has extraordinarily high levels of titanium, aluminum, beryllium and other metals. Doctors were at a loss to explain how, as a toddler, he was alive given his levels of contamination. Today, at sixteen years of age, he is in excellent health."

"As I previously mentioned, Chad was observed by multiple eye witnesses transforming into a silver alien. I also want to point out that these young men were questioned separately at length and their accounts remained consistent. Unfortunately, we have not had any additional sightings of Chad's transformation nor have we had the resources to continue surveillance."

Major Talbot paused to look at all the Joint Chiefs.

"That being said, it is my conclusion that Chad Stone was never contaminated. Rather, he is an alien and was aboard the small craft that crash landed in New York. I am also convinced that he was dropped off at the hospital by one or more aliens."

The Joint Chiefs of Staff conferred briefly before the Chairman Spoke.

"Major, that is quite a story. But even if it was true, *and I am not saying that it is*, what is the connection to the recent communications blackouts and the alleged alien vessels heading toward our planet?"

"Sir, please look at page 16 in my summary. There you will see photos taken by the amateur astronomer of the metallic object in outer space. These pictures were taken at or about the time of one of the initial incidents of the blue hue around the Moon. On page 18, you will see a second sphere that our Military satellites captured during a subsequent power outage. That time, a similar blue hue was seen around Earth."

"Upon detailed review, the objects appear to be identical. We were fortunate to track the sphere from the second sighting as it returned to Earth. We lost contact with it as it neared the planet's surface in upstate New York in the vicinity of the crash site. It is my theory that the sphere is being piloted by Chad Stone."

"It is also my theory that whatever or whoever is headed this way from outer space, they are connected to Chad Stone in some manner. The recent wireless communications outages and associated blue hue around the planet may have been an attempt by Chad to contact his home planet, or at the very least, direct them toward Earth."

Major Talbot paused briefly to study his notes.

"I would like to remind the Joint Chiefs that over the last several years, we have detected the unexplained appearance of what appeared to be small outposts on the Moon —"

"Major," interrupted General Woods, "are you referring to the Lunar Reconnaissance Orbiter incidents?"

"Yes, General, I am. If you recall, those sightings appeared in three distinct locations over a period of five years."

"Yes, I do remember that," General Woods replied.

"In each instance they were classified as small dome-like structure of unknown origin supported by what appeared to be solar panels. They would vanish soon after being located. Some experts thought it was one structure that was being moved around somehow —"

"But I recall that you disagreed."

"Yes Sir, I did."

"Remind me why."

"Based on a review of the surveillance images, Sir, I concluded that each structure and panel seemed to be somewhat different in size and shape."

"Oh, that's right," nodded General Woods. "I do remember you saying that at the time."

"Yes Sir. And there were no other space exploration programs being conducted by the United States, or any other county at the time of those sightings. I believe they represented a series of camouflaged reconnaissance outposts that, in my opinion, are also connected to recent events."

Major Talbot then stopped talking and stood silently in front of the Joint Chiefs.

"Interesting theories Major. Is it also your theory that these UFOs are coming to *rescue the boy*?" asked Admiral Black.

"That is a possibility, Sir, but Chad may have also called them here for reasons yet unknown. He may be trying to create a diversion until they arrive. In either case, I recommend that we act immediately."

"And what are you recommending, Major Talbot?" asked General Dempsey, stroking his chin.

"Sir, I think it is time to detain Chad Stone and interrogate him. As a documented United States citizen, I know this may represent a violation of his constitutional rights. But in the interests of National Security and the authority granted under the Patriot Act, we must take action before Chad Stone does, and before *whoever* or *whatever* it is that is headed this way, arrives."

"Let us recess for ten minutes to discuss this matter," responded General Woods.

With that, the MPs approached the front of the desk as the chamber erupted into a loud discussion among the spectators. The Joint Chiefs quickly huddled.

Not too long later, the MPs motioned that the Joint Chiefs had concluded their discussions. Major Talbot jumped up from his chair and approached the desk as they settled back into their chairs.

"Major Talbot, we have discussed the matter," said General Woods. "And we agree that you should take whatever steps necessary to locate, detain and question this young man."

"You mean Chad Stone Sir?"

"Yes, young Mr. Stone. Detain him until you are satisfied with your findings."

"And what about his adopted parents, family and friends?" asked Major Talbot.

"I will leave that up to you Major. If you feel that they can be of assistance in your investigation then yes, seek them out as well. The entire United States Military will be available to assist you in whatever capacity necessary."

"And what if he resists Sir?"

"I will leave that up to your discretion Major. These are clearly unusual times and we all agree that we need answers and we need them *quickly*."

"Thank you, Sirs," Major Talbot replied with a nod and a salute before briskly walking out of the Pentagon Chamber room.

CHAPTER TWENTY-TWO – GETTING READY

Chad slept poorly all week. Like the rest of the world, he stayed up late every night to watch the news coverage of the approaching UFOs. The Mitel threat was becoming real and he was scared.

On Friday afternoon, Chad decided to go to the Fort to talk with Janus and Markus. Sitting on his bed, Chad studied the tree branches outside his window which were starting to shed their leaves. He took a deep breath and tried to shake all the negative thoughts.

Time to get going.

Chad hurried downstairs and through the kitchen. On his way out the back door, he stuck a note on the refrigerator. It read:

I AM GOING TO THE FORT. CHAD

At the end of the driveway, Chad looked around for the brown sedan, but it was nowhere in sight. He jogged down Grove Avenue and turned up Main Street toward Randall Park. The crisp autumn air felt good in his lungs and he found himself running at a brisk pace. Reaching the park entrance, Chad quickly turned and headed up the dirt road past the old stone Civil War Monument and into the woods before stopping at the entry point. He pretended to stretch while scanning the area for signs of other people.

Good. Nobody is around.

Chad darted into the dense pine forest and made his way to the first opening. Upon entering the clearing, he noticed Markus's monitoring orb hovering in the center about six feet above the ground. As he approached the small sphere, Markus's hologram materialized.

"Hello there, lad," Markus said with a gentle smile.

"Hi Markus."

"Come to see your father?"

"Yes. And you too."

"Ok. How are you Chad?"

"Nervous."

"Listen to me. You have trained *very, very* hard. Mayla and the Battle Hologram will be with you every step of the way. You have got to believe in them — and *trust* them."

"I *know.*"

"But *will you*?"

"Yes Markus. I will."

"Good," smiled Markus. "Don't forget to believe in yourself too."

Chad sighed and looked up at the blue sky.

"That's probably the hardest part Markus. I don't know if I *can* trust myself."

Seeing the worry on Chad's face, Markus stepped forward and looked him straight in the eye.

"You have to believe in yourself, because we believe in you," whispered Markus before stepping away to study Chad closely. "Janus would *not* send you out there unless he was confident that you could do this. But he also never said it would be easy."

"I know."

"We have studied the Mitel battle techniques and we have painstakingly trained you to be successful. They will have traveled a very long way and will be tired and vulnerable."

"What if they've changed their fighting techniques?"

Markus let out a big laugh.

"Lad, if there is one thing I can *guarantee* you, it is that the Mitels will not change how they do things, *ever*. They would not be coming here otherwise. You will see. They will help defeat themselves."

"Do you really think so?"

"Yes Chad I do, and listen, you — on your own — developed a new weapon that could be of great assistance against the Mitels."

"You mean the plasma shield?"

"*Yes*. Janus is quite impressed and he does not impress easily, I can assure you."

Chad cracked a smile as Markus rubbed his long black hair.

"Let's go see what Janus is up to, shall we?"

Chad nodded in agreement.

They quickly made their way through the second portion of the dense forest. Arriving at the pond, a misty fog hung over the water. Entering the second clearing, the Fort suddenly appeared. Chad hurried inside.

"Hello Chad."

"Hi Janus."

"Markus sent me a message about your concerns."

Chad glanced over at Markus briefly as Janus stood up and faced him.

"Markus is right. You are well trained and the Mitels have traveled a long, long way, and as a result, their morale and concentration will be compromised."

Suddenly, rustling sounds could be heard from out in the woods. Janus activated the plasma shield causing the Fort to disappear while he and Markus focused their orbs on the area of the disturbance.

Within seconds, they had processed the data. Markus smiled broadly as Jim, Molly and Melissica stepped out of the woods carrying backpacks and boxes of supplies. Janus disarmed the shield and the Fort reappeared. Markus exited the structure to greet the visitors.

"Let me help you with those," Markus offered.

Suddenly, the boxes levitated all by themselves.

"Where do you want them?" Markus asked.

"In the large building," said Jim.

"Very good," smiled Markus as he walked toward the largest enclosure. Everyone watched as the boxes trailed along behind him.

"Do you have any more items to unload?" asked Markus over his shoulder.

"Yes, why?" replied Molly as she wiped her forehead.

"If you unload them discreetly by the edge of the forest, I will meet you there and bring them back the same way."

"That would be *awesome*," beamed Jim as the boxes disappeared into the largest structure. He then noticed Janus who had strolled outside to observe the group.

"Hello Janus," said Jim "What is the latest news on the Mitel Fleet?"

"They are almost here. The world's governments are transmitting messages in several languages in hopes of eliciting a response. I expect that the Mitel Fleet will answer very soon."

Molly looked at Janus apprehensively causing Janus's monitoring scans to quickly register her concern.

"Molly," said Janus "please try not to worry —"

"It's hard not to."

"Hi Mom," said Chad stepping out from the communications structure. Molly hurried over to Chad and hugged him, with the kind of hug that warms you from the inside out, before stepping back to wipe her tears. She then turned toward Janus.

"Isn't there any other way?" she asked.

Janus could see the pained look in Molly's eyes. It was the same look his wife gave him when it became clear that their daughters were fighting for their lives.

"No. I'm afraid not. Unfortunately, the Mitel leaders have used fear, intimidation and force to compel their people to be obedient."

"But why don't they just rebel against their Leadership?"

"The Mitel Leadership has been in power for a long time. The resistance movement doesn't possess the resources or weaponry to mount a sustainable opposition."

"Did your planet ever try to help the resistance?"

Janus sighed as he considered Molly's question. He looked over at the grave marker before responding.

"Our World Council dealt aggressively with terrorist attacks and their networks on our planet. We also responded decisively to attacks meant to disrupt our interplanetary transportation and trade routes. Sanctions were also imposed. Unfortunately, we never challenged the Mitel Leadership directly, on their planet. If we had done so, we may have stopped their aggression once and for all. In hindsight, the failure to act in that regard was our single biggest mistake."

Janus's voice trailed off as he again looked out at the pond and grave maker.

"This is now the place where Markus and I call home. We must do what we can —"

Suddenly, Janus's hologram deformed for a few seconds before returning to normal.

"What was that?" asked Molly as she stepped back slightly.

"It's a long story," replied Jim.

Chad and Markus laughed.

"You are full of surprises Janus Stone," smiled Molly as she wiped the tears from her cheeks. "And you are also quite special."

"That's *one* way to describe him," laughed Markus.

"What now, Janus?" Jim asked eventually.

"We need to continue our preparations. Which includes making sure you brought adequate supplies here."

"*Oh*, speaking of supplies," said Jim. "Markus — I want to take you up on your offer to help us!"

Jim motioned everyone to follow as he headed toward the trees. Janus watched the five of them disappear into the woods before heading back to his monitoring station.

As the doors slid open to his darkened quarters Zan, now mentally exhausted from meticulously checking the mission plan against status preparation logs, flopped on his bed and let out a sigh. A few minutes later, he heard a familiar clunking noise from across the room. Lia was once again seated in his desk chair.

"How did you — let me guess, your friends let you in," he said matter-of-factly.

"Yes," smiled Lia.

"What is it this time? Are you about to blow up my cruiser?"

"No. At least not yet anyway."

"Well, that's comforting . . . *I think.*"

"Zan — I'm here to tell you that the Leadership Member was *not* killed by the resistance."

"Then by who?"

"I think we both know *who.*"

"Rexx."

"Yes."

"But *why?*"

"He probably has ambitions of his own."

"*Ambitions? Lon?*" scoffed Zan. "He can't control his temper long enough to have any ambitions."

"Maybe, but for the safety of all of us, don't underestimate him. Do you hear me?"

Zan nodded and smiled weakly.

"Good boy," smiled Lia before exiting his darkened quarters.

On Saturday morning, Chad awoke from yet another restless night's sleep. Chad threw off his blankets and jumped out of bed. He threw on clothes from off his closet floor and rushed down the stairs two at a time. When he entered the kitchen, Molly and Jim were sitting at the kitchen table in their robes and pajamas.

"Good morning."

"Morning," Jim and Molly responded in unison.

From the looks on their faces, it was obvious that neither one of them had slept much the night before either. Chad decided to bring them to the Davis Farm to see the Battle Hologram for themselves and watch him transform. When they arrived, Jim scanned the street scene before parking the car in an open area along the road about three hundred yards beyond the entrance gate, hidden from the street.

"Why are you parking so far away?" Molly asked.

"Don't forget," Jim explained. "Major Talbot and his people know what our car looks like."

"And?" she asked a bit impatiently.

"*And* — we don't want to lead them right to Chad's Battle Hologram."

The trio walked quickly along the side of the road to the farm entrance. Chad helped Jim and Molly climb over the stone wall before scrambling over it himself. Suddenly, the sound of approaching vehicles could be heard off in the distance. Chad hopped back over the wall and looked down the road. Coming around the bend were a series of dark brown vehicles. As they approached, he realized that it was a Military convoy.

"Quick! Down behind the wall!" ordered Chad as he scrambled back over the stone wall. "Military vehicles headed this way!"

They crouched along the base of the wall as the vehicles roared by. Chad counted twelve vehicles in all. As the noise of the vehicles slowly faded, he stood up cautiously and brushed off his pants. He then let Molly and Jim know it was OK to get up.

"We need to get going before they return," ordered Chad as he started up the dirt road. Jim and Molly quickly followed. Chad occasionally glanced back toward the farm entrance until they were directly across from the grove of trees on their left.

"This way," motioned Chad.

Jim and Molly followed Chad through the field of tall grass. Approaching the wooded area, Chad once again motioned to his parents.

"We are almost there."

They entered the large tree grove opening. On the other side was the Battle Hologram. Jim and Molly could see the shapes of the hologram personnel as they moved about inside. Seconds later, Mayla and Teri appeared at the main entrance. By the briskness of their pace, Chad knew that something big was happening.

"Good morning Commander."

"Hi Mayla. I want you to meet my parents, Jim and Molly Johnson."

"It's indeed an honor to meet you. Chad and Janus have talked about you a great deal."

"I hope it wasn't *all* bad," smiled Jim sheepishly.

"On the contrary, it was quite complimentary," replied Mayla with a slight grin before turning toward Chad, her face becoming serious.

"Commander, Janus and Markus intercepted several transmissions confirming that the Military has initiated a search for you."

"See, I *knew* it," said Jim triumphantly.

"Mr. Johnson?" asked Mayla glancing at Jim with a confused look on her face.

"We just saw a small convoy of Military vehicles as we headed here," explained Jim.

"Do you think they spotted you?" asked Teri.

"No. We hid behind the stone wall along the road. I don't think they'll see our car either — it's parked up the road hidden behind some trees and bushes. And besides, I don't think they'll be looking for it anyway."

"Not *yet*," responded Mayla. "But they will be looking for your specific transportation device eventually."

Mayla quickly glanced back toward Chad.

"Commander," she said. "We believe your parents are in danger. Janus wants them to head to the Fort *immediately* to ensure their safety. He also doesn't want any of you returning to your home. The Military will likely have that location under constant surveillance. They are probably searching it right now."

"OK," said Jim.

"Markus is on his way to transport you both to the Fort."

"How?" asked Molly.

"He will take you by van," explained Mayla. "Janus is confident that the Military will not be searching for that particular transportation device."

Jim frowned.

"What's wrong honey?" Molly asked.

"The piece of the pod."

"What about it?"

"It's hidden in my office at the college. If they find it, they'll start connecting the dots. I need to get that out of there before they find it."

"I wouldn't worry about that now, Mr. Johnson," said Mayla.

"What about today's training?" asked Chad.

"What about it?" responded Teri.

"Hey Mom, Dad, this is Teri," said Chad. "He looks after me when I transform into a Battle Sphere."

"Hi Teri," smiled Molly "Thank you for looking after our son."

"You are both quite welcome," nodded Teri. "But I'm just one of many assigned to protect Chad."

"Am I still going to practice?" asked Chad.

"Do you think we would let the Military get in the way of *that*?"

"It is decided," said Mayla. "Commander, please prepare for launch."

"OK," replied Chad. "Can my parents watch me transform before they go?"

"It's best they get to the Fort as soon as possible," responded Mayla firmly.

"I guess you're right," Chad groaned.

"Prepare for launch," boomed Denton across the encrypted communications system.

"Markus has arrived at the entrance to this location," instructed Teri. "He said you need to hurry and get there before the Military passes this way again."

"OK, thank you," said Molly "Jim, let's go!"

Jim and Molly waved to Chad then rushed across the forest opening. Teri watched in silence as they disappeared into the forest before speaking into his communications device.

"Hi Markus — it's Teri."

"Hello Teri. Where *are* they?"

"The Johnsons are crossing the field now. They should be there in less than five minutes."

"OK great. I'll look out for them."

Markus glanced into his rearview mirror.

"Things are getting complicated," he said.

"As we all expected," replied Teri while monitoring Chad's performance data on his hand held instrumentation screen.

"Indeed," nodded Markus.

Zan entered the ICC and sat down in his command console chair. Upon seeing him, Ard strolled up from the navigation console to join him. Before either of them could speak, Lia approached the command console carrying an encrypted communications tablet.

"Excuse me, Emperor Liss," said Lia. "I've received a series of updated mission logs for your review."

Zan stared intently at Lia for several seconds.

"Emperor Liss?" she asked blankly. "Is something wrong?"

There was not even a hint in her expression that indicated she had been in his quarters eight hours early.

"No," replied Zan as he reached out for the tablet. "Thank you."

Ard watched Lia walk back to her communications station before leaning towards Zan.

"Now what?" he whispered, "another bad dream?"

Zan shot a quick glance towards Lia before responding.

"Yes," he frowned. "I guess you could say that."

CHAPTER TWENTY-THREE – MORE COMPLICATIONS

Jim and Molly walked quickly toward the entrance to Davis Farm, where a white van idled along the side of the road.

The van backed up rapidly and came to an abrupt stop on the gravel shoulder right next to them. The passenger door window slowly lowered.

"Get in folks," Markus ordered.

"Markus, what should we do with our station wagon?" asked Molly.

"Janus is moving it to a more secluded spot closer to town."

"But he doesn't have the keys," replied Jim, "how is he going to start it?"

"He'll *hot wire* the machine's ignition."

"Here, give him my keys."

"How will he get back to the Fort?" asked Molly.

"The same way I would," Markus replied, nodding toward the rear of the van where his orb hovered silently.

As they approached Coopers Falls, they passed one, then two, then three groups of Humvees heading in the opposite direction.

"The Army is all over the place," said Molly.

"They are indeed," replied Markus softly.

As the van approached Randall Park, Markus checked the rearview mirror, then closed his eyes.

"What are you doing Markus?" asked Jim.

"*Shhhhh*! I'm analyzing data."

"You're what?" asked Molly softly.

Markus quickly opened his eyes.

"I'm tracking the Army's motorized positions. Or rather — my monitoring orb is. It's one of the many benefits of being integrated into it."

"That's amazing," Jim said softly.

Markus drove past the stone Civil War Monument towards the densely-wooded area before abruptly turning and coming to a stop in a small opening along the side of the road.

"Time to get out," Markus instructed Molly and Jim.

Markus climbed out of the van. He headed up the dirt road, followed closely by his monitoring orb, Jim and Molly. "We must get to the Fort as quickly as possible."

"Are you just going to leave the van here?" Jim asked.

Markus did not answer and a few seconds later, the van disappeared. Jim cautiously walked over where the van had been and reached out his hands and felt an invisible wall which repelled his touch. As he held out his hand a second time, he felt the shield rising into the air.

"*Wow* — I guess that answers that question."

The Fort appeared in front of them as the trio emerged from the forest. Upon entering the circular shield boundary area, the shield was reset and the Fort disappeared from site.

"Where's Janus?" asked Jim.

"He's likely monitoring the activity," replied Markus, as he headed to the communications building. Melissica suddenly stepped out from inside the largest structure.

"Melissica, what are *you* doing here?" Molly asked.

From the look on Melissica's face, Molly could tell that she was frightened.

"My mom went to Seattle on business three days ago. She can't get a flight back because so many are being cancelled. I told her I was going to stay with you guys until she gets back. It made her very happy and I guess I am telling the truth, *right*?"

"Are you OK honey?"

"I'm really scared. I didn't know what else to do."

"It is going to be OK," Molly said, taking Melissica's hand. "I've got an idea. Let's go for a walk together?"

Jim watched silently as the two walked slowly toward the pond. Molly paused suddenly and looked back, a bewildered expression on her face. She reached out into the air, only to quickly pull her hand back.

"Molly, is something wrong?" asked Jim.

Molly didn't respond. Instead, she turned and kept walking with Melissica, glancing back over her shoulder every so often.

"What was that all about?" asked Jim to nobody in particular.

"They passed through the plasma shield," explained Markus. "It's permeable from the inside out. It takes a little getting used to."

Jim followed Markus into the communications structure. Janus was seated inside at his computer.

Janus turned around to greet them. "Hello James. The Military is conducting an extensive search for Chad. And it appears they are looking for you and Molly as well."

"They are all over the place. We saw several Humvees on our way here. But why are they looking for Molly?"

"They will detain and interrogate *anyone* if they think it might help them locate Chad," explained Markus.

"Not to worry, though. They can't find you at this location," added Janus.

"What about Chad?" asked Jim. "He is out there all by himself."

"He is by no means alone."

"By that, you mean his Battle Hologram?"

"Yes. Mayla will instruct Chad to land in the adjacent forest opening once he completes today's training exercises. The Mitel Fleet is fast approaching Earth so Chad will cease further training to avoid detection, while we make final preparations."

"Does Chad need more practice? Is he ready?"

Janus stood up and looked Jim in the eye.

"He is ready James. But he must remain mentally prepared, and that means being free of distractions."

"Where is he now?"

"His Battle Sphere just completed another successful plasma shield test around the Earth. It's likely the Military will heighten their search for him as they try to figure out what he's doing and why."

"Why don't we simply tell them the truth?"

"That's certainly an option. However, I don't think the world's military can be trusted right now. They'll want to do more than question Chad. They will analyze him to determine what threat he poses. That will only interfere with our mission —"

"Why can't we just tell the government that the Mitels are the bad guys coming here to harm us?"

"Do you really think they will believe you?"

"Probably not. More likely, they would throw me in a padded cell."

"Precisely," replied Janus.

The computer beeped.

"It's Mayla. Chad just landed in the clearing between this location and the dirt road. Markus, would you please go and escort him back here."

"On my way," Markus responded, as he exited the structure. Molly and Melissica were just returning from their walk. Janus momentarily disabled the plasma shield allowing them to reenter the Fort. Markus waived as his hologram returned to his orb and darted into the nearby woods.

"Where is Markus going?" Molly asked as she entered the communications building.

"He's getting Chad. With all the military activity, Mayla and I think it's safer for Chad to be here."

"I agree."

Several minutes later, Markus returned with Chad, whose face brightened upon seeing his parents and Melissica.

"How did it go?" Jim asked.

"Great," Chad said confidently. "I think I have the plasma shield down pat."

"What's next?" asked Molly.

"Mayla told me to come here and sit tight for now. Not sure what's next, but one thing I do know is that I'm starving!"

"Let's get some dinner going," Molly said to Jim.

They set up the camping stoves and cooked hot dogs and beans. They ate dinner sitting along the pond, listening to the crickets and tree frogs. When asked, Janus told Jim he parked the station wagon a few miles away behind the abandoned Long's Dairy factory next to the old railroad tracks.

Later that evening, when Jim, Molly, Chad and Melissica went to bed, Janus and Markus returned to the communications building to continue monitoring the approaching Mitel Fleet. They reviewed what seemed to be a never ending stream of communications from around the globe. The entire world was talking about the approaching alien crafts.

Zan was lounging in his quarters located in the center section of Cruiser Number 1 when his intercom beeped.

"Liss here."

"Emperor Liss, this is Zia Saar," replied the ICC communications specialist. "We've just received confirmation that two more supply craft have been destroyed. Scans show that there are no survivors."

Zan did not immediately answer.

"Emperor Liss?"

"I'm here. Please summon Commander Lindar to my quarters."

"Yes, my Emperor."

A few minutes later, Ard entered his ID number into the keypad located on the wall next to Zan's quarters followed by the request button. The doors slid open.

"Heard the news," said Ard as he strolled into Zan's quarters.

"We clearly still have a resistance fighters imbedded in our fleet," replied Zan somberly.

"That's for sure."

"We *must* find a way to bring it to an end, once and for all. Every time this happens, morale takes a hit."

"I agree," acknowledged Ard as he flopped into Zan's desk chair.

"Do you think they would be willing to negotiate?"

"What's the incentive? It's in their best interest for this fleet never to return to Mitel."

"True —"

"And besides, the Mitel Leadership will *never* negotiate with them."

"But the Leadership isn't with us, and the success of our mission may depend upon it."

"Do you want my opinion?"

"I'm not sure actually."

"I'll give it to you anyway. If you try to negotiate with the resistance, the entire fleet will turn against you."

"But —"

"Maybe that's what Rexx is hoping for, you know?"

"You're probably right," Zan sighed.

"What are you going to say to the people of Earth?"

"About the Thraen?"

"Yes."

"I'm going to tell them that we are looking for one of our own."

"One of our own? You can't be serious."

"Why not? Ard, do you really think they'll hand him over if we tell them the truth?"

"Probably not. Did you notice how we never received a final report on the assassination?"

"Maybe it's still being finalized."

"I'm not holding my breath waiting it. And besides, should we believe its conclusions given that it came from Lon?"

"Probably not," Zan sighed again.

The two sat in silence for a time.

"I've been told not to underestimate him," announced Zan eventually.

"Who told you that?"

"Someone in a recent dream I had."

"Sounds more like a nightmare to me," laughed Ard. "I think you need to lay off those energy drinks a bit."

"Maybe you're right," Zan grinned.

Lon Rexx sat at the desk of his spacious quarters in Cruiser Number 2, as the commander of Cruiser Number 6 appeared on the center monitor.

"Rexx, we have caught four resistance members posing as medical personnel."

"Torture them for information," growled Lon.

"As you wish. "

"Then I want you to jettison them into outer space. *Alive*."

"But —"

"*But nothing*! Afterwards, I want you to inform the entire fleet about the execution. It's time to fight fire with fire."

"What about Emperor Liss?"

"He has no reason to know," replied Lon impatiently.

"As you wish," nodded the commander as the monitor went black.

Soon enough thought Lon. *It won't make any difference what Liss does or doesn't know.*

That night, Jim couldn't sleep. As he lay in his cot, he kept thinking about the piece of the pod wreckage he had hidden in his office. 12:00 midnight turned into 1:00 a.m., then 2:00 a.m.

They won't think to search my office at the school, will they? he contemplated.

Jim began to devise a plan in his mind to retrieve the evidence. He would sneak out before dawn and make his way to the old train tracks about a half mile away and follow them to Long's Dairy. From there, he would get into the station wagon and drive to school in less than five minutes, grab the wreckage and retrace his steps back to the Fort. He checked his watch. It was 3:15 a.m. *If I go now, I'll be back before anyone wakes up.*

Jim sat up in his cot, quietly slipped out of bed and got dressed. He grabbed his car keys, tiptoed out of the largest structure and walked past the communications building. *They're still at it* he thought, hearing the muffled sounds coming from inside.

Jim felt himself passing through some form of membrane. It didn't hurt, but he felt a slight resistance as he passed through it. When he turned back around, the Fort was gone. Jim reached out his hand only to have it repelled by the same invisible wall that hid the white van.

I guess there's no turning back now he thought as he walked quickly through the dark woods, every so often tripping over a tree root and scratching himself against a tree branch. He eventually reached the adjacent clearing where he stopped for a few minutes to look at the bright moonlight before continuing back into the forest. When Jim reached the dirt road, he walked briskly toward the side entrance to Randall Park. He paused to look in both directions. It was eerily quiet.

Jim jogged up Maple Street about three hundred yards to a dirt path on the opposite side of the road which led back into the woods along Sandy Brook. After about a half mile, he reached the old railroad tracks where he made his way along the long straight stretch for a little over a mile. Off in the distance, the headlights from an occasional car could be seen crossing the railroad tracks along Ridge Street.

This took longer than I expected. I better hurry he thought as the sky lightened. Jim stayed close to the tree line to stay hidden as he approached Long's Dairy, making his way around back. Stopping to scan the area, Jim spotted the station wagon. Satisfied that the coast was clear, he jogged over to his automobile, opened the driver side door and got in. He inserted and turned the ignition key, starting the engine.

Great! Now to my office.

Jim's heart was pounding, as he drove around the front of the building and turned left onto Ridge Street. He kept glancing in all directions for anything unusual as he made his way through a four-way stop and along the long straightaway leading to the college entrance.

So far so good! he thought. *Just stay calm and everything will be fine.*

Jim turned into the entrance to the college and drove along the access road at the rear of the campus. He scanned the area carefully as he pulled in behind the science building.

All quiet, no one in sight.

Jim put the car in park and turned off the headlights. He glanced up at his faculty office window on the third floor. It was dark. As Jim got out of the car, he noticed that it was now almost completely light out.

In and out! He told himself. *I'll leave the car running.*

Jim hurried to the rear entrance, fumbling for his office keys in his coat pocket. He unlocked the rear door and raced up the stairs to his office door. Entering his darkened office, Jim immediately saw that his office had been ransacked.

Oh crap! They've already been here!

Jim instinctively looked out the window. Two soldiers stood next to his station wagon, their Humvee right behind it.

I've got to get out of here, now!

Jim raced to the door. Standing right outside his office was Major Michael Talbot, flanked by three armed Marines holding M16A2 assault rifles. In one hand, Major Talbot held the cloth containing the piece of wreckage. In the other was the medallion.

"Looking for these Mr. Johnson?" asked Major Talbot tersely.

Jim stared at Major Talbot in stunned disbelief.

CHAPTER TWENTY-FOUR – CONTACT

Molly awoke and noticed Jim's pajama top lying on his cot next to his sheets and blanket.

He's up early, she thought.

On the other side of the structure, Chad and Melissica were still fast asleep in their cots. Molly quietly threw on a pair of jeans and a sweatshirt and brushed her hair. Stepping outside, the early morning air was surprisingly warm inside the Fort's perimeter. Molly gazed at the mist over the pond for a time, then headed to the communications building. Janus and Markus were at their monitors.

"Good morning," announced Molly as she walked in. "I could use a cup of coffee right about now."

"Good morning Molly," said Janus without looking up from the computer console.

"Where's Jim?"

Janus and Markus glanced at each other.

"What's wrong?" she asked, sensing that something had happened.

"There were two very important developments during the night Molly," responded Janus cautiously.

"Oh?" Molly answered hesitantly. "Is everything OK?"

"The Mitels entered the furthermost boundary of your planet's solar system and initiated contact. Emperor Zan Liss of the Mitel nation opened a channel of communication, broadcasting a message in every major language on Earth.

Janus paused momentarily.

"Fifteen years ago, I knew him as *Commander* Zan Liss. It appears he has risen through the ranks of the Mitel hierarchy. That is no small feat given their cannibalistic power structure."

"*Oh my god*," replied Molly quietly. "What did he say?"

"I will replay his message for you shortly," replied Janus as he stood up. "The second important development is that James left the Fort during the night to retrieve the piece of our escape pod and silver medallion that he had hidden at his place of work," announced Janus.

"He *what*?" uttered Molly in shock.

Janus glanced at Markus before continuing.

"James was worried that if the wreckage and medallion were discovered by the United States Military, they would have conclusive evidence linking Chad to our crash landing. I didn't think he would actually go back to retrieve it."

"Is he there *now*?"

"We intercepted several Military transmissions confirming that James was taken into custody at the college by a Major Michael Talbot early this morning. I am truly sorry for this latest development. It was quite unexpected."

Molly was in shock. After a time, she looked up at Janus. "Now what, Janus?"

"We must proceed as planned and get Chad relocated to one of our Moon based enclosures. Hopefully James does not lead them here."

"What was he *thinking*?"

"I think Jim believed that he was doing what was best for his family," responded Markus quietly.

"Is there anything we can do to help him?" Molly asked hopefully.

"Markus and I are considering going to the location where James is being detained, to assess the situation. But we don't think it would be prudent to attempt securing his release."

"What do you think they will do to him?"

"They want to know why the Mitels are coming here and the extent of Chad's involvement so they will likely interrogate him until they are satisfied with his response."

Molly let out a long deep sigh as she slowly shook her head.

"That brings me back to the first major development," explained Janus. "I can replay Emperor Liss's message for you now."

Janus typed a few instructions and sat back.

"This is Zan Liss, Emperor of planet Mitel, located six hundred light years from Earth. Our military fleet has crossed that great distance for one purpose: to secure the release of one of our people who is of special significance to us. The individual we seek is a young male approximately sixteen years old. We demand his immediate release upon our arrival to your planet. We also seek the release of his inner circle to accompany him back home."

There was a brief pause in the transmission.

"If you are unwilling to deliver both he and his inner circle, we will take whatever steps necessary to secure their release on our own. If you do not comply, or interfere in any way with our stated mission, my Leadership Council has instructed me to interpret such conduct as an act of aggression against our civilization. Our forces are due to arrive on your planet in less than three days. You have until that time to procure the young male and his associates for transfer to our fleet. In the meantime, our communications channels shall remain open."

"Why are the Mitels also looking for Chad's *inner circle*?" asked Molly.

"As hostages I presume — to insure his compliance," replied Janus. "When Chad awakens, we will begin final preparations. Given the delay in receiving the transmission, we only have about forty-eight hours before the Mitels arrive."

"What are the world's governments doing to address the situation?"

"We have surveilled thousands of communications during the night since the Mitel's pronouncements," Markus began. "Countries are scrambling to assess the Mitel threat. The President of the United States has been in contact with the leaders of Russia, China, India, and Europe and he appears to be organizing with these leaders to pull together a military coalition. Unfortunately, there is little that can be done, given the technological superiority of the Mitel Fleet."

Molly paced and became visibly agitated.

"Then what's the point?" she exclaimed.

"Molly, please. We *must* remain calm. Chad is our best hope. We must help him remain focused and assist him in every way possible. Can you do this for him?"

Molly stared at Janus, taking another deep breath.

"Yes," she responded softly.

Jim was taken to the Coopers Falls Armory, which was now being used as the temporary Army and Marines command headquarters. He was placed in a small windowless ten by ten holding cell in the basement. In the center of the room was an old metal desk with three metal chairs, a single light bulb hung from the ceiling. The Armory's heavily fortified walls were made of two-foot thick granite blocks. The only access to the room was via a solid steel door with a small glass window.

Jim paced around the room for several minutes like a caged animal before stopping to glance out the small window. In the hallway, two armed Marines stood guard. He slumped into the metal chair facing the door and placed his hands on the desk.

How could I have been so stupid? He thought. *They were just waiting for me to show up. I wonder if Janus and Markus have figured out that I've been captured. Regardless, I must stay calm and not tell them anything.*

There was a loud bang and then a squeak as the door slowly opened. A Marine entered the room followed by Major Talbot.

"Hello again, Mr. Johnson. It has been quite a while since we last met."

Major Talbot approached the desk and slowly sat down across from Jim and, without taking his eyes off him asked, "Where's your son?"

"Why do you ask?"

"*Come on* Mr. Johnson, I don't need to spell this all out for you, *do I?*"

"Maybe you do, because I am not really sure why I'm here —"

"You're here, Mr. Johnson because it appears that an alien force has come a long way looking for your son *and his inner circle.*"

"What makes you think they have come here looking for Chad?" replied Jim tersely.

"Listen to me Mr. Johnson," said Major Talbot in a softer tone. "The whole world knows that a large fleet of alien space craft is heading toward us from somewhere in deep space."

As Major Talbot spoke Jim stared stoically, struggling to control his emotions.

"You would have to be living on a deserted island not to know about it at this point. The world's largest telescopes discovered the approaching formation by chance and at this point, every military satellite around the world has confirmed it. And now, just last night, the aliens — who call themselves the *Mitels* — issued an ultimatum."

Major Talbot noticed Jim react ever so slightly.

"So, you *have* heard of the Mitels, haven't you Mr. Johnson?" asked Major Talbot pointedly. "Their leader, an *Emperor Liss*, said it was to secure the return of one of their own. A *sixteen-year-old boy.*"

Jim lowered his head as Major Talbot slowly leaned towards him.

"Mr. Johnson. The planet's entire population is on edge. The discovery of the approaching spacecraft comes on the heels of a series of unexplained communications outages, not to mention the discovery of a spherical UFO beyond Earth's outer atmosphere. In my opinion, these events are somehow linked. And quite frankly, I think you know how."

After a brief silence, Major Talbot continued in a louder, more direct tone.

"Listen, Mr. Johnson, I don't know what these beings can do to this world, but I am guessing that if they have the technology to send a fleet of space ships across the universe, then they probably have the firepower to destroy this planet. Is that what you want? *Is it*?"

"*No!*"

"Then tell me what you know," pleaded Major Talbot. "Tell me where Chad is."

"Why?" Jim asked defensively.

"So we can talk with him and figure out what to do," replied Major Talbot. "The Mitel leader said that we have less than three days to deliver him to them. He said they have come to retrieve one of their own who is of very *special* significance. Eye witnesses have seen Chad transform into an alien being. Why are you protecting him? Are you working with the Mitels too?"

"No!"

Jim fidgeted in his chair before looking away from Major Talbot.

"Their transmission, Mr. Johnson, which took over six hours to get here — was received almost eight hours ago. The clock is ticking."

"*Look*," said Jim earnestly as he turned back toward Major Talbot. "I don't know what the Mitels may have told you, but they are *not* here to pick up one of their *own*."

"And why do you say that Mr. Johnson?"

"Yes, OK," explained Jim nervously. "Chad is not from this world. But he is *not* from their world either. The Mitels *destroyed* Chad's planet when he was a baby. He escaped the carnage at the last minute. The Mitels are responsible for the deaths of over two *billion* beings just like us!"

Major Talbot stared at Jim intently, his heart racing.

"So, the Mitels are lying to us?"

"*Yes!*"

"OK then. Let's assume Chad is *not* one of them for the moment. Is he working alone Mr. Johnson?"

Jim did not answer.

"I don't think he is Mr. Johnson. Do you want to know how I know?"

Jim again did not answer.

"Because he was left at the hospital by other survivors of the UFO crash."

"Look, Major Talbot! Chad is not the *problem*. He is the *solution!*"

"What do you mean by that Mr. Johnson?"

Jim did not answer.

I have got to shut up before I give the whole thing away and jeopardize everything Jim thought.

The two men sat silently for several seconds.

"What's the *Fort* Mr. Johnson? And where is it?"

"I have no idea what you are talking about."

"I think you do," insisted Major Talbot as he placed a hand-written note on the table. It read:

I AM GOING TO THE FORT. CHAD

"We found that note on your refrigerator."

Jim did not respond.

"Where is the *Fort* Mr. Johnson?"

"There is one up by Lake Edward," smiled Jim nervously. "You know, the Revolutionary War fort called Fort William James?"

Major Talbot studied Jim's face.

"We both know that is *not* the Fort we are talking about."

Jim looked at the wall next to him.

"Chad is at the Fort right now, isn't he Mr. Johnson?"

"I don't know."

"You're lying!"

Jim quickly turned and stared at Major Talbot as he grew furious.

"And you have *no* idea what you're doing!" he yelled. "You — and the rest of the military — you are getting involved and interfering with something that is beyond anything you could ever imagine! You need to stay out of it!"

Jim's heart was pounding. He wanted to run right through the door and keep going until he got back to Chad and Molly.

"It's too late for our government to *stay out of it* Mr. Johnson," lectured Major Talbot. "Our country — our entire world — is being threatened by an alien force. I need answers from you and I need them *now*. Before it's too late!"

Jim glared angrily at Major Talbot.

"I have nothing more to say to you."

With that, Major Talbot stood up and walked out of the room. The door closed behind him with a loud bang.

Chad woke up to see Melissica still sleeping in the cot next to him. Crawling out of the cot, Chad quickly got dressed and exited the structure. The mist still hovered over the pond as he made his way to the communications structure. Janus, Molly and Markus were huddled around the computer console as he entered.

"Good morning everybody. Hey, where's Dad?"

Molly stood up from her chair and approached Chad.

"Chad, your father went out during the night to retrieve the space pod wreckage and medallion from his office. When he got there, he was taken into custody by the Military and transported to Coopers Falls Armory —"

"*What?*" interrupted Chad loudly.

"Chad, I know —"

"*Major Talbot?*" asked Chad.

"Listen Chad. We must stay calm and move ahead from here."

"No. What I need to do is transform and go get him!"

"That will only add to the problem Chad," Markus interjected. "It will only serve to reinforce their belief that you are one of them."

"But why? How?" asked Chad in a somewhat calmer tone.

"Zan Liss," Markus began. "Who is the current Mitel Emperor, transmitted a message to Earth overnight *demanding* the release of a sixteen-year-old male *along with his inner circle*. He claimed this boy is "*one of our people*" and gave an ultimatum that everyone is to be delivered to them upon their arrival in less than three days."

"He said that *I* was one of their people?" asked Chad incredulously.

"Yes. And they believe him it seems. This World understands that the Mitels represent a threat far greater than anything they have ever seen. Therefore, they will want to comply with the request to avoid a global catastrophe."

"Which means capturing me and turning me over to the Mitels," concluded Chad. "Along with Mom and Dad?"

"Correct," replied Janus. "Chad, based on the transmissions, Major Talbot has already determined that you are the individual the Mitels want. And he has told his superiors."

"But —"

Janus was getting impatient. "No buts, Chad. Everyone knows it's you. We can't risk you going to get your father."

"Janus, I just want to get my dad, so we can all be together. And what if Major Talbot turns him over to the Mitels?"

Molly glanced over to Janus for something, anything, that would make sense of what to do. Janus paused before answering.

"If you transform now and seek out your father you run the risk of being detected by the Mitels' advanced scanning technology. If that happens, they will immediately come here to Coopers Falls."

"They are going to detect me sooner or later. There is still time for me to get to the Moon enclosures and wait to ambush them. We need to rescue my dad before he is forced to tell the authorities where we are, or even worse — is turned over to the Mitels."

Janus glanced around the communications structure for a moment before looking over at Markus.

"The lad has some very good points. And you know it, Janus," Markus said.

Janus then looked at Molly who nodded in agreement as she wiped tears from her eyes.

"What's your plan, Chad?" Janus asked quietly.

"I fly to the Armory and create a diversion long enough for you and Markus to get Dad out of there and back to the Fort."

"And what should we do about the Mitels?"

"Once everyone is back at the Fort, I will go to one of the Moon enclosures and wait until you give me the signal to attack. Then, we fight."

"I agree with Chad," nodded Markus. "Let's fight the Mitels on our terms, not theirs. Both times the Mitels invaded, we simply reacted to their aggression. Let's do what we need to do, but do it first. There is still time for Chad to get to the Moon enclosures. Let's get Jim back first."

Janus did not respond.

"Janus, the boy is ready. Probably more so than the two of us ever were."

"OK. Let's map out a plan and coordinate with Mayla and the Battle Hologram team," replied Janus eventually. "We also need to show Molly and Melissica how to activate and disarm the invisibility shields in our absence."

"Where are the Mitels now?" asked Chad.

"They passed Neptune about four hours ago. They've reduced their speed to 0.1X now," confirmed Markus.

"They will reach the Moon in about thirty-six hours," concluded Chad after running the numbers in his head.

"Then let's get to it," urged Markus.

Jim felt helpless as he sat in his Armory cell. Suddenly, he heard a bang followed by a long squeak as the door opened. Major Talbot walked in followed by a burley Marine and a third man who looked vaguely familiar.

"Mr. Johnson, this is Lieutenant Jason Miller. We've been working on your son's case for quite some time. We have decided that if you tell us everything you know about Chad and the aliens, we will release you on the condition that you remain in Coopers Falls."

"Let me go and hope that I lead you right to Chad?"

"No, Mr. Johnson, we would just let you go."

"So, what's the catch?"

"There is no *catch*. We just want answers."

The group had a plan. First, Janus and Markus would park close to the Armory and perform final assessment scans of the target area, before getting into position at the rear of the building. Chad would transform in the first clearing and proceed directly to the Armory at high speed and low altitude to minimize detection. At the Armory, Chad would create a diversion by firing a series of low energy laser bursts to distract the Military personnel just long enough for Janus and Markus get Jim back to the van and drive off without confrontation.

Melissica, who had recently woken up, sat in the corner eating a breakfast bar as she listened to the group. Chad, Janus and Markus then discussed the operation details with Mayla and Teri over the encrypted communications system. Right after that, Melissica and Molly practiced turning on and off the invisibility shields under Janus's supervision.

"Molly, these shields not only make you invisible to the outside world, they provide a significant level of protection from intense heat, debris and weaponry. You are *not* to leave the safety of this place under any circumstances."

Molly and Melissica nodded to Janus in agreement.

"Markus and I have added a few extra features to the shield. For example, while it is in operation, it emits specific frequencies and odors that flood the senses of tracking dogs within a two-mile radius of the Fort making it impossible to track any predetermined scent."

Satisfied that Molly and Melissica were now proficient in operating the shields, Janus turned his attention back to his son. "Chad, *please* remember, you are only to create a distraction. You are not to hurt *anyone*. We don't want —"

"Anyone to mistake me for a Mitel aggressor," interrupted Chad.

Molly hugged Chad.

"Please be careful," Melissica whispered to Chad as she hugged him.

Janus and Markus returned to their monitoring orbs and raced through the woods to the van. They quickly materialized and Markus climbed into the driver's side seat and started up the van.

"Let's get this operation started," said Janus as he opened the passenger door for his monitoring orb.

Markus backed the van up onto the dirt road and headed toward the main entrance to Randall Park.

CHAPTER TWENTY-FIVE – THE ESCAPE

A cloud of dust rose behind the white van as they passed the old Civil War Monument before turning onto Main Street. Janus stared out the passenger window as Markus weaved his way through Coopers Falls. Their monitoring orbs gathered and processed relevant transmissions and conversations in the area. As they approached the Armory, they passed several Humvees, armored personnel carriers, Strykers and other military convoy trucks parked along either side of the road. Off in the distance, armed soldiers stood guard behind large cement barricades at the entrance to the Armory complex.

"Turn down this side street," pointed Janus.

Markus drove very slowly along the side street as they surveyed the scene.

"Not a lot of activity here," said Markus.

"Good thing. Turn right here."

Markus pulled over. On Janus's signal, they each initiated scans of the Armory area.

"I confirm one hundred and three Army and Marine personnel, armed with hand held projectile weapons," announced Markus.

"Have you located James?" asked Janus.

"Yes. He is on the basement level, lower left rear corner. Access to the room is through a single door at the end of central interior hallway, no windows. The exterior stone walls are approximately two feet thick. There is a rear entrance on the basement level which intersects the central hallway."

"OK," nodded Janus. "Once we confirm that the diversion has been successful, you will enter through the rear and head straight to the room. Remember to secure the hallway for Jim to escape. At the same time, I will enter through the rear wall and inform him of the plan."

"And if I'm *not* successful?" asked Markus quietly as he glanced out his rear and side mirrors.

"I will come out to assist you. I will also instruct Mayla to intensify the laser barrage."

"Sejus, once outside, you could levitate Jim to the van. I will return to my orb, dart to the van and be ready to drive away."

"That sounds like a plan," smiled Janus.

"I've also instructed my monitoring orb to begin plotting our escape route."

"To Davis Farm as we discussed?"

"Yes. We will rendezvous there with Chad before he heads to the Moon enclosure."

Janus paused to review the plan.

"My monitoring orb calculates a ninety-one percent probability of success."

"I calculate a ninety-two percent chance of success," smiled Markus.

"You always were an optimist," grunted Janus as he looked toward his side mirror.

They sat quietly as their orbs processed the last set of updated scans.

"Several military vehicles are exiting the Armory complex," announced Markus.

"Good. They are intensifying their search for Chad. That should mean fewer guards when we go in for James, but it may impact our escape to the launch area"

"I don't think we can assess that part until we are on our way. As it stands now, there are already dozens of vehicles patrolling the area."

"Agreed," nodded Janus. "As we retreat, Chad should be able to block their interception routes where necessary."

"How do you propose he do that?"

"These petroleum-powered vehicles are not very maneuverable. He could fire minimum strength laser bursts to render their travel routes impassable."

"That sounds like a good plan."

"OK then," said Janus. "I'm relaying the Armory coordinates and current personnel positions to Mayla with instructions for Chad to transform."

Mayla responded almost immediately:

HYBRID TRANSFORMATION COMPLETED. HE IS ON HIS WAY TO THE ARMORY.

"*Quickly Markus*, let's get in position." They exited the van followed closely by their orbs. Approaching the Armory from the North, Chad's Battle Sphere decelerated rapidly.

"Target at 5000 feet," confirmed Teri. "2000 feet. Now 500 feet."

Passing over a fourteen-story apartment building in the Center of town, the Armory complex came into view. On the ground, several soldiers looked up at the approaching silver Sphere.

"What the hell is *that*?" said one soldier.

"I don't know," responded another.

A communications specialist quickly grabbed his field phone.

"A UFO is approaching! *Repeat*, spherical UFO approaching the Armory from the north!" he shouted.

Chad descended upon the Armory, hovering some thirty feet above the entrance. Trees swayed as dust and small debris whirled up into the air. Army soldiers and Marines scrambled from around the perimeter to confront the UFO. Several soldiers climbed into their Humvees and armored personnel carriers to arm and point their M2 and 105 mm caliber machine guns towards the object. A few dozen Marines positioned themselves at the front of the building, pointing their M16A2 assault rifles at the spinning sphere. Troops on the second and third levels of the Armory took positions in every front window.

Spinning in position, Chad was unfazed by the activity. He knew their weaponry would be useless against his plasma shield.

"Target assessment Denton," instructed Teri.

"We've locked onto several unmanned military transport vehicles located on either side of the main structure," confirmed Denton. "We've also identified an old water storage facility diagonally to the right as well as several trees, lamp posts, retaining walls and fencing and an abandoned subsurface petroleum storage facility in proximity, referred to it as a *gas station*."

"Let's start with those," recommended Teri. "We can expand the perimeter if necessary,"

"Affirmative," said Mayla as she monitored the activities from her station in the Command Cube. "Open fire."

Low energy laser bursts exited Chad's Battle Sphere in all directions. The transport vehicles detonated on contact. The water tower disintegrated sending water crashing to the ground in all directions. Trees surrounding the Armory exploded and burst into flames.

"We're under attack!" yelled the Armory Commander as he crouched at the entrance foyer to the Armory. "Return fire! *Return fire!*"

The Humvees and armored personnel carriers immediately opened fire signaling the rest of the positioned soldiers and Marines to also shoot. From inside the Armory, the communications team sent out an urgent transmission confirming that they were under attack from an airborne UFO. In response, three F15 Eagle jet fighters were dispatched from the Massachusetts Air National Guard's 104th Fighter Wing stationed in Westover, Massachusetts. Within a matter of minutes, the fighters were racing down the runway. Sixty seconds later, they were cruising at an altitude of twenty thousand feet headed for Coopers Falls.

From their windowless room, Major Talbot, Lieutenant Miller and Jim heard the gun battle unfolding outside.

"What the hell is going on?" asked Major Talbot tersely.

"It sounds like we are under attack Sir!" shouted Lieutenant Miller.

"Let's go!" instructed Major Talbot racing out the door followed closely by Lieutenant Miller and one Marine. As he ran down the hall, Major Talbot yelled back to the remaining Marine.

"Guard the prisoner. He is *not* to leave the building!"

"Yes Sir!" responded the remaining Marine as he raised his M16A2 assault rifle and took position at the entrance to Jim's holding cell.

Major Talbot, Lieutenant Miller and the Marine sprinted up the heavily fortified stone stairway, across the first-floor hallway to the Armory's main entrance. As they cautiously peered out the front foyer, they saw the spinning silver Battle Sphere hovering up above.

"That's the object in the pictures!" yelled Major Talbot.

The two men scanned the chaos unfolding in front of them. Trees and vehicles were on fire in every direction as embers swirled in the air. The sound of automatic fire was thunderous as troops returned fire at the whirling UFO. Major Talbot focused his attention toward the Battle Sphere. It was clear that the barrage of gunfire was having no effect on the spinning object.

Behind the Armory, Janus's orb hovered silently next to the rear wall, burning cinders whipped around him.

"Let's go Markus. My scan shows that the lower level of the Armory is empty except for one soldier guarding the entrance to James's room."

"On my way," Markus responded and sped over to the rear entrance. After materializing, Markus reached forward and pulled on the handle but the door would not budge.

Markus quickly reached through the door with his right arm and concentrated his focused energy in his fingers. He turned the inside knob and quickly pulled the door open with his other hand.

"I'm in," he announced, walking briskly down the short rear hallway.

Turning the corner, Markus saw the lone Marine who instinctively raised his rifle and pointed it directly at Markus. "*Don't move!*" the Marine bellowed.

At the rear wall, Janus projected his hologram before passing through the thick Armory wall and into Jim's holding area. Jim was sitting in a metal chair staring expectantly at the front door.

"Hello James," said Janus calmly.

Jim spun around and jumped up from his chair.

"How did you get in here?" he asked incredulously.

"I'll explain later. Now let's get out of here. You must do *exactly* as I say."

"How are we going to get out?"

"Through that door," pointed Janus.

On the other side of the door, Markus quickly approached the Marine.

"Get down on the ground!" the Marine yelled. "Get down *now* or I'll shoot!"

Markus ignored the ultimatum and after a slight hesitation, the Marine shot at Markus. The bullets simply passed through Markus's hologram.

"What the . . . ?"

Markus continued to walk toward the soldier.

The Marine swung the butt end of his rifle forcefully toward Markus who in response, raised his right arm and easily stopped the approaching weapon which sparkled brightly on contact. Markus then used his other arm to quickly pin the Marine against the wall.

"Sejus, the hallway is secure! Come quickly!" he shouted.

Janus reached through the door, turned the handle and pushed the heavy steel door wide open. He quickly made his way past Markus followed closely by Jim. Markus wrenched the weapon from the Marine's hands, and threw him into the cell, before closing the door with a loud bang.

That should hold you for now, he thought.

Markus placed the assault rifle on the floor and headed toward the rear entrance.

At the front of the Armory, Chad's Battle Sphere was still hovering in position. Denton performed an updated computer scan of the immediate vicinity and located several additional targets which included two vacant buildings across the street and several street lights, fire hydrants and trees along the street.

As Mayla nodded, Denton instructed the weapons specialists to fire a second round. The vacant buildings and adjacent trees exploded, and burst into flames with a roar. Water gushed from the hydrants while street lights disintegrated with bright flashes of light. The Army soldiers and Marines continued to return intensive gun fire to no avail. As he crouched near the main entrance, it suddenly dawned on Major Talbot what was really happening.

That sphere is not shooting at us, he thought. *This is all an elaborate diversion to rescue Jim Johnson!*

"Lieutenant, we need to get back downstairs immediately!" Major Talbot jumped up and re-entered the Armory.

"Sir?" asked a confused Lieutenant Miller.

"Look at the UFO. It's not attacking us. It's a diversion to help Mr. Johnson escape! Let's go!"

The two men raced back inside toward the holding cell. They pulled out their handguns and peered down the hallway. Seeing that the Marine was no longer standing guard at the door, they cautiously approached the holding cell and noticed the assault rifle on the floor.

Major Talbot exchanged his pistol for the rifle, pointed it toward the door and nodded to Lieutenant Miller to pull it open. The Marine was standing by the door unharmed, but visibly shaken.

"The prisoner has escaped!"

"How the hell did that happen?" asked Major Talbot sternly.

"Two creatures came and took him. They were not *human*."

"What do you mean *not human*?"

"They were like ghosts Sir. I shot one at point blank range several times and the bullets just went right through him."

Major Talbot handed the assault rifle back to the Marine.

"They must have gone out the back. Let's go!"

Janus and Markus made their way along the rear of the building, followed closely by Jim. Smoke, dust and burning cinders whipped about while the gunfire continued. Janus turned and looked at Jim.

"Take my hand James," he instructed.

"What?"

"Take my hand!"

Markus returned to his orb and quickly darted across the street and around the next corner. Janus grabbed Jim's outstretched hand and levitated Jim toward the same street corner.

Exiting the rear of the Armory, Major Talbot quickly surveyed the scene. There was no sign of Jim or the two creatures.

"This way!" motioned Major Talbot as he sprinted along the rear of the Armory building. Turning the corner, he caught a glimpse of what looked like Jim and a translucent being disappear around the next corner followed closely by a small metallic sphere.

"Follow me!" yelled Major Talbot.

Lieutenant Miller and the Marine chased after Major Talbot as he disappeared around the next corner. Major Talbot sprinted up the street, looking for any sign of Jim and the other being. Reaching the next corner, he watched a white van with dark tinted windows pull away from the curb.

That must be them, he thought.

Just as Lieutenant Miller and the Marine arrived, the trio watched in silence as the white van disappeared around the next corner. Seconds later, the silver Sphere streaked overhead in the direction of the van. The sounds of gunfire had all but ceased from the Armory.

"Chad was piloting the UFO!" shouted Major Talbot. "I'm sure of it."

Lieutenant Miller nodded in agreement.

"There was a — I don't know what — helping Jim Johnson escape," exclaimed Major Talbot excitedly. "Did you see it? It was translucent, and they were gliding through the air somehow."

"It was probably the translucent beings from the hallway Sir," explained the still shaken Marine. "One overpowered me with incredible strength while another exited the cell with the prisoner."

Major Talbot wiped the sweat from his forehead, took a deep breath and raced back in the direction of the Armory.

"We have to track them down!" he yelled over his shoulder. "We can't let them escape!"

When he reached the Armory, Major Talbot ordered all available personnel to assist in locating and capturing the white van with the dark tinted windows. His commands were relayed throughout the Armory and the surrounding area. Several Humvees and armored personnel carriers out on patrol doubled back toward the vicinity of the Armory.

Jim crouched silently in the rear of the van, while Markus drove quickly down the narrow side streets. Using his monitoring orb, Markus plotted their escape, while Janus's orb kept track of any approaching Military vehicles.

"Markus, we are going to be cut off shortly. There are simply too many of them. We need Chad's help."

"Agreed."

Janus activated his encrypted communications network.

"Mayla, we need Chad to obstruct —"

"We see them Janus," interrupted Mayla.

"Intercepting targets 3, 6, 8, 13, 17 and 19 now," confirmed Teri.

Chad's Battle Sphere raced above the tree tops, his weapons specialists firing a series of low energy laser bursts which ripped open craters and ditches making the roads impassable for the Military vehicles.

"Good work!" responded Janus as he confirmed that the targets had stopped. "We need you to do the same to targets 1, 2, 4, 7, 9, 10, 12 and 15."

"Preparing to fire," replied Teri.

Janus glanced over at Markus.

"Will we need to make a course correction?"

"Not if they are successful," responded Markus.

Janus confirmed that one by one, the second group of approaching vehicles had stopped and that the earlier targets had turned around in search of alternate routes.

"Chad," announced Teri "there are three new airborne targets approaching from the Southeast."

"I see them, Teri. What are they?"

"Military jet fighters."

The F15 Eagles were now closing in on Chad, as they descended rapidly to 1000 feet.

"This is Casino Royale 81. Preparing to lock missiles on the boogie," the flight leader confirmed.

"That is a negative Casino Royale 81! Repeat. That is a *negative*! We are under strict orders not to fire on the UFO. Make visual contact only. *Repeat*. Make visual contact *only*!" responded the Westover Base Control Tower over the Airborne High Frequency Communication System.

"Please clarify," responded the flight leader.

"HQ says the UFO is likely being piloted by the individual the alien fleet is looking for," explained the Control Tower. "We are under strict orders not to engage weapons fire at this time."

"Roger," responded the squadron commander. "But what if the boogie fires on us first?"

"You are to disengage immediately."

"Roger that."

Markus made a sharp right onto Ridge Street and accelerated as he raced past the cemetery. Suddenly, Janus's orb identified a Humvee quickly approaching them from an intersecting street.

"Chad! A new target will intercept us in approximately ten seconds!" said Janus urgently.

"Closing in," responded Chad as he went into free flight and swooped down toward the van. The Humvee and the van were about to collide. Unfortunately, his side of the intersecting street was heavily wooded preventing him from getting a clear view of the street scene.

"*Chad,*" said Markus nervously as he continued to track the approaching target.

Jim grabbed the rear passenger seat and prepared for impact. Suddenly, Luna fired a series of laser bursts creating a crater in front of the Humvee, forcing it to veer off the road. Chad quickly changed course and raced back up into the sky at supersonic speed to assess the overall situation.

"Chad!" yelled Teri "Watch out!"

Before Chad could react, his Battle Sphere clipped the tail section of the flight leader's streaking F15 Eagle. The impact redirected Chad's Battle Sphere into the path of the two remaining F15s flying in close formation behind the flight leader.

Chad's Battle Sphere tore off the left wing of the second jet then crashed directly into the third fighter aircraft, obliterating the F15 on impact, mere seconds after the pilot ejected.

The remaining two F15 Eagles spiraled out of control. The pilots ejected themselves before the jets spiraled downward, exploding on impact. Enormous yellow fireballs and billowing black smoke clouds rose from the wreckage.

Chad's Battle Sphere stopped spinning and deceler-ated rapidly toward the ground.

"Chad!" yelled Mayla. "Can you hear me?"

There was no answer.

"*Chad!*"

Jim, Markus and Janus watched as black smoke billowed up into the sky. Chad's Battle Sphere descended across Main Street and into Randall Park where it plowed into the open area with a shuddering thud that could be felt for miles. The impact created a large crater, partially burying Chad's Battle Sphere.

"Quickly Markus!" ordered Janus. "We must reach Chad before the Military does!"

"He's landed in a large opening in Randall Park," Mayla reported. "We are performing a damage assess-ment now."

"Is he going to be OK?" asked Jim, his voice trem-bling.

"His plasma shield is very strong," replied Janus cautiously.

"Our system scans did not reveal any internal damage," confirmed Mayla. "But we believe Chad is unconscious."

"We are almost there," replied Janus.

Markus sped to the park entrance.

"This is all my fault!" muttered Jim in an agitated tone. "I should have never left the Fort."

"There's no time for regret, Jim," Markus said firmly. "We must stay focused and help Chad."

Markus navigated around several downed trees to the crater. They heard the sound of emergency vehicles in the distance.

"My monitoring scan indicates that several military vehicles will arrive here in less than two minutes," announced Janus grimly.

"Confirmed," replied Markus as they reached the edge of the crater.

Chad lay motionless in the twelve feet deep crater, covered in dirt from his waist down. He had transformed back into his silver flesh and blood form.

"Sejus , we must hurry," urged Markus.

Janus's hologram descended the crater, scooped Chad up in his arms and floated back up and out.

"OK, let's go," said Markus as he hurried back toward the van.

Jim opened the rear door and Janus glided safely inside the vehicle with Chad in his arms. After Jim scrambled into the passenger seat, Markus accelerated across the open field toward the dirt road.

"Why are you driving across the field?" asked Jim while he looked for something to hold onto.

"To minimize a dust cloud," explained Markus.

They reached the dirt road and Markus continued into the dense forest towards the van's hiding spot. At the same time, several military vehicles led by Major Talbot and Lieutenant Miller turned into Randall Park and raced along the dirt road toward the crater.

After Markus parked in the hiding spot, he opened the rear doors. Janus carefully exited the vehicle cradling Chad. Markus then levitated Jim out of his passenger seat before the group floated silently toward the woods trailed closely by their silver monitoring orbs. Jim watched the van as it rose above them eventually disappearing from sight.

Major Talbot and Lieutenant Miller rushed to the crater followed closely by two dozen soldiers and Marines. The contingent cautiously peered over the edge with their weapons drawn.

"Do you think he is under there somewhere Sir?" asked Lieutenant Miller.

"Not by the looks of it," responded Major Talbot pointing toward the ground by the edge of the crater.

"I see only one set of foot prints Sir," concluded Lieutenant Miller.

"The other beings probably don't leave footprints Lieutenant, which probably explains why we didn't find any at the crash site fifteen years ago."

"Of course."

"I don't see why the silver sphere's wreckage isn't here, even if the pilot is gone," mumbled Major Talbot. "In any event, *we are obviously too late. They are gone.*"

Additional Military vehicles poured into the park from all directions.

"Lieutenant, seal this Park off *immediately*. Search every inch of it for Chad and his father and *who* or *whatever* else is helping them!"

"Yes Sir. Right away Sir!"

"And Lieutenant," Major Talbot said, as he reached into a small backpack and tossed Lieutenant Miller a tee shirt. "It's Chad's. Give it to the dog handlers."

"Yes Sir!" responded Lieutenant Miller before making his way back to the convoy followed by several Marines.

We must find them quickly, thought Major Talbot as he stared back down at the empty crater.

The Mitel Fleet moved steadily at one-tenth the speed of light and would arrive on Earth in just thirty-two hours.

CHAPTER TWENTY-SIX – TURMOIL

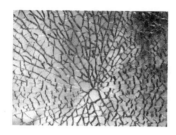

Janus cradled Chad in his arms as the group weaved their way through the forest to the clearing at the pond to get back to the Fort.

"Molly, Melissica, disarm the invisibility shield immediately," instructed Janus firmly.

The Fort appeared at the edge of the pond near the grave marker. Janus floated over toward the largest structure followed by Markus. Once inside the shield periphery, Markus lowered Jim to the ground. Seconds later, Molly rearmed the shield then ran toward Janus.

"Is he alright?" she asked fearfully.

"He's unconscious but he doesn't appear to have suffered any permanent damage, but he will need time to heal."

"Oh thank God."

"I'm going to check on the progress of the Mitel Fleet," said Markus quietly.

After carefully placing Chad on a cot, Janus also exited the structure, leaving Molly and Jim alone with Chad.

Molly gently rubbed Chad's cheek as she studied his face then turned to Jim. "What were you thinking, Jim?"

"I'm sorry Molly," Jim said. "I really thought I was doing the right thing."

"You thought you were doing the right thing?"

"I wanted to conceal Chad's link to the crash," Jim said, almost in a whisper. "I thought it would keep people like Major Talbot off his trail."

"Well *that* certainly wasn't the case."

"No," he whispered.

"What you did was reckless," lectured Molly. "You put your son in danger, not to mention Markus and Janus."

"I'm truly sorry."

"Let's hope Janus is right, and Chad recovers from this."

Jim could only nod in agreement.

Molly grabbed Jim's hand and squeezed it tightly and then let go. They sat down side by side on the adjacent cot to keep watch over Chad.

Several minutes later, Janus re-entered the structure followed by his monitoring orb. As Chad lay motionless on a cot, his orb performed a series of scans.

"How's he doing," asked Molly quietly.

"He has a few bruises and a small contusion on his left hand, which I'm not concerned about, but he suffered a concussion when he collided with the aircraft fighters. Unfortunately, it's the second one he's suffered."

"When did he have the first one?"

"On the first day of practice out in the asteroid belt."

Janus and Molly watched Chad breathe in and out for a few minutes.

"There's another concern."

"What's that, Janus?"

"It's unclear what the long-term effect may be of the trauma, and the forced transformation back to human form."

"Is he in danger?"

"No, it's not that. But he may have lost the ability to transform."

"*For good*?"

"Correct," nodded Janus.

"*Oh my god* — what would we do then?"

"I don't know," responded Janus.

They continued to observe Chad in silence for several minutes. His eyes and left arm occasionally twitched as if he was having a vivid dream.

"Is there anything we can do to help him?" Molly asked.

"He needs to sleep and to heal — physically *and* emotionally. In the meantime, I must return to the communications structure to monitor for new developments."

"I would like to stay here with Chad."

Jim nodded in agreement. They remained with Chad while Janus and Markus monitored communications between the world's military and political leaders, as well as the chatter among the Military units in Coopers Falls. Melissica shuttled back and forth between the two buildings with updates.

Thousands of additional troops poured into the area to assist in the search. Based on the limited information Jim had provided Major Talbot, the Pentagon instituted a gag order on the Coopers Falls mission. It was determined by the world's leaders that it was in the best interests of national security to make no mention of the incidents in Coopers Falls, until Chad was detained and interrogated. Major Talbot would have to speak with the press without revealing any details about the events that transpired. He explained that the Coopers Falls mission was a strategic training exercise, in preparation for the alien arrival. There was an unfortunate accident, and two warplanes collided. The destruction in and around the Armory was a simulation of potential attacks.

Janus knew the Mitels were intercepting and reviewing the countless transmissions from Earth, to determine Chad's whereabouts. Luckily, the Military did not disclose details about the events at Coopers Falls.

Under the direction of Major Talbot and Lieutenant Miller, Randall Park was sealed off. They ordered a massive manhunt across the Park, and the entire region. Helicopters with infrared cameras combed the area at night. On the ground, the dogs quickly established Chad's scent in the crater only to lose it once they climbed out. The dogs picked it up again along the dirt road where Chad had jogged several times in recent weeks and then lost the scent again at the edge of the dense woods. The dogs were unable to focus. One of the canine officers went to speak with Lieutenant Miller about the dog's unusual behavior:

"Sir, it's as though they have sensory overload. I've never seen anything like it before. One minute they're tracking the scent and the next thing you know, they're running around in circles."

At the same time, rows of Marines fanned out in the woods, in search Chad and the others. They continued their search into the night, arriving at the first clearing around midnight. They stopped and listened briefly for any sounds, then crossed the opening toward the woods on the far side.

As the Marines approached the pond, Janus carefully directed the invisible Fort to come to a stop over the middle of the pond. At the second opening, the Marines again stopped and listened for any hint of movement.

The soldiers were now only thirty yards away from the Fort. The Marines inspected the vicinity, but found no signs of activity. Eventually, the signal was given to move ahead and they made their way around both sides of the pond before disappearing back into the woods to continue their search. The process was repeated two more times during the night as troops approached through the woods from different directions. Helicopters flew back and forth overhead all night long.

The intense ground and air searches turned up nothing. It was as though Jim, Chad and the others had disappeared into thin air. Time was running out and Major Talbot was getting increasingly impatient. When it became evident that the intensive ground search through their section of the Park had ended, Janus reset the Fort back onto its invisible rotation around the edge of the pond before heading over to the largest structure.

Inside, he found Molly asleep on the cot next to Chad, and Jim curled up on the floor. On the other side of the structure, Melissica was fast asleep. Janus's orb ran a series of scans of Chad, which disclosed no significant change in his condition. He stood silently, watching his son for a time before heading back to the communications building.

"How's the lad?" Markus asked.

"No change. Where's the Mitel Fleet now?"

"They will be passing Saturn in just over an hour. At their current velocity, they will reach Earth in approximately twelve hours. Time is indeed getting short," said Markus somberly.

"Indeed it is, Markus. We should have relocated Chad's Battle Sphere to the Moon enclosure by now."

"Yes, you are right, my friend."

On the Mitel battle cruiser's ICC, Zan waited impatiently for the Mission Arrival Teleconference or 'MAT' to begin. Zan was intrigued by how one power structure on Earth, the United States of America, was recognized by the other nations to be the most powerful. It was a far cry from what he and his people were accustomed to on Mitel. Contemplating his own situation, Zan knew that his rise to power had provided him with two important resources: access to information and the ability to maintain a reasonable level of secrecy. To ensure his survival, Zan knew that his thoughts and plans must remain a closely guarded secret. Suddenly, the faces of several cruiser and transport vessel commanders appeared on the ICC monitors for the teleconference.

"Commander Lindar," boomed Zan over the cruiser's intercom. "Where are you? The meeting is set to start any second!"

"Almost there," replied Ard from the HorVert elevator.

Seconds later, the elevator doors slid open.

"I thought you hated these meetings," smiled Ard as he stepped out of the elevator.

"I do. I hate them even *more* when I have to do them by *myself*."

Just then, the stoic face of Lon Rexx appeared on a monitor.

"He looks like his usual happy self," whispered Ard.

"Yeah, right," grunted Zan.

With Lon's appearance, Zan turned on the volume and initiated the meeting.

"Thank you all for joining today's call. After a long and challenging voyage, we are now only ten hours away from our destination. And as you all know, we've intercepted and analyzed countless transmissions both before *and* after my message to Earth. Here is what we know: there have been recent sightings of a small spherical object in outer space. For reasons yet unknown, it is believed that this sphere has caused the disruption to Earth's worldwide communications on several occasions. In *my* opinion, the spherical object is in fact the young Thraen operating in his hybrid Battle Sphere mode. We don't know where he's hiding, and neither does anyone on Earth it appears. Does anyone have anything to add to that?"

"I do," replied Lon in his deep monotone voice.

"Commander Rexx. Your thoughts?" asked Zan.

"When will you initiate your mission orders?"

"What do you mean?"

"You know exactly what I mean — the preemptive strike."

"You are getting ahead of yourself Commander," replied Zan, trying to mask his disdain.

"With all due respect, Emperor Liss, I don't believe that I am," replied Lon. "I am confident that I am speaking for my fellow Commanders when I say we must take swift and decisive action to pressure the people of Earth to release to us the immortal Thraen."

Zan did not respond.

"Anything else would go against the explicit mission orders of the Mitel Leadership."

"I am fully aware of the mission orders," replied Zan, his anger rising. "But we can't risk killing the young

Thraen or his inner circle in the process Commander. *Don't you agree?*"

"I am not implying that we do Emperor Liss. And for the record, I agree with you that the spherical object is in fact the young Battle Sphere. If we attack, he will easily avoid our cluster pods with the aid of his Battle Hologram and be forced out of hiding in the process."

"But again Commander, his inner circle will not have that same ability."

"Agreed," nodded Lon grudgingly. "But it's a risk we will have to take."

"And once he is *exposed* Commander? Then what?" asked Zan curiously.

"We will engage him with our strike fighters until we force the inexperienced Battle Sphere into outer space."

"And then?"

"We use our enhanced gravity control beams that you yourself helped develop, to initially immobilize him. The crushing weight of the beams will eventually render him unconsciousness causing his transformation back to human form. At that point, he will be ours."

Zan sat in silence for several seconds as he considered Lon's plan.

"I am impressed Commander Rexx. I mean, other than the part about the preemptive cluster pod strike which will force us to use our finite resources on civilian targets. Please explain what *exactly* you are suggesting we do in that regard?"

"It is quite simple, actually. I'm suggesting we target only a select number of Earth's largest and most densely settled population centers, omitting for now the United States of America."

"Why omit them?" Zan inquired.

"From the transmissions we have heard, the United States is Earth's largest military power. We should only use our resources against them when it becomes necessary," explained Lon. "Given our technological superiority, I believe their military will have no choice but to stand down."

"I see," replied Zan. "And what about the dozen civilian population centers you have targeted? Our cluster pods would probably kill upwards of one hundred million people. Men, women *and* children."

"Based on an eighty percent kill rate," replied Lon. "I calculate one hundred and forty-seven million."

"And you are convinced that this kind of attack is our best option, Commander?"

"I believe —"

"And may I point out Commander Rexx, that you are recommending the exact tactics that were ruthlessly used against our *own* fleet on our voyage to Earth."

"What *I believe* Emperor Liss," growled Lon tersely, "is that we must follow the explicit mission orders from our Leadership. A preemptive attack will either force the Thraen out, or terrify the people of Earth enough to give him up."

"Understood. I will certainly give your suggestions careful consideration. Does anyone have anything else to add?"

There was no reply.

"Very well, then. We will continue on our approach to Earth. In the meantime, I want everyone to continue monitoring as many transmissions as possible and notify me immediately if you obtain information that may lead us to the Thraen."

With that, Zan ended the MAT and headed for the HorVert.

"Follow me," Zan motioned to Ard to get in the elevator. The doors slid closed behind them. "Rexx has not changed. He's as crazy as ever."

"*That's* an understatement. I also think he wants your job."

"Oh really? He can have it."

"I'm serious, Zan."

"What makes you think so?"

"He's *hiding* something. Or waiting for a chance to get back at you for what you did to him in CCCF."

"Maybe you should have been a behavioral specialist instead of a Mitel cruiser commander," Zan said sarcastically.

"What are you going to do?" asked Ard.

"About Lon?"

"About his suggestion for the preemptive strike . . ."

"I don't know yet."

The elevator doors opened and they stepped out into the officer's cafeteria.

"Let's get a protein drink," suggested Zan as they headed for a table in the corner.

"Zan, you seem convinced that the young Thraen is already transforming into a Battle Sphere."

"I am. Have you seen the images we intercepted?"

"Yes."

"Well? What do *you* think? After all, you are the expert on all things Thraen."

"I think an argument could be made that it's a Battle Sphere. Or a satellite or — "

"It's him. I am certain of it."

"In that case, what should we do?"

"What do you mean?"

"If it turns out that the young Thraen is a fully functioning Battle Sphere, then we may be in more danger than we realize," cautioned Ard.

"Nonsense," scoffed Zan. "He is just a boy, *years* away from realizing his full potential as a fighting machine capable of defeating our fleet."

"And what if you're wrong, Zan? A trained Battle Sphere can destroy a fleet much larger than ours!"

"Understood. But there's no way he has been trained."

"I think —"

"The answer is he can't be."

"How can you be so sure Zan? If you're wrong . . ."

Zan took another long sip of his protein drink while he thought for awhile about the USEP pod.

"Do you remember when the Thraen pod escaped?"

"I do," smiled Ard. "I was a young Navigator and Third Officer under your command, fresh out of the Academy."

"We thought we had all the answers back then, didn't we?"

"That's for sure. But why do you ask?"

"Well, remember how we detected two small probes in the Thraen escape pod at the time of their escape?"

"Vaguely. What about them?"

"We intercepted transmissions between the small USEP and a larger craft that had appeared nearby."

"I'm sorry but —"

"Do you think that it's possible Thraen holograms could have somehow imbedded themselves in those probes — and traveled across the universe with the boy?"

"It's possible I guess. That may explain how the infant survived the voyage in the first place," Ard began. "After all, embedding holograms into all kinds of technologies was one of Thrae's signature achievements. But projecting a hologram into a probe? That seems highly unusual. But then again, our surprise attack was also unusual."

"Indeed. And if you recall, both vessels were scanned and determined to be unmanned other than the Thraen child."

"Thraen Holograms would not have registered as life forms."

"That is precisely my point!"

"But if that's true, you are also proving *my* point."

"How so, Ard?" Zan frowned.

"Because the young Battle Sphere will know we were responsible for the destruction of his home planet. He will be expecting our fleet to attempt the same thing to Earth."

"More reason for us *not* to launch a preemptive strike."

"Exactly! Listen, Zan. The fierce determination of the Thraen Battle Sphere is legendary. If this young Battle Sphere was in fact trained by experienced holograms, I fear that he will either prevail or fight to the death attempting to do so. Either way, it will probably not end well for us."

"Let's hope you're wrong," replied Zan somberly.

Janus again checked on Chad while Molly and Jim sat together on the adjacent cot. Seconds later, his monitoring orb darted into the structure to conduct several detailed scans.

"Any progress?" asked Molly as Janus reviewed the scanning reports.

"Unfortunately, no," replied Janus with a hint of frustration.

"What are we going to do?" asked Jim quietly.

"We must continue to wait," replied Janus somberly as he turned and headed back to the communications building.

Over the next several hours, Jim, Molly and Melissica kept a close watch over Chad, hoping for any sign of improvement. Every so often Chad would wince or twitch his left arm giving hope that at any minute, he would open his eyes and sit up.

Markus suddenly appeared in the doorway with a somber look on his face.

"Markus. What's wrong?" whispered Jim.

"The Mitel Fleet has arrived."

CHAPTER TWENTY-SEVEN – THE STRUGGLE

Thirty-six hours after his midair collisions, Chad finally opened his eyes. He smiled seeing his parents seated next to him in the safe confines of the Fort.

"Hello Son," Jim said softly.

"Hi Dad, hi Mom. I guess our rescue plan worked."

"It sure did," grinned Molly lovingly.

Janus and Markus entered. They both smiled seeing Chad sitting up in bed.

"It's good to see you awake and alert my boy. How are you feeling?"

"Hi Markus. I feel OK."

"We are all very grateful that you are OK," said Janus.

"What is the latest on everything?" asked Chad quietly.

"What is the last thing you remember?"

"I remember flying above the van."

"You collided with three Jet fighters and crashed in the park," explained Janus. "We were able to reach you just before the Military arrived and brought you back to the Fort. You've been unconscious for nearly thirty-six hours."

"What? *Thirty-six hours*?"

"Yes."

"What about the Mitels? Where are they now?"

Janus glanced at Jim and Molly before answering.

"They are positioned just above Earth's atmosphere."

"*No!*"

"The escape did not go *exactly* as planned but we must go forward from here."

"Everything you planned for. It's all too late now," said Chad sadly.

"Let's not dwell on past events. While you were unconscious, the Military conducted an intensive air and ground search of the park. Fortunately, the invisibility shields successfully concealed both the Fort and the van."

"What about Mayla, Teri, Luna and the rest of the team?"

"Your Battle Hologram is still operating safely concealed in the tree grove," confirmed Markus.

"What about the jet fighters?"

"They crashed into several nearby homes lad."

"Listen, Chad. What happened, although tragic, is just the beginning," explained Janus. "You must prepare yourself for much worse when the Mitels attack."

Janus lowered himself to one knee, so he could be eye to eye with Chad.

"Son, you could have been badly injured, or worse. You *cannot* afford to make a third mistake. You must promise me that you will *not* override your Battle Hologram ever again."

"But free flight allows me to react in ways I can't otherwise."

"Understood. But you are still learning. You must *promise* to follow orders."

"I promise."

"Very well then," smiled Janus as he stood up. "The Battle Hologram is assembling a plan right now, based on the current positioning of the Mitel force."

"I need to transform!" Chad said, jumping out of bed, feeling weak and dizzy.

Markus immediately ran a series of scans on Chad.

"Do you feel up to transforming?" Janus asked cautiously.

"There is only one way to find out." Chad headed for the pond, abruptly turning around to face the others. He took a deep breath, closed his eyes, and positioned his arms and legs.

Nothing happened.

Chad repositioned himself and tried again. Still nothing happened. He spun around to face the pond and tried again without success before turning back toward the structures to try one last time. Still nothing.

Chad lowered his arms and opened his eyes. His expression was a combination of disappointment, bewilderment and frustration. Janus and Markus knew that feeling all too well.

"I can't transform!"

Janus placed his hand on Chad's shoulder.

"Chad, you've been through a lot. You're bruised and have experienced a severe concussion. You need to rest and be patient."

"I can't be patient. We're running out of time!"

"You must rest so your body *and* your mind are equally ready to respond."

Over the next few hours, Chad attempted to transform without success. In the communications structure, Janus, Markus, Molly and Jim listened to news broadcasts and military transmissions. Melissica sat nearby, keeping an eye on Chad.

"What do you think?" asked Markus.

"I'm convinced it's all in his mind," replied Janus.

"Do you think it makes a difference where he is?" asked Molly.

"What do you mean Mol?" asked Jim.

"All of the previous transformations occurred over at the Davis Farm. Maybe that's where he is most comfortable transforming."

"You may be on to something Molly," said Janus. "But getting him there undetected won't be easy."

"We need to try *something*," reasoned Molly.

"They won't be looking for me," announced Melissica from behind.

"What do you mean?" asked Janus as everyone turned to look at her.

"The Military. They aren't looking for *me*. I can go get my Mom's Subaru and drive it back here. We can hide Chad in the back seat and drive him over to Davis Farm."

"The Park has been sealed off to the public," Molly said as she considered Melissica's plan.

"Maybe I could meet you somewhere else close by?"

"*Yes*," said Jim. "We can go the same way I went the other day. If we leave from the Park's North entrance, go through the woods along Sandy Brook and then up the old railroad tracks, Melissica can wait for us behind Long's Dairy. It will be a short drive to Davis Farm from there."

"*We*?" asked Markus.

"Yes, we," replied Molly firmly. "We have no intention of waiting here."

"Getting you all out of the Park all at once won't be easy," Janus said.

"Why can't we use one of your invisibility shields? Why can't we just drive the van to Davis Farm under its protection?"

"Unfortunately, our shields operate statically or under extremely slow speeds."

"OK, but couldn't we use one to get out of the Park on foot?"

"I can't see why not, although it will take a few hours for me to create one big enough for all of us."

"I think we should go at night to minimize the potential of being seen," Markus added.

"Agreed," nodded Janus. "Unless you hear otherwise, Melissica, you are to drive to the rear of the Long's Dairy building at three o'clock in the morning and wait for us," Janus said, turning to Markus. "Please escort Melissica out of the Park under the protection of the small invisibility shield."

Melissica followed Markus outside and went over to Chad.

"Hey," she said tenderly. "I came over to say good-bye."

"*Where are you going?*"

Before Melissica could answer, Janus appeared and began to speak.

"She's going home to get her mother's car."

"Melissica, we should get moving," said Markus from across the enclosure. "Are you ready?"

Chad grabbed Melissica and hugged her.

"*Coming.*"

Melissica and Markus made their way into the woods. Chad was exhausted so he went inside and quickly fell asleep.

On the ICC of Cruiser Number 1, Zan stared at Earth on the center screen in front of him. He wanted desperately to escape the confines of his artificial environment and breathe natural air. The planet below was breathtaking and inviting. The HorVert doors slid open and Ard stepped out.

"A pretty impressive sight, don't you think?"

Zan nodded but didn't respond.

"I understand our forces have branched out and have now encircled the planet," continued Ard.

"That's correct."

"Any update on the Thraen?"

"No."

"Not surprising. What should we do?"

"I have been mulling over Lon's plan."

"Oh?"

"The plan has some merit, if you ignore his suggestion to use a sizeable portion of our cluster pods on a preemptive strike against the general population."

"Emperor Liss," interrupted Lia from her communications station. "Commander Rexx would like to speak with you."

"Put him on," Zan sighed.

Lon's stern expression appeared, along with the faces of the other commanders on the monitors.

"What is the meaning of this Commander Rexx?" asked Zan. "I don't recall scheduling a follow-up meeting to the MAT."

"I called this meeting," replied Lon. "It is time to take action. We have waited long enough."

"Is that so?"

"Yes. It's time to order a pre-emptive strike."

"I don't think we should waste our cluster pods on the general population in the hopes of forcing the Thraen to confront us. We don't even know his capabilities at this point."

"He has no capabilities!"

"We don't know that!"

"I see they have gotten to you," announced Lon.

"What are you *talking* about?"

"The Mitel resistance. They have corrupted your integrity!"

"I always thought you were crazy, but — "

"I *personally* interrogated several resistance fighters and they all confessed that you have spoken with resistance leaders."

There were surprised gasps among the ICC personnel.

"Those conversations happened during a terrorist attack on one of our development facilities!" Zan said, dismissively.

"Before I killed them," smiled Lon. "The pathetic resistance scum also confessed that the *facility* you mention was not sanctioned by the Mitel Leadership!"

Zan did not respond.

"So, you don't deny it?"

"Deny *what*?"

"That you are a traitor!"

"Rexx, you will pay dearly for your insubordination!"

"Empty rhetoric from a corrupt Emperor," Lon taunted. "I will initiate the preemptive strike myself!"

The monitors went black.

"Is it true?" asked the weapons specialist abruptly. "What Commander Rexx said about you?"

Zan spun around to see his third officer pointing a hand-held electro laser. The Navigator and scanning specialist had also drawn their weapons.

"Rexx is delusional!" Zan said defensively. "Not to mention a liar and a cheat!"

"He may be a cheat, but he is a true Mitel warrior!" replied the third officer as he prepared to fire his laser.

"*Don't!*" Zan pleaded, reaching for his weapon.

There was a series of bright flashes and suddenly, all three crewmen were dead, their torsos emitting a smoldering gray cloud. Stunned, Zan glanced around the ICC. Lia and the two assistant specialists were holding their electro lasers.

"Well," said Lia calmly. "That takes care of that. Are you OK Zan?"

"Yes. I guess those weren't dreams after all."

"No, they weren't."

Red lights began flashing on the navigation, weapons and propulsion consoles.

"That's not good," said Zan as he rushed to the auxiliary console.

"What's happening?" asked Lia.

Zan studied the displays before he began to type furiously.

"We are under attack," he replied. "Cruisers 2 and 3 have launched laser bursts and cluster pods!"

Everyone rushed to their stations while Ard scrambled over the railing to the weapons console.

"Can we avoid them?" asked Lia.

"There isn't enough time for evasive maneuvers," replied Zan, sprinting over to the navigation console.

"Then what are you doing?" asked Ard.

"Energizing the high-speed shields," replied Zan without looking up.

"Wait, you can do that before we are up to speed?"

"Don't forget — I ran the entire high-speed development program. I made sure this cruiser had capabilities the others didn't . . . Mat — Status report. Now!"

"Incoming fire in ten seconds!" At nineteen, Mat Wall was not only the cruiser's assistant scanning specialist, but also a third generation Mitel resistance fighter.

"Navigator. Full power *now!*" instructed Zan, "Hard right!"

"Yes Sir," replied Dax Bann. At twenty-one, he was the cruiser's assistant navigator and a fourth-generation resistance fighter.

"Bracing for impact!" announced Mat.

The cruiser shuddered violently, and the lights flickered before returning to normal.

"Damage assessment," requested Zan.

"We are slowing down," replied Dax. "The propulsion units are damaged."

"We're on auxiliary power," confirmed Lia. "Not sure how long that will last."

"You guys OK back there?" asked Zan over the intercom system.

"Affirmative," replied Dru. "Are you going to keep us in one piece?"

"I'm trying."

"Thanks." Dru's intercom beeped again.

"Who was *that*?" asked Ard.

"My mechanic. He has looked out for me since I was a boy."

"Tell him to watch out for me too," replied Ard.

"I'll be sure to do that right after you establish a target lock on those two cruisers."

"Already done."

"Launch two cluster pods," ordered Zan.

The pods exited the twin weapons tubes located beneath Cruiser Number 1 and raced toward their targets, releasing several small warheads. As Cruiser Number 2 circled around an enormous transport vessel, Lon stared at the ICC's primary monitor in disbelief.

"How was he not destroyed?" he bellowed in frustration.

"It appears the cruiser activated its high-speed shields, absorbing or deflecting the brunt of the impacts," replied the scanning specialist."

"How did he activate them?" demanded Lon.

Suddenly, several red lights flashed on the console panels.

"Incoming cluster warheads!" blurted another scanning specialist.

"Where from?" shouted Lon.

"The *Emperor's cruiser!*"

"Navigator, get us behind the transport vessel!"

"Yes Sir!"

Just after Cruiser Number 2 slipped from view, several cluster warheads detonated along the side of the transport vessel, tearing it apart. Then, multiple warheads plowed directly into Cruiser Number 3, causing it to violently explode.

"Cruiser Number 3 and Transport Vessel 14 have been destroyed!" announced the scanning specialist.

"Arrghh!" roared Lon angrily. "I will *not* let him defeat me again!"

Janus spent the next few hours creating the digital "mesh" for a new rectangular invisibility shield. He energized the mesh with a magnetic field before injecting it with plasma. After a series of diagnostic tests, the shield was ready. There was sudden flurry of short radio bursts. He instinctively knew what was happening.

"Markus, did you notice that?" he asked quickly.

"Indeed I did."

"What's going on?" Jim asked.

"We've picked up transmissions indicating some activity from outer space," replied Janus.

"Is it the Mitels?"

"Yes. It appears their vessels are attacking one another."

Zan stood on the ICC of Cruiser Number 1, demanding a status report.

"Cruiser Number 3 has been destroyed, Sir," confirmed Mat.

"What about Lon and Cruiser Number 2?"

"It ducked behind a transport vessel, and only the vessel was destroyed Sir," replied Mat."

"I'm picking up transmissions from Cruiser Number 2," interjected Lia. "They are retreating beyond our effective firing range and have instructed all cruisers to return to this region."

"That doesn't leave us much time," said Zan. "We need to check the status of the primary propulsion system."

"How will we do that with 160 Mitel loyalists between here and there," Ard asked.

"I don't know yet. But we must get out of here before those cruisers arrive."

"I have a plan," Lia said.

She quickly made her way to an auxiliary wall cabinet to retrieve several oxygen masks and backpack units.

"Everyone — put one on," she motioned.

"*Why?*" asked Ard.

"We're going to put the rest of the crew to sleep. Zan do you remember the series of *devices* I mentioned earlier?"

"When you were in my quarters?" asked Zan.

"*Wait,*" exclaimed Ard. "*You* were in *his* quarters?"

"It's *not* what you think," replied Lia quickly. "Anyway, the devices — they *aren't* bombs.

"Well *that's* a relief," replied Zan sarcastically.

"They are remote-controlled time released airborne opioid devices. They are extremely effective *and* depending on the length of exposure, very lethal."

Zan spoke into the intercom.

"Dru, are you still there?"

"Yes. But the crew is getting restless down here."

"Understood. Everyone is to put on oxygen units immediately. We 're going to sedate the entire crew."

"OK. Will do."

Jim followed Molly back to the largest structure to rest up while Janus and Markus monitored the Military transmissions. The ongoing chatter confirmed that there had been two large explosions beyond Earth's outer atmosphere.

"What do you think?" asked Markus curiously.

"Something's clearly going on up there Markus," said Janus incredulously. "I just wish we knew what that *something* was."

"Indeed," nodded Markus.

On the ICC of Cruiser Number 1, Zan reached for his laser as he walked toward the HorVert.

"Lia, I'm placing you in command," he instructed. "Ard and I are going to check out the propulsion area."

"Understood," nodded Lia.

"Hopefully your devices worked," said Ard uneasily.

"I would stake my life on it," nodded Lia.

In the HorVert, Zan and Ard sped toward the propulsion area.

"Dru, can you hear me?" Zan said through the intercom.

"Yes."

"Are you —"

"We're fine. Everyone else appears to be unconscious."

"Good. We are on our way. I want you and your assistants to inspect the propulsion units for damage."

"Inspections are already underway."

Zan looked through his oxygen mask at Ard, who was visibly anxious.

"Are you OK?" he asked Ard.

"Yes. I guess this means we're not going back to Mitel."

"Probably not."

"Zan," Lia said over the intercom. "The six remaining cruisers are on route here. Cruiser Number 2 appears to be waiting for them beyond weapons range."

"How much time do we have?"

"About a half hour."

As the doors to the HorVert slid open, Mitel crew members lay motionless along the length of the corridor. Zan and Ard gingerly stepped around them, lasers drawn. Entering the propulsion area, Dru and his three assistants were just finishing up a series of diagnostic tests on the two large propulsion units.

"Any news?" asked Zan.

"Unit number 1 is destroyed and unit number 2 is at thirty percent capacity."

"Well, *that* explains things."

"We're screwed!" moaned Ard.

Dru shot a quick glance at Ard but did not respond.

"Have you started to swap things over?" asked Zan.

"Yes."

"How much longer will it take?"

"Twenty minutes, maybe twenty-five."

"Wait, how much longer will it take to swap *what* over?" Ard asked.

"To switch to propulsion unit number 3," replied Zan.

"What are you *talking about*? There *is* no propulsion unit number 3!"

"There is here," smiled Dru.

"You guys are unbelievable!" Ard said.

"I'm not," smiled Zan as he patted Dru on the back. "But my *father* is."

Dru nodded in appreciation and over the next several minutes, they all worked feverishly to swap out the interface modules from unit 1 to unit 3. They also replaced two damaged modules on unit 2. Once the units were back on line, it was time to put their work to the test.

"Lia, can you hear me?" asked Zan over his mask's intercom.

"Loud and clear."

"Move away from the planet at full power. We need to buy some time to figure out our next move."

Seconds later, a deep humming sound filled the propulsion area as the large cruiser sped forward.

"*Excellent!*" shouted Zan. "Lia, we are on our way back."

He then turned to Dru.

"Thank you. I want the four of you to go to the *tube* and make sure everything is ready, OK?"

Dru nodded before leaving to gather up his three assistants.

"What was *that* all about?" asked Ard.

"I'll explain later," replied Zan.

Ard rolled his eyes in frustration.

"You say that *a lot* — you know that?"

CHAPTER TWENTY-EIGHT — THE MITELS ATTACK

Lon paced Cruiser Number 2's ICC like a caged lion.

"I *knew* Liss was a traitor!" he muttered to himself. "I should have acted before his renegade ship was able to attack our fleet!"

Lon then let out a long deep sigh.

"Status report on our remaining cruisers," he inquired.

"They are almost here," confirmed the communications specialist.

"Good. Make sure all transport and weapons vessels remain out of range. We can't afford to lose any more of them —"

"*Commander!* Cruiser Number 1 is accelerating and heading away from the planet," exclaimed the scanning specialist.

"Looks like the coward is fleeing. Have you heard anything from our sources over there?"

"Still nothing Sir," replied the communications specialist.

"*Strange.* I don't understand why they've all stopped checking in."

"Their communications devices register as operational," confirmed the communications specialist.

"It doesn't matter anymore," muttered Lon. "Notify the fleet. It's time to strike."

At 12:30 a.m., Janus took a break from monitoring.

"Everything seems too quiet," he said softly.

"Agreed," replied Markus.

At 1:30 a.m., Markus went over to the largest structure to wake Jim, Molly and Chad. It took everyone a little extra time to fully wake up and become alert. As they prepared to leave, Markus noticed that it was now 2:15 a.m.

"Sejus, we really need to get moving," he said anxiously.

Under the protection of the new invisibility shield, Janus and Markus guided the group diagonally through the woods to the Park's north entrance. Up ahead, a Humvee idled on the dirt road, two heavily armed soldiers on either side of it. Janus motioned the group to follow him past the soldiers and into the middle of the adjoining street.

Just then, Headlights of another Humvee appeared from up the road. Janus motioned everyone to stand still as the Humvee roared past them within inches of the shield before abruptly turning into the park. Janus gave the signal and the group continued across the street, up the path along Sandy Brook and back into the darkness.

Once out of view, Janus and Markus returned to their orbs and raced ahead while Chad, Molly and Jim made their way to the abandoned railroad tracks. Once the trio arrived at the old dairy building, Janus's hologram reappeared and motioned for everyone to stop.

"This area is highly patrolled. We need to move quickly. Melissica is waiting for you behind the building."

As the group approached Melissica's car, she opened the door and got out.

"You guys are 25 minutes *late*. I was really worried!"

Molly quickly got in on the passenger side, while Jim and Chad climbed into the back seat and crouched down as low as possible. Seconds later, Janus's hologram reappeared next to the car.

"Head directly to the farm's main entrance," he instructed. "Markus and I will be right behind you in our monitoring orbs."

Lon paced the ICC of Cruiser Number 2.

"The cruisers are awaiting your orders."

"Order the strike," Lon told the communications specialist.

"Yes Sir."

On command, each of the seven cruisers launched a series of eleven cluster pods targeting the most densely populated cities on Earth: Tokyo/Yokohama, San Paulo, Seoul/Incheon, Mexico City, Manila, Mumbai, Jakarta, Kolkata, Cairo, Moscow, Shanghai and Beijing.

Zan and Ard stepped from the HorVert elevator onto Cruiser Number 1's ICC.

"Zan! The fleet has initiated a preemptive strike on Earth!" Lia shouted.

"*Rexx*," muttered Zan angrily. "Navigator, turn us around *immediately*!"

"Ard, lock onto as many pods as possible!" shouted Zan.

"I'm on it."

"Reengage the high-speed shields!" Zan ordered.

"Done," confirmed Dax.

"Activate the slip ring and head directly toward the pods!"

"*Sir*?" asked Mat incredulously.

"The slip ring is nowhere near energized," added Ard.

"We must get as close to those warheads as possible. *Do as I say!*"

"Yes Sir," replied Mat before the cruiser lurched forward.

"Ard, have you locked on the targets?"

"Yes."

"*Prepare to fire!*" Zan commanded.

"Are you sure? At this speed, we risk spontaneous detonation."

"Do it!"

"OK, *OK!*"

Cruiser Number 1 accelerated directly towards Earth.

"But the planet!" yelled Dax apprehensively.

"*Fire!*"

Ard launched twelve cluster pods in rapid succession aimed at the preemptive strike. For good measure, he fired three dozen laser bursts targeting the strike's last three rounds.

"Disengage the slingshot, hard right!" Zan directed.

Cruiser Number 1 decelerated rapidly and vibrated violently as it scraped along the edge of Earth's outer atmosphere. Seconds later, the vibration was replaced by the normal hum of the propulsion units.

"The laser bursts destroyed the final twenty-one cluster pods, Sir," Dax announced.

"And the pods?"

"They destroyed another thirty-five."

"That means twenty-one got through," Zan said, pounding his fist on the console in frustration.

The remaining pods passed Earth's outer atmosphere releasing their missile clusters which quickly activated and separated before streaking toward the surface. They plowed into the targeted metropolitan areas with incredible precision. Approximately one hundred twenty million men, women and children were killed instantly. Another sixty-five million were badly burned and would eventually succumb to their injuries.

"Sir!" the scanning specialist on Cruiser Number 2 announced. "A significant number of our pods were intercepted and destroyed by Cruiser Number 1."

"The traitor is trying to undermine our *entire mission!*" bellowed Lon.

"Emperor Rexx," said the communications specialist. "I just received confirmation that another transport vessel has unexpectedly disintegrated."

"*The Mitel resistance!*" yelled Lon. "I thought we had eliminated them!"

Ian Micron, second in command and Lon's special assistant, stepped out from the shadows of the ICC. Ian, not a typical Mitel warrior — was short, thin and somewhat frail. The great grandson of a Leadership member, Ian was fascinated with Thraen culture, often finding himself torn between the two worlds while at times openly critical of his own.

"The resistance appears to have perfected our signature calling card, wouldn't you agree *Emperor* Rexx?" proposed Ian.

"We stopped using terrorism a long time ago," scoffed Lon.

"Have we?"

"Yes."

"Then what do you call the preemptive strike we just launched?"

"I'm merely following orders!"

"That fact does not allow us to wash our hands of the ugly truth."

"Which is?"

"That we *never* stopped using terrorism. We murder innocent men, women and children in the name of the Mitel Empire. We choose to call it something else, but it is still genocidal terrorism."

Lon turned away and did not respond.

"The remaining pods have successfully reached their targets," confirmed the scanning specialist.

"And?" asked Lon impatiently.

"Infrastructure damage is significant Sir," replied the scanning specialist. "Our modeling algorithm is estimating over one hundred million killed."

"That's not enough," Lon hissed. "Prepare to launch a second strike."

"Sir?" asked the weapons specialist incredulously.

"We must carry out our express orders." explained Lon tersely. "And since the Mitel resistance continues to deplete our resources, we must act quickly and forcefully to ensure that this world complies with our demands! DO AS I SAY!"

In Washington, DC, the President held an emergency meeting with the Joint Chiefs. The fact that the United States was spared from the initial onslaught was not lost on them. After a brief discussion, the decision was made to reach out to Emperor Liss.

"We have information concerning the location of the individual you seek," said the radio wave and message beam transmissions. "Cease fire immediately and we will provide it to you."

Cruiser Number 2 intercepted the communication. Seconds later, Lon responded.

"This is Lon Rexx. I am the acting Emperor of the Mitel people. You are in *no* position to negotiate. However, if you provide his exact location and do it quickly, I will consider your request."

Soon thereafter, the communications specialist received another transmission and passed it on to Lon which read:

Emperor Lon Rexx:

Our military has been conducting an intensive ground and air search for the teenage male we believe you are seeking. The search area is centered in or about Coopers Falls, New York in the United States of America (latitude 43° 18' 33" N longitude 73° 38' 39" W). He was recently observed by military personnel in the immediate vicinity of two unidentified holographic beings and a small metallic sphere. We request that you cease your attacks. Once the youth is apprehended, we will arrange to deliver him to you unharmed. In return, it is our expectation that you will leave our world in peace.

The President of the United States

"Abort the second strike," ordered Lon. "Contact the closest transport vessel and instruct them to send seven groups of strike fighters to attack this *Coopers Falls*. We will force him out of hiding."

"Are you sure?" asked Ian.

"Yes. History tells me that if there is one thing I can rely on, it is that a Thraen Battle Sphere will make a critical mistake."

On Cruiser Number 1, Lia relayed the news of the destruction on Earth; then shared the transmissions between Lon and the United States President.

"Navigator, swing us back around," ordered Zan.

"Yes Sir," nodded Mat.

"What are you going to do now?" asked Lia.

"We need to take out as many Mitel vessels as possible before they launch another strike."

"Uhh, that might be difficult," said Ard.

"Why?"

"Even with the additional supply, we are going through our cluster pods very quickly."

"What do you suggest we do, Ard?"

"Focus on the cruisers for now. We can go after the transport vessels later, assuming we are still around to do it."

"Sounds good to me!" replied Lia.

"Let's do it," nodded Zan.

Melissica drove cautiously down Ridge Street past the college before turning right onto Route 4 toward the Davis Farm. It was now beginning to get light as Melissica approached a long curve about a half mile from the farm entrance. Suddenly, from the other direction, a Military convoy appeared around the bend.

"*Oh no!*"

"Stay calm Melissica," instructed Molly firmly. "Jim, Chad, crouch down as low as possible!"

Humvees, jeeps and armored personnel carriers roared past Melissica's Subaru wagon. As the last Humvee drove by, someone yelled from inside as it screeched to a halt. Glancing at her rearview mirror, Melissica could see a column of bright red tail lights. Seconds later, the vehicles started to turn around.

"I think they discovered us!" said Melissica in a panicked voice.

"Melissica, we must go *now*!" ordered Chad.

Melissica hit the gas and the Subaru sped off around the bend. From the back seat, Jim and Chad watched the convoy as it disappeared from view.

"Chad, what do we do when we get there?" Molly asked.

"We don't have time to hide the car like we did before," replied Chad. "We'll have to ram through the metal gates at the farm's entrance."

As they approached the farm, Chad saw that the gates had already been opened.

"Janus and Markus opened the gates for us!" exclaimed Chad. "Quickly, just follow the dirt road."

Melissica did as Chad directed. A thick gray morning mist covered the fields.

"Melissica, turn off the car lights and drive as fast as you can."

Chad noticed the faint reflection of the convoy's head lights against the power lines as they made their way around the bend.

"Melissica, turn off here and stop! Right now!"

Melissica followed Chad's orders. The Subaru bounced to a stop in the tall grass. They waited silently for the convoy to go by the farm entrance.

"Now what?" asked Molly.

"Let's try to get closer," instructed Chad.

Melissica backed up on to the dirt road and drove closer to the tree grove.

"Turn here," Chad said, directing Melissica to head back onto the field.

"We should stop here," suggested Jim. "The car will get stuck if we go much further."

The group piled out of the car and headed toward the grove as the two monitoring orbs sped by overhead. Off in the distance, the convoy could be heard making its way back up the main road.

"They're looking for us," Jim said.

Cruiser Number 1 headed back toward the Mitel Fleet at high speed.

"Cruiser Number 4 is almost within range," confirmed Dax.

"Where's Lon's cruiser?" asked Zan.

"It's not registering Sir."

"Keep looking. He's out there somewhere."

"What about the gas? Shouldn't we start flushing it out?" Ard asked.

"It won't make much difference for the crew," explained Lia. "None of them could have survived such a lengthy exposure."

"Let's do it anyway," replied Zan. "Our oxygen tanks won't last forever. Ard, initiate a system purge."

"The cruiser is within weapons range," announced Dax. "Scans register a transport vessel much further out, on our right side."

"Incoming cluster pods!" shouted Dax.

"Navigator, hard right," instructed Zan.

The propulsion units hummed as Cruiser Number 1 accelerated and banked in the direction of the transport vessel. Seconds later, the incoming cluster pods streaked harmlessly past.

"Ard, *return fire on the cruiser!*" shouted Zan.

After launching the pods, the group waited silently.

"A series of direct hits on Cruiser Number 4!" exclaimed Dax. "The transport vessel is now within firing range."

"Prepare to fire," ordered Zan.

"But I thought we decided to wait," said Ard.

"It's too close to pass up."

"*OK.*"

He launched two cluster pods followed by several laser bursts causing the entire side of the giant craft to explode and then disintegrate. As they streaked past the stricken vessel, several red lights flashed on the consoles.

"What the —" muttered Zan.

"*Cruiser Number 2!*" yelled Dax. "It was shielded by the transport vessel —"

Before he could finish, a cluster warhead plowed into Cruiser Number 1's high speed shields, dispersing the explosive energy before involuntarily shutting down. A second warhead tore through the front end of the vessel jerking it sideways, and hurtling everyone across the ICC. Up front, the sudden decompression pulled everything into outer space before the emergency environmental monitoring system closed the nearest bulkhead doors. A third warhead tore through the massive slip ring hardware stored beneath the spacecraft, flinging debris in all directions and shutting down Cruiser Number 1's power completely.

"I want a status report!" demanded Lon from the ICC of Cruiser Number 2.

"Three confirmed hits, Sir. The cruiser is drifting without power or propulsion," the scanning specialist said. "Air quality within the vessel registers as uninhabitable. Scans confirm that ninety percent of the crew is dead."

"*Excellent*! I have *finally* defeated the great *Zan Liss* once and for all!"

"Sir, the strike fighters are descending on Coopers Falls."

"More good news," Lon smiled. "Navigator, take us closer to the attack zone and redirect the cruisers there as well."

"Yes, Sir."

Chad walked to the center of the tree grove and sat down to clear his head. Molly, Jim and Melissica watched silently from the periphery. After several minutes, Chad stood up just as Markus and Janus appeared through the woods in their hologram forms. Teri, Mayla and the rest of the hologram team monitored Chad apprehensively from inside the Command Cube.

"Chad, are you ready to try?" asked Janus.

"Yes," Chad said as he walked to the far side of the tree grove opening and got into position.

"OK Chad, now concentrate," coached Janus softly.

At that very instant, helicopters could be heard off in the distance. As the sound grew louder and louder Chad lowered his arms.

"Back into the woods, everyone," instructed Markus.

Two large CH53D Sea Stallion helicopters circled over the open field a few times before one of them passed slowly over the tree grove, coming to a stop directly over its opening. The noise was deafening and the large rotors caused the treetops to sway back and forth fiercely. The Sea Stallion hovered in place for what seemed like an eternity before slowly moving on.

"Do you think they saw us?"

"Possibly. They likely identified Melissica's vehicle."

"What should we do?" asked Jim.

"Help Chad focus and transform."

"Chad, are you ready to try again?" asked Molly.

"Yes." Chad walked back over to the far side of the opening and got in to position. As he watched from the perimeter, Markus's orb confirmed that the Military convoy was entering through the Davis Farm gate.

"Janus, the convoy is making its way through the entrance right now, with Major Talbot and other members of the Military right behind them."

"Damn it!" shouted Chad in frustration before lowering his arms.

"Markus and I will go look," Janus said before they sped off through the woods.

At the entrance to the Davis Farm, Army soldiers and Marines poured out of the military vehicles parked along both sides of the dirt road. Seconds later, Major Talbot and Lieutenant Miller arrived in an Army jeep followed by more Humvees and armored personnel carriers. After driving past the parked convoy, Major Talbot jumped out of the jeep and began barking orders.

"We're out of time. We must find the boy and apprehend him *unharmed*!"

Military personnel quickly fanned out into the fields followed by Major Talbot and Lieutenant Miller.

"What are we going to do?" asked Molly nervously.

"Chad, do you want to try to transform again?" asked Jim.

"I don't know," muttered Chad as he closed his eyes. "Maybe I should wait for Janus to return."

"But what if he doesn't return?" asked Melissica anxiously.

"He *will* be back."

"Maybe he's going to try to talk to them?"

"Talk to who?" asked Chad.

"You know, Major Talbot." replied Jim uncertainly.

Chad studied the looks on each of their faces. He then took a deep breath and started walking toward the fields.

"Wait for me here," he instructed.

"Where are you going?" asked Jim.

"To talk to Major Talbot myself," said Chad as he headed into the woods.

CHAPTER TWENTY-NINE — THE SURFACE WAR BEGINS

Chad exited the tree grove and stopped at the edge of the open field. The sun had all but completely burned off the thick morning mist. He paused briefly to look up at the bright blue sky before striding into the tall grass.

"Don't go out there," Jim warned.

"It's going to be all right Dad. I promise. Please go back and wait with Mom and Melissica."

"OK. But please be careful."

"I will," promised Chad as he continued deeper into the tall grass. Chad froze, and strained to listen to the rustling sounds in the distance.

"Janus? Markus?" he asked cautiously.

There was no answer.

"Janus, Markus?"

As the sounds got louder, Chad saw the tops of helmets approaching. Then their faces came into view, their expressions serious and determined.

This is it, he thought.

Chad was quickly surrounded by several troops cautiously pointing their M16A2 assault rifles directly at him.

"Don't move!" shouted one of the soldiers. "Put your hands above your head!"

Chad slowly raised his arms. Major Talbot appeared from the tall grass. He studied Chad for a short time before walking past the perimeter of armed soldiers.

"You can lower your arms Chad," instructed Major Talbot.

Chad silently complied without taking his eyes off Major Talbot.

"Listen carefully, Chad. It's over. You must surrender peacefully. We don't want to hurt you."

Chad did not respond.

"I want you to surrender your spherical craft and any other devices you have. Do you understand me?"

Chad nodded.

"I also want you to tell me who else is here with you."

"My mother and father are here along with my girl-friend."

"That is not what I mean Chad. Who else from your planet came with you?"

Chad again scanned the field for any signs of Janus and Markus.

"We know that your people have come for you."

Chad abruptly stopped scanning the fields and looked directly at Major Talbot.

"Chad, we only want to return you to your people so that all of you can go back home in peace."

"They are *not* my people. My father, Jim Johnson, tried to explain that to you but you wouldn't listen."

"Jim Johnson is not your father Chad."

"Yes, he *is*!"

"Whether you consider him to be your father is not important at this point. What *is* important is that an extraterrestrial invasion force has attacked our planet, bombing several major cities. Our country is next."

"Janus was right."

"Who is *Janus*? Did he come here with you? Is he also one of them?"

"I already told you that I am *not* one of them. They have *not* come here to rescue me. They are here to *capture* me. My father tried to tell you that but you wouldn't listen."

"Why should we believe *him* or *you* for that matter? You have lied to us before."

"I'm telling you the truth."

"The only *truth* I know is that our planet is under attack!" Major Talbot said angrily.

"Major Talbot. I'm sorry about this whole situation. But you have to believe me. I'm not one of them. I am trying to *defend* this planet!"

"What are you talking about? They have agreed to stop the attacks if we return you to them."

"They're *lying*!"

A few Marines standing behind Major Talbot turned and pointed toward the sky.

"Major, UFOs approaching," a soldier said.

Several soldiers turned and pointed their automatic rifles toward the two approaching spheres. Major Talbot turned and studied the small orbs.

"They're peaceful," said Chad. "They're also here to help protect our planet."

Major Talbot turned back toward Chad and studied his expression.

"STAND DOWN," Major Talbot ordered as the orbs approached. They hovered on either side of Chad. The soldiers stood dumbfounded as Janus and Markus's holograms appeared.

"Michael Talbot, I am Janus Stone. To Chad's left is Markus Kilmar."

Major Talbot nodded at Janus.

"The three of us are from what *was* planet Thrae, located six hundred light years from Earth along our galaxy's spiral arm. Your planet is in grave danger. You must allow Chad Stone to move about freely. He is your planet's only hope to avoid total destruction."

"Tell me more," Major Talbot said unconvinced.

"The Mitels have not come to rescue Chad. They want to capture him and then decimate your planet."

"Why do they want to capture him?"

"Because Chad is truly special. He is the last of our kind in flesh and blood, and he is also an immortal. Thrae's *last* immortal. More importantly, Chad is also the last of our kind with the rare ability to transform."

"What do you mean *transform*?"

"Chad was born with the ability to switch from flesh and blood to predominantly machine."

"He can change *into a machine*?" Major Talbot asked incredulously. "What kind of a machine?"

"The most incredible fighting machine in the universe," responded Markus. "On our planet, it was called a *Battle Sphere*. It was Chad that your satellites and telescopes recently photographed in outer space."

"You are telling me that Chad *is* the spherical craft. *Not* the pilot of that thing?"

"Yes," responded Janus.

"That . . . that's . . ."

"Incredible, but true."

"But why interrupt the world's wireless communications?"

"Chad was practicing placing a plasma defense shield around Earth to protect it in anticipation of the Mitel invasion."

"*Protect us*? Then why did he attack the Armory?"

"Chad did not go there to hurt anyone nor did he —"

"He attacked and destroyed three of our jet fighters! Several innocent civilians were killed on the ground!"

"That was an unfortunate accident," replied Janus. "The three jets you speak of inadvertently collided with Chad as they passed one another. I presume that your pilots confirmed that they were not fired upon."

"Yes, but —"

"The people of Earth are *not* our adversary. It is the Mitel Empire that is our shared enemy. They have come here under orders from their Leadership to seize the last Thraen immortal and his Battle Sphere technology."

Suddenly, Janus's hologram deformed for a second with a buzzing noise. Major Talbot, confused, studied Janus.

"It's a long story," said Chad.

Major Talbot looked towards the sky briefly before looking back at Janus.

"I want to believe this incredible story. If it's true, then we must tell the President and warn the rest of the world."

"That will make little difference," explained Janus. "Your planet's military is no match for The Mitel Fleet."

A shrieking noise came from off in the distance, unrecognizable to everyone except Janus and Markus. An instant later, 44 Mitel attack fighters raced overhead. The white 'V' shaped craft with angular markings and a silver underbelly were thirty-five feet long with thick, distinctive delta wings. Each fighter contained two vertical stabilizers in the rear positioned at sixty-degree angles from the wing surface and a rectangular shaped propulsion slot in the rear.

"What the hell *are they*?" yelled a Marine as the crafts streaked overhead. The ground shook from explosions in the distance, where the Mitel Fighters leveled buildings.

"My god, you're right!" said Major Talbot. "They have no intention of leaving here peacefully."

"Orders, Sir!" asked a stunned Marine.

"Notify Central Command that we are under attack!" instructed Major Talbot tersely. "We need air support and we need it *NOW*!"

From the White House underground bunker, the President and Joint Chiefs of Staff were meeting, joined by the Vice President, Secretary of State, Senior Staff and the Secretary of Homeland Security.

"We are at war on our own soil, "the President told his assembled team.

Within minutes, twenty F15 Eagles left Otis Air Force Base in Mashpee, Massachusetts for Coopers Falls at supersonic speed. A similar contingent of F15 Eagles headed southwest from the Pease Air National Guard Base in Portsmouth, New Hampshire. From the northwest, another ten Eagles quickly mobilized from the Massachusetts Air National Guard's 104th Fighter Wing in Westover, Massachusetts.

At Langley Field in Hampton, Virginia, the 1st Fighter Wing scrambled forty F22 Raptors and another thirty F15C Eagle jet fighters. Once airborne, they headed to Coopers Falls to provide additional support. The remaining bases around the Country were placed on high alert, prepared to enter the battle on a moment's notice.

Cruiser Number 2 detected the American fighter squadrons as they reached altitude on their way to Coopers Falls.

"Emperor Rexx, it appears Earth's air defense forces have mobilized one hundred and twenty aircraft from four territories," a specialist reported.

"Based on the data we have gathered on their defense technology, they will be nothing more than a nuisance," smiled Ian.

"Then let's show them what *our* fighters are capable of," smiled Lon. "Deploy two additional groups of strikers to engage and destroy them."

"Yes, my Emperor," nodded the communications specialist.

Amid all the commotion, Markus noticed Chad becoming increasingly nervous. He needed to get Chad somewhere safe and quiet so he could focus on his transformation. Markus then glanced toward the tree grove.

The tree opening, he thought. *My orb can emit a low energy magnetic shield that should produce enough of a negative refraction to deflect much of the incoming sound waves.*

"Come with me, my boy, back to the opening so that you can concentrate and begin your transformation."

"I don't know if I can do it Markus," admitted Chad anxiously.

"You can do it Chad!"

"How do you *know*?"

"I just know lad. Here, take my hand and hold on tight!"

As they rose into the air, Markus's orb calculated an exit trajectory.

"Here we go," said Markus.

A Marine noticed Markus levitating Chad toward the tree grove followed closely by his monitoring orb. He tapped the shoulder of the Marine standing next to him and pointed toward Markus.

"They are trying to escape!"

The first Marine prepared to fire with the second Marine quickly following suit. Markus's monitoring orb registered their activity.

"Stop *or we'll shoot!*" yelled the first Marine.

Major Talbot spun around to see Markus pull Chad tightly in front of him while instinctively initiating his focused energy throughout his hologram. Before Major Talbot could speak, the Marines opened fire. Markus sparkled brightly as the bullets entered his projection. He squeezed Chad's hand tightly, his hologram jerking forward violently. Sparks and arcs of energy discharged from Markus's nearby monitoring orb as they too were hit by multiple rounds.

"Hold your fire *God damn it!*" yelled Major Talbot lunging toward the soldiers.

Markus's hologram fell to the ground sparkling brightly, his orb rolling to a stop right next to him. Chad, who had tumbled to the ground, sprung back to his feet and stared down at Markus in stunned disbelief. Janus rushed through the tall grass to where Chad was standing. As he knelt down, Janus could see that Markus was trying to talk to him.

"I am sorry my friend," mouthed Markus just before his entire hologram glowed a brilliant white and disappeared.

"Markus. *NOOOOOOO!*" screamed Chad.

His eyes opened wide and turned metallic silver quickly spreading across his face and down his neck in a shard like mesh pattern. Chad's eyes turned bright white as he glared at the Marines who nervously stepped backwards a few paces. In his fury, Chad stepped forward to annihilate the soldiers with a plasma laser burst from his eyes.

"Chad *NO!*" commanded Janus, quickly positioning himself between Chad and the soldiers.

"Do *not* seek revenge against these men. They acted out of fear and confusion."

Chad did not respond.

"Chad. Listen to me. Focus your anger toward the Mitel Fleet. They are the ones who caused this. They are also the ones who initiated the destruction of Thrae."

Chad's expression changed from fierce anger to grim determination. Without another word, he stepped back several paces, raised his arms and moved his legs apart. His silver body slowly ascended several feet into the air just before the blue translucent plasma sphere surrounded him. Swirling clouds of small metallic particles appeared from every direction and began swirling around the sphere. The soldiers watched in amazement as Chad's hardened silver skin peeled away to form the outer spin surface of his Battle Sphere.

"Unbelievable," Major Talbot whispered.

Jim, Molly and Melissica, having exited the tree grove, hurried across the field to where Janus was standing. As they approached, the Battle Hologram rematerialized in the field behind the troops. This time however, it was much larger. Chad's pent up anger converted into additional plasma energy, causing the Hologram Matrix to grow and extend. Instead of the initial three cube height, the hologram matrix now stood five cubes high extending more than three hundred yards in length.

Sensing the structure behind them, Major Talbot and the Army soldiers and Marines turned to see the brilliant blue and yellow translucent glowing Battle Hologram.

"What is that?" exclaimed Major Talbot.

"*That*, Major Talbot, is Chad's battle operations center," replied Janus.

Inside the Battle Hologram, dozens of personnel were at work. Mayla appeared at the Hologram entrance and after locating Janus's tall frame and white hair in the crowd, made her way across the field, passing directly through one, two, and then a third incredulous Marine.

"Commander, the planet is under attack. Orders please."

Major Talbot and Lieutenant Miller stood and stared at Mayla in amazement while the troops glanced back and forth between the Battle Hologram and Chad's transformation.

"Michael Talbot," said Janus motioning toward Mayla. "This is Mayla Tallis. She is Chad's battle operations Commander. Mayla commands the Battle Hologram you see projected behind you. She runs Chad's battle operations, flight and weapons systems."

"You mean they assist Chad *up there*?"

"Yes."

"We presume they are trying to draw Chad's Battle Sphere out into the open," she announced.

"And they are succeeding," Janus said, as he turned back toward Chad's transformation. By now, his outer shell had completed its silver patchwork construction within the swirling particle cloud. The two short cylinders slowly extended to reveal the glass fragments which began to flash in a red, yellow and orange random pattern for several seconds before pulsating back and forth around the cylinder like a multicolored wave.

"Chad!" shouted Janus as he stepped toward the Battle Sphere. "Don't let your anger interfere with your mission. Is that understood?"

Having attained his final form, Chad looked down at the field in front of him.

"Understood."

Chad watched silently as four technicians raced out of the main entrance to retrieve the orb. They carefully placed it on a hovering tray and headed back to the entrance, only to be jerked backwards by the Battle Hologram's magnetic field, signaling that access had been denied. The technicians quickly tried a second time but the orb was again repelled by the magnetic charge. On their third try, they disappeared through the opening. Chad heard a series of loud explosions off in the distance. The time had finally arrived for him to confront the Mitel Fleet.

"Chad! It's time for me to affix my monitoring orb to your outer skin surface," shouted Janus.

"No. I must go *now*."

"But I'm going with you."

"No. I won't risk losing both of you. You knew the Mitels would eventually come here. You trained and prepared me for this. And now, you must trust me to do what I need to do."

Janus turned to look toward Mayla who nodded in approval.

"OK, I'll stay here. But remember your promise. You must listen to your Battle Hologram team and not —"

"Override their instructions and go into free flight. I *promise*."

A series of loud explosions shook the ground.

"Let's get this mission started!" boomed Denton.

"OK everyone, ready when you are," said Chad resolutely.

"Shields up and energy levels at one hundred percent," confirmed Denton.

"Propulsion system ready to go," said Cantor.

"Laser cannons armed and operational," added Sami.

With that, Teri engaged Chad's internal flywheel causing his Battle Sphere to slowly begin rotating. The tall grass whipped furiously in all directions as the Battle Sphere spun faster and faster until it was revolving at full speed. Mayla waved to Chad before rushing back to the Battle Hologram. Teri detected a second group of Mitel Fighters descending on the Davis Farm.

"Chad!" shouted Teri. "Mitel Fighters are —"

"I register them Teri."

"Launch sequence activated," confirmed Mayla.

"Commencing takeoff in three, two, and one, *launch*," announced Teri just before the Battle Sphere darted away at supersonic speed to intercept the approaching Mitel Fighters.

"Soldier!" barked Major Talbot.

"Yes Sir!" replied the communications specialist.

"I want you to relay an urgent message, and I want you to make it *absolutely* clear to all of our air and ground forces."

"Sir?"

"The silver sphere is *one of ours*! Repeat, the silver sphere is on *our side.* Do you understand me?"

"*Yes Sir!*" shouted the soldier as he rushed to relay the Major's message up the chain of command.

Accelerating up into the sky, Chad heard Mayla's familiar calming voice.

"Commander, we are here to get you through this."

"It's payback time," announced Luna as she ran through her target tracking system one last time.

"You got that right," added a second weapons specialist."

Chad checked his monitors as his laser cannons opened fire. Within seconds, the entire first wave of approaching fighters lit up brightly on impact and disintegrated.

"Take that, you bastards!" Luna said triumphantly.

Before anyone could respond, a second wave of Mitel Fighters quickly approached, followed by a third and then a fourth.

"There are so many," muttered Chad as he raced through the pulverized debris of the first wave of fighters.

"Two hundred and twenty targets approaching," said Teri.

As Chad's Battle Sphere closed in, his laser cannons discharged even faster than before. In half a minute, the entire second and third waves of the attacking fighters were completely obliterated. Chad became more confident as he streaked toward the fourth wave. Just before reaching firing distance, the Mitel Fighters veered off in all directions. Caught off guard, the Hologram weapons specialists scrambled to maintain their weapons locks. As the fighters streaked past, only a handful of them were destroyed.

What are they doing? Chad thought.

It then dawned on him.

They're bypassing me!

Chad's diagnostic monitors flashed, warning that a fifth wave was approaching. He instinctively shifted to free flight mode, reversed direction, and raced down after the fourth wave.

"That promise didn't last long!" boomed Denton.

"Mitel Fighters approaching!" Teri warned.

On the ground, Janus, Major Talbot and the rest of the group heard the now familiar shriek as the white and silver fighters streaked toward them in a random attack pattern.

"We're sitting ducks!" yelled Major Talbot. "*Prepare to fire!*"

The Army soldiers and Marines aimed their M16A2 assault rifles while Major Talbot reached to his side for his 9mm pistol.

"Get down behind me!" he ordered Jim, Molly and Melissica.

Janus moved next to Major Talbot and activated his focused energy across his entire hologram. He then instructed his monitoring orb to target the lead Mitel Fighter with a small but powerful laser in the hopes that it might disrupt their attack.

Realizing that he only had a few seconds left, Chad closed his eyes and focused his attention on the open field. A hemispherical-shaped blue translucent plasma shield appeared over both the Battle Hologram and everyone in the field just as the Mitel Fighters opened fire. The shield successfully blocked the Mitel's laser weapons and high energy explosives. Several fighters exploded on contact with the shield, while the remaining Mitel Fighters frantically veered off in all directions.

"It worked!" exclaimed Chad.

The weapons specialists opened fire on the remaining targets and the fleeing Mitel cruisers flashed bright white before disintegrating. Chad circled over the open field before streaking skyward to engage the fifth wave. On the ground, Army soldiers and Marines cheered loudly.

"Thank you, Commander," said Mayla.

"No problem Mayla. I should have spotted their bypass formation. I won't make that mistake again."

"*Please don't*" laughed Denton loudly.

Racing skyward, Chad checked his diagnostic monitors for signs of the next wave of Mitel Fighters. To his surprise, he saw nothing.

"The fifth wave has changed course," announced Mayla.

"To where?"

"They are headed toward the population center of Coopers Falls," replied Teri.

Chad turned and darted toward the center of town.

"I see them," declared Chad as Mitel Fighters approached from all directions.

"Do you guys see all the other fighters?" he asked.

"We're tracking them," replied Teri. "They are part of the initial wave that randomly attacked the region. Most likely, they are trying to get you to go toward the population cluster."

From his command console, Lon tracked the Mitel group's maneuvers. After the fourth wave of Mitel Fighters was confirmed destroyed, he addressed Ian across the ICC.

"This Battle Sphere appears to be well trained. Not what we were expecting."

"Indeed, Sir. And he seems to have intimate knowledge of our attack patterns."

"That's impossible!"

"His accuracy and skill remind me of what I have read about Zebulon Park."

"*Zebulon Park?* The Battle Sphere who defeated us in battle?"

"Yes. "

"It's well known that Zebulon Park died at the end of that invasion!"

"That was never confirmed."

"For Zebulon Park to still be alive now, that would most certainly mean he is *immortal*."

"There are more than a few historians who believe that."

"You want me to believe that Zebulon Park is immortal, is *here* on Earth *and* has personally trained the young Battle Sphere who, by the way, is also immortal?"

"The thought crossed my mind, yes," admitted Ian softly.

"*Ridiculous!*" boomed Lon rolling his eyes in frustration.

Downtown Coopers Falls, lined with brick and stone faced four and five story buildings from a bygone era, had been transformed into a vibrant restaurant and shopping hub for the region. Mingled in with the historically significant structures are four modern high rise buildings, constructed during a revival of sorts after a long period of stagnation.

Mitel Fighters formed rows of three as they approached the downtown area. The citizens of Coopers Falls grabbed their children and ran for cover, but it was too late. Each fighter released small high energy disks which detonated in rapid succession just above the city skyline. Like dominoes, the buildings exploded in rapid succession collapsing into piles of rubble. The entire downtown area was flattened in less than ten seconds. The explosion wave hurtled large chunks of debris and materials over a mile in every direction. The destruction was absolute. There were no survivors.

Approaching the city center from the north, Chad was unable to see through the smoke and debris. His Battle Hologram identified and locked onto their intended targets. Within seconds, Chad's weapons specialists opened fire in all directions.

"Another group approaching your location from multiple directions," confirmed Teri. "Prioritizing and locking onto targets."

The weapons specialists cycled back and forth between the two groups with devastating proficiency, striking and vaporizing most of the Mitel Fighters.

"That's how it's done, Mitels!" shouted Luna as she led the laser cannon weapons barrage with her usual pinpoint accuracy.

In all the chaos, some laser cannon bursts inadvertently struck large chunks of airborne rubble allowing a few lucky Mitel Fighters to evade the on-slaught. They retreated toward the outer atmosphere. Chasing after them, Chad's Battle Sphere tore a temporary opening through the billowing smoke cloud.

Cruiser Number 2's scanning specialists feverishly tracked the movements of the young Battle Sphere.

"My Emperor, the Thraen is giving chase to six of our returning fighters," said the scanning specialist.

"Excellent. Is the swarm ready to engage him?"

"Almost," confirmed Ian.

"What is taking so long?"

"We are coordinating one thousand strike fighters into a single attack unit as quickly as possible."

"I don't want excuses! We must lure the young Thraen into a surprise attack! We may not get a second chance."

"I want another 500 fighters ready to enter the swarm," Lon ordered.

"As you command."

Chad raced toward the upper atmosphere, checking for signs of the Mitel Fighters. The light patterns on his cylinders flashed a predominately red hue.

"Identifying targets" Teri confirmed.

"Wait," said Mayla. "Fifty United States planes are about to be intercepted in Coopers Falls by a group of Mitel Fighters. Another group is heading south to confront the seventy more jet planes headed their way."

"The jet fighters don't stand a chance."

With this latest update, Chad reversed direction and raced back down toward Earth.

"My Emperor," announced the lead scanning specialist. "The Thraen has unexpectedly changed direction. He is now heading back toward Earth."

"ARRRGH!" growled Lon.

"It appears he is turning around to engage our surface fighters," concluded Ian.

"We *almost* lured him into our trap!"

"At the expense of over three hundred fighters."

Lon stared defiantly at Ian.

"I trust we will be ready for him the next time, assuming there *is* a next time!"

"I will make sure of it."

Racing back to Earth, Chad saw the U.S. Jet fighters being systematically decimated by the much quicker and agile Mitel Fighters. One by one, the F15s burst into flames and crashed to the ground in huge fireballs. After downing the last of the US warplanes, the strike fighters turned and headed south in unison.

"Identifying targets," said Teri.

"Take that!" exclaimed Luna.

She cycled through her first sequence of five targets, then a second, and a third before the other hologram weapons specialists could begin firing. Luna destroyed all fifteen targets without a miss. The remaining Mitel Fighters were eliminated by the rest of the weapons specialists shortly thereafter.

Janus stood in the Command Cube entrance to monitor the communications chatter and data results.

Luna's proficiency is simply incredible, he thought.

Janus then headed down the stairs to the Diagnostics Cube. Stopping at the doorway, he watched the seasoned team methodically inspect the damage to Markus's orb. By now, the majority of the orb's outer skin had been removed and several fiber optic probes connected to its inner components.

"Please Markus," said Janus softly. "Please be in there somewhere."

The lead technician put down his equipment when he spotted Janus observing his work from the doorway.

"Commander. The monitoring orb is simply too badly damaged. We don't have the necessary equipment and materials to repair it."

Janus did not respond.

"We've not been able to register any type of signal. It appears the hologram is gone."

"Is there anything you can do?"

"I'm afraid not. I am truly sorry."

Janus headed back toward the Command Cube, closing his eyes momentarily. The person he had known longer than anyone else in his life was gone.

"Goodbye my friend."

Chad circled the downtown area surveying the damage. The entire area was destroyed, not a building left standing. Further out on the horizon, dozens of fires raged and smoke billowed up like silent markers of where the F15 fighters had crashed. It was a surreal scene.

"The second group of Mitel Fighters is preparing to intercept another contingent of US Jet fighters," Teri informed Chad.

"Where are the Mitel Fighters now?"

"Due West of New York City."

"And the jet fighters, what is their position?"

"Southern New Jersey headed due north."

"You must get me there NOW!"

"Establishing coordinates," confirmed Canton.

"Commencing all out speed in three, two, and one," announced Teri.

Chad's Battle Sphere roared south to chase down the Mitel Fighters, its speed quickly increasing to 700, then 3500, then 8000 miles per hour.

Squadron Commander Coronel Kevin Haller piloted his F22 Raptor accompanied by sixty-nine other fighter jets. He had just received word that all fifty F15s had been downed by alien craft, with no survivors. He studied the small photo of his wife and two children as a transmission from the Langley Air Force Base Control Tower came over the Airborne High Frequency Communication System.

"Accura, this is Langley Control, do you copy?"

"Roger Control."

"We have confirmed forty-four UFO craft heading your way due south."

Coronel Haller had already started tracking them over the F22's AN/APG-77 active electronically scanned array (AESA) radar.

"Roger that. We have initiated radar contact," he confirmed. "Are these the same ones that took out the squadrons in upstate New York?"

"Negative, Accura. These are *new* boogies."

"What about the UFOs over upstate New York?"

"They abruptly disappeared from radar."

"They what? *Disappeared*?"

"Affirmative."

"Please clarify."

"Multiple eyewitness reports say they were taken out by another UFO, possibly the silver sphere said to be friendly. Do you copy?"

"Roger Control. Where is the silver sphere now?"

"Unknown."

"We could sure use its help here."

"Roger that."

Just then, Coronel Haller's radar identified the approaching UFOs.

"This is Squadron leader. Forty-four UFOs confirmed approaching. Prepare to engage," he announced to the F22 Raptor pilots flying alongside him. "Good luck gentlemen and give it your all."

The Mitel Fighters were approaching.

"Control, I have a visual."

Out of the corner of his eye, Coronel Haller saw a bright flash. Seconds later, the silver sphere bore down on the UFOs. In response, a few of the Mitel Fighters broke formation and streaked skyward.

"*Damn* that thing is fast."

The Battle Sphere opened fire and within seconds, all but two were hit and destroyed. As the last two craft headed skyward, Chad switched to free flight and darted after them.

"Langley Control, this is Accura."

"Roger Accura."

"Visual from our present location confirms the silver sphere took out the enemy fighters."

"Please repeat Accura?"

"The silver sphere. It eliminated the boogies. It happened so fast, as if they were never there."

"Are you *sure*?"

"Yes. If I hadn't seen it with my own eyes, I wouldn't have believed it! That thing flies faster than anything I have ever seen! I am sure as hell glad it's on our side!"

"Roger that."

Chad's Battle Sphere bore down on the two fleeing Mitel Fighters just as they reached the upper atmosphere.

"Targets locked," confirmed Teri.

Before Chad could respond, Luna fired two quick laser bursts. Chad watched the two retreating fighters light up then quickly disintegrate.

"Got them!" shouted Luna.

Chad's Battle Sphere sped through the speckles of debris and through thermosphere and the final layer of Earth's atmosphere before decelerating rapidly. Cruiser Number 2's lead scanning specialist excitedly confirmed that the Battle Sphere was approaching.

"Emperor Rexx. The Thraen is within striking distance!"

"Excellent! Quickly, order the swarm! *Do it now!*"

"Yes, my Emperor."

Mayla paused as she double checked the data display.

"There are 1,522 targets in your immediate vicinity. It appears the Mitel Fleet is —"

"About to initiate a swarm strike," interjected Janus.

Suddenly, one thousand Mitel Fighters raced toward Chad from several directions.

"Chad!" shouted Teri. "Get out of there!"

Before Chad could react, the fighters descended upon him.

"Here they come!" shouted Teri as he furiously typed commands. "One thousand targets locked."

"We can do this!" declared Luna as she cycled through her laser cannons along with the other weapons specialists.

To the swirling Mitel Fighters, the Battle Sphere looked like a gleaming star emitting bright rays of pulsating light in all directions. Dozens upon dozens of Mitel

Fighters were obliterated as Chad dodged and weaved. He also used the flip maneuver each time a fighter moved in right behind him.

The extreme battle conditions were draining Chad's power levels rapidly. Several red flashing signals confirmed that the Mitel Fighter barrage was piercing his weakening defense shields. The signals eventually indicated that the laser cannons were being destroyed.

In the Battle Hologram itself, individual weapons cubes went dark as specialists and their supporting equipment, were being destroyed. The Mitel battle plan was becoming clear: systematically beat Chad's Battle Sphere into submission.

"Energy reserves down to 23 percent!" shouted Denton.

"Commander, you must withdraw and recharge *now*!" instructed Mayla anxiously.

Chad spotted a small pathway in the swarm and darted through it at full speed.

Having escaped the swarm, Chad raced back through the upper atmosphere toward Earth. The Mitel Fighters pursued him, but their chase speed was no match for Chad's explosive acceleration. They were left far behind as Chad neared Earth's surface.

"Mayla, are you able to disarm the Fort's invisibility shield?" asked Chad wearily.

"I don't think so," she replied.

"I can do it remotely from here," Janus said as he sat down at Mayla's computer.

Chad descended upon the Fort as Janus feverishly typed commands.

"Let me know when you reach the pond."

"I'm there now," Chad said in a tired voice.

Janus entered the final code and the Fort suddenly appeared. Chad darted across the pond coming to a stop next to the largest structure.

"I'm in."

Janus reentered the code and the Fort and Chad disappeared inside the shield.

CHAPTER THIRTY — THE CONFLICT WIDENS

With the auxiliary power now back on line, Rad Aarden and the rest of his medical staff weaved their way past the dead crew members to the HorVert elevator. He had recognized the warning signs for the opioid gas and immediately instructed his team to put on their oxygen units. Once their hand-held scanners confirmed that the cruiser's environment had returned to safe breathing levels, they removed their masks.

"I hate these things," Rad mused as he clipped his oxygen mask to his belt. The HorVert elevator then beeped indicating that they had reached the ICC. As the doors slid open, the team stepped out to find everyone unconscious on the floor. Starting with Zan, the team spread out to revive the crew.

"Ard? Lia?" Zan muttered.

"Here, I think," groaned Ard from off in the corner.

"I'm OK," replied Lia. "Mat? Are you OK?" Dax?"

Neither Dax nor Mat responded. Lia struggled to her feet and rushed around the consoles to find the two sitting on the floor surrounded by medical personnel.

"They are pretty shaken," confirmed a staff member. "But OK otherwise."

With Rad's help, Zan staggered to his feet.

"Thank you," nodded Zan.

"I assume that your failure to warn us of the opioid gas release was an oversight."

"Yes. Sorry about that."

Zan unsteadily made his way over to the intercom.

"Dru? Are you ok?"

There was no answer.

"*Dru,* answer me!"

"Dru here. We're OK. Next time we're attacked, could you give us a head's up?"

"You knew when we did. How do things look back there?"

"The engines are down again. We are evaluating them now. Don't expect much from them going forward."

Ard gingerly made his way over to the scanning computer. He entered a report request and then scrolled through the results.

"Good news and bad news," he said eventually.

"What's the bad news?" asked Zan.

"Lon blew off the front of our cruiser. Luckily for us the airlocks closed before the power went down. The majority of our slip ring systems and equipment are also gone. "

"What about our weapons tubes?"

"Right side is gone, but the left side appears to be active."

"At least we can still defend ourselves."

"*That,* by the way, is the good news."

"What do you plan to do next Emperor Liss?" Rad asked.

"Haven't you *heard*? I am no longer Emperor. I am no longer *anything* other than an alleged traitor. Is that a problem for you?"

"As a medical staff, we try to avoid political and military entanglements."

"Good to know.

"Who is in charge then?"

"Lon Rexx."

"*Rexx!*" snorted Rad.

"Do you know him?"

"Yes. He is an egomaniac. A power hungry, butchering psychopath."

"That's our guy!" chirped Ard.

"What do you plan to do about *him*?" asked Rad.

"We have been trying to prevent him from committing total genocide on this planet. Unfortunately, he has already started."

"How can we help?"

"For starters, keep monitoring the air quality and check the rest of the ship for any survivors. Our Mitel resistance team can help you."

"*Our what*?

"The Mitel resistance."

"The same faction who keep blowing up our spacecraft?"

"Yes," replied Zan, motioning toward Lia, Mat and Dax.

"Don't your people believe in peaceful resolution?"

"Sometimes that isn't possible," replied Lia.

"Rad Aarden," said Zan. "This is Lia Saar, communications specialist who also happens to be responsible for saving my life."

"I am honored," nodded Lia. "You and your team are very dedicated. For the record, the Mitel Leadership will *never* give up power peacefully. Their families have been ruthlessly ruling Mitel for generations and have murdered millions of our people. Since they will not step aside, we have no alternative but to bring the fight to them."

"I see," responded Rad. "Are you with them Zan?"

"The Mitel resistance? That's a good question."

"When you decide, please let us know. In the meantime, let's get started."

Once his flywheel disengaged from its outer spin surface, Chad's Battle Sphere slowly came to a stop. As the recharging process continued, he took in the scene around him, noticing off in the distance, several dark columns of smoke rising silently into the sky.

"Plasma reserve levels increasing to 24 percent," confirmed Teri.

Chad listened to the chatter of the hologram technicians as they relayed their damage assessments to the Command Cube for further evaluation.

"Chad?" asked Teri. "Are you hanging in there?"

"I think so. How are the weapons specialists doing?"

"You are down twenty-seven cannons. That's roughly fourteen percent."

"How is Luna?"

"Luna is *fine*," reassured Teri. "We are rerouting three laser cannons over to her."

"Any word on Markus?"

"He's gone Chad. I'm truly sorry."

On Cruiser Number 2's ICC, the scanning specialist expanded the scope of his scanning perimeter, but the results were the same.

"Emperor Rexx, the Battle Sphere has disappeared."

"He *must* have hidden behind an invisibility shield to recharge!" growled Lon. "We have squandered an excellent opportunity!"

"What do you suggest we do?" asked Ian from behind.

"We must draw him back into battle before he can fully recharge," explained Lon as he spun around in his console.

"But how?"

"Order our Fighter groups to begin a staggered attack on three population centers in close proximity to the Thraen's last known location. I want them to attack the first two in rapid succession. The young Battle Sphere will feel compelled to help, coming out of hiding before he is adequately recharged. I want four other groups to attack the largest of the three immediately thereafter. His reserves will deplete rapidly. If we can draw him back into outer space, we will have him."

Ian nodded in agreement.

"Relay an urgent message to all remaining cruisers," Lon continued. I want a battle perimeter set up around our current location. Every vessel is to be *absolutely* certain that their gravity control beams are fully operational, and activated."

"As you command," replied Ian before turning and making his way toward the communications console.

Hovering silently, Chad struggled with intense guilt over the enormous loss of life inflicted by the Mitels. He tried to distract himself by monitoring his power level which was now at 60 percent. Off in the distance, Chad heard the faint sounds of fire engine sirens.

"We have a problem," announced Teri.

"What is it?" Mayla asked from across the Command Cube.

"Six more Mitel Fighter groups are descending rapidly."

"Where are they headed?"

"The northeast United States."

"I can't just *sit* here!" complained Chad anxiously.

"You must complete your recharging process," replied Mayla.

"How is that going to save innocent people from being killed? I need to get back up there!" pleaded Chad. "I will withdraw as soon as we take care of them, OK?"

"Power levels at 65 percent," confirmed Teri.

"Janus, *please.*

"Alright Chad. Stay cognizant of your energy reserve levels, and when the Command Cube tells you to withdraw, you do it. *Do you hear me*?"

"I *promise.*"

"Propulsion system checks completed," announced Denton.

"Launch sequence activated," confirmed Mayla.

"Commencing takeoff in three, two, and one, *launch*," instructed Teri.

Chad's spinning Battle Sphere darted through the outwardly porous shield before turning and racing south toward the descending Mitel Fighters.

Several hours earlier, three Nimitz class nuclear powered aircraft carriers, the USS Abraham Lincoln, USS Theodore Roosevelt and USS Harry S. Truman, headed north from their home port of Norfolk, Virginia. On their way, a fourth carrier, the USS Dwight D. Eisenhower, joined the group from its home port of Portsmouth,

Virginia. All four vessels were overloaded with 20 F/A-18E Super Hornets and 48 F/A-18C Hornets.

Once confirmation was received that Mitel Fighters were approaching, the F18 hornets took off from the carrier flight decks. Simultaneously, the 4th Fighter Wing stationed at Seymour Johnson Air Force Base in Goldsboro, North Carolina, scrambled 92 F15E strike Eagles from the 333rd, 334th, 335th and 336th Fighter Squadrons.

While Chad headed south, the first wave of Mitel Fighters swooped down in rows of five on Albany and released their high energy disks which detonated in rapid succession just above the city skyline. Albany's tallest building, the 44-story Erastus Corning Tower, shuddered under the barrage before imploding and toppling to the ground in a gigantic cloud of smoke and dust. The second-tallest building, the Alfred E. Smith State Office Building collapsed next, followed by the four Empire State Plaza Convention Center towers. Massive black and gray plumes of smoke and debris rose to the sky from the piles of rubble and twisted steel.

"I'm too late!" shouted Chad, closing in from the North.

"Identifying targets," said Teri.

Chad's abrupt approach forced the Mitel Fighters to scatter. Flying close to the surface, his Battle Sphere vanished into the massive cloud of smoke shooting laser cannon bursts in all directions trailed by smoke spirals.

All forty-four Mitel Fighters were destroyed. Luna herself destroyed eighteen fighters. Little consolation, knowing that upwards of fifty thousand men, women and children had just been killed.

"Targets eliminated," confirmed Denton. "Cease fire."

"Albany is gone!" shouted Chad.

"Scanners indicate a second group of Mitel Fighters are approaching the planet's surface to your west," announced Teri.

"Where are they headed?"

"I am trying to figure that out. It looks like the population center called Philadelphia."

"We are redirecting you now," confirmed Mayla.

After the Albany attack, 75 F16C/D Fighting Falcons from the 20th Fighter Wing and 77th, 78th & 79th Fighter squadron located at Shaw Air Force Base in South Carolina and another 25 F16s from the 113 Wing Air National Guard at Andrews Field Washington, DC raced down the runway and took off northward.

At Langley Field in Hampton, Virginia the forty F22 Raptors and thirty F15C Eagles which had all returned unharmed from their previous flight, headed north. At the request of their NORAD (North American Aerospace Defense Command) partners, 40 single-seat CF-18As and 14 two-seat CF-18Bs of the Royal Canadian Air Force stationed in Quebec joined the others.

In all, 516 American and Canadian jet fighters, the largest airborne collection of ultra-modern fighter aircraft the world had ever seen, raced toward the northeastern corridor of the United States at supersonic speed.

From his console station aboard Cruiser Number 2, the lead scanning specialist registered the jet fighter activity. He then double checked his data to confirm numbers and trajectory.

"Emperor Rexx, a much larger contingent of surface aircraft is headed in the direction of our strike fighters."

"How many have you detected?"

"Approximately five hundred craft."

"No need for concern. In fact, these aircraft will likely help us achieve our ultimate objective."

The Mitel Fighters swooped down on Philadelphia in rows of six and seven across. People frantically ran from the shrieking noise. The fighters once again released their lethal high energy disks which detonated just above the city skyline. The sixty-story Comcast Center and twin Liberty Place towers shook violently before disintegrating. The glass exteriors of the BNY Mellon Center, Three Logan Square, G. Fred DiBona Jr. Building and 1414 South Penn Square sent shards of glass raining down on to the streets below before collapsing. The downtown and surrounding area had been reduced to piles of rubble and twisted steel. Fires raged out of control in every direction.

Before Chad's Battle Sphere reached the Philadelphia area, Teri noticed additional activity in the vicinity.

"Does anybody see what I'm seeing?" he asked.

"Yes," nodded Mayla. "Four Mitel Fighter squads are descending on New York City."

"I'm always one step behind!" shouted Chad in frustration.

"Stay calm and focus Chad," instructed Mayla.

Janus jumped from his chair and raced outside to find Major Talbot, who was standing with a large group of soldiers closely huddled around a Single Channel Ground and Airborne Radio System (SINCGARS) combat radio.

"It sounds like all hell is breaking loose," said Major Talbot.

"The Mitels are systematically attacking your population centers trying to deplete Chad's energy reserves," explained Janus.

"What can we do to stop them?"

"Redirect your air fighters immediately. Send them all to New York City."

"OK, but why?"

"To hold off the Mitels until Chad arrives. If you can do that, we should be able to save the City."

"Will do," said Major Talbot.

Less than a minute later, squadron commander Coronel Kevin Haller received a transmission from the Langley Air Force Base Control Tower over the Airborne High Frequency Communication System.

"Accura, this is Langley Control, do you copy?"

"Roger Control," Haller replied.

"You are instructed to change course immediately."

"To where?"

"New York City."

"What about Philadelphia?"

"Reports on the ground confirm the city has been destroyed."

"My god . . ."

"Intel indicates that approximately one hundred seventy additional UFOs are headed to New York City. All airborne U.S. and allied fighters are being redirected there to intercept, do you copy?"

"Roger Control. We are just about there," confirmed Coronel Haller. "Any word on the silver sphere?"

"It's headed to New York to back you up."

"Roger Control."

"Get Chad to New York City. *Now!*" Janus ordered.

Mayla entered Chad's new coordinates while Teri programmed the Battle Sphere's approach speed at Mach 10.

"Chad, you will arrive in New York City in approximately one minute," confirmed Mayla.

On the ICC of the heavily damaged Cruiser Number 1, Ard turned towards Zan.

"What now?" he asked.

"We need to figure out what Lon is up to," replied Zan.

"That is going to be tough, since he went dark and locked us out of the fleet communications system."

"No, it's not," said Dax.

"What do you mean?" asked Ard.

"Lia. She is the best systems hacker the resistance has ever seen."

"*Oh really?*"

"Lia is this true?" Zan asked.

"I wouldn't go that far, but I was able to hack into the communications system and download all of the fleet logs," she smiled.

"Nice work. While Dru checks the propulsion units, I'm going to scan the logs to see if I can figure out what Lon is up to."

"Good idea," replied Ard as he sat down at an adjacent computer. "Go to log set A.24.5. Look at the notation. A strike fighter pilot reported seeing a translucent blue protective shield over the Battle Hologram."

Zan read the entry and paused momentarily.

"I remember coming across similar information during our approach to the planet. Earth transmissions reported brief disturbances around their satellite and then the planet itself."

"How do you know they were protective shields?"

"I don't, but they were also translucent blue and coincided with sightings of the Battle Sphere."

"Do you think the Battle Sphere is projecting the shield?"

"Yes."

"In all my research on Thraen culture, I have never come across that ability before. Now look at entry C.42.2"

"From the President of the United States requesting that we stand down? I am sure Lon had a good laugh over that one."

"No, not that part."

"You mean the part about the hologram and orb sightings?"

"*Yes!*"

"So?"

"Don't you find that strange?"

"The Battle Hologram *only* has holograms Ard."

"I know *that!*"

"Then I don't see how —"

"Battle Sphere support holograms never travel far from the Matrix."

"And you know that because?"

"I just know. Something strange is going on here."

Zan rolled his eyes as they continued to scan the logs.

"Hey!" Ard shouted. "Go to D.13.7."

"OK," Zan replied eventually. "*Swarm pilots observed the Battle Sphere executing an instantaneous roll maneuver.* I don't see what —"

"Don't you see? He went from the pursued to the pursuer in the blink of an eye!"

"I *understand* Ard. Other than it being an insanely cool maneuver, what does it have to do with anything?"

"I have read about that maneuver being used by a Battle Sphere only once before!"

"*Seriously*? Who?"

"Zebulon Park."

"You're kidding, right?"

"No, I'm not! I *knew* it!"

"Knew *what*?"

"*He's here*! Park is here."

"You think he came over on the USEP?"

"*Yes*! For whatever reason, he converted his body into a hologram projected by one of the small monitoring orbs we detected during the invasion. That is how the boy survived the trip. And there is no way he could have learned that maneuver all on his own!"

"That means he is also an immortal."

"Many Thraen historians said he was."

Zan sat back to consider what Ard was telling him.

"If what you say is true, then the boy knows we attacked his planet."

"Yes. "

"And Park must believe that Thrae was destroyed."

"Probably. "

"That means they both have incentive to defeat the Mitel Fleet."

Ard paused.

"Actually, it's probably much worse than that."

"Why?"

"Zebulon Park believed more than anything else that a Battle Sphere's duty was to protect and defend his planet and people at *all* costs."

"Do you think —"

"That Earth is now his *home* planet? Yes, yes I do."

As Chad's Battle Sphere was heading to New York, U.S., Canadian and Mitel Fighters swarmed over the city, with more jet aircraft approaching from the north and southeast. Denton decreased Chad's approach speed as Teri locked onto the Mitel Fighters.

"Identifying targets," Teri said hesitantly, eyebrows furrowed.

"What's wrong?" asked Janus.

"There are so many U.S. aircraft among the Mitel Fighters, it's almost impossible to tell the difference."

"What should we do?" asked Chad impatiently.

"Set up an engagement zone and shoot down all Mitel craft that exit the zone," Mayla ordered.

"Engagement grid defined," confirmed Sami.

"Tracking computer synching 3-D matrix," said Teri.

Chad approached Manhattan from New Jersey. Slowing to a stop over the Hudson River, his laser cannons fired intermittently, destroying a handful of Mitel Fighters.

The battle now raged over Manhattan. The Mitel Fighters dominated, sending U.S. and Canadian jets plummeting into the Hudson and East Rivers, while others spiraled and crashed into the buildings below.

"I've *got* to get in there and help!"

Mayla and Teri looked across the Command Cube at Janus, who nodded his approval.

"OK, Chad, we are ready on this end," replied Teri.

"All set here," added Luna.

Chad switched to free flight and lurched forward into engagement zone toward Central Park, surrounded by Jets and Mitel Fighters. F22 squadron Commander Coronel Haller noticed the distinctive reflective flash of

Chad's Battle Sphere as he maneuvered between the dueling aircraft.

"Looks like backup has arrived!" Coronel Haller informed the fighters. "Remember everyone — he is on *our* side!"

Suddenly, a burning F18 Hornet plunged in front of Chad. As he braced for impact, Luna destroyed the plane. Chad flew through the plane's remnants before circling back around toward lower Manhattan.

"Planes and Fighters are falling everywhere!" shouted Chad.

A burning Mitel Fighter tumbled and exploded next to him, releasing its high-energy plasma ordnance in all directions. Arcs of white plasma energy raced around Chad's outer spin surface before disappearing.

"What was that?" exclaimed Denton.

"My laser cannons aren't firing!" shouted Luna.

"Mine either!" barked a second weapons specialist.

"Same here," added a third.

"Cycling through weapons system reset," announced Sami.

"Still nothing!" confirmed Luna impatiently.

"Trying again," said Sami as Teri raced over to her station.

"Chad, the energy discharge from the Mitel Fighter has caused your laser cannons to malfunction," explained Teri.

"For how long?" Chad asked.

"Assessing that now."

Chad's mini-screens flashed brightly indicating that several Mitel Fighters were approaching.

"Withdraw from the conflict immediately, Commander. We need time to correct the damage to your weapons system," ordered Mayla.

"I can't leave the fighter jets alone against the Mitels," argued Chad. "They will all be destroyed along with the City!"

"You are defenseless. You must withdraw *now*!"

"I have an idea." Chad accelerated down to street level and then over the Hudson River, with eight Mitel Fighters in hot pursuit.

"Commander, what are you doing?"

"I'm trying to draw some Mitel Fighters away from the fight until you guys figure things out."

Chad headed north toward the George Washington Bridge, the water immediately below him a blur. Six additional Mitel Fighters heading toward him from the opposite side of the bridge. His sensors blinked that all fourteen fighters were set to converge at the bridge.

Waiting until the last possible second, Chad darted skyward. Trying to give chase, five strike fighters veered into the massive cabling system along the center span, exploding on impact. Two additional fighters clipped each other's wings under the bridge before cart wheeling into the water. Now disoriented, the remaining seven fighters plowed into the superstructure, causing their ordnance to detonate. The entire center section of the bridge fell into the Hudson River, sending a surge of water into the air which engulfed six more fighters swooping down to provide backup. Chad adjusted his orientation 180 degrees just long enough to watch the bridge plummet into the river before circling over the Bronx, across the Harlem River back into the engagement zone toward Central Park.

On the ICC on Cruiser Number 2, the communications specialist received several transmissions that the

Battle Sphere had abruptly disengaged and retreated close to the surface.

"Emperor Rexx, pilots are reporting that the Battle Sphere may be damaged. It is not engaging our fighters."

"*Very interesting*. Instruct our fighters to pursue him vigorously. This may be the break we have been waiting for."

"Yes Sir."

Lon then spun his console toward Ian.

"Is the second swarm in place and ready to go?"

"Yes," nodded Ian.

"Excellent!"

Dru and his team did the best they could to bring the propulsion units back on line but without more advanced tools and replacement modules, their options were limited. In the end, they stripped several modules from the more damaged unit two and installed them on unit three to bring it back to 90 percent capacity. With only one working propulsion unit, the cruiser's overall capacity was down to 45 percent. It was not ideal, but as Dru would say: *it was better than nothing*.

On the ICC, Zan and Ard scanned for the Mitel Fleet.

"The Fleet is concentrated above the northern portion of Earth's Western Hemisphere," concluded Zan.

"Strike Fighters are actively engaging airborne forces above a major population center. They appear to be preparing for a second swarm."

The intercom light flashed.

"Liss here," said Zan.

"It's me," replied Dru.

"By the sound of your voice I can tell you have bad news."

"It's not all bad actually. We got unit number three back up to 90 percent.

"*Outstanding*! And unit —"

"Gone."

"Well, good work keeping unit three."

"Thanks. But if number three goes, that's it."

"Understood."

"Oh, one more thing. The high-speed shield generators are gone."

"*Gone* gone?"

"Yes."

"Got it."

With that Dru's intercom beeped again.

Lia, Mat and Dax stepped out of the HorVert elevator and headed to their stations.

"Excellent timing," said Zan. "How did it go?"

"No survivors."

"Sorry to interrupt," said Ard," but I'm hearing chatter from the surface that something is wrong with the Battle Sphere. Pilots report that it is no longer firing and appears to be in a defensive mode. What are we going to do?"

"Go after Lon Rexx and the rest of the fleet," replied Zan. "Navigator, full power."

Chad raced over Central Park as six Mitel Fighters descended upon him. They opened fire, the barrage causing huge columns of water to rise along either side of his Battle Sphere as it passed over the Reservoir. Chad swerved and continued South over the park as dozens of trees exploded into balls of fire. Reaching the edge of the park, Chad darted down Madison Avenue just inches above the pavement. The six Mitel Fighters split into groups — four followed Chad in single file while the other two streaked down Third Avenue just a few streets over. People in the buildings stared out their windows as the fighters roared by.

Coronel Haller saw the silver flash of Chad's Battle Sphere below and instinctively dove toward the fighters. Just ahead was a wall of thick black smoke where an F16 Eagle had crashed.

Madison Avenue starts at East 23rd Street thought Chad just before his Battle Sphere disappeared into the smoke plume. Exiting the other side, Chad darted left ninety degrees down East 23rd Street just as Madison Avenue ended. Exiting the smoke, the Mitel Fighters banked sharply to their right before crashing into the high-rise condo buildings. Chad continued three blocks along East 23rd Street before turning right onto Third Avenue just ahead of the two other fighters.

Approaching Third Avenue, Coronel Haller activated the afterburners at the back end of his two Pratt & Whitney F119 turbofan engines. The short burst of speed enabled him to close in on the two Mitel Fighters.

This is going to be tight he thought.

He lowered his 44-foot wingspan into the sixty-foot wide steel and glass ravine, settling in behind the second Mitel Fighter. He opened fire with his M61A2 Vulcan 20 mm cannon, setting the craft on fire as it crashed onto the street below. Coronel Haller pulled up slightly before settling in behind the second Mitel Fighter as they reached the Bowery. He opened fire until the strike fighter burst into flames and plowed into a series of buildings. Major Haller banked and raced skyward.

Chad glanced briefly at the streaking Raptor before making a right onto Canal Street then Seventh Avenue.

"Any luck with those cannons?" he asked anxiously.

"We're working on it, but nothing yet," replied Teri.

"*Hurry!*" snapped Chad.

His attention shifted to two more Mitel Fighters coming after him.

"I feel useless!" shouted Luna, pounding her fist.

As the first fighter closed in, Chad performed the flip maneuver. Stunned and confused, the pilot clipped the corner of the nearby building with his wing, somersaulting diagonally across the street and crashing in a ball of flames. Up ahead, Chad saw smoke clouds rising from several downed jets and Mitel Fighters. His mini-screens indicated that another Mitel Fighter was approaching in the opposite direction along Seventh Avenue.

If I hurry, I can make it to 34th street Chad decided. He accelerated across West 14th Street shadowed by the Mitel Fighter. Chad blew through two more walls of smoke as he crossed West 23rd Street. Up ahead, Chad saw a dense black wall of smoke. He raced passed Madison Square Garden on his left bursting through the wall of smoke. Just ahead, the Mitel Fighter was bearing down on him. Before the pilot could open fire, Chad turned right onto West 34th Street heading east. Chad heard a loud explosion as his monitors confirmed that the two strike fighters had collided head on.

He slowed down considerably as his Battle Sphere approached the Empire State Building coming to a stop at Macy's, where he hovered in place.

"How are those cannons coming Teri?"

"We are working on it."

"You said that already."

"*I know.*"

"Why aren't they responding?"

"The electrical impulses that activate your cannons were shorted out. The diagnostics teams say it needs to clear itself out."

"When will that happen?"

"They don't know. Hopefully soon."

"I'll just keep moving then."

Chad sped forward turning right onto Broadway back toward lower Manhattan. Three more Mitel Fighters had descended onto Broadway just behind him. Approaching 23rd Street, Chad saw the twisted wreckage of the four Mitel Fighters that had chased him along Madison Avenue minutes earlier. The billowing black smoke from the burning debris filled the street.

Chad shifted to the right as he approached the wall of smoke. Just beyond the intersection was the Flatiron building which Chad avoided crashing into by a matter of inches. One by one, the three pursuing fighters sheared off their right wings against the building before crashing on to the street below. Seconds later, he was surrounded by weapons fire pelting the street and buildings.

"Ten Mitel Fighters descending from two thousand feet," confirmed Teri. "Chad, you need to get out of there!"

Chad raced in a zigzag pattern across Union Square before swerving right on Broadway.

"Find cover. Use the tall buildings," urged Teri as Chad accelerated.

Teri locked onto the incoming targets in the hopes that Chad's cannons would come back on line while Luna and the other weapons specialists continued to rotate through their selected targets.

"Some good news, the Mitels have lost over one hundred-fifty fighters."

"How many have we lost?" Chad asked.

"Around three hundred jet fighters. The population center is taking quite a beating, but it would be completely gone otherwise."

"Understood, but —"

"Commander, you must *focus!*" scolded Mayla.

Chad sped past City Hall Park in lower Manhattan before circling around One World Trade Center. He darted upwards along the southern face of the building while five Mitel Fighters streaked past him on either side of the skyscraper before circling back around. Chad quickly made his way around to the north side of the building to avoid them. As he hovered in place close to the steel and glass exterior, he watched five Mitel Fighters speed past on his left before once again circling around back toward him. Chad quickly darted back around to the southern face to see the five other fighters heading directly toward him.

"*Crap!*" shouted Chad.

"Locking targets," Teri announced as the weapons specialists tracked the Mitel Fighters. As Chad frantically decided what to do, his laser cannons fired.

"We are back up and running!" hollered Luna as one by one, the incoming Mitel Fighters broke apart, debris crashing into the World Trade Center. As soon as the five other fighters appeared, they were quickly eliminated. Everyone in the Command Cube cheered while Chad raced skyward to engage the remaining Mitel Fighters.

"Got a bunch of them," Luna announced, as she cycled through her weapons tracking.

At that instant, a stray F22 AIM-120 AMRAAM missile detonated against Chad's outer defense shield, causing it to ripple slightly. A millisecond later, a Mitel Fighter's laser slipped through Chad's outer defense shield.

"Getting ready to —" Luna started, before her communications link went silent.

"Chad! Are you OK?" yelled Teri.

"I think so. Luna, are you OK?"

There was no answer.

"*Luna!*" shouted Chad.

"Luna was hit. She's gone," confirmed Teri.

"*NOOO!*" yelled Chad.

The glass fragments of each cylinder flashed crimson red as he streaked past ten F22 Raptors and another five F16 Fighting Falcons that had begun to pursue the fleeing Mitel Fighters.

"Chad!" Do *not* follow the Mitel Fighters!" said Janus sternly "Do you *hear me*?"

Chad wouldn't listen. He passed through the Earth's troposphere while Teri locked onto the remaining Mitel Fighters. Within seconds, Chad's laser cannons opened fire. They glowed brightly for a few seconds and were gone. Before he could change direction, his diagnostic mini-screens alerted him that Mitel Fighters were approaching from every direction.

"Identifying targets," said Teri quickly.

"They're everywhere. There must be thousands of them," said Chad.

"Two thousand one hundred and fifteen," said Teri as the Mitel Fighters swarmed and opened fire.

CHAPTER THIRTY-ONE — THE FINAL BATTLE

Chad's remaining laser cannons fired nonstop in all directions as his weapons specialists quickly eliminated 100, then 250, then 500 Mitel Fighters.

"The Thraen is more than a match for our Fighters," Lon muttered as he tracked the unfolding battle.

"Do you *still* believe we can defeat it?" asked Ian.

"I don't, however, that's not our goal. By coming back into outer space, he has made a critical mistake. And this time, he will *not* escape."

"We have destroyed over 600 Fighters," confirmed Teri. "But they just keep coming."

"Chad's energy reserves are back down to the low threshold," announced Denton.

"Chad, you must withdraw and recharge," instructed Teri.

"Emperor Rexx," announced the lead scanning specialist. "The Battle Sphere's energy levels are extremely low."

"Are the cruisers and transport vessels in position and ready?"

"Yes," nodded Ian.

"Order tracking protocols on the Battle Sphere!"

"Already done."

"Which vessel is the closest?"

"Cruiser Number 6," confirmed the lead scanning specialist.

Lon rushed over to the scanning console.

"Wait for my signal," he instructed.

"Chad! Retreat *now!*" Teri urged. "Reserve levels are dangerously low!"

"I'm picking up tracking signatures — several of them," announced Denton from across the command cube.

"What do you make of it?" asked Mayla.

"They are preparing to fire their cluster missiles."

"No," said Janus. "They are preparing to activate their gravity control beams."

"Order Cruiser Number 6 to initiate its gravity control beam. *Now!*" ordered Lon sternly.

"Yes, my Emperor," replied the communications specialist.

Searching for a slight opening in the swarm, Chad felt the sudden jolt of the corkscrew gravity beam as it locked onto his plasma defense shield.

"The first beam has been successfully attached," confirmed the scanning specialist.

"Outstanding!" shouted Lon excitedly. "Quickly now, direct the next five vessels in the perimeter to do the same!"

Chad struggled to free himself by accelerating but his Battle Sphere would not budge. He tried for a second and then a third time, but the result was the same. His energy reserves were now down to 18 percent and his laser cannons were unable to fire. He stayed still to conserve power.

"Is there anything we can do to break free?" asked Chad.

"We are assessing the situation," responded Mayla glancing around the Command Cube.

"The beams are just too powerful," replied Cantor.

"The force has shut down his laser cannons," said Sami. "We can't even shoot our way out."

"I don't understand," muttered Janus. "They should *not* be able to contain Chad's Battle Sphere. Their technology is significantly more advanced than what we've seen in the past."

Then it suddenly dawned on him.

"That must have been their plan all along," Janus concluded. "They used the Fighters as a decoy."

"Mayla," said Chad. "I've got an idea."

"Commander?" asked Mayla.

Chad closed his eyes and focused on his internal core. He concentrated on allowing the helium plasma of the gravity control beams to be absorbed through his outer skin surface to replenish his own plasma energy reserves. The extreme discomfort of the gravity control beams began to dissipate and then leave his consciousness altogether.

The energy absorption caused Chad's Battle Hologram to increase rapidly. Rows upon rows of new modules appeared across the Davis Farm field before spreading vertically. Mayla, Teri and everyone else in the Command Cube were in disbelief.

"Simply incredible," said Janus. "Chad is absorbing energy from the gravity control beams for his own use."

"Energy reserves have jumped to 65 percent!" boomed Denton.

"Chad, can you break free?" asked Mayla hopefully.

"I'll try."

Suddenly five more corkscrew beams locked onto his Battle Sphere. Chad strained to accelerate at full power but the crushing force of the gigantic magnetic fields held him firmly in place.

"Can you move at all?"

"*No!*" Chad yelled as he struggled to change his view just enough to see Earth. It then occurred to him: the gravity control beam represented a double-edged sword.

They can't escape me either he thought.

"Mayla! The gravity control beams. How strong are their magnetic fields?"

"Beyond *any* machine generated levels we have ever encountered. Why?"

"I want you to jack up the speed of my antigravity field."

"I don't understand."

"*I want to speed up my core.*"

"We can do it one of two ways," explained Mayla. "One way is to increase the speed of your plasma core to almost the speed of light. In that case, we could still maintain control over the process."

"And the other?"

"Have the Battle Hologram initiate an override sequence. Your core would eventually surge out of control."

"I'm thinking the *first* one," Chad replied.

"But even if we speed up your core, I don't see how that will help you escape."

"It won't right away, but the high energy electrons will generate huge quantities of positrons."

"And initiate a scattering process and produce *antimatter*."

"*Exactly*!" replied Chad.

"But Chad, as soon as the antimatter comes into contact with *anything*, it will cause an instantaneous annihilation!" Teri warned.

"I think I know how to contain it."

"With the gravity control beam magnetic field," concluded Janus.

"Yes!"

"Denton," said Mayla, "run a detailed scan of the beams' magnetic field and map out its characteristics. Q*uickly*!"

"Doing it now. OK, the magnetic field is uniform *and* stable."

"Is it strong enough to quarantine the antimatter?"

"Yes, but Chad will need to add a second *inverted* plasma shield to encase it."

"Do you hear that Commander?" asked Mayla.

"Yes. Attempting that now."

Chad struggled to create the reverse shield and then push it out just far enough to create a small cavity. At the same time, Janus entered commands into the energy monitoring console.

"I've created a charge pattern for both inner and outer shields that should shift the surrounding magnetic field just enough to contain the antimatter. I just sent the results to you."

"Got it. Confirmed," replied Denton. He then ran a series of simulations. "It appears that the modified pattern won't hold for very long."

"It doesn't have to. The entire process will happen very quickly. Once the exterior shield is released, the antimatter will cause an *immediate* annihilation of both the antimatter *and* the gravity beams."

"Let's do this," instructed Chad.

Janus signaled to Denton to speed up Chad's plasma core. Chad felt a new sensation, a tingling, deep within him. He then noticed several brilliant white marble sized balls of developing antimatter emerge through his porous skin cells. In less than a minute, he was surrounded by a mass of brilliant white antimatter.

On Cruiser Number 2, the scanning specialist detected the antimatter.

"Emperor Rexx," he said nervously.

"What now?" Lon asked impatiently.

"My scanners have detected significant amounts of *antimatter* emanating from the Thraen Battle Sphere."

"*Antimatter*?" uttered Lon in disbelief.

"Yes, two hundred pounds worth, and increasing!"

"*That's ridiculous!*" barked Lon. "The presence of such quantities in the known universe is unheard of. Give me a visual, NOW!"

The unfolding scene appeared as a panoramic view on the ICC monitors. Six Mitel craft were emitting streams of light on an intensely bright star-like object at the center.

"That must be the *antimatter*!" exclaimed Ian.

"If you are right, then why hasn't it triggered annihilation?" scoffed Lon.

"He's somehow containing it —"

Before Ian could finish, Chad released his outer shield. Unconstrained, the antimatter expanded outward to the gravity control beams. In the blink of an eye, the beams and their six large source craft exploded violently in a brilliant white flash. Only Chad's silver Battle Sphere remained as a small dot on the monitor.

"What just *happened*?" shouted Lon.

"The gravity beams, Cruiser Number 6 and the five transport vessels are gone!"

"It worked!" shouted Chad.

"*YES!*" boomed Denton from his station in the Command Cube. He decelerated Chad's antigravity propulsion core to normal speed while Teri calculated Chad's exit trajectory.

"Send him to one of our hidden Moon enclosures," instructed Janus. "He can recharge as we perform a damage assessment."

"Initiating high speed exit in three, two, and one," said Teri.

Nothing happened.

"OK, Teri — *let's go*," said Chad impatiently.

Teri frowned before typing furiously.

"What's wrong?" asked Mayla.

"Chad's propulsion system is not responding."

"*What*? Why not?"

"The plasma core energy signature has shifted and antigravity propulsion is no longer working."

"Laser cannons are offline too," said Sami.

On the ICC of the Cruiser Number 2, the scanning specialist stared at his computer screen.

"Emperor Rexx," he began.

"*Now what?*" asked Lon angrily.

"The Battle Sphere appears unable to move or fire its weapons."

"A silver lining! Order twelve more vessels with gravity control capability to move into position!"

"What?" exclaimed Ian incredulously. "You *can't* be serious!"

"I'm quite serious," smiled Lon. "You heard him. The Thraen is disabled and unable to defend itself. Let's get him once and for all."

"A dozen Mitel craft closing in on you," Teri announced.

"What should I do?"

"We're trying to reset your core pattern, Chad. Hold tight."

Janus compared Chad's earlier magnetic field with that of his current signature.

His superconducting disc's critical current density has decreased, greatly weakening his propulsion force he thought.

"Janus?" asked Chad.

"Yes my Son?"

"Can you *fix* me?"

"Chad, I . . . we're trying."

"You can't fix it."

"Chad, we are trying everything we can to get you moving again."

"But you can't fix me, can you?"

"The damage to your propulsion system was unanticipated."

"The Mitel craft are closing in," said Teri.

On the battered Cruiser Number 1's ICC, Zan listened to the chatter over the hacked interfleet communications channel.

"Something is wrong with the Battle Sphere," he muttered. "Navigator, how much longer until we arrive."

"Two minutes, Sir," confirmed Dax.

"Hopefully we can sneak up on them while they're focusing on the young Thraen."

"And then what?" asked Ard.

"I haven't figured that out yet. Lia, do you think you can hack into the Battle Sphere's *communications system*?"

"I can sure try."

She took a deep breath then inserted a program module into her computer launching a series of high-speed searches of encrypted communications signals. Almost immediately, streams of data appeared. Lia refined her search twice before focusing her attention on an unusual series of tight bandwidth signals that coincided with prior scans of the Battle Sphere.

"I think I found something," she announced. Lia instructed her module to search for the encrypted communications 'back door'. A few seconds later, she heard a long beep.

"I'm in."

"Can anyone hear me?" asked Zan.

"Who's this?" asked Teri.

"Zan Liss."

"*Emperor Liss*?" asked Mayla incredulously.

"Not anymore."

"How did you —"

"That's not important. Who am I speaking with?"

"This is Janus Stone. What is it that you want Liss?"

"*Stone*. That name is familiar. Yes, of course, you were GDC Commander during our second attack of the Thraen planet."

"That's correct. Are you trying to broker the surrender of planet Earth?"

"Hardly," snorted Zan.

"Then *what* do you want?"

"To prevent Lon Rexx from killing more innocents."

"Who is *Lon Rexx*?" asked Teri.

"A murderous psychopath who anointed himself Mitel Emperor," responded Ard.

"Then I take it you're with the resistance."

"Which one?"

"There is *more* than one Mitel resistance?" asked Janus.

"No. I thought you might be referring to the Thraen resistance."

"The *Thraen* resistance? Thrae *survived* the second invasion?"

"Yes. Not that the Mitel Leadership wants anyone to know. I was sent there years ago to crush the Thraen resistance once and for all, but instead got captured and struck a deal with them in exchange for my life. I found your high speed pods in the old defense fortress —"

"And reverse engineered the technology and adapted it to your fleet."

"Correct."

"Your voice sounds *very* familiar," Ard said. "I know I've heard it before. Listening to historical archives I think. Wait — you're an immortal, *aren't you*?"

"Yes," replied Janus.

"Are you Sejus Theron?"

"I am."

"You are also Zebulon Park, aren't you?"

"Yes."

"See!" yelled Ard clapping his hands. "*I told you*!"

"What about the sporadic outer space explosions we detected?" Janus asked.

"That was us *and* elements of the imbedded Mitel resistance," acknowledged Zan. "We tried to intercept the cluster pods fired on the planet. At this point, our ship is pretty banged up."

"What are you doing now?"

"Heading to the Battle Sphere to take out as many vessels as possible. If we can destroy Lon's cruiser, the remaining fleet *might* withdraw and head home."

"Or they might decide to come after us," replied Ard.

"Yes, that's a possibility too," acknowledged Zan.

"I'm not sure I like this plan."

"Do *you* have a better one?"

"No."

"I'll send a message requesting assistance to any resistance fighters still out there," added Lia.

"Thank you," replied Janus. "In the meantime, we will try to get the Battle Sphere's propulsion and weapons systems working again. We are running out of time."

"Hopefully we won't need much," replied Zan.

"Emperor Rexx, our craft are almost in position. What are your orders?" the lead scanning specialist asked Lon.

"Initiate tracking protocols. I want the gravity beams in place before he can escape. *We will crush him into submission!*"

Mat tracked twenty-two Mitel warships.

"A dozen vessels are forming a perimeter around the Battle Sphere," he announced.

"How many cluster pods do we have left?" asked Zan.

"Eight in each tube according to the computer," replied Ard. "But don't forget, the right tube doesn't work anymore."

"There isn't time to manually shift any of them over," muttered Zan. "We'll just have to work with what we've got. Ard, program the remaining pods to release their missiles at multiple targets."

"Doing that now."

"Any word on Lon's whereabouts?"

"No Sir," Mat replied. "I register three transport vessels directly up ahead. The first two are located close together, the third farther out. *Wait*, scans show *something large* located in between the first two."

"*Lon's cruiser*," Zan said. "Dax, close in on the first transport vessel. Ard, prepare to fire a cluster pod. We'll flush him out of hiding."

"I'm on it," replied Ard. With a series of keystrokes, he quickly activated the pods. "Ready when you are."

"We are within target range," confirmed Mat.

"Fire!" ordered Zan.

The cluster pod released its missiles, which exploded along the right side of the large transport vessel. Almost immediately, several alarms sounded throughout Cruiser Number 2 indicating that shrapnel from the adjacent blast had penetrated portions of its outer hull.

"*What is happening?*" growled Lon.

"Transport vessel 17 has been destroyed!" announced the lead scanning specialist.

"Another terrorist attack?" asked Ian.

"No Sir. Cruiser Number 1 is *bearing down on us*!"

"*WHAT?*" Lon yelled incredulously. "That's *impossible!* Navigator, full power ahead, then swing us around!"

"That got his attention," Zan smiled. "Quickly, target the vessels around the Battle Sphere."

Ard tried firing four reprogrammed pods. Nothing happened. He tried again. Still nothing.

"We have a couple of problems," Ard announced.

"*Which are?*" asked Zan impatiently.

"Number one. We are no match for Lon's speed."

"Not yet anyway. And the other?"

"The left tube malfunctioned."

"*That's definitely a problem.*"

"Sir," said Mat. "Cruiser Number 2 is turning back around"

"Circle in behind the second transport vessel, but not *too* close," instructed Zan.

"Yes Sir," nodded Dax.

"Where *is* he!" barked Lon.

"Straight ahead," confirmed the specialist. "Next to Transport Vessel Number 12 — "

"Fire!" shouted Lon. "*Full cluster barrage!*"

"But it's too close to the transport vessel!"

"Do as I say!" yelled Lon.

"Yes Emperor Rexx."

Just as Zan's cruiser disappeared, the transport vessel exploded in a series of bright flashes, throwing debris in all directions.

"That was close," Ard sighed.

"Swing us behind the third transport vessel. Quickly!" ordered Zan.

On Cruiser Number 2's ICC, Lon was furious.

"*WELL*?" he boomed.

"Transport vessel number 12 has been destroyed," replied the lead scanning specialist meekly.

"*ARRGHH!*" Lon snarled. "What about Cruiser Number 1?"

"It is retreating toward Transport Vessel Number 20."

"Something must be wrong with its weapons systems," concluded Lon. "Destroy it, *before it can escape!*"

"But the transport vessel is in the direct line of fire," warned the scanning specialist.

"We *must* stop destroying our own ships!" shouted Ian.

Lon spun around and stared angrily at Ian before slowly regaining his composure.

"Navigator. Hard right. Swing us around the transport vessel. We *must* destroy Zan's cruiser."

"Yes, my Emperor."

"In the meantime, order the perimeter vessels to activate the gravity control beams!"

Cruiser Number 1 slowed to a stop behind the large transport vessel. Seconds later, alarms signaled that the cruiser was being hit by small laser fire from the vessel's protective weapons ports.

"T20 just finished off our last weapons tube!" confirmed Ard angrily. "I know some of the guys over there. During maneuvers they couldn't hit anything!"

"How about our lasers, are they still working?" Zan asked.

"There's only one way to find out."

Just then, Cruiser Number 2 appeared from around the front of the transport vessel.

"Rexx's cruiser!"

"I see it!" shouted Ard, unleashing a barrage of lasers at the craft as it banked towards them. The onslaught tore apart both weapons tubes, the entire slip ring undercarriage and both propulsion units setting the cruiser adrift.

"You got it!" shouted Mat excitedly.

"*Whoo hoo!*" yelled Ard. "Take that you lunatic!"

Alarms suddenly sounded as Cruiser Number 1 received additional weapon fire from the transport vessel.

"Not again!" shouted Ard.

"Navigator, get us out of here!" ordered Zan tersely.

"Doing it now," replied Dax as the cruiser slowly lurched forward.

In the lower section of Transport Vessel T20, the last surviving resistance fighter detonated a large bomb that had been hidden in a solid oxygen fuel container. The catastrophic explosion sent fragments flying. Chunks of debris tore through the exterior skin of Lon's cruiser forcing the crew to scramble for their oxygen masks and backpack units. The explosion also finished off propulsion unit number 3, sending Zan's cruiser adrift.

"Status report!" shouted Lon through his oxygen mask.

"Transport Vessel Number T20 has been destroyed," replied the scanning specialist. "Our propulsion units and weapons systems are inoperable. Auxiliary life support won't activate. We must abandon ship."

"Where's Zan's cruiser?"

"It's drifting to our right, about a mile away and appears to be disabled."

"Order the closest cruiser to proceed to our coordinates. In the meantime, begin preparations to launch the escape pods."

Zan reached for the intercom.

"Dru, are you alright?"

"We're shaken up but OK. I thought I told you to warn us next time."

"Sorry about that. Let's get ready to go."

"Already on it," confirmed Dru before the intercom beeped.

"Lia, can you access the Battle Sphere's communications system again?" asked Zan.

Seconds later, there was another beep.

"This is Teri."

"Liss here. We can't move or defend ourselves."

"What about Rexx?" asked Janus.

"Still alive unfortunately, although preparing to abandon ship. A cruiser is on its way to rescue him and finish us off in the process. We have no choice but to flee."

"But how?"

"In two large USEP pods stored in this cruiser."

"So *that's* what you meant all this time!" Ard exclaimed.

"The fleet is preparing to launch another dozen gravity control beams," continued Zan. "They plan to capture the Battle Sphere and take him back to Mitel."

"And what are his plans for Earth?" asked Janus.

"I think you already know the answer to that question."

"Where will you go?"

"Returning to Mitel would mean certain death. Our best option is to return to Thrae."

"*Thrae?*"

"Yes. From there we can fight to free your people. And then, who knows? Maybe ours too."

"Understood."

"I'm sorry we couldn't do more. I regret not standing up to the Mitel Leadership sooner."

"Zan," said Ard, "Cruiser Number 7 will be arriving soon."

"We must go now. Good luck."

In the Command Cube, there was a long silence.

"What now?" Mayla asked eventually.

"We must find a way to get Chad's propulsion system working again," replied Janus resolutely.

"It's no use Janus," said Teri. "We've tried everything. The core alteration can't be reset,"

"How about if we reconfigure it?" offered Cantor.

"We could calculate a modified core pattern," added Denton.

"We're out of time," said Chad quietly.

"We need to do *something*," said Mayla.

"The second option."

"Commander? *What did you say?*"

"The override sequence . . ."

"*What?*" exclaimed Teri.

"The cosmic *annihilation* — my Battle Sphere can take out the entire fleet."

"Listen, Chad —"

"I can't move. I can't shoot. And now I'm about to be captured. I didn't follow your directions and as a result, I've put billions of innocent people in danger."

"Chad, don't blame yourself —"

"The Mitels are going to increase the number of gravity beams to make sure I can't escape this time. Our only option is for me to channel all of *that* energy into producing enough antimatter to wipe out the entire fleet."

"But Commander," pleaded Mayla, "that amount of instantaneous energy release will be devastating. You can't possibly survive!"

"I understand."

"It will also cause *significant* damage to Earth, killing countless people we are trying to save."

"No, it won't."

"What? *Why not*?"

"After you initiate the override, I'm going to channel some of the gravity beam energy into a plasma shield around Earth."

Chad paused for several seconds to create a much larger exterior spherical shield.

"Emperor Rexx, I detect an energy surge from the Battle Sphere."

"Launch the gravity control beams. NOW!" shouted Lon. "We must not squander this opportunity."

"As you command," replied the communications specialist.

The first gravity control beam grabbed Chad's outer plasma shield followed quickly by three, then six, then eleven more corkscrew beams from several directions.

Chad's voice was now laboring under the crushing force of the beams. "It's starting . . . now tweak my shields like you did before . . . *hurry*."

Teri and Cantor quickly ran a series of computer simulations. Mayla looked at Janus who was desperately trying to figure out how to free Chad from the gravity beams.

"Janus, are you still there?" asked Chad.

"Yes, I'm here."

"I know how you feel about this."

Janus did not respond.

"I remember what you told me about Hybrid duty and the responsibility to fight until the very end."

Janus's heart was breaking.

"That's just the opinion of a stubborn old man," he replied sadly. "Chad listen, there *must* be another way. Hang in there while we figure it out —"

"We both know there isn't."

Janus felt helpless.

"Son, I —"

"You were right Janus. You knew all along. The Mitels won't stop attacking Earth until they completely decimate it. This is our last chance."

Janus paused as his mind raced to come up with an idea to free Chad's Battle Sphere. Realizing there was nothing he or the Battle Hologram could do, Janus then struggled to face the inevitable.

"But Chad, what am I going to do without you?"

"You'll keep doing what you've always done. Helping others and leading by example."

"But Chad, I —"

"I love you Dad."

"I love you too my son . . ."

"Initiate the override," Chad ordered. Focusing his thoughts, he felt the shield energy leaving him. The sensation of the enormous energy drain was like stepping out of a warm tub into the crisp cold air. In one sense, he

felt chilled and naked. In another, he felt unburdened from his enormous responsibility. Chad paused briefly to place a second small shield around the International Space Station. Seconds later, he was jerked toward Cruiser Number 8 by the corkscrew gravity beam.

From his scanning station on Cruiser Number 2, the specialist tracked Chad's energy surge followed by an even greater decrease. He performed a second and then a third scan to confirm his initial findings. The results were the same.

"My Emperor. The Battle Sphere's energy levels spiked dramatically before falling back to minimum levels."

"Is it another antimatter surge?"

"No."

The scanners detected the protective shield around the planet.

"I've located the energy displacement," he announced. "There is a plasma shield *around* the planet."

"How is that possible?"

"I have never heard of a Battle Sphere capable of doing such a thing," said Ian.

"What is your recommendation?" asked Lon.

"This shield is not getting any energy input. It will decay soon enough."

"*When*?"

"An hour, probably much less."

"A desperate final act by the young Hybrid to protect his new planet. Pathetic . . ."

In the Command Cube, Teri, Denton and Cantor completed their simulations and then cross referenced their calculations.

"It looks like we're in agreement," concluded Teri. "While the void between the shields is much larger, we can still tweak the magnetic field enough to contain the antimatter, at least temporarily."

"Agreed," announced Denton.

"OK then," said Teri as he began to type. "I'm entering the instructions now."

From her Command station, Mayla stared at the override keypad and switch before looking back up at Janus. He also stared at the switch as if in a trance. Everyone in the Battle Hologram was wondering the same thing: is this the end? Will they die six hundred light years away from their home planet?

Janus looked around the Command Cube. Teri, Denton and the rest of the Hologram team stared silently back at him. He then looked at Mayla directly and gently nodded.

"I *can't* do it," whispered Mayla.

Teri knew what had to be done. He quickly typed the security code, activating the switch. Teri hesitated for a second or two, before he flipped the switch.

High above the planet, Chad felt his core surging faster and faster as it absorbed and processed the incoming plasma energy from the gravity control beams. Marble sized balls of antimatter collected between the plasma defense shields until once again Chad was surrounded by a brilliant white light. The Battle Sphere glowed like a star.

Images of his life flashed across Chad's mind, slowly at first, and then faster and faster. He saw his high school and the home observatory followed by the Fort. He saw Jim's boat, the islands from the camping trip on Lake Edward, playing out in the back yard as a little boy and the doctors at the hospital. He then heard Molly's soothing voice when she first held him in her arms and felt at ease.

As Zan and the others prepared to leave the ICC, Mat noticed a dramatic growth of antimatter from 100 pounds to almost 60,000 pounds in less than a minute.

"Sir, I'm detecting significant amounts of antimatter around the Battle Sphere."

"How *significant,* Mat?" asked Zan.

"65,000 pounds. *Wait.* Now 70,000 pounds."

"Give me a visual," instructed Zan as he approached the monitors.

A white star-like object extended outwards into each of the individual corkscrew beams.

"It's absorbing the energy of the gravity control beams!" Zan marveled.

"The Thraen legend is true," mumbled Ard.

"What legend?"

"A Battle Sphere can speed up its energy core before ultimately self-destructing on a cosmic scale. The override process *must produce antimatter*. He is using the gravity beams to accelerate the process."

"How is he containing it?"

"I have absolutely *no* idea."

"How much antimatter will he produce before detonation?"

"I'm guessing about a million pounds of antimatter should get rid of everything."

"*A million pounds*? How long do we have?"

"Around ten minutes, maybe less."

"That doesn't give us much time. What about the planet?"

"I'm also guessing that's where the plasma shield comes in."

The interfleet communications channel signal flashed.

"It's Lon Rexx," confirmed Lia.

"Put him on," replied Zan.

The stoic face of Lon Rexx appeared on the monitor.

"What is the Thraen doing?" snarled Lon.

"He's not going to allow himself to be taken alive," replied Zan.

"How do you know?"

"Thraen folklore," said Ard. "And he's going to take the entire Mitel Fleet with him."

Lon became visibly alarmed by this news, before turning angry.

"*You* sabotaged our mission!" he hissed. "You knew our orders! And you didn't carry them out!"

"I can't condone murdering innocent people! Not any-more," replied Zan.

"You attacked your own vessels! You killed your own people!"

"We attacked military vessels that fired on defenseless men, women and children."

"They had no choice."

"We all have a choice Lon! *You* kill and destroy without hesitation! You've *always* done that!"

"And *you* have been corrupted by the resistance!"

"300,000 pounds," announced Mat.

"My parents were Mitel resistance officers," Zan continued. "They were murdered in their own home in cold blood when I was a boy. Does any of that sound vaguely familiar?"

"I don't understand your question," replied Lon defensively.

"Your *father* and most of your family — they were murdered because he also was a resistance fighter!"

"That's preposterous!"

"It's true. I saw it all in the restricted database."

"The resistance is nothing more than a bunch of t*errorists*!" barked Lon angrily.

"And the Mitel military is *not*?"

"No!"

"We *invented* terrorism Lon!"

Lon did not answer.

"Sir," proclaimed Mat. "Antimatter levels have increased to 450,000 pounds."

"My one consolation is that all of you will *die*," Lon hissed.

"Sorry to disappoint you, but that's not going to happen," replied Zan. "I have two high-speed escape pods ready to go."

"*What*?"

"OK everyone, let's get going. Good bye, Lon," Zan motioned everyone toward the HorVert as he turned off the interfleet communications system and the monitor went black.

"ARRRGGGHH!" howled Lon.

Zan, Ard, Lia, Mat and Dax piled into the elevator. Before the doors closed, the interfleet communications signal flashed once again.

Zan entered the intercom code.

"Dru here."

"Are we ready to go?"

"Yes."

"Good. We have very little time."

"I know."

Mat continued to monitor the antimatter on his handheld scanner.

"600,000 pounds."

Zan reset the intercom and entered a second code as the elevator changed direction and headed to the bottom of the cruiser.

"Rad Aarden speaking," said the voice.

"Rad, it's Zan. Get yourself and your staff down to the auxiliary launch tube *immediately*!"

"There is no auxiliary launch tube," replied Rad.

"There is. Punch in the code A39A into the HorVert keypad. It will bring you there."

"On our way."

On the Cruiser Number 2 ICC, Lon sprung from his console seat.

"Where is Cruiser Number 7?" he demanded impatiently.

"It is almost here," replied the scanning specialist nervously.

"Shall I give the order for the fleet to withdraw?" asked the communications specialist.

"*NO!*" ordered Lon, as he hurried toward the HorVert doors. "If we give the order now, we will be left behind. Is that what you want?"

"Of course not, Emperor Rexx."

"Order the closest supply vessel to head towards the outer reaches of this galaxy until further notice."

"My Emperor?"

"I will explain later. Then prepare to abandon ship. Once we have been picked up, I will give the order for the rest of the fleet to depart."

"Yes, but —"

"Do as I say!" ordered Lon tersely before the HorVert doors closed behind him.

"Now I understand why you went snooping around the old Thraen command center," Ard said. "You planned this escape from the very beginning, didn't you?"

"Do you *really* think I became Emperor on my good looks alone?" replied Zan just as the HorVert came to a stop.

The group raced down the hall to a large reinforced door. Zan entered the keypad code and the door slid open. Sitting inside a large cylindrical launch tube were two bright silver oversized USEP² pods. The oversized curving ring components could be seen under each craft. As Zan approached the first pod, its airlock doors slid open. Dru quickly poked his head out.

"Rad and his six people are in the second pod with the mechanics," said Dru. "The other three are in the first pod with me.

"Let's go," motioned Zan.

After the HorVert doors slid open, Lon rushed down the hallway to the primary launch bay. Looking through the large reinforced clear acrylic panels, Lon saw a dozen escape pods ready to be launched into outer space. He waited impatiently for the familiar hiss of the bay pressurization system. After what seemed like an eternity, the "all safe" light flashed yellow releasing the clear acrylic sliding doors. Lon entered the bay followed by a dozen transport and safety personnel.

"I must get to Cruiser Number 7 immediately!" instructed Lon.

"I'm sorry, but in accordance with evacuation protocol, the escape pods are launched all at once," replied a safety officer.

"I cannot wait for that. You must launch me now."

"But —"

"If I get there first, I will coordinate the withdrawal of the fleet while the rest of you are being rescued."

"Yes, my Emperor," nodded the officer.

The safety and transport personnel scrambled out the bay before the panels slid closed. Once depressurization was completed, the silver bay doors slid open, revealing countless stars against the blackness of deep space. Cruiser Number 7 was waiting nearby.

Zan entered the pod and took a seat in the first row of twin seats. Ard sat down next to him, and Zan ran through the final launch checklist.

"875,000 pounds," announced Mat nervously from behind.

Zan flipped a series of switches on the console in front of him which resealed the airlock doors, depressurized the chamber, and opened two large doors at the far end of the battle cruiser. Staring out into space, it suddenly occurred to him.

"Lia, are you able to send a message to the Battle Sphere from here?" he asked.

"Yes. I downloaded the communications database before leaving the ICC."

"Good. Tell Chad to place a protective shield around *himself*."

Lia typed quickly and sent the message.

"OK. Preparing to launch."

Zan pressed the launch button, sending the pod streaking out the rear of the cruiser. The second USEP shot out a few seconds later. Zan studied the system readouts and controls. Satisfied with what he saw, he pushed a second button initiating maximum normal speed. The USEP lurched again and accelerated. Once Zan confirmed that the energizer gauge had reached *100* percent, he initiated the slip ring which was now deployed into position.

Zan pushed a third button to activate the departure sequence. The USEP pods accelerated forward above the speed of light and were gone.

On Cruiser Number 7, the doors to Lon's small escape pod opened as several medical and safety staff helped him get out.

"I'm fine," growled Lon. "Order the fleet to retreat. Immediately!"

"But what about the rest of the escape pods?" a staff member asked incredulously.

"There isn't time!" explained Lon. "The Battle Sphere is about to detonate and if we don't retreat now, he will take all of us with him!"

"Yes my Emperor," replied a safety officer.

Lon watched the officer rush to the wall intercom. He then made his way to the HorVert and headed for the ICC.

High above the Earth, Chad's antigravity superconductor disk was now fully depleted from converting plasma energy into antimatter. His core was shutting down, and his Battle Sphere began its reverse transformation process. Weak and exhausted, Chad faded in and out of consciousness. Just then, he noticed Lia's message. He read it just before the screens terminated. Chad tried to place a small but strong plasma shield around his body without success. He tried again before everything went dark.

The HorVert doors opened and Lon stepped onto the ICC of Cruiser Number 7. On the center screen was an intensely bright star like object.

"The Thraen!" Lon barked.

He then looked towards the commander.

"Is the slip ring energized?" he growled.

"Yes —"

"Then let's go, NOW!"

"But what about your crew?"

"There isn't time. Instruct the rest of the fleet to withdraw! LET'S GO!"

With Lon's cruiser well in the lead, the remaining Mitel Fleet sped away from Earth.

"Approaching maximum normal speed," announced the propulsion specialist.

Now unconscious, Chad's outer defense shield dissolved, releasing the antimatter. The cosmic explosion was far beyond anything Earth had encountered in over sixty-five million years. The protective plasma shield around the planet held its ground, deflecting the flash wave away from Earth. Janus, Mayla and everyone else on the release side of the planet covered their eyes from the brilliance of the explosion.

On Cruiser Number 7, the propulsion specialist tracked the slip ring's progress.

Suddenly, the ICC monitor turned white.

"The explosion wave!" shouted the scanning specialist.

Lon jerked his head toward the screen.

"Activate the slip ring!" he howled.

The propulsion specialist reached for the start button while the annihilating wave swept over the rest of the escaping Fleet.

"Departure activated," blurted the specialist.

Cruiser Number 7 lurched forward as the flash wave bore down on it.

"The wave is still gaining!" shouted the scanning specialist. *"It's right on top of us!"*

"NO!" yelled Lon.

An instant later, the cruiser accelerated faster than the speed of light, and pulled away from the expanding energy.

"We made it! But it appears we were the only ones," shouted the scanning specialist.

"What do we do now?" asked the communications specialist.

"Is there any sign of the Battle Sphere?" asked Lon.

"No. Nothing."

"Then we head back to Mitel," replied Lon wearily. "If it wasn't for the acts of a lone traitor, this mission would have succeeded. We face another long voyage. But it will provide me time to devise an explanation of what happened. Navigator, let's catch up to the supply vessel."

As the annihilation wave expanded, a concentrated pocket of energy grazed the Moon causing a section of its northern hemisphere to disintegrate.

The energy wave finally dissipated and the plasma shield surrounding Earth disintegrated as well.

"Status report on the Mitel Fleet," instructed Mayla.

"The scanners show nothing Commander," responded Teri.

"What do you mean?"

"Everything's gone."

"Please explain."

"The Mitel Fleet: the battle cruisers, Fighters, supply vessels, transport vessels, the weapons pods. *Everything* is gone. As if it never existed."

There was a long silence.

"What about Chad?" Mayla asked. "Are you able to make contact with him?"

"Commander, our scanners indicate that there's *nothing* out there, *nothing* at all. Wait — I'm picking up a lone signal from the International Space Station. Chad must have placed a shield around that too. But that's it, nothing else . . ."

Janus struggled to process what just happened. Before he could fully comprehend it, he realized Mayla was no longer a Hologram. He was now staring at a real live woman. Janus looked around the Cube. Teri, Denton and the rest of the Battle Hologram team were also human and the Battle Hologram itself was now a permanent free standing building. Its translucent hazy glow was gone and its components had been replaced by metal, composites and plastic.

Janus raised his hands and stared at them. He too, was human. Technicians were running back and forth, yelling and laughing and hugging each other. The miracle of life process had been completed, just as the Thraen folklore had described. Just then, Luna walked into the Command Cube with a confused look on her face.

"Luna?" yelled Teri. "Luna is that you?"

"Yes," she replied, somewhat confused.

"But we thought you were gone."

Luna smiled weakly. "The last thing I remember was shooting at the Fighters. And now, here I am, a person."

"Your Hologram signature was somehow re-embedded in the Battle Hologram," Janus explained.

"Simply incredible," said Mayla softly. "How did this happen?"

"It was Chad," replied Janus. "He freed us. The energy from the antimatter detonation released all of us from our hologram state."

"You mean the miracle of life?"

"Yes."

"Deep down, I thought it was just Thraen folklore," Mayla whispered.

"Your ancestors were right for once," mused Janus.

"We must try to register a signal from Chad right away," Mayla announced.

Janus looked away in silence.

"Janus, we *must* try!" Mayla repeated.

She reached out her hand and touched Janus's arm, as he gently nodded for her to try.

Mayla quickly sat down and paused briefly to acclimate herself to her new surroundings. The sensation of touching the keyboard was new and exciting. While Janus watched silently, she waited for a response from Chad.

Nothing.

Mayla tried a second and a third time.

Still nothing.

Refusing to accept the results, she shifted over to the next computer and repeated the process.

He must be out there somewhere she thought.

Mayla sent off signals and messages to Chad from every computer in the Command Cube. She waited silently for a response as tears streamed down her cheeks.

No response.

Mayla then tried to reach him through the encrypted communications system. Chad did not answer. She tried a second time and then a third. Mayla finally slumped back into her chair, buried her face in her hands and sobbed. She realized what Janus had already known. Chad was gone. Janus walked over and placed his hand gently on her shoulder. She forced herself up from the chair and Janus took her in his arms, holding her for a long time.

Jim, Molly and Melissica entered the control room looking for Janus and Mayla. They noticed the two across the Command Cube. Jim and Molly immediately knew what had happened. Molly fell to her knees and began to cry.

"*No, no, no, no, no!*" she wailed.

Jim knelt beside her and hugged Molly tightly. Janus took Molly's hand and squeezed it tightly. Jim looked at Janus in disbelief.

"Chad freed us all," Janus explained.

"I don't understand," Jim said as he wiped tears from his face.

"Chad made the decision to speed up his energy core. That created a substantial amount of antimatter. The subsequent annihilation reversed the hologram transformation process, and freed us from that confinement."

"What happened to the Mitel Fleet?"

"They were destroyed."

Teri watched the group from a few steps away, before making his way outside the Battle Matrix and looking up at the blue sky.

"Thank you, Chad. Thank you for everything."

A visibly shaken Major Talbot with Lieutenant Miller and several other soldiers walked past Teri into the Battle Matrix.

"Janus, what the hell just happened?" asked Major Talbot as he reached out and touched Janus on the shoulder.

"The Mitel Fleet has been destroyed. Your planet is no longer in danger," responded Janus somberly.

"What about Chad?"

"I am afraid that he is also gone."

Major Talbot studied Janus intently.

"You're human."

"Yes. That was also Chad. His enormous energy surge released us from our hologram state."

"That's incredible. I want to tell you how sorry I am, Janus. For everything."

"Thank you Major Talbot. But you could not have been expected to comprehend everything that was going on. Perhaps now, your world will be ready to listen and work together."

"Maybe," replied Major Talbot.

"Major Talbot Sir!" a Marine shouted "It's the Pentagon. They want to speak with you!"

"Excuse me, Janus," said Major Talbot as he turned and followed the Marine. He looked back over his shoulder. "I will personally see to it that you and your people are taken care of from here on in."

Janus watched Major Talbot leave the Command Cube before he too made his way down the stairway and out the main entrance. Looking at the afternoon sky, he noticed the reshaped Moon which had risen above the trees out on the horizon. Studying its new contour, Janus's thoughts drifted back to the time when he had placed Chad in the USEP pod next to Markus back on Thrae. He remembered how he felt when he prepared to launch the two of them up into space. As he stood there alone, tears streamed down his checks.

Goodbye my son.

CHAPTER THIRTY-TWO – MOVING ON

The outer space explosion that destroyed the Mitel Fleet, while quick, had lasting effects on the World. The blast obliterated all satellites orbiting the Earth beyond Chad's plasma shield. While internet service was minimally affected due to its heavy reliance on trans-continental cables, GPS and most cell phones no longer worked. National television stations no longer broadcasted since they relied heavily on satellites to deliver their programming worldwide. Commercial air travel became less safe and predictable without GPS satellite data to guide flight routes or identify bad weather and turbulence.

Instability of the global food supply, which relies in part on accurate weather data, loomed on the horizon. The world scrambled to figure out how to replace as many satellites as quickly as possible in order to bring global satellite communications systems and GPS back on line.

The global-wide loss of life was staggering. An estimated two hundred million people perished during the short yet devastating Mitel attacks. Infrastructure around the world was destroyed and would take years, even decades to rebuild. In the face of this massive devastation, the people of the world were coming together, helping each other. It no longer mattered what country you were in, what religion you practiced or the color of your skin.

Scientists around the world scrambled to determine the effects of the Moon's new shape. Initial results showed that the ocean's tides and the wobbling nature of the Earth's spin were not impacted to any measurable extent.

As details of Chad's heroics made their way around the globe, the world quickly realized that they were forever indebted to his selfless act of bravery. Everyone wanted to know more about Chad, Janus, Mayla and the rest of the surviving Thraens.

Two days after the incident, the President of the United States addressed the nation and the world. During his address, he reminded everyone that the simple act of looking up at the Moon to see its missing section would be a lasting memorial to Chad Stone's noble and heroic actions.

"May the scar that will forever be part of our Moon be a constant reminder to all of us, and all of those who follow, of the courage and sacrifice of one individual who stood up to evil."

Under the direction and guidance of General Michael Talbot, most of the surviving Thraens from Chad's Battle Hologram were given new identities and places to live, as they assimilated into Earth's culture. A small group of the Thraens would be staying on to work at the Battle Matrix. The Davis Farm would eventually be transformed into a quasi-military base site.

Some of the surviving Thraens were assigned positions at high tech companies, research organizations and think tanks around the world based on their skill set.

Janus accepted an offer to work for General Talbot.

"I will only assist when and where I know it will be for the benefit of everyone, and not just a few," Janus told Mayla in private.

"As it should be," smiled Mayla.

Janus, Mayla, Luna and Teri were planning a private memorial service for Chad and Markus before they went on their separate ways, but news leaked and soon the President of the United States invited Janus to speak in Washington D.C. at an event that would be broadcast around the world.

Janus did not know what to do, but Mayla gently urged him to speak.

"Do it for Chad and for Markus," she told him.

Janus reluctantly agreed.

Preparations were quickly made for the historic speech that he would give from the Lincoln Memorial, looking out over the reflecting pool and the National Mall.

The headline on most news websites read:

ALIEN SURVIVOR JANUS STONE TO ADDRESS THE WORLD IN WASHINGTON D.C.

People from all over the world headed to Washington. More than twenty million people were expected to attend in person, and some five billion people worldwide were expected to watch online.

The day before his speech, Janus, Mayla, Luna and Teri were escorted by the Secret Service to the Capitol.

They spent the night in the White House as guest of the President.

Janus and Mayla sat in the dark most of the night gazing out the windows while Janus reflected on his life and what he planned to say the following day. He wrote various thoughts down on a notepad.

The next morning was beautiful and sunny, the air cool and crisp. They were escorted by the Secret Service to the Mall. When they arrived, Janus slowly climbed the stairs to the main stage. Mayla, Luna and Teri stood off to the side and out of view from the crowd, and were soon joined by Jim, Molly and Melissica. Security personnel were everywhere. Approaching the podium, Janus glanced out at the enormous crowd that seemed to go on forever.

Janus looked up at the sky before carefully placing his notes on the podium. He then looked to make sure Mayla was still there. She was now the most important thing in his life, and for that, he felt both lucky and grateful. She nodded at Janus and smiled slightly, as if to gently urge him along and reconfirm that he should do this. Janus took a deep breath and began speaking:

"People of planet Earth" he started slowly. As he spoke Janus heard the slight echo of his voice reverberating across the Mall.

"My name is Janus Stone. I am from a planet named Thrae, located approximately six hundred light years away. Physically, it is much like your planet Earth. As a civilization, we had evolved into a truly global society under a single leadership committee called the Word Council. We also had regional and local leadership groups which operated in many ways like your state and local governments. Like anything in life, it was not perfect, and it had taken us a very long time to get to that point, but it worked.

I am not here today to tell you that you need to do as we did, or to be more like us. But after our 4ᵗʰ global war, we as a people were weary of conflict. As a result, we made the decision *as a civilization* to fundamentally change how we did things. A worldwide vote for change was almost unanimous and it sent us down a path of unprecedented peace and prosperity.

One thing I do believe is that your civilization is on its way down a somewhat similar path and will be faced with many of the same challenges. How you choose to respond will ultimately determine your long-term existence.

I came to your planet fifteen years ago with my lifelong friend Markus Kilmar and my infant son Chad. In doing so, we escaped a second, and ultimately catastrophic, invasion of our planet by the very same beings that recently assaulted your world: the *Mitels*.

I want to offer my deepest apologies for subjecting your planet to their relentless aggression and death."

Janus paused to glance over at Mayla who smiled broadly and nodded for him to continue.

"My initial reason for coming here today was to honor the life and memory of my friend and my son who both died trying to protect their new home from the Mitels. But as I thought about it more, I realized that a truly dynamic and vibrant civilization is not about a few individuals but rather the population and the entire planet. Chad and Markus did what they did because they too believed in that principle. But make no mistake; the danger of attack from an extraterrestrial threat should *never* be considered a onetime occurrence.

I firmly believe that the people of Earth *must* come together, and begin to prepare for the inevitable contact with other hostile worlds. By means of an example, our world had been aware of Earth for quite some time. We referred to it as 5.1.18.20.9. Given the substantial distance between us, it was not a priority."

Janus paused to look up at the sky before continuing.

"Observing your culture over the past fifteen years, I have witnessed the growth of something that my planet came to abhor — *terrorism*. It is something the Mitels used extensively and effectively to advance their own empire. In my opinion, it is also something that prevents an advanced society from achieving its true potential.

Terrorism, by its very nature, is meant to eliminate rational discussion, cooperation and trust. It most often triggers military retaliation that ultimately blurs the line between terrorist and victim. I believe that terrorism serves no legitimate purpose and its goals are directly opposite those of a freely advancing civilization. That is why it is crucial for the people of Earth to listen to each other and embrace the beauty and diversity that is your world. If you can find ways to come together in ways that allow you to get beyond the types of behavior that trigger terrorism and war — your future as a civilization is limitless."

Janus paused one more time as he gathered his final thoughts.

"You, the people of Earth, have tremendous promise. While I cannot predict the future, I am here today to warn you that you must also remain wary of the negative effects and uses of technology. Your planet does not require the threat of another exterior invasion to bring it to an end. You are currently quite capable of doing it to yourselves.

Going forward, I ask, no, I implore you to accept one another and help one another. Not sometimes, *but all the time*. That is the only real way that your planet will move forward and develop into a truly great civilization. Thank you."

Janus picked up his notes from the podium and slowly walked off the stage. As he did, the applause began. It started as mild clapping, and intensified into a thunderous roar. It was the sound of jubilation. It was the sound of change. It was the sound of hope and promise. As he reached Mayla, she gave Janus a long hug.

"There is hope," he said, his eyes filled with tears.

"I agree," replied Mayla as she reached up and wiped the tears away before giving Janus a long affectionate kiss.

The group was whisked away by the Secret Service Agents to another secret location.

CHAPTER THIRTY-THREE – A NEW BEGINNING

Janus, Mayla, Luna and Teri made plans to meet Jim and Molly at a lodge on Lake Tahoe to get away from the lime light. General Talbot arranged for a private flight to Sacramento International Airport and insisted on arranging a protection detail of six Navy seals in two unmarked SUVs to accompany Janus's car to the lakefront lodge.

After they settled in, Jim and Molly drove the group across the Nevada state border to a secluded beach along Lake Tahoe's eastern shore. They had previously visited the beach when Chad was seven years old.

The descending trail, a winding dirt path bordered by pine trees and other scrub bushes, became steep as they got closer to the lake. At the bottom was a beautiful, deserted sandy beach. The water was crystal clear with several large partially submerged boulders near the water's edge. Even though it was late fall, the temperature was still in the low to mid sixties. Snow was visible on the mountain peaks off in the distance.

Mayla spread a blanket and sat down while Janus, Jim and Molly walked along the beach. Jim, as was his hobby, looked for oddly shaped and colored stones along the way. Teri and Luna waded out into the water to sit on the large boulders.

Out in space, approximately two hundred miles above Earth, a small blue translucent enclosure circled the planet. Inside of it was Chad's silver body. He had been unconscious from the trauma associated with his core reversal and subsequent annihilation event.

Chad was able to wrap himself in a thick protective plasma shield just as he lost consciousness. The enclosure protected him from the expanding core energy that culminated in the cosmic explosion. It also retained and stored large quantities of oxygen, hydrogen and nitrogen released during the final stages of his reverse transformation. And now, a breathable mixture was slowly being discharged into the shield enclosure; while combining with the hydrogen to form small pockets of water.

As the plasma shelter circled the planet fifteen times a day — at over 17,000 miles per hour — it absorbed and attenuated the scorching heat of the sun; and kept Chad comfortable at night when temperatures plummeted to minus 250 degrees Fahrenheit.

A tiny pocket of slowly dripping water onto Chad's chest helped him finally regain consciousness and open his eyes. He awoke to a million shining stars around him.

Where am I? He thought just before it all came rushing back to him.

How long have I been out here? He wondered.

He turned to see Earth below. It was just as beautiful as ever. He then glanced around. The Mitel Fleet and fighters were gone. Chad's heart began to race.

We did it! He thought.

Chad then looked down at himself to see that he was naked, but still covered in silver shard mesh. He tried unsuccessfully to complete his transformation into Battle Sphere mode. He then tried to open a communications link with the Battle Hologram. Nothing.

Think Chad he said to himself before suddenly remembering his emergency beacon located just behind his left ear. He slowly reached up and activated it.

Denton was in the Battle Hologram command room re-programming one of the many system computers when he noticed Chad's emergency beacon blinking on the console.

Could it be? He thought.

Denton quickly switched on the Battle Hologram communication system.

"Battle Matrix, Denton speaking. We're receiving your distress signal. Please respond."

There was no response. Then the signal stopped.

Denton's heart began to race.

"Is that *you* Chad?" he exclaimed.

Still nothing.

Denton thought for a moment. Then he got an idea.

"Chad if it's you, flash your beacon once for yes and twice for no."

The beacon light flashed once.

"Wahoo!" boomed Denton as he instinctively opened the communications system to the rest of the Battle Matrix.

"Chad, are you OK?"

The beacon light again flashed once.

"Alright, that's great news Chad! Are you in Battle Sphere mode?"

The beacon light again flashed twice.

"OK, OK. I understand. Are you able to transform to full battle sphere mode?"

The beacon light again flashed twice.

Within seconds, Thraen personnel flooded the command center and activated the full monitoring system. As it came on line, the familiar hum could be heard throughout the building. Denton fed the beacon signal directly into the Battle Matrix primary computer. After several seconds, the computer began to track Chad's trajectory.

"We found him!" said Alnanda, a tracking and communications specialist. "He is currently over Australia orbiting about two hundred miles above the planet," she added.

"Chad, we've located you," confirmed Denton. "We'll find a way to get you down. Sit tight!"

The beacon light flashed once.

Denton immediately switched communication systems and contacted Mayla. As Denton explained the news, she jumped up from her blanket and sprinted as fast as she could toward Janus and the others.

Janus, Jim, Luna and Molly were walking along the beach. When they heard Mayla yelling, they stopped and turned to see her running toward them. When she reached them, Mayla placed her hand against her chest as she struggled to catch her breath.

"What's wrong Mayla?" Janus asked. "Please tell me."

Mayla's cheeks were flushed as she stared at Janus lovingly.

"We received a beacon signal from Chad!" She exclaimed, hugging Janus with all her strength. "He's alive!"

ABOUT THE AUTHOR

With a graduate degree in thermo-fluids engineering, a financial MBA, and now a practicing lawyer, Keith has always had a thirst for learning, adventure, and trying new things. He has always had a creative side – drawing his first cartoon called *Bill Liss* at age 11 – and an imagination that knows no limits. His love of science fiction and the possibilities of the Universe led him to write this action packed and thought provoking science fiction novel. Keith loves to be outdoors and is an avid stone wall builder, collector of marble patterned ocean rocks, and science enthusiast.